Beyond Desire

GWYNNE FORSTER

BeyondDesire

ARABESQUE®

BEYOND DESIRE

An Arabesque novel published by Kimani Press/September 2008

First Published by by Kensington Publishing Corp. in 1998

ISBN-13: 978-0-373-83109-8
ISBN-10:   0-373-83109-9

© 1998 by Gwendolyn Johnson-Acsadi

his is a work of fiction. Names, characters, places and incidents are
either the product of the author's imagination or are used fictitiously,
and any resemblance to actual persons, living or dead, business
establishments, events or locales is entirely coincidental.

www.kimanipress.com

Printed in U.S.A.

ACKNOWLEDGMENTS

To my stepson, Peter, who willingly uses his
skills as an electronic engineer to keep me
abreast of ever-changing computer lore;
to my husband, who rescues me from
day-to-day computer calamities, designs my
promotional fliers, bookplates and bookmarks
and whose love, encouragement and unfailing
support sustain me; and in memory of my
deceased friend, Phyllis M. Harewood, who
knew the meaning of true friendship.

SOURCES OF QUOTATIONS

Most of the quotations that appear in this book were taken from the following sources: Evan Esar, ed., *The Dictionary of Humorous Quotations,* Dorset Press, New York, 1989; R.T. Tripp, *The International Thesaurus of Quotations,* Harper & Row, New York, 1970; Beatrice Rosenthal, *Webster's Dictionary of Familiar Quotations,* Galahad Books, New York, 1974; and Elza Dinwiddie-Boyd, *In Our Own Words,* Avon Books, New York, 1996.

Chapter 1

Jacob Graham patted her arm affectionately, his smile sympathetic. "I'm afraid so. There's no chance of error. Have a seat in the waiting room while I write a couple of prescriptions for you." She dressed, walked back to the gray carpeted little room and sat in one of the red leather chairs. Not a chance, he'd said. She'd gone to Elizabeth City—forty miles north of her Caution Point, North Carolina, hometown—for the examination, because the old doctor had been her family's physician for more than forty years; she trusted Jacob Graham. Her gaze captured the man who sat across from her beneath a painting of the perfect family gamboling in pristine snow. She wanted to turn her back to it. Engrossed in the *Carolina Times,* the man seemed oblivious to her presence. Would he also get bad news?

Dr. Graham appeared, saw the man and greeted him with a smile. "I see you've finished it ahead of time. My grandson is going to be one happy boy." He opened the violin case, examined the instrument and exclaimed, his weathered white face wreathed in smiles, "It's beautiful, just like new."

"It's as good as new, too," the stranger said. "Ought to last Jason until he's ready for a Stradivarius." She shrugged off the tremor of excitement that shot through her when she heard the husky, sonorous voice.

Dr. Graham rubbed the wood gently, as though respectful of its value. "Now, tell me how things are going with you these days. Any better?"

"Nothing new; not a thing." She reflected on the weariness apparent in the man's voice and vowed not to let her circumstances whip her. She hated gloom, and she wasn't going to let it cloud her life. Anxious to leave, she cleared her throat, and the doctor turned toward her.

"Are these my prescriptions?" she asked him as she stood preparing to leave, and pointed to the two sheets of paper that he held.

"Yes, sure." The doctor looked from her to the tall, dark man beside him, rubbed his chin as though in deep thought and glanced back at her. "Have you two met?" Before she could respond, the big man shook his head more vigorously than she thought necessary. "You two ought to talk," Jacob Graham declared.

"Why is that?" the man inquired with an exaggerated note of skepticism and without so much as a glance her way. Not that she cared, she told herself.

Her doctor seemed to like his idea better the more he thought of it. "I've known both of you for years." He looked at her. "And you I've known all your life. If the two of you were prepared to act sensibly, you could solve each other's problems." He shook his almost snow-white head. "But sensibleness seems to be too much to expect of you young people these days." He handed her the prescriptions and patted her on the back. The other man nodded, but seemed preoccupied and hardly glanced in her direction as she left them.

"Just a second," Jacob Graham called after her. She waited until he reached the door where she stood. "Lorrianne's having one of her barbecue brunches Sunday, and I know she'd love to have you come."

Amanda diverted her gaze from the piercing blue eyes. "I

don't want her to know about this yet. I have to get used to it myself. You understand, Dr. Graham?"

He removed the pencil from behind his ear and made a note on his writing pad. "How will she know if you don't tell her? I don't give my wife an account of everything that goes on in this office. You come on over. The garden's at its peak this time of year, and you know how she loves to show it off. Noon, Sunday. Don't forget, now."

Though anxiety boiled inside of her, she raised her head and squared her shoulders with an air of calm and walked out into the April morning, chilled by the Atlantic Ocean's still wintry breeze.

Amanda plaited her long, thick and wooly hair in a single braid, twisted it into a knot, surveyed the result and made a face at herself in the mirror. She couldn't bring herself to cut her hair, though she spent a good fifteen minutes every morning braiding it and wrapping the single braid around her head or making two French twists at the back of her head. It would be easier to manage if she straightened it but, as a teenager, she had decided to leave it as nature had ordained. She finished dressing, got into her car and drove to Elizabeth City, giving herself plenty of time to arrive before other guests; joining a crowd of cocktail-sipping strangers was not anything she relished on that particular day. Her concerns were too serious for light chatter. But in spite of her efforts, she arrived to find at least a dozen people milling around, chatting and drinking coffee. No cocktails. She had forgotten Lorrianne's rule about not serving alcohol before six o'clock. Lorrianne claimed that Americans spent too much money and wasted too much energy on alcohol. Not that any of it mattered to her; a glass of wine was as much as she ever drank.

Her hostess introduced her to the other guests, but she couldn't muster any interest in the things that concerned them—mostly local gossip and politics—and after a few polite exchanges she focused her attention on the garden. Lorrianne Graham had created a magnificent retreat for a troubled spirit, Amanda decided, as she strolled among the profusion of red, white and pink peonies, pansies, hyacinths, and flowering dogwood and fruit trees. What a pity the tulips had no perfume, she thought, gazing at their array of colors and the many shapes of their petals. Flowers from several fruit trees floated to the ground, leaving behind their tiny green treasures.

She leaned against a wrought-iron bench and inhaled deeply, enjoying the fresh spring air and the fragrant hyacinths. But her weight toppled the three-legged bench and, to her amazement, she lay sprawled across a patch of purple and yellow pansies. Her cheeks burned in embarrassment as she looked around, hoping that she'd escaped notice.

"Here, let me give you a hand." She had to quell the impulse to ask him to leave her to her own devices, summoned her dignity and smiled politely. Of all people: the man she'd seen that previous Thursday in the doctor's office.

"Give me your hand," he persisted. She raised her left hand, because her right one lay trapped beneath her side. "You're lucky you missed that raspberry bush," he said, friendlier than she thought necessary. She accepted his assistance with as much dignity as she could muster, thanked him and hoped he'd leave her and join the other guests. She couldn't think of a way to dismiss him without appearing rude and ungrateful. So she strove to be her normally gentle, courteous self and to make conversation, but her personal problems bore so heavily on her that she couldn't summon the will to friendliness. *I'm in bad shape,* she conceded, *if I can't focus well enough to carry on an impersonal conversation with such a man as this one.*

"Your head is almost covered with pink and white petals," he told her, evidently oblivious to her discomfort. That voice. Could he hear the melodies in his speech? Of course, she immediately concluded; enough women must have told him about it. She forced herself to turn slowly toward him, gaining time to restore her equilibrium.

"Oh? Flowers in my hair?" She hated that he disconcerted her to such an extent that she lost her poise.

"Yeah," he answered, no doubt unperturbed by her aloof-ness. "Lots of them." He picked off a few and showed them to her. She backed away, sensitive to the feel of his fingers on her scalp, and resisted the urge to remove her dark glasses. Remove them and get an unobstructed look at eyes she remembered as being the color of dark brown honey and at a flawless almond complexion. She breathed deeply in relief when a beautiful, sepia woman with a mannequin's build and carriage claimed his attention and took him away. *All I need right now is to lose my head over a guy like that one,* she told herself, amused that the possibility existed.

She didn't tolerate the medicine well and went back to her doctor two weeks later for a new prescription.

"Nothing has changed," Jacob Graham told her when she asked again whether he was certain of the diagnosis. "Only time will change this; you know that, so you might as well start right now to adjust to it. It won't be easy, but I'm confident you'll manage."

"Don't worry; I'll be fine. Give my love to Lorrianne." She doubted that anything could have depressed her more than his declaration that he knew she'd manage. How was she supposed to do that?

An hour and a half later, she slid into a booth at Caution's Coffee Bean. She had heard it said that, if you went to the popular eatery often enough, you would eventually see most of the town's fourteen thousand inhabitants. She barely remembered driving from Elizabeth City to Caution Point, North Carolina, or even parking her car. The waiter brought her usual breakfast of coffee and a plain doughnut and would no doubt have paused for their morning chat, had she not been preoccupied.

She sipped the coffee slowly, without tasting it. In two weeks, just two short weeks, she had tumbled from a state of euphoria to one of despair. She almost wished she hadn't gotten that promotion; a department head might get away with it, but never a school principal. It couldn't be happening to her. But it was and, somehow, she had to find an acceptable solution.

"It's ridiculous," she heard a man in the adjoining booth say. "How can they charge like that? It must be illegal."

"They can, and it's legal," his companion replied in a deep, resonant, almost soothing voice, a familiar voice. "One hundred thousand dollars for my child's future. A hundred thousand and she'll be able to walk like other children. She's had fourteen months of operations, tubes and needles. Fourteen months in intensive care, and now this. Those doctors charge as much as ten times what the insurance pays. I've sold my car, mortgaged my home and my business and borrowed on every credit card I have. And now because the insurance company will pay only thirty thousand of it, I have a little more than a week to come up with seventy thousand dollars, or Amy will never walk again." Amanda couldn't help listening to the two men.

"And the bank turned you down flat yesterday afternoon?"

"Yeah. Wouldn't you? I'm a poor risk right now. A year ago, I could call my shots, but now I can't even take care of my child's needs. I told the bank officers that I have a strong damage suit in this case, but all that got me was sympathy."

"Have you tried Helena? Maybe she'd be willing to help. After all, that British polo player she married is rolling in money."

"I wrote her about the accident the day after it happened, and I got a note about six weeks later saying that she hoped everything was all right. Not that I expected more; Helena doesn't have the maternal instincts of a flea. She hasn't written since and doesn't know what her four-year-old daughter's condition is." Amanda empathized with the man; compared to his problem, hers seemed slight. If she could solve her problem with seventy thousand dollars, she would stop worrying. As heir to the wealth of her parents, grandparents and great-aunt—derived from their interests in one of the regions most prosperous fish and seafood canning businesses, money was the least of her problems. She wanted to peer around the coat tree to get a look at him, but she wouldn't know which one was Amy's father. Surely that voice couldn't belong to the man she first saw in her doctor's office and then at Lorrianne's barbecue brunch. But how could two men have that same voice? She sipped some water. Great-Aunt Meredith had always said that sipping water slowly was very calming. The men continued to search for a way to pay for Amy's surgery.

"Can't you pay the doctors on installment?"

"They want it upfront," she heard him say. "Every dime of it. But look, Jack, you'd better go. You'll be late for work, and you've sacrificed enough for me."

She looked up as "Jack" passed her on his way out, then focussed on the man who remained. Good Lord! He *was* the same one she'd seen in Dr. Graham's office and at his home. She regarded Amy's father, a handsome, clean-cut man whom she thought any woman should be proud to have for a husband. Dr. Graham had said that they could solve each other's problem. Her gaze held him, seemingly deep in thought, as he stared into his coffee cup. Perhaps... No. She pushed back the absurd idea, paid for her breakfast and left.

Amanda drove home thinking that spring recess would soon be over and she hadn't done any of the things she'd planned. Instead, she had been struggling with the most difficult problem she'd ever faced. She didn't put her car in the garage as she usually did, but left it in front of the house. She had lived alone in the comfortable, two-story home with its spacious grounds since her aunt Meredith's death and, though she loved the house with its memories, ghosts and treasures, there were times when she had to struggle with the loneliness. The telephone rang just as she closed the front door.

"Amanda, can you come to my office tomorrow morning?"

"Why, yes. Is there a problem, Dr. Graham?"

"Maybe a solution. I have an opening at eleven o'clock. Would that suit you?" She agreed and hung up. A solution. Solution to what? Well, she'd find out when she got there.

When she walked into Jacob Graham's office, Amanda supposed that his cheerful greeting was meant to put her at ease but, instead, his smile alarmed her.

"What is it?" He wasn't wearing his white coat, and he didn't indicate that he wanted her to go to the examining room. "Is something wrong, Dr. Graham?"

"Amanda, I want to talk with you as an old family friend. Caution Point is a small place, and you've just been made principal of the junior high. Small-town people are conservative; you know that. I saw you talking with my friend, Marcus Hickson, in the garden the day Lorrianne had that brunch. Both of you have a difficult problem that you could easily solve together. Marcus is a fine man by any measure, or I wouldn't say this."

"Say what?"

"Well, he's got a problem with his daughter's health, and…"

"I know," she said when he hesitated as though not wanting to betray a friend's confidence. "I overheard him telling someone. What does that have to do with me?" The skin seemed to roll on her neck as she anticipated his next words, and her breath lodged in her throat when he leaned back in his old-fashioned swivel chair, made a pyramid of his hands and prepared to continue.

"Amanda, the answer to your problem and Marcus', too, is for the two of you to get married. Don't look so shocked. You pay his daughter's medical bill, and he'll be a buffer against what you'll face otherwise."

"You're not serious!"

"Oh, yes, I am. He's a good man." Tremors spiraled down her back at the thought of being married to the man she remembered having passed a few minutes with in Lorrianne Graham's garden.

"But marry a perfect stranger? I couldn't." Agitated, she stood abruptly and began to pace. "Do you realize what you're suggesting?" His gentle smile failed to soothe her, and he must have realized it, for he added, "If the two of you found that after one year you couldn't get along and didn't want to stay married, you could separate. Of course, that means you couldn't consummate the marriage during that year. In fact, I'd counsel abstinence unless and until the two of you learned to care for each other." She felt the heat scorch her face; she hadn't been thinking of a marriage of convenience. She sat down and gazed at her feet. Dr. Graham wanted what was best for her, and she couldn't reject his proposal out of hand.

"What about him?" she asked. "Would he do it?" She was almost certain that he wouldn't. Jacob Graham looked toward Heaven and slapped his hands on his thighs.

"Probably react same as you, but considering what he's facing, he may have no choice. Do you want his phone number?" She shook her head.

"I'll have to think about this."

Amanda started down the walk toward her car and stopped short. A picture of Iris Elms, a female colleague at the junior high school, flashed before her mind's eye. Iris, gloating triumphantly. Iris victorious at last. The woman had lost her bid for school principal, but there would be no end to her boasting and baiting if she got the job anyway because of Amanda's mishap. Amanda was convinced that Iris' antagonism toward her was more than envy and hatred because she'd lost her bid to become school principal. For months, the woman had derided her at every opportunity. She reached her car and leaned against it. Half of the joy of getting that promotion to principal had come from knowing that Iris would have to treat her with respect. Dr. Graham had said that Marcus Hickson had no options. Did she?

Fighting a feeling of gloom, Amanda got into her car and drove to General Hospital in Caution Point, where she volunteered several afternoons a week. She got in the short cafeteria

line, bought a pint of milk and a peanut butter sandwich for her
lunch and found a table. Soft music from overhead speakers proclaimed the soothing charm of a wide, sleepy river in the moon-
light, and she felt it sweep away the darkness of her mood. Since
childhood, she had loved peanut butter and jelly sandwiches, and
she rose to get back in line for grape jelly.

"Leaving? I was going to ask if I could join you; the place is
practically deserted." She looked up to see Marcus Hickson
holding a tray of food.

"Oh, no. I don't mind." Flustered, she pointed to the chair.
"Please sit. I'm just going for jelly." She couldn't imagine his
thoughts as he glanced toward the chair, shrugged one shoulder,
hesitated and sat down. She took her time getting back to the
table, because she wasn't in a hurry to talk with him and
wondered why he had decided to sit with her when there were
at least twenty vacant tables.

"If you'd rather not have company..." he began and let it drift
off with a seeming diffidence that she thought didn't ring true.
She remembered that he had a sick daughter and assumed that
he had come to the hospital to visit her.

"Please stay," she said, compassion winning over wariness.
"I'm glad for the company." When she asked if he was visiting
a patient, she couldn't understand his reluctance to admit it. And
the dark cloud that seemed suddenly to mark his features troubled
her. She thought of Jacob Graham's advice earlier that day. If this
man was as desperate as he looked...

"How is your...your little girl?" She could see that her question surprised him.

"Are you clairvoyant?" She wasn't, she told him, and waited
for his answer.

He didn't seem to recognize her, but that didn't surprise her,
because she had been wearing dark glasses when they'd encountered each other in the Grahams' garden and, at their previous
encounter, he hadn't looked straight at her. She braced herself
for his reaction to what she was going to say.

"I overheard your conversation with your friend in Caution's Coffee Bean yesterday morning. I hope she's better." He told her that the child was no longer in danger, but that there was a chance she would be crippled permanently. She reached toward him to comfort him when he propped his head with his left hand, his elbow resting on the table, and released a long breath, but she withdrew self-consciously. He stirred his coffee idly, seeming to look through her, lost in his thoughts. If he wasn't desperate, she decided, the thought of his child's condition pained him so much that he might… She girded her resolve and seized the moment.

"Since you apparently aren't married, I have a proposition for you."

He frowned in disapproval. "I wouldn't have thought you the type."

"Please. I'm not trying to pick you up, but you have a problem and I have one, and together we can solve both of them."

He leaned back, observing her more closely. "Are you by any chance the woman I pulled out of Lorrianne Graham's flower patch a couple of Sundays ago?"

"Yes." She bristled at his perusal but, considering what she was about to suggest, he was entitled to appraise her. "Yes, Dr. Graham has tried twice to introduce us, but somehow, it didn't come off."

His skepticism was apparent even before he replied. "I suppose you've got seventy thousand dollars lying around unused."

All right, if he didn't believe her; she knew she didn't look as if she had a penny. "Yes, I have that much money, and I'm willing to strike a deal with you. I need a husband. At the end of one year, if either of us wanted out of the marriage, we'd call it quits. We could even sign an agreement to that effect. Up to that point, we'd be married in name only. We'd live in the same house, and I'd give you a certified check for seventy thousand." Both of his eyebrows shot up, his mouth opened, and he stared at her, seemingly speechless.

"I'm only suggesting a marriage of convenience, unless we decided to change that, though I kind of doubt that you'd want to. That way, your little girl can have her operation and I can get out of this predicament I'm in." He leaned farther back in the chair and looked at her. She saw nothing sensual in the way that he regarded her, but she blushed, obviously surprising him.

"Why do you need a husband desperately enough to put out this kind of money?" She folded her hands in her lap and had to control an urge to squirm, because she hadn't considered that she would have to give this stranger intimate information about herself. His barely checked sigh suggested that he wasn't a patient person, and that she'd better hurry and get it out.

"I'm two months pregnant." That seemed to stagger him, but only for a second, as he blinked eyes that she thought were the most beautiful honey-brown ones she'd ever seen.

"Then you're talking to the wrong man. You should be talking to the guy who had the pleasure of putting you in this predicament." She winced, unable to hide her embarrassment, and he apologized.

"I don't know where he is, and if I did I don't think I'd marry him. I'd rather be disgraced."

"Many single women have children outside the sanctity of marriage. Why would you be disgraced?"

"Those women aren't principal of Caution Point Junior High School. I am. I just got the appointment week before last, and I don't think the Board of Education would like having an unmarried pregnant principal as a role model for fourteen- and fifteen-year-old girls."

He knew how to whistle: it was long and sharp. "You don't have to have it, you know. You're only two months along."

Her lips quivered, and she closed her eyes, fighting back the tears. No point in getting annoyed, she told herself, as she gathered her purse to leave, then felt rather than saw his hand lightly on her sleeve, detaining her.

"Why do you want to have it?" he asked softly, showing sympathy for the first time. "You obviously don't like the father. Why?" She hadn't had anyone with whom she could discuss personal things since her aunt Meredith's death eighteen months earlier, just after her friend, Julie, had married and gone to live in Scotland with her husband. She had turned to Pearce Lamont out of loneliness and the need for more than casual contact with another human being, and she had convinced herself that she cared for him and that the feeling was mutual.

"I didn't plan…that is, I was unprepared for…I mean I wasn't taking the pill, and he told me that he would protect me. I had every reason to believe him and to trust him, but I found out that he was just stringing me along; he didn't really care. I'd rather not be pregnant, but I am, and I don't expect ever to conceive another child. I'm thirty-nine years old, and neither boys nor men ever found me irresistible."

"At least one man did." He said it softly, gently, as if he didn't want to hurt her. "Go on."

"I don't have any family, and if I had a child at least there would be someone who needed me and cared about me."

"Are you sure you're doing the right thing by not trying to find the child's father?"

"I cared for him, and he knew it. But I discovered that I was just fun to him, a game, a challenge. He was one of the summer people, the first man who'd showered me with attention, and I wasn't wise about such things and fell for him. He strung me along through the winter, but I refused to have an affair. Aunt Meredith said that men could change their minds once they got what they wanted. I finally gave in and proved her right. He wasn't very kind, and I never saw nor heard from him after that night." She searched her handbag, found her business card and handed it to him. He read: *Amanda Ross, Ph.D., Chairperson, English Department, Caution Point Junior High School,* followed by her school and home phone numbers.

"I haven't gotten my new cards printed yet," she told him, trying to display the cool dignity that was so natural to her. "Please call me after you think about it." *If you refuse, I'll probably have to resign and leave town,* she thought. He put the card in his shirt pocket.

"You have to find that man." He took the card out and looked at it. "Amanda. The name suits you."

She smiled. "I've always liked it."

"Amanda, no man is going to take responsibility for a child without knowing something about the father's whereabouts and his reaction to the whole thing." For a minute he seemed deep in thought, letting his left hand lightly graze his strong square chin. "Are you being wise to consider marriage to a stranger? You'd be sharing your property as well as your life with me, and you wouldn't have much protection if I proved to be unscrupulous. Legally, a marriage is a marriage, no matter what kind it is."

"I am not entirely naive. Taking a chance on a man who would mortgage his life for the health of his four-year-old daughter is no gamble whatever. Besides, Dr. Graham seems to think highly of you. You're an honorable man, Mr.... Do you realize that this is the second time we've talked and that we've been sitting here nearly an hour, and we've never introduced ourselves."

"Marcus Hickson. This is a lot of money we're talking about, Amanda. Will it put you in a hole?"

"No, it won't. If you can't give me your answer now, will you call me tomorrow or the next day?" He stood and offered her his hand. Her trembling reaction to the current that shot through her at his touch must have shocked him as it did her, for he quickly withdrew his hand. She couldn't look at him, merely picked up her tray with the half-eaten peanut butter sandwich and fled.

"I'll phone you," he called after her. He looked at the card, then back at her, knowing already what his answer would be. He'd gotten his food, started for a table and noticed her sitting in a far corner of the nearly empty cafeteria shrouded in despondency. Thinking that she might have just left one of the patients and sensing a kindred soul, he'd stopped at her table on an impulse. He hoped she got out of her predicament, but he wasn't her solution. He'd find a way to pay for Amy's surgery, and marriage wouldn't be in it. He had just been curious; he never expected to marry another woman as long as he inhaled oxygen and exhaled carbon dioxide.

Marcus put Amanda's business card back in his shirt pocket and stood where she'd left him, staring in her direction until she was out of sight. As he stood shaking his head, he didn't think he'd ever heard of a more ridiculous idea; she had to be out of her mind. Or desperate. He'd had a lot of experience with desperation, and he couldn't help but empathize with her, but he did not want any part of her scheme. He carried his tray to the disposal carousel and stepped out into the spring sunshine, dreading going to his daughter's room, abhorring the expectant looks he knew he would see on the faces of the nurses. But they no longer asked him when Amy would have her operation, because they could read the answer in his face. He had to find a way, and it wouldn't involve Amanda Ross.

Unable to postpone it any longer, Marcus walked past the nurses' station, relieved to see it unattended, and hurried to his daughter's room. During the last fourteen months, he had spent so many hours in that corner watching her sleep that he imagined he'd be lonely for it when he no longer had to go there. She opened her eyes, smiled at him and closed them again. He supposed the painkillers made her drowsy. Leaning over her carefully, so as not to touch the tube in her arm, he kissed her forehead, and his heart kicked over when her little fingers brushed his cheek.

Clouds had begun to darken the sky when he left the hospital for the short walk to the railroad station. He ignored the fine mist that soon dampened his cotton poplin bomber jacket and made his way at a normal pace. He grabbed a copy of the *Carolina Times,* tossed the newsboy fifty cents and boarded the train for Portsmouth, Virginia, and home seconds before it left the station. But he couldn't concentrate, couldn't even decipher the words; visions of Amanda Ross flitted around in his mind, troubling him. A couple and their twin daughters around Amy's age got on at Elizabeth City and sat across from him. He realized later that he'd ridden thirty miles without being aware that he'd covered his eyes with both hands, shutting out the pain of watching that couple with their healthy little girls.

"How'd it go?" Luke, his older brother asked when he opened the apartment door. Marcus walked in, comfortable in his brother's home, but it galled him that he might be forced to rent out his own house and move in with Luke in an effort to conserve his resources. Yet, he knew that, barring a miracle, the move was inevitable.

"Same old. Same old, man. But I haven't given up. I can tolerate anything, but I want Amy to have a normal, healthy life and I have to do whatever I can for her."

"Of course you do. If I hadn't just bought that resort property on the Albemarle Sound, you wouldn't have a problem." He handed Marcus a piece of paper. "The surgeon wants you to call him."

After the doctor's first few words, Marcus stopped listening. What was the use?

"I'll get back to you in a couple of days," he told the man, but he knew the futility of the gesture.

"Something wrong?"

Marcus pulled air through his teeth, leaned back in the kitchen chair, crossed his knee and took a hefty swallow of the beer that his brother put in front of him.

"Yeah. Plenty. The doctor and his team have two dates open during the next month. After that, it will be too late. They can help some, but if we wait any longer, she'll be deformed." A deep sigh escaped him. "Hell must be something like this." He pushed the beer aside. "I'm going down to Elizabeth City. See you tomorrow."

"You want to take my car?"

Marcus shrugged. "Thanks, but I'd better take the train."

An hour later, Marcus sat in Jacob Graham's living room questioning him about Amanda. "Her suggestion stunned me. She doesn't know anything about me, except that she saw me here twice and yet she makes this preposterous offer. I shouldn't mention this to you, and I doubt I'll do it, but as things stand now I have to give it some thought." Marcus couldn't think of a reason for his friend's smile and happy mood. He frowned. "Am I to think you're enjoying this, Jacob?" The smile dissolved into a grin.

"Yes, I suppose I am. This is precisely the solution I wanted to propose, but you seemed to find it preposterous that anything involving Amanda would interest you. She's a fine woman, and she'll honor any commitment. You could do much worse."

He spent the next day reviewing his options and concluded that he didn't have any. At six o'clock that evening, he forced himself to smile and walked into the intensive care room that had been his little daughter's home for more than a year. At least, she was out of danger now. She would live, but would she ever walk? Her multitude of internal injuries had been repaired, and the web of tubes that for months had reminded him of the frailty of her life had been removed—the last one just that day—and he was thankful. But he wanted his child to be whole, to be like other children. The nurses had propped her up in bed, combed her hair and plaited it with two big yellow bows. Sometimes he thought the doctors and nurses on Amy's ward ministered to him as carefully as they did to her. He leaned over to hug her and caught a whiff of a lovely, feminine scent. She smiled brilliantly, as if she knew he needed cheering.

"Hi, Daddy. Tomorrow, I'm going to be in a room with other children. I don't have to be by myself anymore."

"That's wonderful. Maybe you'll make some little friends." He gathered his child into his arms and hugged her again. He had to do his best for her. The poor child had been in that bed so long that she'd forgotten what living in a real home with him was like. He thought about Amanda and her crazy scheme. He couldn't, wouldn't marry again. Marriage as he knew it was hell, and he would challenge anyone to prove differently. *I can't go that route again: I won't. There has to be another way,* he told himself.

"Am I going to get a wheelchair like Brenda and Terry, Daddy? The nurse brought them to see me today in their new chairs."

Marcus crushed the child to him. "I don't know, baby. We'll see." He held her until she was asleep and then slipped quickly past the nurses' station to avoid a discussion of the inevitable. Four years old and already inured to pain and discomfort as a way of life. He let a tear roll down his face untouched. Too drained to make the trip back to Portsmouth, he decided to spend the night with his friends, Jack and Myrna Culpepper.

He hadn't meant to unload his dilemma on his friends. It poured out of him: his child's health or his freedom.

Flabbergasted, Jack stared at Marcus. "My God, man, don't look a gift horse in the mouth. This is the answer to our prayers. It's not 'til death do us part, man. It's just a year out of your life, and you get more of your problems solved than the money for Amy's operation."

"I'd like to know what they are," Marcus said, losing his taste for the discussion. "What is so good about being bought by a woman for a year? It's one thing to borrow money and another thing entirely to barter yourself. I have never been beholden to others. And since Helena, I've been careful not to owe any woman anything. You get screwed even if you don't owe them. Until Amy's accident, I didn't owe one penny. I don't like being indebted to *anybody,* much less to a woman in whose house I would be living and who, for whatever reason, would bear my name." Myrna sat on the floor between her husband's knees and turned to face their long-time friend, whom she regarded with sisterly affection.

"Look," Jack explained, "if you stay with her, you'll be right here in Caution near Amy and won't have that four-hour daily and expensive commute from Portsmouth. You can lease your house in Portsmouth for the year, and the income will cover the mortgage you put on it. And you can visit the factory from time to time, which is about as often as you get there these days, anyway."

Marcus stopped pacing and sat down. He hadn't thought about

Amanda's problem and, suddenly, he did. "Please don't mention any of this. I wouldn't like to see her hurt more. As it is, she has a rough time ahead. If it's all right with you I'm going to call Portsmouth, talk to my brother and turn in."

Luke Hickson listened to his younger brother's story about Amanda and her offer. Marcus had always looked up to Luke and would be the first to acknowledge his brother's sobering influence. He knew that he could be hotheaded at times and stubborn, and he valued Luke's judgment. He told himself to be open-minded.

"She needs you just as much as you need her," Luke told him. "Sounds to me like the hand of Providence working here. Not all women are like Helena. The very fact that she wants the child and plans to have it is a major difference. Don't forget that." How could he? It was the reason for his divorce. Helena had blithely informed him that she wasn't having their second baby after all and that it was a fait accompli, a done deed, giving him no choice. And then she'd left him and Amy. But he had wanted no more of her and would never forget the pain that she'd caused him.

"Thanks, Luke. I'll keep you posted." He hung up. A man shouldn't be faced with such choices; he was damned if he did and damned if he didn't.

The following evening, Amanda sat on her upstairs back porch looking over at the Albemarle Sound that had been a part of her life ever since she knew herself. She had stopped by the Caution Point Public Library after leaving school and collected books on the North Carolina and Virginia coast towns. Her heart wasn't in it, but a week had passed and she hadn't heard from Marcus, so she had to start looking for a new home. Amanda hated the thought of leaving the place where she belonged, where people knew her name and she could distinguish the churches by the ring of their bells, knew the cracks in the sidewalk, the names of the dogs that barked at night and which trees had broken limbs. She would have to move; she couldn't expect the ultraconservative citizens of Caution Point to accept unwed motherhood from the principal of their junior high school. After all, a lot of people thought it disgraceful that fifty-six-year-old Minnie Carleton, a spinster, had gotten married. A woman in her position wasn't supposed to think of such things.

Amanda leafed idly through a book on the outer banks of North Carolina, listening to the swirling waters of the Albemarle Sound. She couldn't contemplate life without it, but she knew she would have to leave if Marcus Hickson turned her down. And he might; the idea didn't seem to have found any favor with him. But she was betting on his love for that girl, a love that she sensed was strong enough to force him to do things he didn't want to do.

She sniffed the air with pleasure as scents of the roasting herbed chicken, buttermilk biscuits and apple pie baking in the oven wafted up. She sat on a low hassock, and when the cool April breeze worried her bare toes, she pulled the burnt orange caftan that she wore down to cover them. She loved the color orange, because it flattered her smooth brown complexion. The wall supported her back, comforting her because it was familiar. And she needed, loved, to have familiar people, things and places around her. But for how long? The telephone ring broke into her thoughts, and her heart seemed to drop to her middle as it had with every ring since she's encountered Marcus at the hospital cafeteria the previous week. She raced to her bedroom.

"Hello." That nervous squeak couldn't be her voice.

"Hello, Amanda. This is Marcus Hickson. If you're not busy, I'd like to come over." She felt shivers rush through her at the sound of his rich baritone.

"When?" she asked, nervous and excited.

"Now, Amanda. I'm at the hospital. How do I get to your place?"

She gave him her address and the directions. But Caution Point was a small enough town, just over fourteen thousand people, and everybody who lived there knew how to get around. Why did he need directions? She figured it would take him about forty minutes walking and took her time about dressing. When he rang the bell in less than ten minutes, she had no choice but to greet him as she was—thick hair billowing, feet bare and burnt orange caftan clinging.

Her impression of Marcus Hickson had been of a refined, sophisticated man, and she wondered why he seemed less poised.

"Hello, Amanda. I assume you're Amanda." He offered her what was barely a smile. "But this is certainly one hell of a metamorphosis."

Amanda at home was very different from Amanda anywhere else. Gone were the severe suits, sensible shoes and the thick twist or braids in which she always wore her hair. In the evenings, her heavy black mane hung loosely down her back, kinky and wild; she wore floor-length, brightly colored caftans, and shoes never touched her feet.

Thinking that he was disappointed in the way she looked, she apologized. "I'm sorry. I thought you'd need more time getting here. I didn't have time to get dressed."

He looked down at her and gave his left shoulder a quick shrug. "God forbid you should make yourself less attractive on my account. I caught a ride. Mind if I come in?" She stepped back and let him pass as she mused over his cryptic remarks. Not an easy man to understand, she decided.

"Before we talk business, let me show you around." She would be foolish if she didn't do everything she could to make him decide in her favor, so she began the tour upstairs, showing him first the guest room and adjoining bath that would be his personal quarters.

"You could rearrange it to suit yourself," she told him, "and I'd change the covers and curtains. You'd want something more masculine." She walked on. "This is my sitting room."

He nodded. "You've got a complete office up here," he said of her sitting room.

"You'd be welcome to use it." They walked out onto the porch.

"This is beautiful, Amanda. Idyllic. Don't you get lonely here?"

She answered him truthfully. "Yes. But the result of my one experience at reaching out after my aunt died is the reason you're here. Believe me, lonely is better."

She's rambling, because she's scared and nervous, he thought, and told himself that he should put her at ease. But he didn't; the little exercise was very revealing.

She took him through the living and dining rooms and, though she didn't invite him to do so, he followed her through the break-fast room and into the kitchen. She took the pie out of the oven and turned the chicken. Her slight body with well-rounded, feminine hips silhouetted through the caftan sounded a warning to him as she bent to her task. This wasn't going to work. She'd upped the ante. He refused to believe that she hadn't presented herself as a little siren just to get him to agree to her mad scheme. He had been astonished when the door was opened not by the lackluster person he'd met previously, but by a lovely and charming woman. He let his gaze travel over her back. Yeah. A real sexy sister. The sensation he experienced was not one that he welcomed.

He brought his left hand up and brushed the back of it against the bottom of his chin. In all fairness, she was entitled to try and win her case, he acknowledged silently; she had plenty to lose. He told himself to lighten up.

"What kind of contract are you offering, Amanda?" The abruptness with which he opened the topic surprised her, but it relieved her, too. If he wanted to discuss it, he hadn't ruled it out.

"Go on in the living room; I'll get us some coffee. Sugar or cream?" He took both.

"The kitchen's fine." She felt oddly secure as she watched him settle his long frame into the straight-back chair.

"Well, I thought like this. You would have no financial respon-sibility for me or the baby. We'd stay married for one year, and then consider the future, though I expect you'll want to end it. You'd live here. Any of your friends or family would be welcome anytime you wanted them to come, because this would be your home. We'd both have physical exams first and you'd get the certified check as soon as we married. We'd divorce after one year on grounds of irreconcilable differences, if that's what either of us wanted. I would bear all household expenses during that time."

He turned sharply and stared at her. "You're proposing to take care of me for one year?" His discomfort with the idea was obvious and, for the first time, she resented what she regarded as his unnecessary defensiveness enough to bristle and show it.

"You've got a more reasonable suggestion? Maybe if I knew a little something about you, I'd manage not to insult you. For starters, why did you need directions to my house? Everybody in town knows this place." She wondered why he seemed pleased at her sharp response. Maybe he preferred women with guts to shrinking violets.

"Amanda, I live in Portsmouth. I'd brought my daughter with me to watch the sailing competition on the Sound, and a building crane fell on our rented car and crushed her almost to death. I was practically unharmed. The emergency squad took her to Caution Point General, and it hasn't been wise to move her. I could now, but she's learned to like and trust the nurses and she's getting the best of care. So I'm keeping her there."

"You've commuted between Portsmouth and Caution Point daily for fourteen months?"

"Fourteen months and two weeks. Sometimes twice daily. I have a business in Portsmouth. I rebuild fine grand pianos, antique harpsichords and spinets. I'll handle a console or a small string instrument, but only if it's of superior quality. Right now, the banks own everything I have."

She shook her head slowly, so slowly that he had to know exactly what she was feeling and that the sentiment was for him.

"Are we going to have a deal, Marcus?" She wanted his agreement, but not at the expense of appearing fragile and vulnerable. He must know that both her future and his child's future were at stake. Her apparent calm as she waited for his answer was as good a piece of acting as she had ever pulled off, she thought proudly.

"It's possible, but there's still the matter of the child's father." She handed him a fax from Dexter and Strange, Inc., dated that day. He read it twice before giving it back to her.

"If you had told me his name, I could have saved you the price of those detectives' fee. Still, it's a good thing to have a copy of that death certificate. Pearce was always a daredevil and totally self-centered. I think I should warn you, though: you'll be better off if Pearce, Sr., never learns about this child; he'd give you plenty of trouble."

She gasped. "How could he? This child is mine."

"Amanda, Pearce Lamont, Sr., is a rich man. He owns two newspapers, an FM radio station, a string of motels, and he doles out a lot of money to both political parties. He can swing any deal he wants to. He's bought his son out of jail, out of parenthood..." Seeing her shocked, hurt reaction to that information, he toned it down. "There've been several paternity suits against Pearce, Jr., but, as far as I know, he and his family won all of them. We'll never know what the truth is. Just pray that you're carrying a girl. Lamont doesn't have a grandson nor another son, and he'd bend rules and break laws now to get a male heir."

The more he talked and the longer she shared his company, the more certain she was that she wanted him there. She felt more secure than ever in her life. "Marcus, you're very big. How tall are you?"

He blinked, obviously surprised by the question. "I'm six feet, three and a half, and I weigh two hundred dripping." She blanched as the image of a dripping Marcus filled her mind and, from his expression, she didn't doubt that he knew her thoughts. "And I'm thirty-five years old," he added gruffly.

"Nothing would frighten a person with you around." She caught her breath when he threw her off balance with a genuine grin, his white teeth flashing and his enchanting, honey-brown eyes sparkling with deviltry.

"There's not much to you, is there?" he teased.

"Well, I'm five-three, and it hasn't hindered me so far."

"You didn't tell me what name you'll put on the birth certificate as the father of your child, Amanda." She was quiet for a long time before looking inquiringly at the man who sat before her, waiting patiently for this most important of answers. The answer that would determine her future. It was best to be honest.

"I want to put your name there, Marcus. Could you agree to that? It's very important to me that my child be legitimate. When it's old enough to understand, I'll explain to her or him. But I won't do it unless you agree."

He studied her for a few seconds. She hadn't made it a term of the contract, but had asked his permission. And instead of doing it surreptitiously, she had chosen to be open and honest about it. Marcus walked over to the window and stared out at the darkness. The eerie shapes of the big, stalwart pines barely moved in the gusty wind, but the little dogwoods—visible by their bright flowers—bowed low as though under a great burden. He couldn't help likening the scene to his present dilemma. He had what he needed to withstand the rigors of life but, as small and vulnerable as she was, Amy could not protect herself. Only he could do that. What was one year of his life for the whole of Amy's? He walked back to Amanda and extended his hand.

"All right, Amanda. If those are your terms, you've got a deal, and my name goes on the birth certificate. I don't know how I'll feel, though, knowing that there's a child somewhere with my name and who thinks I'm its father, but to whom I give nothing. It's never going to sit well with me, but I don't suppose you're crazy about the idea, either. *Something for something,* I suppose. But, honey, this is one tough bargain." He'd have to tell her not to hope for more than a year; he didn't see how he could push himself to accept it longer than that. Her face glowed with happiness, and he waved off her thanks. She had tried to make it as palatable as possible, he knew, but it still went against his grain and tied up his guts. *Married!* After all the promises he'd made to himself and God about tying himself to a woman. Still, it didn't seem right to make her miserable just because he was. He tried to shake it off.

"Do I have the right to offer a little advice?" When she nodded, he continued. "For the sake of privacy, let's see a lawyer in Elizabeth City. And I suggest that we get married there, too." He looked at his watch. "Good Lord, I've got to go. I'm just about to miss the last train to Portsmouth." Amanda glanced at her own watch.

"I don't see how you can get to the station and on that train in eight minutes, not even if I drive you. So, suppose you stay over and try out your room tonight. Supper's ready."

"I hate to put you out, and I don't want to eat up your meal."

"Marcus, I've never eaten a whole chicken at one sitting in my life. There's plenty. I made a fresh batch of buttermilk biscuits and there's a pot of string beans." It occurred to Marcus that he could stay with Jack and Myrna as he had done many times, but for reasons that he refused to examine, he dismissed the idea.

"What's that over there?" He pointed to the pie.

"Apple pie."

He loved home cooking, though he rarely got any. But just the thought of a home-baked apple pie could make him delirious. What was the point of polite pretense?

"You're on. I love that stuff."

He finished his third piece of pie and stretched lazily. "Happiness is having 'a good bank account, a good cook and a good digestion.' Two out of three's not bad." Amanda Ross turned sharply around and stared at the man who'd just eaten half of a roasting chicken, seven biscuits and more than half a pie. He leaned back, watching her. Had she thought he wouldn't know anything except the way in which wires and hammers functioned on string instruments? From the look on her face, she hadn't expected a housemate knowledgeable in literature, which he assumed was her specialty.

"I see you've been reading Rousseau."

He smiled wickedly, enjoying her surprise. "And I see you've mixed up your metaphors."

She got up and began to clear the table. "You've got many sides; we'll get along." Nodding in agreement, Marcus rose and took the plates from her.

"The one who cooks shouldn't wash dishes. And we'll do the housework and other chores together. You should have put that in the contract." And he should have put it in a contract with Helena. She hadn't done much more than sleep at home, not even after Amy's birth. Oh, but she had punished him!

"It's been my experience that one ought to look ahead and start the way one can finish. And that's from Ross. Amanda Ross."

"Yeah? Well 'the only thing that experience teaches us is that experience teaches us nothing.'" He waited for her to identify the quote.

"Maurois, right?" He nodded. She showed him the washer and dryer so that he could wash his underwear, socks and shirt, gave him a large beach towel and bade him good-night.

For the first time since she had learned of her pregnancy, she didn't dread going to bed. She would sleep. All still wasn't right with the world, but the outlook was certainly improving.

Several days later, Amanda sat in Jacob Graham's waiting room. The same painting hung facing her on the wall, and the simple red and gray furnishings hadn't changed but, to her eyes, the old looked new and what had seemed dull now glowed. She stood when the doctor walked toward her.

"I hope you've got something good to tell me," he said, draping an arm around her shoulder. "Come on in the examining room." She told him about her agreement with Marcus.

"That's the best solution for you two; I'm glad you worked it out by yourselves." She explained about the health certificate she needed.

"All right, and while I'm at it, we'll see how the baby is coming along. You're in good shape," he told her later and advised her to choose a gynecologist in Caution Point. As she left, he assured her, "You will never meet a finer man than Marcus Hickson. I hate to see him down on his luck this way, but I don't doubt for a minute that he'll snap back. If you need me, you know where I am."

She skipped down the walkway to her car, picked up a green crab apple from the lawn and sent it sailing through the air. Turning, she waved to the doctor who stood in the doorway smiling, got in her car and drove off. She stopped at Caution's Coffee Bean and ordered a chocolate shake from the lone waiter who nodded and asked whether she'd hit the lottery.

"Haven't seen you this bright in a while now," he said.

"Haven't felt this bright," she answered, smiling to herself. She walked out into the sunlight and looked up and down State Street for her friend Sam, the rag man, who'd been sweeping that street for as long as she could remember, but he was nowhere to be seen. She stopped by the Albemarle Kiddies Roost and bought a book on pregnancy and two on child care. At last, she could have the pleasure of planning for her baby.

Chapter 2

Four days later, in the presence of Jack and Myrna Culpepper, Lorrianne and Jacob Graham and Luke Hickson, Amanda married Marcus in the parsonage of the Mt. Pisgah Baptist Church in Elizabeth City. She had stamped her foot belligerently and made Marcus understand that, even if theirs wasn't a real marriage, she would not repeat her vows before a Justice of the Peace. When he realized that she was not going to relent, he had conceded defeat and agreed, flashing his charismatic smile and shrugging as if to say, you win some and you lose some. He had also been elegant in an oxford-gray pinstriped suit, pale gray on gray shirt and yellow tie, and his lingering, appreciative look made her glad that she had splurged on a flattering Dior blue silk suit and matching hat. Her eyes misted when Marcus handed her a bouquet of six calla lilies just before the ceremony began; the flowers made it seem like a real, lovers' wedding. But she noticed the glances that passed between the two brothers when she showed her pleasure and wondered which of them had thought of the flowers.

Two days after the ceremony, on the morning of Amy's scheduled operation, Marcus stumbled into the kitchen. The rain pouring down in sheets, and a visibility of barely three feet failed to daunt him. He'd be soaked when he got to the hospital, but he wouldn't think of complaining; Amy meant everything to him, and she would finally have a chance to be well again. He stopped abruptly at the kitchen door, hands on his hips and the surprise on his face unmasked. He hadn't thought he'd find Amanda there, the table set for one and the odor of food permeating the room at six o'clock in the morning. And when she asked him to sit down and eat a meal of scrambled eggs, country sausage patties, home fries, hot buttermilk biscuits, orange juice and coffee, a feeling of discomfort pervaded him.

"Aren't you eating?" he asked. He didn't want to be treated like a husband. He wasn't a husband; he was a man caught without options and paying a harsh penalty for it. He knew that she sensed his suddenly dark mood and that she even understood the reason for it. Though he tried to hide what he felt, her forced smile was evidence that he hadn't succeeded. But what was he to do? He didn't want to hurt her, but neither did he want this cozy husband-wife relationship with her. He didn't even know her.

"I'd love to be able to eat that," she said, apparently deciding that it would be she and not he who would set the tone of their relationship. "It's what I usually have but, these mornings, crackers and club soda are as much as I can manage."

In spite of himself a feeling of protectiveness toward her sprouted within him. "Bear with me, Amanda. My nerves are raw this morning, what with the operation and all." Her refusal to take offense at his cool manner was as much punishment as he needed. He told himself he'd make it up to her.

"It's pouring outside. I'll drive you." But as they reached the attached garage, she handed him the keys, and he took them without hesitation, all his battered ego needed right then was for her to drive while he sat beside her like an underaged kid. They drove to Caution Point General in silence, and he wondered whether he'd be able to endure the year ahead. Amanda parked, while he rushed in to comfort and reassure Amy before the doctors anesthetized her. A few minutes later, Amanda walked into the waiting room and sat down, giving him another surprise.

"I thought you'd gone home."

"I couldn't leave you here alone for hours, maybe all day, waiting for the outcome of the operation. I'm human, Marcus." He looked at her through long, slightly lowered lashes. She was human, all right, and she had an old-fashioned mother instinct. Amy would fall in love with her and, when they separated, his child would be motherless again. But this time, she'd be old enough to feel the pain of separation. A sense of foreboding engulfed him. He didn't want his child hurt because of the bargain he'd made with Amanda. But what choices did he have? He dropped his head into his hands; helplessness was foreign to him.

He had always prided himself in having the intelligence and the mother wit to anticipate and circumvent problems, and the mental stamina and physical strength to handle whatever caught him unaware. He had never shirked a responsibility nor dodged an obligation. And he knew how to be a friend. But it was quid pro quo with him and Amanda, and he didn't want to be more obligated to her than he was. Like that breakfast this morning. He hadn't had such a wonderful breakfast since he'd left his parents' home more than a dozen years earlier. He didn't know how he could stop Amanda from behaving like a wife without crushing her spirit, and he'd be less than a man if he added to the emotional battering under which she was struggling. But he couldn't let Amy form an attachment to her. He knew Amy would need and love Amanda, because Amanda was lovable, and then they'd go their separate ways. Not on your life, he swore silently, as he tried to banish a persistent thought: You're already going to miss her. Give her a year and see how you'll feel. He stiffened. If his hunch was correct; keeping her own child out of old man Lamont's clutches would be a full-time job, and that problem was bound to surface as soon as Amanda had her baby. He'd better be prepared for it.

* * *

In spite of her lack of experience with men, Amanda wasn't so naive that she thought she could change Marcus or that he would look upon her as his salvation. He hated and resented that he had been forced to relinquish his personal freedom. She knew that, and she hardly blamed him. What she didn't understand was why he wouldn't try harder to make the best of it for both their sakes. Why wouldn't he acknowledge that she was also a victim and that she might find their situation just as repulsive as he did?

She looked at the big clock hanging on the wall near the nurses' station in clear view of the waiting room and shuddered. What a thoughtless reminder of passing time for anxious relatives and friends! One o'clock. They had been waiting for five hours, and barely a word had passed between them. Did he know she was there? She left the room just as Marcus buried his head in his arms.

"Marcus." He looked up in response to her gentle touch. "I've brought us a little something to eat."

"What time is it?" She told him, and watched helplessly as the color drained from his face.

"She's so little. What could they be doing to her all this time?" Amanda risked draping an arm over his shoulder as she sat beside him and handed him a paper container of coffee.

He glanced up at her. "Thanks." Encouraged, she passed him a ham sandwich. He bit into it.

"Have you been here all this time? Wouldn't you think they'd have enough feeling to come out and tell me something? It's my child in there."

"Have faith, Marcus. You hired a team of the best physicians in the country. Isn't it good that they're taking their time and doing it right so she won't have to go through this again? I know it's tough, but it can't be much longer." As she spoke, she let her left hand move gently over his broad shoulders, circling and patting him, in an offering of support. He seemed barely aware of it. She talked on, keeping her voice very low and soft, trying to soothe him. It wasn't difficult. He seemed to be hurting too badly to rebuff her tenderness and caring.

An hour and a half later, huddled together with Amanda's left arm around Marcus and her right hand grasping his right forearm, they didn't see Luke as he approached. "How's it going? Any word, yet?"

Marcus shook his head. "They're still with her." He knew that Luke loved the child and was as glad as he that she would have the chance to be like other children again. He felt the comforting arm around him and settled into it, neither caring nor wondering why it was there. He needed it. No words passed between them until finally the doctor appeared, still wearing his surgical greens.

"We've done all that we can. The rest is up to God, the therapists and Amy." Marcus didn't want to hear that and, at his profane outburst, the doctor assured them that she would be as good as new *if* instructions were followed to the letter.

"May I see her? I just have to see that she's all right." The doctor's assurance that she was all right, but asleep and in intensive care, didn't satisfy him.

Marcus turned to Amanda. "I'm going to stay here until I see her. You go on home. And drive carefully. Ocean Avenue was very slippery this morning."

Amanda didn't want to leave Marcus, but she did as he asked when Luke promised her that he would remain with his brother. She shopped at the supermarket and had just turned into her lane when she saw a stray kitten, the worst for having been in the heavy morning downpour. Amanda didn't like pets, because she thought that animals should be free. But she couldn't bear to see a being suffer, so she took the kitten and her groceries in the house, dried the weak little animal, fed it and put it in a padded basket. She changed her clothes and started dinner, but the kitten cried until she gave it her attention. Marcus arrived several hours later with Luke to find her lounging in an oversized living room chair with her bare feet tucked under her trying to calm the little creature.

Luke paused in the doorway, as though fearing to intrude further; the sight of this adult woman lovingly stroking a kitten while singing it a lullaby, albeit out of tune had dumbfounded Marcus. Luke turned to his brother, intending to remark on the drollery of that bizarre little scene but, one look at him, and the words died unspoken in his throat. With her head bowed and her voice low and sultry, Amanda sang softly, slowly stroking the little cat. Marcus' eyes sparkled rustic fire, his lips were slightly parted, his face open and filled with emotion. Luke knew that he had never before seen this Marcus, this man smoldering with desire. And he didn't doubt that Marcus wanted to exchange places with that kitten. What a pity that Amanda didn't see her husband's face!

As if she sensed their presence, Amanda looked up, her eyes locking with Marcus' heated gaze. Luke watched as she caught her breath and lowered her gaze, flustered; surely his brother must see that Amanda was vulnerable to him, aware of him as a man. He shook his head sadly; she was a tender, gentle woman, but would Marcus give up his cynicism and allow himself to see that? He didn't hold out much hope for it.

Marcus stood rooted to the spot, speechless, remembering how she had held him, caressed and soothed him while he had waited in agony for news about Amy's surgery. And ingrate that he was, he told himself, he had repaid all of her caring with rudeness. He hadn't even wanted Luke to come home with him, hating to dignify his circumstances by sharing his temporary home with his brother.

"How is she?" Amanda's obvious embarrassment as she managed to break the silence aroused his compassion.

"She recognized both of us." Marcus banked the desire raging in him and tried to smile, but he was so shocked at his unexpected reaction to Amanda that he managed little more than a grimace. "She's bandaged from her hips to her toes, and she's heavily sedated, but the worst is over." He walked slowly over to her. "Thanks."

"For what?"

"For being there when I needed someone."

She smiled. "You would have done the same for me." She turned to his brother. "Luke, you're more than welcome to stay for dinner. I cooked with you in mind."

"No need for that; we'll go out," Marcus said, still unwilling to accept the place as his home and unable to hide his concern for his status there. He saw that Luke's sympathies were with Amanda when his brother shook his head, and he could almost read Luke's mind, could almost hear him saying for the nth time: "It's time you let go of the past and stopped nursing the hatred and bitterness that you've wrapped yourself in ever since Helena betrayed you." *Well, I'm the one wearing these shoes, not Luke,* he told himself.

Luke scowled fiercely at Marcus, then smiled at Amanda. "I'd love to stay for dinner, Amanda. I get enough of restaurants." Marcus knew that Luke didn't care how much he fumed; Luke took the commandment about justice and mercy seriously, even when it wasn't in question.

"I want to find out what kind of cook my sister-in-law is." Marcus wasn't fooled by the remark; it had been intended to please Amanda and to put her at ease. If it made him furious, Luke didn't mind. He watched Amanda put the kitten in the basket and start toward the kitchen. But when it was deprived of her body warmth, the little animal cried, and Amanda stooped to take it into her arms.

"When did you get a cat?" Marcus asked. He wasn't fond of cats. More accurately, he disliked them. Amanda explained how she got it and that she planned to take it to a shelter on Monday. A picture of Amanda nursing her baby, coddling it and loving it flashed through his mind's eye; that child was a lucky one. His Amy hadn't had that kind of loving from her mother. Could he deny her the sweetness, the loving acceptance that Amanda would shower on her? He glanced at the woman he'd married and couldn't believe that he hadn't previously noticed her café au lait complexion and large wistful black eyes. Heart-stopping eyes. *Cut it out, man,* he admonished himself.

Amanda went on to the kitchen, through the long hallway and past the dining room, wondering why not having a cat around had pleased him so much. He didn't want them to get too close; she was sure of that. But when he had needed her, she'd had a glimpse of the man without the veneer, without the antiwoman armor that he wore either naturally or for her benefit, she wasn't sure which. A minute earlier, he'd silently told her that she was in some way special. He confused her. She sensed that Luke was different, more open. When she met him at her wedding, she knew at once that he was an easier, gentler man than his brother. A man with Marcus' aura of danger but without his anger.

Luke looked around the living room, attempting to glean something of Amanda's personality, while his brother paced the floor. Her taste in art appealed to him, because he, too, loved the paintings of John Biggers, Elizabeth Catlett and Jacob Lawrence, artists who dug deep into the black soul. Realizing that Marcus hadn't placed anything of his own in the room because he'd probably decided that the arrangement was temporary and didn't want to forget that, Luke faced him.

"I've got to talk to you." He could see that Marcus wasn't ready to give up the pain he felt because of his circumstances, that he found that pain enjoyable, like a balm for his wounded pride or a nice safe place to put his worries.

"It's a free country," Marcus told his brother.

"Lighten up, will you, Marcus? Don't you realize that she's doing everything she can to make life as pleasant as possible for the two of you? What do you think having to ask you to marry her in these circumstances and paying you to do it has done to her pride? You're too old for this stubbornness. Can't you see that you've gotten so used to having problems—pretty awful ones, I grant you—that you've closed your eyes to the truth. You have struck gold, man, but you don't even recognize relief when you have it." He moved to put an arm around his brother's shoulder, but Marcus stepped away.

"You're annoyed, but you'll think about what I've said, because you're a man of conscience and honor. You've been reliving Helena's treachery and betrayal long enough."

Luke didn't wait for a reaction. He had already decided that he wanted to talk with Amanda, see what she was like. Even before meeting her, he'd been impressed with her refusal to let Marcus treat their marriage as though it was an incident of no special significance and with her request that they have a dignified ceremony. And after what he'd seen of her today, first with Marcus at the hospital and then with that kitten, he felt that he pretty much understood her, and he had a hunch that she could light up Marcus' life.

Amanda flipped on the oven light and bent to check her pork roast. When she straightened, a wave of dizziness almost sent her sprawling, but Luke must have stepped into the kitchen just in time to see it. She felt his steadying hand.

"Easy there." He guided her to a chair and sat her down.

"Where do you keep the glasses?" But even as he asked, he'd found them and was at the sink getting a glass of cold water.

"Drink a little. It will help steady you." Amanda sipped while Luke waited for her to empty the glass. *He's got a low, gentle voice,* she thought, *but you wouldn't dare disobey it.*

"Thanks. That's the first time *that's* happened. I thought that once I got over the morning sickness, that would be it for the day." She didn't mean it as a complaint, just an observation.

"When are you expecting the baby, Amanda?"

Her lashes swept up quickly. Marcus hadn't bothered to ask. "November seventh. The doctor was certain, because there's only been that one time." She could see that her remark had made him curious, though he tried to appear casually interested. She was thirty-nine years old, after all; any man would wonder about that statement.

"What do you mean, 'that one time'?"

"Maybe I shouldn't be telling you this. But there's so much I don't understand. I never discussed anything personal with my father and I'm an only child, so there wasn't a brother to talk with. And Marcus hasn't invited any intimacies between us. I feel closer to you than I do to him, but there are things that I could ask him that I don't think I should be discussing with you." When Luke glanced toward the kitchen door, she realized he didn't want to offend his brother, but that he wanted to help her if he could.

"What are you talking about, Amanda?"

She laced her fingers and looked first to the ceiling and then to the floor, before settling her gaze on the refrigerator. "I thought the baby's father cared for me like I cared for him. But it seems I was just a challenge. He'd made a bet with his buddies, and he won it. He wasn't nice to me, Luke, although he must have known…he had to know that he was hurting me and he wouldn't stop. I had to go to the emergency room. He had courted me persistently for six months, but after that night he never called or wrote, and I never saw him again. I had been lonely after my aunt Meredith died, and I didn't know much about men. I have nightmares about it sometimes. Luke, isn't there any gentleness in men? If there is, I have never experienced it, not in my father, my baby's father, nor my coworkers. And so far, not much in my husband."

Luke bit back an explosive expletive. "I always thought that most men are gentle with women, Amanda. Are you telling me that Marcus mistreats you? I can't believe he'd lay a finger on you. He's not that type of man."

Amanda stood and began to set the table. "Of course not. I know he's a gentleman, Luke. It's just…well, if I do anything for him… This morning, I fixed him a good breakfast, but that made him uncomfortable, and anytime he finds himself being nice to me, he quickly withdraws. It's like he's trying to make me pay for something I didn't do." Luke rested a hand lightly on her shoulder.

"He had a hard time with Amy's mother, but he's softening. You can help him, and he can help you. In fact, if the two of you were ever to communicate, really communicate, you'd see that you need each other."

His words failed to placate her. She had realized earlier that evening that she was vulnerable to Marcus, that she was attracted to him, and it frightened her. She walked to the back door, pretending to look for something on the porch, while she restrained the tears. She didn't want Luke's pity or anyone else's, but her feelings about Marcus, her situation and their relationship troubled her. She stepped back inside and closed the door and, with her back to the kitchen, looked into the darkness. She spoke to him quietly, resigned. "I'm going to pay for that one night for the rest of my life."

Luke shook his head. "You don't have to go through with it, you know."

"Yes I do. Anyway, I don't have anyone now. At least I'll have someone to love and to love me. But Marcus says that the baby's grandfather might try and take the child from me, if he learns about it."

Luke had heard Marcus walking toward the kitchen, but didn't look in his direction; it wouldn't hurt Marcus to know what his wife had experienced and what she feared.

"Who is he?"

"Pearce Lamont, Sr. He lives in Portsmouth."

"I know him and I know where he lives." He walked around to face her and handed her his business card: Lieutenant Luke Stuart Hickson, Detective; Portsmouth Police Department. "Don't worry about Lamont. If he gives you any trouble, let me know." He acknowledged her thanks with a nod, thinking that she had a lovely smile. But her smile faltered and, glancing around, he frowned in concern. Had she stopped smiling because she'd seen Marcus?

"Where's this dinner you were promising?" She glanced at Marcus and then smiled when his relaxed manner indicated that the three of them would spend an enjoyable evening. She had wondered what Marcus was doing alone in the living room, whether he was brooding about Amy. She took pleasure in having controlled her urge to go to him, suspecting that he had needed to be alone in order to recoup from the trauma of their long wait for the doctors' verdict.

Amanda asked Marcus to say grace, explaining that her aunt Meredith had always said that, in a civilized home, the head of the house always says grace before meals. Marcus looked as if he wasn't sure he was head of that house, but a smirking Luke bowed his head and waited. Marcus said the grace. Amanda wouldn't have admitted that she had set out to impress Luke with her cooking, but that was the effect she got. He had as big an appetite as his brother, and as he swallowed his fifth biscuit, he told her, "If you feed Marcus like this every night, you'll never get rid of him." In a reflexive action, she reached over and gently wiped the scowl from Marcus' face and got an embarrassed grin for her effort. Her innocent gesture seemed to surprise and please Luke, and she was happier than she'd been at any time since her marriage. She felt that she had a friend and ally in her brother-in-law, and her instinct told her that, in the months to come, she would need his support.

Innocently desiring to communicate to Marcus the feeling that Luke gave her, she told her husband, "I like your brother, Marcus."

Marcus fingered his emerging beard and shrugged his left shoulder. "Why doesn't that surprise me? Liking Luke is something women just seem to do automatically."

Rather taken aback, she responded honestly. "Oh, I can see that Luke is very handsome, Marcus, but not more so than you. Perhaps even less. Do you have any more brothers?" Marcus stopped eating and looked at his wife.

"No. You really think I'm better looking than Luke? You're pulling my leg. You've got to be. Luke's on the stud list of every matchmaking matron in Portsmouth. If a celebrity beauty comes to town, he's the man they ask to escort her. He once squired Miss America around Portsmouth. Tell her how many tuxedos you've got, Luke."

Luke's gruff response reflected his discomfort and belied his commanding presence. "He's overstating it, Amanda. They all know that I'm a widower, and they take advantage of it." Amanda postponed commiserating with Luke over his status as widower and turned to her husband. First things first.

"Luke *is* nice, Marcus, but you've got the most bewitching eyes I've ever looked into in my life." She plowed on; make hay while the sun's shining, Aunt Meredith had always said. "Have you been wearing dark glasses, or are the women in Portsmouth all blind?" Marcus actually blushed, and Luke clearly delighted in it. The exchange gave Amanda food for thought: The brothers enjoyed each other's company; they loved each other. So this was what she had missed in not having a sibling.

"What's so funny?" Marcus blustered, but both his wife and his brother could see his delight in Amanda's compliment.

Luke watched Marcus clear the table, scrape the dishes and put them in the dishwasher while Amanda made coffee and got the dessert. What interested him most was that they did it without uttering a word. *Teamwork,* he thought. *Don't they know that they would make a great team if they tried?* He'd never seen Helena and Marcus cooperate on any level; they had always seemed to be at cross-purposes.

* * *

When Amanda served the deep-dish apple pie à la mode, Luke threw his head back and roared with laughter. Marcus knew from his brother's cheshire grin that Luke was delighted at his discomfort. He scowled. Sure, Amanda was catering to his passion for apple pie. Well, let her. Nobody could blame her for trying. Beside, she made the best apple pie that he'd ever eaten. He didn't miss her smothered smile.

"The hell with both of you," he told them amiably, as he gave himself another serving. "You grin and I'll eat."

A few minutes later, walking through the hall toward the living room feeling as if she had progressed in her effort to make friends with her husband, Amanda glanced toward him, saw that he had just called the hospital and waited for him to give her news of Amy. He hung up, turned and went to the kitchen apparently to give Luke the information. Sorely disappointed that he hadn't told her how Amy was progressing, she waited at the bottom of the stairs in the hope that he would realize her concern and rectify the oversight. But he remained in the kitchen and, convinced after a long wait that he didn't think it necessary to tell her, she pondered what to do. Fighting a growing annoyance, she walked back to the kitchen, interrupted the conversation and asked him if he'd planned to tell her.

"Look, I…she's…doing fine."

"But you weren't going to tell me. Didn't you think I cared?"

"I'm sorry, but…well…I'm so used to talking with Luke about this…" Realizing his error, he added as an explanation, "He's her uncle."

"And I'm nothing to her, right?" He grimaced, but she didn't care that she'd made him uncomfortable.

"Amanda, please be reasonable. This situation is difficult enough without…"

She didn't wait to hear the rest of it, but fled to her room, tears stinging her eyes.

* * *

"Proud of yourself, Marcus?" Luke asked him. "Are you touched in the head, man? You don't recognize a good, honest woman when you see one. How could you do that to her, when you know how badly she's been hurt?"

Marcus braced his elbow against the wall and supported his head with his hand. "Lay off, man." He shook his head, perplexed. "No, I'm not proud of myself. I don't understand why it's so difficult for me to behave naturally with Amanda. I do know that I can't let her establish any contact with Amy. If Amy starts to like her, she'll be hurt when we go our separate ways—as you and I both know we will—and she's already suffered too much. Having her mother reject her is enough."

"You go right ahead and fool yourself. Where do you keep the bedding? I'm going to turn in. Good night... Oh, Marcus."

"What?"

"If you'd just try to be your normal self, this would be a peaceful, maybe even a happy home. Amanda is a terrific woman."

In the quiet house, only the wind could be heard bending the trees as the storm moved off the coast and out to the ocean. Marcus leaned his big muscular frame against the banister at the bottom step and looked up the stairs. How could he have done it, he asked himself. He felt protective toward her, had from the very first. Yet he'd deliberately hurt her when she was only expressing concern. *You go right ahead and fool yourself,* Luke had said. He wasn't fooling himself, he argued to himself, he was protecting his child. And he didn't want any involvement with Amanda or any other woman. He had taken care of Amy by himself since she was two years old, and he would continue to take care of her. "I should have asked him how he knew Amanda was a terrific woman after a mere half-hour conversation with her. Oh, hell. I know she probably is, and that's the trouble," he murmured, as he forced himself to climb the stairs.

He saw the light shining beneath her door and paused. She'd been up there nearly three hours, he estimated, and was still awake. What had he done to her? Marcus struggled against his deeply ingrained ethics and lost the battle. He raised his hand, uncertain of his move and, for the first time, knocked on Amanda's bedroom door. He did it not knowing what he would say. After he knocked several times, she opened it and looked up at him, her wide black eyes reddened by hours of tears. Marcus stared at her, the epitome of femininity in a lacy peach peignoir that covered her from her neck to her bare toes. He wanted her. And the knowledge shook him. He stood there speechless as desire washed through him with such stunning force that he would have left if she hadn't spoken.

"Marcus…" It was barely more than a sigh, falling off her tongue as if pulled by the force of gravity. His hypnotic gaze bore into her like a sharp drill. He exuded pure magnetism, and the female in her responded to his maleness. She gasped, remembering what she'd felt when she'd caught him watching her right after he and Luke walked in the house, and wrapped her arms around herself for protection as she shivered, rooted to the spot.

"My God!" he muttered, stepping into the room and opening his arms to her. She went into them without a second of hesitation. Her thoughts centered on her need to be held, and when he pulled her to him and cradled her head against his broad shoulder, she moved into him. She relished the comfort of his hand roaming her back, shoulders and arms, caressing her. Zombie-like, she tiled her head back in order to look at him, and he lowered his head. *He's going to kiss me,* she thought, and knew that she wanted it. Wanted him. But he stopped and drew back, shaking his head as if in wonder. At her puzzled expression, he pulled her closer and hugged her, then stepped back.

Marcus took her hand and walked into her sitting room, away from that enticing bed. He hadn't meant to make a move on Amanda, not then, not ever. But his body hadn't taken his intentions into account. One look at her, red-eyed and miserable, her brown face open and unadorned, and he had wanted her at a gut-searing level. He sat there with both of her hands in his big one, not talking, hardly breathing. Recovering his equilibrium. That had been close.

"I know it isn't enough to say I'm sorry. We both know you didn't deserve what I did. I...I hope you won't hold it against me and that you'll be able to forget it. I don't ever remember being so unnecessarily unkind to anyone. It's been a rough day, and that may account for it; I don't know. Anyway, I wanted you to know that I regret being rude to you."

"But you meant it, Marcus. Maybe not so harshly, but you meant it." He spread his legs, let his elbows rest on his knees and clasped his hands. He knew his response was important to her. But if he told the truth...he had to; he hated lying and liars.

"Yes, I meant it. But I didn't mean to appear vicious. I know you're concerned about Amy, but we'll separate, and that's it. So I don't want her to become attached to you."

Amanda let her hands fall into her lap. As an apology, it was one of the poorest she had ever witnessed.

"And your telling me about her condition would attach her to me?" She was pushing him, but she didn't care; he deserved it.

"No. Hell, I don't know. Talking it over with you seemed like the beginning of something that I don't want." It wasn't much of an explanation, and she was tempted to tell him so, but Aunt Meredith had always said that you got more flies with honey than with vinegar.

"It seemed like such a natural thing for you to do," she said, softly, although she didn't feel that she should apologize. Oh, the devil with sweetness, she decided, as her anger surfaced. "Any person who knew what that child went through today would be concerned, and you're old enough to know that. I'm not going to apologize for showing an interest in her. You're just paranoid, and it wouldn't hurt you to take a good look at yourself. I was being friendly, Marcus, because I really want us to be friends, but I won't give my blood for it."

She got up to dismiss him, then surprised herself by asking, "What happened to make you so wary of people?" That marriage, she thought, and sat back down. "Marcus, what was your wife like?"

"You don't want to know, believe me."

"Oh, yes I do."

"Why, for heaven's sake? You don't believe in giving a man one bit of privacy, do you?"

Amanda wasn't going to be put off. "She must have been exceptional to have driven you to such bitterness. Did you love her so much?"

"I loved her." He gave her the bare facts.

"Is she beautiful?" Amanda wasn't sure she wanted to know, because she thought herself plain, but she couldn't force herself not to ask.

She stared at him in amazement when he laughed, harshly. Nastily. "Beautiful? Helena? Oh, yes, she's that, all right. Not many women can claim to be the top fashion model on two continents. Oh, yes. Not one processed, glossy strand is ever out of place. Why, the very thought of me seeing her without her famous face made up to perfection annoyed the hell out of her. I still wonder what made her disfigure herself enough to have Amy, and why it came as a surprise to me when she decided that she wasn't doing it again, no matter how I felt, made certain of that and damned the consequences." Amanda couldn't hide her shock, nor her sadness at the obvious strength of his bitterness.

She looked at him then, but spoke mostly to herself. "If I had been in her place, I would have cherished what I had. Some people have all the luck, blessings or whatever you want to call it. And how do they treat it? They practically laugh in God's face."

Marcus was sitting beside her, and he had to turn so that he could see her face fully. Her words had touched him more than any statement of intended sympathy ever could have, but when he saw her tears, he had a sense of unease. "Don't cry for me, Amanda."

She let the tears roll, as if she hadn't heard him, but she looked him in the eye and told him, "I never realized that a person could find bitterness to be such a loving, congenial companion." Then she left him sitting there and didn't say good-night. But she couldn't have gone far, he figured, maybe to the middle of her room, before she was back. He sat where she had left him, immobile, contemplating her parting words. The frown that he hoped would discourage further conversation brought another of her big smiles.

"Marcus, you could really use a sense of humor." At that, he stood up, his imposing physique looming over her. *She doesn't give an inch,* he thought, when her smile got broader.

"Why are you suddenly so happy?" he queried, his words tinged with gruffness.

She grinned, her eyes sparkling in a way that he hadn't seen before. "Because the operation is over, and the doctors expect that she'll be as good as new. And I'm happy about it, even if you are a grouch."

"I'm not a grouch, and my sense of humor is as good as the next guy's," he informed her. "I'm just a troubled parent. Wait until you get to be a mother. You haven't worried yet, believe me."

Amanda regarded him steadily, her face still beaming. "If you've got any advice, I'll gladly take it." A softer, less defensive mood pervaded him, as he took in her smile, her guileless demeanor and her cheerful warmth. The woman wasn't beautiful, but she was charismatic, and in that flowing peach gown and peignoir, she was the epitome of feminine softness. A man could get used to that kind of woman. If she wasn't beautiful, she sure seemed like it. He felt a rush of blood and the swift tightening of his groin and ordered his libido under control. He wouldn't let her do this to him, he told himself for the second time that night.

His self-control in working order, Marcus grazed her cheek lightly with the back of his left hand and admonished her, "Go

to bed, Amanda, before you get into trouble." She raised one
eyebrow, and he watched her smile slowly evaporate as she
examined his face. "You heard me." He said it gently, but in such
a way that she couldn't mistake his meaning nor his sincerity.
She went into her room and closed the door.

Amanda hung her peignoir in the closet, opened the window
wider and went to bed. She had a sense of unease as she turned
out the light on her night table. She might have undertaken more
than she could handle. She sensed trouble if she didn't watch her
step with that sleeping giant across the hall. She didn't doubt that
he could be trusted, that he was a gentleman, but she had to admit
that her feelings for Pearce Lamont never even approached what
she'd felt for Marcus a few minutes earlier. If she had to live in
that house with him for a year... She let the thought slide and,
as though to banish it altogether turned over so quickly that the
bed seemed to swirl around and she had to grasp the side of the
mattress to steady herself.

Reminded that she hadn't had any options before he agreed
to their arrangement, she told herself to be thankful and not
grumble; being susceptible to a man like Marcus only meant that
she was female and human. Even so, her reaction to him had
surprised her, and it was he who had stopped that almost kiss
when she should have done it. But she had no intention of con-
gratulating him on having such self-control; men had never found
it impossible to withstand her charms. "I'm safe from him and
from me, too," she told herself unhappily just before she started
counting sheep.

Chapter 3

Ten days after he'd stopped himself from kissing Amanda, Marcus made another trip down to earth and had another hard battle with his feelings. Having just arrived home, jolted by the sound of what seemed like thunder, he raced up the stairs four at a time, feeling as if his heart had fallen into his stomach. What on earth was that noise? He had walked into the front door and gone to the kitchen for some thirst-quenching iced tea. The doctors had told him that Amy was progressing even more rapidly than they had anticipated, and that her therapy would start in a week, so he had come home feeling more relieved and more lighthearted than he had in more than a year. And now this. Where had the noise come from? Something had literally shaken the house, or at least it had sounded that way.

"Amanda! *Amanda!*" Where was she? He knew she was at home; she hadn't even put her car in the garage. He ran into her bedroom and found it empty. He listened, heard the water and momentarily froze. If she was in that bathroom with the door locked... He tried the door, pushing it with full force as he did so. "Amanda? Amanda, my God. Are you all right?" He took in the incredulous scene. She lay on her back in the tub, the shower rod, curtain and part of the wall were in the tub with her, and

water from the shower sprayed her face. Quickly, he turned off
the tap, cleared the debris away from her, lifted her naked body
into his arms and stumbled into her bedroom, where he lay her
gently on the bed. Then he raised the edge of the bedspread and
threw it across her body.

"What happened, Amanda?" He leaned over her. "Amanda,
answer me!" His gaze roamed from her head to her feet. "I'm
taking you to the hospital. You may have done some damage.
What were you doing? Amanda, talk to me!" She opened her
mouth to speak, but no sound came. He dried her body, got a pair
of slacks and a robe from her closet and dressed her as best he
could, but by the time he got her in the car, her continued silence
had alarmed him. He was thankful that the trip to the hospital
was a short one. What if she lost it? He paced the floor in front
of the emergency room for what seemed like hours, until the
resident opened the door and beckoned him.

"Mr. Hickson, your wife is mildly in shock, but otherwise all
right. We've given her some medication, and here's a prescription for some more. Give this to her at bedtime, as instructed.
Nothing is broken, but she'll probably be sore tomorrow. And I'd
see that she stays off her feet for a few days."

Marcus fought to make himself ask that most important of
questions. In the end, he didn't ask it. He just said, "She's three
months pregnant, doctor."

The doctor smiled, seeming to understand his reticence. "Yes,
I know. That's why she reacted this way. Going into shock, I mean.
She was afraid that she had injured the baby or that she might lose
it. But she's healthy and strong so as, I said, she won't have more
than a little soreness. Just keep her in bed for a few days."

Marcus nodded. "May I see her?" He wanted to see for
himself that she was all right. Since he'd met Amanda, he had
never known her to be speechless, and he didn't think that was
a good sign. He stood looking down at her, so small in that
ridiculously ungainly, utilitarian hospital gown. She opened her
eyes and lifted her hand to touch him.

"Thanks for helping me and bringing me to the hospital, Marcus. I was so scared. I slipped while I was taking a shower. Then when I grabbed the shower curtain rod for support, it came out of the wall, and I lost my balance and fell. I was scared to death that I was going to lose the baby."

"I'm glad I was there. Actually, I had been in the house less than a minute when I heard that noise. The doctor's going to let me take you home, but only if you promise to stay in bed for three or four days. Will you?" He contemplated the strangeness of the situation. He wanted to comfort her, to hold her, but that wasn't the kind of relationship they had. Unable to resist at least a minimum display of tenderness, he caressed her cheek and had the pleasure of seeing her turn her face fully into his palm, her eyes bright with unshed tears.

Marcus combed her still damp hair with his fingers, and put her robe on her while they waited for the wheelchair, as the hospital regulations required. And he was very much aware that, within the past hour or so, his relationship with his wife had undergone a subtle change. He wheeled her out to the car, lifted her to put her in the backseat and stared down at her in wonder. He'd had her naked in his arms and had been so alarmed that he'd barely looked at her. That thought brought a half smile from him. Must be getting slack in testosterone, he told himself derisively.

Marcus laid Amanda on her bed, realized it was still damp from his having placed her there earlier, and took her into his room instead. He noted with considerable amusement that she offered no objection. Didn't even seem concerned. Where was the feisty, independent woman who had turned his life around?

He fluffed the pillow, propped it against the headboard and let her rest there. "Your bed's wet. Stay here while I get some fresh sheets and try to make it presentable." When she didn't answer, merely nodded, Marcus straightened up and looked down at her. There she was in his bed, completely agreeable to his every suggestion, soft and submissive. A woman who could

tie him into knots with her big black eyes or her come-here-to-
me smile. Who said he didn't have a sense of humor? Marcus
threw his head back and roared with laughter.

"What's set you off?" she asked him testily. He ignored her
peevishness and grinned.

"'Never trust a husband too far, nor a bachelor too near.' I'm
about as close as you can get to a combination of the two."

She glared at him, trying to ignore the mischievous dance of
his luscious eyes. That quote was not only to the point, he could
hardly have found one more fitting.

"Why on earth would you read Helen Rowland? She wasn't
exactly enamored of the human male."

So he had thought that this time he'd outwitted her, had he?
He shrugged in the manner of a man caught loafing on the job.
"Helena was always quoting her to me, so I read the stuff in order
to defend myself. *Phooey* was my judgment."

That was the opening she wanted. "'The average man's
judgment is so poor, he runs a risk every time he uses it.'"

Marcus spread both hands, palms out, in surrender. "Okay,
you've got me. What pseudo genius wrote that?"

"Ed Howe. And I don't know whether or not he was a genius."
Her interest in their fun game waned, and she had begun to favor
her left shoulder. He remade her bed quickly, carried her to it,
lay her there carefully and gently tucked the covers around her.

"I'm going to the drugstore for your medicine."

"Could you help me into my gown before you go, please?" It
worried him that she favored both her left shoulder and her lower
back and that she seemed reluctant to move. And the silent plea
in her eyes… Was she praying for her baby's safety? He couldn't
think of anything but that the woman whom he had loved and
who had taken his name in a solemn vow had not wanted either
one of the children he gave her.

Marcus looked down at Amanda, rooted in his tracks, as the
picture of her completely nude in his arms floated back to him.

In his mind's eye, he could see her beautiful and generous breasts with the glistening beige tips, the soft brown flesh of her body, her slightly rounded belly and, below it, the thick, curly black patch that guarded the seat of her passion. He turned quickly, hoping that she hadn't seen the sudden and unmistakable evidence of his desire for her, and tried to deal with the wild sensation that had him suddenly shackled.

"I'll be right back" was all he could manage, as he moved away from her bed. He found the peach gown, choosing that one because it was so feminine, and managed to help her into it without looking at her. Perspiration beaded his forehead. He patted her in a self-conscious gesture of comfort, but he wasn't looking at her and was unprepared for the feel of her erected nipple under his palm. Shocked, he looked over at her to apologize and swallowed it when he saw that she was as disconcerted as he. Best to pretend that nothing had happened.

The medicine she took in the emergency room had begun to make Amanda sleepy, but that light touch of Marcus' big hand on her breast brought her fully awake. It was accidental, she knew, but that made it all the more erotic. She didn't like being vulnerable to a man who didn't want her close to him or to his motherless child. And she certainly didn't want to feel the raw attraction for him that had begun to suffuse her with increasing frequency. Thank God, he didn't seem to know it.

There was much about her that Marcus didn't know and that she didn't want him to learn. Her almost total lack of experience with men wouldn't gain her any kudos with him, she reasoned, and might even place her at a disadvantage. And it wouldn't help if he knew how low her self-esteem had sunk when she learned of her pregnancy. Only that would explain her willingness to bargain marriage with a stranger. She rubbed her tingling breast, wanting his hand back there. "Slow down, Amanda," she admonished herself. "Only the man responsible finds a pregnant woman attractive, and even for some of them, it's a turnoff."

She looked up at the ceiling. Lord, was it too much to ask that a man care deeply for her just once in her life? Forever was too much to hope for. But couldn't she know what it was like, how it felt, just once? She almost wished that Marcus—when he was tender and caring—hadn't taught her what was missing in her life.

Marcus returned from the drugstore and found her asleep, her body curled into a fetal position. He stood over her for all of ten minutes, wanting her. Then, in a fit of disgust with himself, he put the medicine on her night table and went to the kitchen, where he dumped the chocolates he'd bought for her safely into the garbage pail. Then he wandered around the kitchen trying to find something to cook for dinner. He hadn't prepared dinner since coming to live with Amanda, and he had gotten used to her mouthwatering meals. He got busy preparing the food, but his mind was on Amanda. An unusually interesting woman; he hadn't counted on that.

He let his mind wander over the day's events. His dangerous attraction to Amanda gave him reason for concern, though he could handle that, but what he'd felt for her when he'd carried her in his arms, dressed and undressed her, was more than lust. He had to watch his step with her. And she was more vulnerable than she knew, he suspected. When he had stopped by the school to report Amanda's illness, the female colleague who had taken the message had been vicious.

He suspected the woman of jealousy. But why? Unless the two had competed for the principal's post—and from the look of her he doubted that—what reason could she have for such blatant animosity toward a person with Amanda's gentle manners? He'd been astonished both at the woman's words and at her willingness to reveal her dislike to her boss's husband. He hated seeing black women with their hair dyed red, and this one looked as though her head was on fire. He shook his head as though to rid his vision of her image.

"You don't mean that Amanda Ross married a number twelve like you. What did you do, make her pregnant?" the woman had asked him. His acerbic reply had definitely not gained Amanda a friend. Sensing that he'd seen her somewhere before, he'd asked her where that might have been. After assuring him that, if she'd ever seen him, she'd never have forgotten it, she replied, "If you're in on Portsmouth's social life, you might have noticed me at the Lamont estate. They're friends of mine." It was clearly something of which she was proud. He had been careful not to react visibly, because he had learned not to show his hand to an adversary. The woman was a potential source of trouble for Amanda, an unsuccessful competitor and a friend of her unborn child's ruthless grandfather. He'd have to find out what she knew. She had wanted to prolong their conversation, but he'd finished it, probably more curtly than was wise given the woman's antagonism toward Amanda.

Odor and smoke from the frying chicken legs warned him that his dinner was in jeopardy, and he brought his mind to the present. He arranged trays of the chicken, baked potatoes, string beans and sliced tomatoes, got iced tea from the refrigerator and hesitated. What the heck? It never hurt to be nice. He'd eat his dinner upstairs with Amanda, he decided, adding glasses of water to their trays. But the minute he saw the glow on her face as he set out their food, he wondered if he was sending her the wrong signal.

Marcus had stayed away from his factory while Amanda was recovering, and he had a backlog of work. "I intend to spend all of Saturday and Sunday in Portsmouth at the factory," he told her as they cleared away the remains of Friday night's supper, "but I'll be here as usual Saturday night."

"Want me to drive you to the station tomorrow morning?" His answer was going to disappoint her, but he couldn't help it. She wanted him to accept their relationship and was looking for a sign of his willingness to do that. But he didn't see how he could accept it, when he couldn't feel like a man so long as she footed the bills.

"That won't be necessary. I need the exercise." It was a pitiable excuse, and he knew it, but he didn't want to encourage her by letting her do things for him. Afraid that he'd hurt her, he looked up from the pan he was scrubbing, ready to gloss it over, and was surprised that her slacks had gotten so tight, showing her pregnancy, and that her breasts were getting larger. But what shook him was the open plea in her eyes. A wordless appeal to his decency and, God help him, to his masculinity. He dropped the brush and didn't bother to dry his wet hands; getting to her was an all-powerful urge, and he gave in to it. He'd barely touched her shoulder, and she was in his arms. She looked up at him, her eyes ablaze with passion, and his defences disintegrated. He lowered his head and brushed her voluptuous lips with his own, then raised up slightly to look into her eyes. To check her submission. Females had craved him ever since his voice had changed. But not like this. He squeezed her to him, one hand at the back of her head and the other spread across her buttocks, and kissed her with all of the yearning and hunger that he'd stored in five weeks of want and deprivation. He ran his tongue around her lips and, when she didn't respond to suit him, he nipped her bottom lip with his teeth. Her lips parted, and he found a place for his foraging tongue within her sweet mouth and let it roam until, as if aching for more, she caught it between her lips and sucked it as if it were the essence of life. He felt her fingers weaving through his thick curly hair, caressing his shoulders and neck, testing his biceps, learning him.

Her response almost brought him to his knees, a position with which he was unfamiliar, and his heart was a pounding drum, beating furiously in his chest, as he gloried in the warmth, the feel, the taste of her. He told himself to pull back, to stop before it got out of hand. But instead, he increased the pressure, deepened the kiss, relishing the fact that she was with him all the way. He told himself to let it go, before it was too late. But he didn't want to stop, and she didn't appear to want him to. She seemed to want and to need exactly what he was giving her. And she clung to him. He kissed her eyes, her ears, her neck and her throat as he murmured unintelligible things to her. She trembled from head to foot, enthralled in his sweet loving and consuming passion, released, as if he were catapulting her into the stratosphere. Learning what a man's tenderness could do to a woman. She craved him in every molecule of her body, and could not have withheld her feelings if her life had depended on it. *I should stop him,* she thought, *because he'll make me suffer for this. But I don't care; I need him. I need this.* She burrowed into him, holding him. His arousal stunned her, but she accepted him without reservation and tightened her grip on his waist.

As if shaken, she swayed unsteadily and he set her away from him. "Don't you know how to say stop?" he asked her, his voice a gravelly whisper. She reached for him as she reeled backward, and he caught her, holding her just a little too long.

"Amanda, the way things were going, I would have been inside of you in minutes. I don't think that's what you want, and I know it isn't what I want. We're both tired and strung out. I'll see you tomorrow night." He headed down the hallway.

She ran after him, amazed that he could turn his feelings off at will, while she still staggered under the impact of the first genuine loving she'd ever had. "What's with you? You may be tired and unstrung, mister, but I'm not."

He paused, his expression bland, as though his energy had been sapped. "Unless angels come down here, Amanda, we're going to separate on April eleventh. You know it, and I know it and, if we ignore that fact, we will both regret it. So let's not fool ourselves. We could easily step across that line and then find the consequences intolerable." His voice softened. "I won't risk it, and neither should you."

"You're not willing to try?"

"Amanda, a sensible man won't stick his bare hand in the fire twice, no matter that the flame is a different color. I can't risk it. I thought I could, but then I remember what is was like... I'm sorry."

Amanda climbed the stairs with difficulty. She couldn't say

she was sorry that he'd kissed her that way, but she knew she would go through hell reliving it for the rest of her life. What a man he was, she mused. He had stood there in all his ebony male glory, a faultlessly crafted colossus, surrounding her with his consummate male magnetism, beguiling her senses. He had shown her the strong, but loving, gentle and tender man that he was so clever at hiding. Then he had gently, but firmly pushed her away. She didn't think she could tolerate eleven more months of it.

Amanda got ready for bed and reached for the light to turn it out. Her gaze caught a reflection of herself in the mirror and she walked toward it. What did he see in her? Why had he kissed her and held her like that? She knew he hadn't wanted to do it and had given in to it against his will. Maybe he just needed a woman, and she was there. That doesn't make sense, she reasoned; a man who looked like Marcus Hickson didn't have problems getting a woman. If he needed a woman, there was probably one waiting somewhere.

Agitated and, for the first time, uncertain that she could handle living with Marcus on their agreed-upon terms, she slipped on a cotton robe and walked out on the porch. She listened for the lapping and sloshing of the waves and heard it, but for once, the tune that had nourished her since birth failed to comfort her. Cool, salty air whipped in from the Albemarle Sound, bringing goose bumps to her arms, and the brisk wind that brought it trapped her long thick hair in the branches of a ficus tree that stood behind her in a corner. She looked out toward the Sound for a few minutes and turned to go back into the house, but she couldn't free her hair. She looked over her shoulder at the tree. *I'll never be able to move it,* she thought, declining to panic.

Amanda had been alone for so much of her life that her next thought was whether she could scream loud enough to attract attention. She relaxed when a light flickered on in Marcus' room. Amused at herself that she could have forgotten his presence after what he'd done to her only minutes earlier, she took a deep breath and called him.

Marcus stepped out on the porch and looked around. "Amanda, did I hear you call me?"

"I'm over here." She disliked the plaintive sound of her voice; after all, any husband could do what she was about to request of him. *Any husband!* "The wind blew my hair into this tree, and I can't get it out."

"Don't you have a light out here somewhere. It would be a pity if you had to stand there until daylight." She told him where to find the switch, and he turned on the light and walked over to her.

"I can't get between you and the tree, so this will take a while." Heat suffused her cheeks, and excitement raced through her when he reached over her and began to free her hair strand by strand. He must have noticed her unsteadiness, because he tried to put her at ease.

"Hold on to me, Amanda. If you lean back, you'll be in a worse pickle than you are now." Apparently searching for levity to abate the rising sexual tension, he added, "And don't act so scared; I don't usually bite."

"I notice you said, 'usually.'" She folded her arms across her middle in an effort to create a buffer between them. But he leaned over her to unthread some of her hair from around a branch, and she felt his chest against her face. She couldn't stop herself from inhaling deeply the scent of his male body. Strength and power emanated from him, and she stifled a rising resentment that it should have such a heady effect on her even as she squelched an urge to wrap her arms around him and let herself soak up the sweetness and know again the torment of holding him close.

He stepped back and looked down at her, his mouth pursed in a rueful smile. "Are you getting the impression that something or somebody is playing tricks on us?" She didn't answer at once and nearly stepped back, but he quickly prevented it, holding her head with his hand.

"You want to undo all this tedious work I've done? You didn't answer my question." Amanda couldn't think of a reason for the dazzling grin that spread across his face, unless it was from a desire to bamboozle her more than the scent of him and the heat of his body had already done.

"How about you're a human trip-hammer, and I'm standing over a trapdoor? Where's the trick in that?" she asked him, unwilling to pretend. He let several recently freed strands of hair cascade over her shoulder.

"You wouldn't be fooling, would you? If you aren't, let me tell you, lady, that kind of joking is dangerous. And if you are…" He shook his head. "It's still dangerous." She wanted him to move away from her, but he didn't give her an inch, just continued unravelling her hair from the ficus branch.

"Have you almost finished?" she asked him, embarrassed by the quake in her voice. "Maybe you ought to get a pair of scissors and whack it off."

"Come on, now. Much as you love this thick wooly stuff, you'd cut if off just to get rid of me? That's hardly flattering." Let him think what he liked. She had learned that Marcus mastered his emotions with the ease of a glider. She didn't know much about men, much less how to handle herself around them. But she figured that even if she'd been an expert on them, Marcus Hickson would still be an enigma to her. That is in the past, though, she assured herself. She had just begun to learn that he could have the kind of feelings he generated in her and she knew that, if he were a different kind of man, she'd be in his bed right then. In court, whose word would have the greater weight? Blood rushed to her face, neck and ears, and she lowered her head to prevent his seeing her telltale facial expression. He reached around her and began to untangle some strands from a branch below her waist.

"Marcus…Marcus, would you…please…"

"Would I please what?" He released her hair, grasped her shoulders and took a step back. She looked up into eyes that burned with want and struggled not to let her gaze drift down to his beguiling lips. His rugged breathing tempted her to test her feminine power, and excitement sent shivers through her, as he seemed to weigh her in some way, to anticipate her next move. His hands tightened on her shoulders.

"You're new at this, Amanda, so listen. Whatever you're feeling, I'm feeling it at least twice as strongly. That's because I know what there could be between us, and you don't. If I get into trouble, Amanda, it's on my own terms. Nobody leads me astray. So don't be tempted to see how far you can go with me." He put a hand behind her head, pulled her hair over her right shoulder and pinched her playfully on her nose. Then he turned and went to his room.

Marcus caught the first morning train to Portsmouth. He'd spent the previous night wrestling with the feelings of tenderness and possessiveness he'd had for Amanda while he picked the strands of her hair from that tree. He wondered where their relationship was headed, but the thought left him when he arrived at the factory and noticed that Jerzy Heiner was already at work.

"I'm planning to ask for an hour off this afternoon," Jerzy explained. "Oh, yeah," he said, as though in afterthought, "you aren't planning to sell the factory, are you?" Marcus stopped raising the window, and turned toward his trusted small-strings expert.

"Of course not. Why do you ask?"

"A man came here just after you left yesterday asking about inventory, profit, outstanding debt and a lot of other things that I told him were none of his business. If you aren't planning to sell, how'd he get the nerve?"

"Beats me. But I'll check on it. Let me know if you see him around." Marcus could hardly wait for his bank to open. He called Allen Baldridge, the president, and learned that it was the bank's policy to list large mortgages on commercial property in the hope of unloading them if the debtor defaulted. The bank had already had several offers for Marcus' mortgage, but had refused in view of its long relationship with the Hickson family. However, in the event of a default, the bank would sell to the highest bidder.

Marcus reflected on that news for a while after hanging up. His father and the man with whom he'd just spoken had been roommates at Morehouse College and as tight as peas in a pod. When you had your hand out, he recalled, you didn't have friends in high places, only some big shots you'd once known who now considered themselves your superior. He'd show them; he'd work that much harder to repay that bank loan. It wouldn't be without a struggle, and he hadn't thought it would. Two hundred and fifty thousand dollars of debt plus what he considered exorbitant interest was an enormous short-term load for any small business. His stomach tightened with uneasiness. He had mortgaged his house and his business, sold his car, Steinway and Stradivarius, given up his credit cards and left himself with nothing but his clothes and his tools. In the end, he'd given up his freedom. But if Amy walked again, he'd have no regrets. He realized for the first time that he could easily lose the fruits of twelve years' hard work. Everything he had.

Three hours later, emotionally drained from grappling with the problems he faced, he put the felt on the last hammer of a concert grand and looked over at an employee working near him. "Let's go out for coffee," he said to the man. "If you feel as old as I do right now, you can use a pick-me-up, too." Surprised that his boss would take a mid-morning break, the man raised both eyebrows and started for the door.

Amanda awoke early the next morning to discover that Marcus had already left. She decided that he'd probably done that to prevent her from giving him breakfast, and that was just as well. When he was untangling her hair, he had suggested that she might have tried to seduce him, and she couldn't help laughing at the idea, wishing she knew how. He had been the seducer, and she figured that if he were as clever as he seemed, he'd know that. She dressed in a navy, ruffled skirt and pink peasant blouse and went to the hospital. Anyone who knew her situation would consider her reckless, but she was beyond caring. After reading the second chapter of a novel to a patient with impaired vision, she made her way to the children's ward, where she identified herself as a volunteer—which she was—and asked directions to Amy's room. She found the child looking listlessly out of the window, ignoring the other children in the four-bed room. She gave Amy a cone of vanilla ice cream that she'd gotten from the vending machine and asked her whether she'd like to read some stories. To her surprise, the child's eyes sparkled excitedly at the prospect of reading stories. Amanda read *Winnie the Pooh* to her, talked with her for a bit and promised a return visit. She had liked Amy, an attractive, bright child, and wanted to see more of her, but she decided not to tell Marcus that she had met his daughter.

Walking down State Street later, after having bought her first maternity clothes, she passed a toy store and couldn't resist the yellow floppy-eared bunny that gazed beady-eyed at her from the window. Amy hadn't had a single toy, so she bought it for her, ignoring the warning that sounded from both her conscience and her common sense. She walked briskly up State Street, humming an old tune, feeling happy and even lighthearted, in anticipation of her Sunday visit with Amy while Marcus worked at his factory in Portsmouth.

"Morning, Sam. Lovely Saturday morning, isn't it?" She hadn't seen him for weeks and had wondered about him. She couldn't imagine State Street without Sam with his archaic four-wheel trash cart, battered hat and highly polished, though worn shoes. She stopped, as always, to greet him, and his black, weathered face immediately became wreathed in smiles.

"Mighty glad to see you feeling better, Miss Amanda." Sam always called her "Miss Amanda," which was the Southern custom even if a woman was married. He leaned against his old trash cart and peered at her. "Last time I see'd you, you was a mite troubled. I said prayers for whatever it was that was bothering you."

Deeply moved at his caring, Amanda reached out to touch his bony shoulder and then, on impulse, leaned over and brushed a kiss on his unshaven cheek. "Oh, Sam, I was troubled, but your prayers must have worked." It was rare that anyone stopped to talk with Sam, and she realized what her brief greetings meant to him. She told the stunned, happy old man, "Since I last saw you I got married. My name's Hickson now, and next year I'm going to be principal of the junior high school. Thanks for the prayers." She waved him goodbye as he ducked his head, but not quickly enough to prevent her seeing the old man's tears.

Amanda looked at her watch. Marcus wouldn't be back in Caution Point for another four hours, so she could go back to the hospital and take Amy the bunny. She had enjoyed the little girl's enthusiasm and warmth and couldn't wait to see her expressions of delight when she gave her the stuffed animal. She went directly to the child's room and found her in a deep discussion with Winnie the Pooh, lecturing the imaginary little bear about his bad habit of sticking his nose in honey. Amanda couldn't resist a laugh, and she thought her heart would burst when Amy's face blossomed in smiles at the sight of her.

"Lady! I thought you were coming tomorrow." She walked over to the bed, and when Amy raised both arms to her, leaned over and hugged her.

"What's in that package, Lady?" *Precocious little thing, aren't you,* Amanda mused. She handed her the package, sat down in the nearby chair and watched in awe at the child's patience; in all her years as a teacher, she'd never known a child to unwrap a package with such care. She supposed pain would do that to a child, but this one showed no ill effects of her ordeal; bright, happy and bubbling with energy, Amy had the personality of a child who had known deep love and caring and who expected to be loved. If anyone knew how much Marcus loved his child, she did. Excitement that dissolved into shivers coursed through her at the memory of his passion and, though she fought the image, in her mind's eye, she saw him as a lover. Her lover. She forced her attention to the little girl, hoping to banish Marcus from her thoughts, but she could have saved herself the trouble. Amy was Marcus incarnate, with the same curly black hair and honey-brown eyes.

"Lady! Lady! Is it mine? I love him. I love him." Her squeals brought a nurse running to the room. In answer to Amy's question, the nurse assured the child that she could keep the bunny. Amanda didn't doubt the difficulty the nurse would have had if she hadn't allowed it.

"Thanks," Amy said, wearing the famous Hickson smile. "I'm going to name him Peter." Amanda left immediately, in spite of Amy's pleading; she couldn't risk Marcus' arriving early and finding her there.

Marcus stared unseeing at the console in front of him. He had been working on that piano for hours, and he might as well have been in Caution Point; he hadn't done anything right. Normally, he would have had those hammers positioned within an hour; he was, after all, a master craftsman. But not today. On that Sunday morning, his mind was not on his work; it was on Amanda Ross Hickson and their torrid kiss a few nights earlier. Why couldn't he keep a level head around her? What was it about her, he mused, that made him lose sight of things that were so important to him? And why couldn't he have found a way to call a halt to it without making her feel as though she might have done something wrong? He'd been gentle, but he suspected that she'd felt hurt nevertheless. She hadn't been the one to start that…that heated kiss. He groaned. He didn't want to think of it. He'd been married, and he had known other women, as well, but he couldn't recall ever having a woman respond to him the way she had. She hadn't cared about anything, except her need of him. Only him. He got up and walked around, trying to shake off the sensation, the feeling that her scent and warmth still surrounded him. He had never known a woman like Amanda, but he knew that if ever she was in his arms in his bed, she would give him everything and drive him wild in the process. He swore loudly as the telephone interrupted his woolgathering.

"Hickson. We're closed today."

"If you're closed, what are you doing there?"

"What's up, Luke?" Luke explained that he'd called Marcus at home and learned from Amanda that he was at the factory.

"How about meeting me for lunch? River Café all right with you?"

"Yeah. Twenty minutes."

"Why so long? It's only around the corner from you."

"Yeah. Right." He hung up. He loved his only brother, but he was not keen on seeing him right then. Luke was the most perceptive person he had ever been around and had been able to read him accurately even when they were growing up.

Marcus didn't remember having seen River Café almost empty at noon, but this was the first time he'd been in the place on Sunday. The thought that he might be out of step with most of Portsmouth's working men didn't give him a feeling of virtuousness; instead, he suddenly felt tired. When would it end? They found their favorite table, sat down and ordered beer.

"Why are you working on Sunday?" Luke asked. Marcus told him of his conversation with his bank's president, adding that he regretted having taken out all of his loans with one bank and paying them off would be a Herculean job.

"Don't blame yourself, Marcus; our grandfather banked there. If that's Baldridge's policy, I'll move my account. What kind of contingency plans do you have if you can't make those payments?"

"I've got an order to repair a priceless seventeenth-century harpsichord. As soon as I get all the parts I need, I'll start on it. I've placed orders with master craftsmen in London and Leipzig. When that job is finished and when my suit with the insurance company liable for Amy's injuries pays up, I'll be in the clear. Otherwise…" He threw up his hands. "It's anybody's guess."

"When is the hearing on your claim or have you decided to settle out of court?"

"I'm going to court, but I'm having trouble getting my suit on the docket." He added that his lawyer was working on it.

"Good. I may be able to call in some favors, if you have trouble with it."

Marcus nodded his thanks. He looked around for a waitress, saw one who wore a short tight skirt and had streaks of yellow in her black hair, reminding him of Iris Elms. He told Luke of his conversation with her.

"She's a source of trouble, Luke."

Luke nodded. "I'll say she is. Have you told Amanda?"

Marcus shook his head. "No. She almost panicked when I told her the old man might try to take the child. I hate to upset her with this."

"I don't agree with you. That's a fox in the henhouse. Amanda is that woman's boss. You have to warn her."

"I'll tell her to watch her back, and I'll do what I can to protect her, but I'm not going to alarm her unnecessarily."

"Yeah. Well, if you need me…" The waitress arrived. Luke ordered pan-fried Norfolk spots (a small sweet fish) with hush puppies, and Marcus settled for Cajun fried catfish, French fries and coleslaw. They each ordered another beer.

The waitress didn't seem anxious to leave. Finally she asked, her tone flirtatious, "Anything else?"

Marcus groaned in disgust, but Luke seemed to think it funny. "Not at noon, honey," he said, winked and dismissed her. Then he turned to his brother. "What's eating you, Marcus? And don't say that nothing is. You can't even appreciate a little harmless flirtation."

"I'm a married man."

Luke snorted. "Really? You've consummated this marriage? Congratulations. That's the best news I've heard since we got the result of Amy's operation. By the way, how is Amy?"

"Amy's doing great, and my marriage is still one of convenience. Don't push me, Luke. I'm not in the mood for it."

"How are Amanda and Amy getting along?" Marcus had low tolerance for Luke's meddling, but he knew Luke didn't care. Lately, his older brother seemed to regard their six-year age difference as a license to interfere in his affairs.

"They haven't met." There was no point in hedging.

Luke narrowed his eyes. "You haven't taken Amanda to meet her stepdaughter? Are you out of your mind?"

"I told you not to push. I'm not going to expose Amy to any unnecessary unhappiness. When this year is up, I'm coming back here, and Amanda will be staying in Caution Point. I don't intend to have Amy's heart broken. This marriage is a bargain, and I plan to treat it like one."

"I'm astonished that you can live in the house with a woman like that one, talk to her, eat with her, joke and tease with her and keep your hands off of her. You *are* keeping your hands off her, aren't you?" It wasn't a fair question and it irritated Marcus, because Luke knew that he wouldn't lie.

"Well, aren't you?" Marcus knew that his silence was worth a thousand words. Not only had he had his hands on her, but he couldn't swear that he would refrain from doing it again. He looked at his all-seeing brother and slowly shook his head.

"She gets to me, Luke, like no other woman I've ever known. I know I haven't given her a fair shake. She gives, and I take. She offers everything, and I'm offering her nothing because I don't have anything to offer. The only time I've felt in control, felt comfortable and at times even contented in this situation was when she fell in the bathtub and needed me. And I was there for her, because I wanted to be, because I needed to be. But I had to back off. She's carrying another man's child, and all of a sudden I don't know how I feel about that. I don't intend for this to be a marriage, but the other night I came pretty close to making it one. I initiated it, but after I got myself in line, I might have made her feel bad. I don't know. I hope not."

Luke laid a hand on his brother's shoulder. "And it's eating away at your conscience. Why are you so afraid to care for her? If you'd talk with her about the circumstances, as I did, you'd be more understanding and less wary. I promised myself that I wasn't going to tell you this, Marcus, but she was a virgin, a thirty-nine-year-old virgin, and the guy showed so little regard for that fact that she had to be treated in the hospital emergency room. She told me that the night I spent with the two of you, and I checked her story. She got there in bad shape."

Marcus brought his head up sharply, as he sucked in his breath, pulled air through his teeth and released a stinging profanity. "Too bad he's not around. I would have loved to smash his face."

"Marcus, go home and look at what you have there. Amanda isn't a shell of a person like Helena. I told you before you married Helena that she was too self-centered, that she wouldn't be able to handle the demands of marriage. You loved her, and that was what she wanted—constant admiration. She enjoyed the glamour of being seen with you, of other women envying her. Good-looking woman with good-looking man. Amanda is different, very different, and you know it. There is great depth to her. Real substance. And you're not going to forget her just because three hundred and sixty-five days have elapsed. You won't ever forget her. Legally and for all practical purposes, it's your child she's carrying. It will bear your name and call you father, and you will always want to know how it's getting along. Always. Like it or not; those are the facts. And don't forget that she's given your Amy a new life; you can't do any less for her child."

Marcus nodded as the bright light of knowledge penetrated his mind, and he mulled over words that found their mark and pitched him into distress. "I know all of that, and you know very well that I'll do the right thing by her. What bothers me is that I don't have any viable options. The chemistry between us is so strong. Most couples go through a process of getting to know each other, having the attraction between them grow, mature. We started backward with both of us at a disadvantage and with a powerful mutual attraction." Luke nodded. Marcus knew that Luke had seen it for himself the night that he had slept at their home.

Marcus spoke reluctantly, unaccustomed to sharing such intimacies, even with his brother. "A man wants to protect and care for his woman but, from the outset, I couldn't have that role. And I don't want to be married again. I won't risk it. Not ever. Amanda is a born mother hen and a special woman, but what she wants from a marriage is the whole nine yards. I don't blame her. It's her right. But not with me, and I'm going to get out as soon as I can. I'm just going to try not to hurt her anymore. She doesn't deserve it." His sigh must have exemplified all that he felt, his hurt and longing, for Luke stared at him. Then he added, "But she's sweet, Luke. God, she's so sweet."

His thoughts of that conversation still plagued him the following afternoon when he went to the hospital, something that he no longer dreaded.

"Hi, Daddy. Do you know about Winnie the poop?"

Marcus beamed at the love of his life. He hadn't thought that he would ever again see Amy smiling and cheerful and free of pain. He leaned over and kissed her. "You mean, Winnie the Pooh. Yes. But how did you learn about Winnie?"

"A nice lady came and read it to me, Daddy. And she brought me a bunny, too." He'd noticed how she cuddled the stuffed toy that was almost as big as she. Her toys had been removed to prevent her moving around too much after the operations.

"So you can have toys now?"

"The nurse said I could have Peter." She kissed the bunny. "Oh, Daddy, bring a book when you come. I already know about Mother Goose and Daddy Goose, too, and I like Daddy Goose the best."

A tired Marcus looked at his precious little angel. She hadn't shown any interest in anything for so long. His heart swelled with joy. "Daddy Goose? She read you a story about Daddy Goose?" he asked, disbelieving.

Amy laughed excitedly. "No, Daddy. She told me that story. I said I wanted a story about a daddy goose. She didn't have the book, so she told me the story. And you know what? Daddy Goose sounded just like you. I liked him much better than Mother Goose. It's my favorite story." It had been a rough weekend. He hadn't gotten much done at the factory and, last night, relations between him and Amanda had been strained. But as he gazed down at the one person who needed him, his mirror image, he felt some of the weight ease from him. His smile came easily, as he squeezed her tightly.

"What's the lady's name, honey?"

"I don't know, Daddy. I just call her Lady." He kissed her goodbye and left. Somehow, he didn't want to go home. Amanda would confront him about his inconsistent behavior with her. He didn't know when, but it was a certainty, and he was not ready for that tonight. Hardly thinking about it, he found himself at Jack and Myrna's home and knew at once that going there was a mistake. He didn't want to talk about himself and Amanda. So he drank a mug of coffee, and after an interminable hour of evading their questions, went home, wondering when he'd begun to think of the place as home.

Guilt shot through him when he found her note in a sealed envelope taped to the outside of the front door. She hadn't told him that she would have an amniocentesis test nor that she had the results. And he hadn't known, either, that the test could pose problems. Now, she threatened a miscarriage and had gone to the hospital. He went in the house and called a taxi, too drained for the long walk back. Marcus wondered what else was going on that he didn't know about, and knew that their lack of communication was his fault. Worried and anxious for his wife, he leaned back in the taxi, strung out.

He caught himself rubbing his chin with the thumb and forefinger of his right hand, a signal that he faced a moment of truth, and exhaled deeply in an attempt to shrug off his thoughts. But he couldn't escape the fact that his feeling for Amanda was not the casual interest that one might have in a friend's well-being, but a deep and personal desire, an increasingly intense concern for her health and happiness. A caring that had nothing to do with lust. When he'd read her note, he'd had a sensation of marbles rattling around in his belly. He didn't want to care for her nor about her, but he had to admit that fate seemed to be refereeing their game with no consideration for his preferences. He leaned forward.

"Driver, can't you get this bus to move any faster?"

"I'm already fifteen miles over the speed limit, mister." Marcus slumped in his seat. One more piece of evidence that he'd better watch his feelings about his wife.

Chapter 4

Amanda sat propped up in bed, almost shaking with fear. The realization that she was spotting had frightened her. She had ignored the slight cramps, but the spots were a more serious matter. And Marcus. He hadn't been at his factory or at the hospital with Amy, and Luke didn't know where he was. She had taken the test because the doctors had said it was important for women who were thirty-five or over, but there was no point in rehashing the past, and she tried to rechannel her thoughts. She wouldn't have planned her life this way, but she would make the best of it.

Finding Marcus had proved to be no less than a blessing. A miracle. She knew he felt trapped, but he gave her a sense of well-being, and he was a gentleman, an honest man, strong and tender, a man who would take care of his own. But she couldn't allow herself to forget that he didn't want her to be a fixture in his life. Her hand slipped idly across her belly as she stroked it unconsciously, lovingly. She couldn't lose the baby; she couldn't. Her child was all she had.

She heard him before he reached her room. "I'm Marcus Hickson. My wife is here. Where is she, please?" Blunt as usual, Amanda thought, smiling and holding her breath until her eyes could verify his presence. He walked straight to her bed, anxious, his face ashen with concern.

"Is it…? Tell me. What happened? Are you still…?" She reached for his hand and placed it on her rounded belly.

He sat on the edge of her bed. "Thank God. Tell me what happened?" She went over it with him, reliving the horror of it but minimizing it for his sake even though she knew her plastic smile didn't fool him.

"I wish I'd been there. Hell, I should have been there. I can imagine what you went through. Don't cry. It's going to be all right; it has to be." Then, he leaned over and brushed her lips with his, before enclosing her in a firm but tender embrace and kissing her gently and sweetly. What he saw when he raised his head and looked at her caused him to wonder, and what she saw in his eyes left her totally befuddled.

The pull between them was of such strength that they couldn't break eye contact. And so much uncertainty. So much unsaid. A bystander would have thought them the most passionate of lovers. A doctor finally disrupted their unlikely trance, clearing his throat after standing there several moments without their knowing it.

The doctor spoke to Marcus. "Mr. Hickson, the news is good, but I want you to encourage your wife to remain in bed for a few days. I've known Amanda for years, and I know she likes to be busy. That's why I'm telling you in her presence. If you can't get her to stay in bed, at least encourage her to stay home. School will be over after tomorrow, so that shouldn't be a problem." He winked, man to man. "She's tough, and we can be glad for that."

Amanda had been at home for a week on doctor's orders, and her relationship with her husband had been nearly all that she could have asked. Of a marriage of convenience, that is. Marcus had been warm, tender and protective. He'd cooked, served and waited on her. They had even exchanged stories about their childhoods, and Marcus had confided that Great-Aunt Meredith was a character from whom he was glad to have escaped. They'd laughed, joked and tested each other's knowledge of English and American literature, and Amanda had learned that her doctors degree in English literature didn't guarantee her winning points on Marcus. A voracious reader, he possessed an awesome memory and stumped her so often that she had begun to wonder what, other than music, was taught at the New England Conservatory of Music where Marcus had gotten his degree. She didn't like being incapacitated, but whenever she was, Marcus allowed her to see a side of him that she cherished with all her heart.

When Amy was unhappy, so was Marcus. The "lady" hadn't visited or read to Amy for a week, and Amy missed her. He was going to tell the hospital authorities not to let that woman near his child again. She had no right to ingratiate herself with a four-year-old and then disappear. And the same thing would happen if he let Amanda get close to her. He still fumed about that when he got home and found his lawyer's letter stating that his suit over Amy's accident was being contested and that settlement could be years away. He needed that money to restore his financial position and to repay Amanda. He didn't want her money, not even as part of a legal contract. And another thing. Her passion for that kid she carried was getting to him. Considering how the child was begot, how could she want it so desperately? He was beginning to get suspicious of her story, no matter what Luke had checked. Helena hadn't wanted either one of her pregnancies, and no man could have been more considerate and loving than he when she conceived them.

He had made the mistake several days earlier of expressing that sentiment to Luke, only to earn a reprimand.

"When did you start letting your emotions overrule your common sense, Marcus? I've never known you to be unfair. If something's eating you, you're not a man to take it out on your wife."

"All right. All right. Forget I said it."

He hadn't meant any of it, deep down, but he was becoming

more frustrated every day. At times, he wanted Amanda so badly he hurt. Every day, she got bigger, but that had no effect upon his desire for her. And that surprised him. Lately, he'd protected himself by being aloof. It was that or give in to his feelings, make love with her and cement their marriage, and he wasn't prepared to do that. He knew that his behavior had begun to disturb her, but he couldn't help it, because they'd gotten too close, too much like husband and wife. He did the only thing possible: He put some psychological distance between them.

A woman who was pregnant with a child other than his was not supposed to attract him. Maybe being his wife made the difference. He thought about it more, examining himself and his role in their relationship. Amanda was the difference. She had an ability to reach him deep inside where he needed healing. Where he was vulnerable. He hadn't counted on the effect that her attractiveness, feminine warmth and close proximity would have on him. He didn't find celibacy enjoyable either, but he knew that he would respect those marriage vows even if the marriage was not a real one.

While they cleaned up after dinner, he told her about the status of the lawsuit, mostly to make conversation, and his eyes widened in amazement when she casually dismissed the seriousness of it.

"Oh, don't worry. I'll speak to someone, an old suitor of Aunt Meredith's. He'll take care of it. You should get a judgment in three or four months at the latest. Probably sooner. Just give me the name of the other principal."

He took her hand, aware that he had rarely touched her since he'd brought her home from the hospital. "You'd do this for me, after all that's gone wrong between us?" he said, unable to hide his astonishment or his happiness. "This is the first time I've been glad I sued in Caution Point rather than in Ashville, where the company's headquarters are located. It's been a problem getting things done here."

Marcus looked at the woman who was his wife and wondered why he couldn't make himself get to know her. Inside. He would swear that she was an extraordinary person, and he didn't know all the ways in which she was. He didn't know her. He squeezed her hand. After all of his coolness toward her and the yo-yo he'd had her on where his affections were concerned, she'd still go to bat for him. The words of gratitude stuck in his throat; he struggled with his feelings and, after several emotionally charged moments, he managed to say, "You can't imagine what this means to me, Amanda. I don't know how to thank you."

She patted him in the rib section. "Don't thank me, Marcus. You and I both know you would do the same for me."

"I know that, but why do you think you know it?"

"Oh, you take a pound of flesh from me from time to time just to make certain that I don't get too comfortable with you," she told him without a trace of a smile, "but every time I've needed you, Marcus, you've been there for me. And you haven't stinted, never let me feel as if I'm imposing on you. You've been generous and giving. Yes. I'm certain you would do the same for me because you've already done much more."

He gazed beyond her at the butterfly mobile dangling whimsically from the light fixture and wondered if heaven and hell hadn't somehow gotten mixed up.

Amanda got out of bed, walked to the window and looked out at the breaking waves. Tonight, however, the lapping water didn't soothe her. She had never been able to tolerate duplicity in anyone, and she was guilty of it now herself. She was deceiving her husband, knowingly going against his wishes. True, it was a marriage in name only, but he was still her husband; she bore his name, and she owed him honor and respect. When he learned what she had done, and fate being what it was he surely would, he would never forgive her. Worse even, he would hate her. She had known she was taking a chance, but she had not known she would fall in love with Amy and that Marcus would come to mean so much to her. She hadn't slept for nights worrying about it. When she had walked into the child's room after not having visited her during the week of her recovery, Amy had screamed with joy.

"Lady! Lady! You're back. You're back. I told my daddy you would come back." It had nearly broken her heart the way Amy had clung to her and then, begged, "Teach me a surprise for my daddy." So she'd taught her the alphabet from *A* to *O* and the first twenty numbers. When she left, Amy was singing first one and then the other. She had to tell him. She wanted to go on seeing Amy, but she couldn't continue going against the wishes of this man who was beginning to invade her heart. *First thing tomorrow morning, I'll tell him,* she promised herself. But when she got downstairs a little after eight, she found a note saying that he would be in Portsmouth all morning and at the hospital with Amy in the afternoon.

When Marcus got home later that day, she knew that she would soon pay the piper. He was obviously in a dilemma and didn't seem inclined to share his thoughts with her, and when she asked if she could help, he held up his left hand as if to push her away.

"I've got a problem, Amanda, and I need to deal with it on my own." Her sharply drawn breath must have impressed upon him the impact of what he'd said and how he'd said it, because he looked closely at her.

"Look, I shouldn't have been so curt," he offered, "but the doctors tell me that they want Amy out of the hospital this week, and they want her to go back every weekday morning for therapy. I'm told that she has to work harder, that Amy considers it normal for a child not to be able to walk, because none of the children she sees at the hospital can walk on their own. She has to see children who are whole and want to be like them. They think that once she's out of the hospital, she'll make faster progress. I've got to figure out what to do with her."

He must have seen her face fall just before she turned her back to him, for he walked around to face her. She couldn't help thinking that he wouldn't even touch her. She didn't care what his reason was; it hurt that he seemed to take every precaution to make sure she didn't become a part of his life.

"*Now* what's the matter?"

"Why can't she come here? It's your home and there's plenty of space. We even have large gardens and a shaded backyard. I'm home every day, now that school is closed for the summer, and you could spend more time at the factory. Why are you doing this, Marcus? I'm not some kind of ogre." She walked rapidly out of the room, grabbed her handbag from the hall table, got into her car and drove off. She didn't know where she was going or even why she had gotten the sudden urge to get away from him. Out of habit, she turned down Port Street toward the Albemarle Sound and sensed the late spring wind beating at her car. She tried to understand her sense of impending doom, and then she knew. It went beyond facing Marcus' anger. Slowly, she turned around; it was already too late. She was in love with him, and he was going to leave her. She hadn't broken the contract, but she had violated his trust, and he had every right to leave. She stopped and rested her head on the steering wheel. How could she face him?

Amanda glanced up when Mike Henley, on his way to the Sound with his two small grandchildren, tapped on her window.

"You all right there, Miss Amanda? I recognized your car. Just wanted to know nothing was wrong." She rolled down the window, gave him a superficial explanation for idling by the side of the road that time of day and thanked him for his concern. She didn't resent the intrusion: small-town inquisitiveness could be a lifesaver if you were alone and desperate. She watched the threesome as they moseyed down the street, the six-year-old boy carrying his little sister's fishing pole. Would Amy ever go crabbing at the Sound's edge the way other local children did? Or would Marcus take the child back to Portsmouth when he learned of her visits with his daughter?

Amanda didn't want to go back home to face the inevitable, but she knew that the longer she postponed it, the worse their encounter would be. It would take an angel from heaven to prevent

Marcus from walking out. And if he were annoyed, who would blame him? A churning began in her stomach at the thought of his leaving her. She hadn't been wise, letting herself dream of Amy as her daughter and imagining the nurturing and guidance that Marcus would give her own child. Their contract allowed either one of them to call it off at the end of one year; and she had no doubt that he didn't intend to stay with her a second longer. It pained her to think of it, for though she hadn't set out to love him, hadn't even dreamed of it, love him she did. She'd suffer for that, she knew, but she would never regret loving him. She only wished that nothing she did would intensify his mistrust of women. Too late, she supposed, because what she'd done gave him more ammunition to fuel his bias.

Marcus was dealing with his own demons. Luke opened the door of his spacious apartment and let his brother enter. "I thought you'd be working late tonight." Marcus nodded a tired greeting, brushed past him and started pacing the black-and-white marbled floor of the foyer.

"You want a drink?"

"No. That's the last thing I need." Marcus got right to the story, and when he'd finished, he had the feeling that he'd sounded like a petulant kid, making a problem where none existed. Marcus appreciated his brother's approval, but having it right then would make him feel disloyal to his wife. He wished that he could be by himself. He had leased his own mausoleum of a house through March, and he was either in Luke's apartment or Amanda's house, and sometimes, like now, he wanted to be as far as possible from both of them. He felt Luke's hand on his shoulder as he turned to leave.

"Marcus, Amanda is offering you exactly what Amy needs. A home. A place where she has the run of the house, where she can have the experiences of any normal child. What are your alternatives? A boarding or rooming house in Caution Point where you're both confined to one room? A cramped apartment with no place for outdoor play? And can you break your contract with Amanda? Anyway, that's legally your home and you're entitled to take care of your child in your home. There's no favor involved here."

"Thanks for nothing. I've been through all of that. Luke, I'm too close to that woman as it is. What's going to happen to me when I watch her loving and caring for Amy? I never once saw Helena coddle my daughter, and that's just what Amanda will do."

Luke grinned. "So that's the real issue. Why don't you just tell her you love her, take her to bed and the two of you get on with married life?"

"I'm not in love with her."

"Of course you aren't. And the Albemarle Sound is in the middle of Kansas City. Haven't you noticed that every time Amanda needs you, some kind of peace settles over you?"

Marcus stopped pacing. "I think I'll take a beer." He walked to the kitchen with Luke, musing over his brother's last words. He wasn't in love with her, but the rest was true. The week that she had been in bed after her near miscarriage and he'd taken care of her, he had been happier than at any time since Amy's birth. And he had felt good looking after her when she was recovering from that fall in the bathtub. He restrained the urge to run his left hand over his hair, a gesture that usually meant he was deep in thought. Or frustrated.

"Save the beer, Luke. Can you give me a lift to the station?"

"Sure. You okay?" Marcus nodded. He was going to take the chance. Amy came first, he rationalized.

Having a strange man open his door for him when he got home—well, it was his home for the time being—annoyed Marcus. Like male animals of all species, he was very territorial, and he didn't like other men in his space. He raised one eyebrow at the man, didn't speak and walked in. "Where is Mrs. Hickson?"

"She's out back in the garden," the flustered man informed

him. "She asked me to come over and paper a room." Marcus spun around and went looking for his wife.

"Marcus, I've got to tell you something. I…"

He interrupted her with, "Can it wait? We've got to talk, Amanda. And where is that man going to put the wallpaper?"

"In my sitting room. I'm going to change it into a nursery. I have to do it anyway eventually, and I thought that now would be a good time, in case you change your mind about Amy."

"That's what I wanted us to discuss. I've decided to, well, to accept your suggestion and bring her here, but I don't want her to be a burden to you, so I'll do whatever extra work is involved. If you put her in the room adjoining yours, she may wake you up at night, and I don't want that."

"It's the best room for her, Marcus. It's very light, there are a lot of windows, and she can see the Sound from the porch. It's true that one door opens into my bedroom, but another door opens into the hallway facing your bedroom door. There isn't a problem, unless you make it one. But there's something else, Marcus, and I'm not sure you're going to…"

"Mrs. Hickson, could you come and see if this is all right?" the paper hanger yelled down from the second-floor porch. Amanda had a feeling that fate was conspiring against her as Marcus walked with her to examine the room. Dancing yellow bunnies and large, smiling green and silver balloons decorated the walls and were replicated on the curtains, the spread on a child's bunk bed and a chaise lounge. A green and yellow rug covered the floor.

Plainly amazed, Marcus gazed around the room. "When did you do all of this?" She didn't reply, only watched him closely for his reaction. He walked to the window and looked out, turned to walk back to her and hit his head with the balloons that danced from the ceiling. She saw him win the battle against his pride about yet another instance in which she gave something to him and hoped he'd be as successful in controlling his temper when she told him about her visits with Amy.

"I did it today," she told him, the thrust of her chin suggesting combat readiness. "I didn't have anything else to do. I wanted to ask you about it, but you left early and I couldn't reach you at the factory." It wasn't accusatory, unless he wanted to take it that way.

"All right. I know I'm taking a chance, but I'm taking it anyway. She'll love the room." His voice and manners softened. "And you couldn't reach me because I was at Luke's place." Why, he wondered, had he found it necessary to explain his absence from work? He looked around. "What did you do with the computer and workstation?"

"I had the paper hanger put them in your bedroom. I'll use them while you're at work when I outline my plans for the next school year. But I'll be at school for only two weeks this fall, and then I'll begin maternity leave, so I won't need the computer again before early next year, and you use it constantly. I hope you don't mind that I put it there."

"No. It's all right. And thanks. I've got to check this inventory report and mail it tonight; there's a lot to do. I'll get a sandwich when I get hungry." He glanced at her as he started into his room and noticed that she clutched her back. Immediately disturbed, he asked her urgently, "What's wrong? Are you having pain? What's the matter, Amanda?"

He crossed the room to her and, seemingly anxious for her or at last having an excuse to touch her—she didn't know which—he put an arm around her thickened waist. "Come on," he said softly, guiding her toward her bedroom, "you did too much today. You'd better rest. I'll fix supper."

Amanda couldn't help being perplexed. Why was he loving and tender only when something went wrong with her? No tears, she told herself. She blinked them back; doggoned if she would cry. At times like these, she could swear that he really cared for her, but an hour or a day later, he'd give the lie to it.

"It happens sometime that my back hurts a little; the doctor doesn't think it's unusual. I'll be all right, but I appreciate your concern. Dinner's in the oven, so you can go on with your work."

He hesitated for a moment and then, "Okay, if you're sure." He went into his room and closed the door. She stood there. Well, she'd tell him tomorrow. Tomorrow proved to be too late.

Amanda hurried to the Board of Education's annual year-end meeting. It would be the last time that she would be able to participate in the evaluations knowing that the criticisms weren't leveled at her as school principal. She greeted several teachers in passing and squirmed at their knowing glances. Then, she squared her shoulders in defiance as she remembered that a married woman had a right to be pregnant if that was what she wanted. The Board's chairman pronounced her new last name a little too carefully, she thought, amused that she'd managed to hoodwink the lot of them. Nevertheless, the old man lauded her skills as an educator and said repeatedly that Caution Point was fortunate to have such a competent and dedicated woman as its junior high school principal. He exhorted the staff to give her its full support and, after half an hour of condemning the increase in graffiti and loud radio playing on school grounds, he dismissed the meeting and wished them all a happy summer. So much for the quality of education, she thought, as he handed her the keys to her new office. Moments later, she raised her hand to fit the key into the lock and glanced toward the sneering face of Iris Elms.

"You might have fooled them, but not me," Iris Elms told her. "I don't suppose you're planning to frame your marriage certificate and hang it on your office wall, are you?" Amanda suppressed her annoyance; she had won hands down, and she could afford to be gracious.

"If I remember well, Iris, courtesy is the second item on every teacher's evaluation sheet, and it counts for fifteen points. You don't want to start with eighty-five, do you? Oh, yes. The only certificate you'll see hanging on my office will be my doctorate degree," she added, knowing that Iris had not gone beyond her bachelor's degree. She opened the door, walked in and closed it.

She wanted to know the reason for Iris' venom toward her, but she wouldn't give her the satisfaction of asking. She supposed, though, that it went further than winning the principal's job; Iris didn't have the qualifications for the position, though she had applied and had campaigned assiduously for the post. Amanda sat at the desk to get the feel of it and looked around. The room needed a bright color, some pictures and a couple of young ficus trees. She locked up and considered herself lucky when she reached her car without having encountered Iris Elms again.

That afternoon, Amanda strolled through her garden examining the peonies. They had been so beautiful, but they had such a short life. Every year she looked forward to their lovely pink, red and white blossoms, and every year she became depressed at the sight of their bowed heads and dying petals. She was again tempted to take them out and put in a swimming pool in that corner, but with a baby coming and another small child in the house, perhaps it wouldn't be safe. She wandered around, on edge. Marcus had left before she awoke, and she hadn't been able to tell him about her visits with Amy. She didn't want her baby in a climate of anger, and she was sure that it wasn't the best thing for Amy, but she doubted that anger would be a broad enough word to describe Marcus' reaction to what she had done. She went to the back porch for her floppy straw hat to protect herself from the sun and heard a car door slam. Curious, she walked around the side of the garage toward the front of the house and stopped, transfixed, as Marcus got out of the taxi and came up the stone walk carrying Amy in his arms. Dear God, he hadn't told her. What was she going to do?

"Lady! Lady! Daddy, it's Lady." The child's excitement bordered on euphoria, as she tried to jump out of Marcus' arms to reach Amanda. "Daddy! Daddy!" she squealed. "It's Lady!" Amanda tried to ignore Marcus' confused and uncertain look and did the only thing that she could. She walked to them and, as if unaware of his presence, she put an arm around Amy and kissed her.

"Hello, Amy, darling." Before she could say more, the child reached for her.

"Lady, I brought Peter. See?" She held out the floppy-eared yellow rabbit that Amanda had given her.

Marcus stepped away. "What the…? What is the meaning of this, Amanda?"

"It's Lady, Daddy." The child informed him again, innocently, as she hugged him with sheer joy.

"I tried to tell you, but you wouldn't listen."

"You tried to tell me? *You tried to tell me?* I don't suppose it occurred to you to *ask* me, did it? Of course not, because you knew my feelings about this. And you wilfully and deliberately ignored them." He backed away, symbolically it seemed to her, as if moving Amy out of her reach.

"Daddy, what's the matter?" Amy asked, obviously aware of the currents that flowed between the two adults. He didn't answer her, merely turned and started back down the walk, certain that he had never been so unsettled in his life. Or so disappointed. How could she have gone behind his back and done a thing that she knew he would dislike? He had thought her above surreptitious behavior.

"Daddy, can I go to the bathroom?" He stopped, swearing under his breath. Now what?

"I have to go now, Daddy." Without saying a word to Amanda, he walked past her and took Amy inside and up the stairs to the bathroom. The door to the room that Amanda had prepared for Amy stood open and, as he carried her out of the bathroom, the child saw the room and squealed in delight. "Is this my room, Daddy? My rabbit is just like that one and that one." She pointed to the rabbits on the wallpaper. "Can I have a balloon, Daddy?"

Marcus regarded his precious child with a smile. She'd played no part in his quarrel with Amanda, and he wouldn't let it touch her. He looked around and saw that two balloons were tied to the post of Amy's bed. He untied the yellow one, and gave it to her.

"Oh, Daddy, there's my chair. You can put me down now."

Marcus hadn't seen the little wheelchair, and he hadn't remembered to buy one. But Amanda had thought of it. When had she done it? It hadn't been there the day before. With a sigh, he put Amy in the chair and sat on the edge of the chaise lounge, exasperated. If Amy hadn't had to go to the bathroom, he would have walked the two miles back to the hospital. The child chattered away discovering things that pleased her, while he wondered how he could take her away when she was so happy. He kissed her, locked her chair and told her that he'd be back shortly. Then he went to find Amanda.

"We won't discuss this right now," he told her, "because I'm too vexed. She's seen it now, and she's seen you. It's been a long time since I saw her so happy, and I can't take this away from her."

He turned and went back into the house. To Amy, she supposed. She allowed a little time to pass and then went up to see the little girl.

"I thought you'd be asleep, Amy."

"I was waiting for you. Are you going to live with us, Lady?" Amanda nodded. "Then you can read me a story before I go to bed?"

"If your father doesn't mind. Maybe he will want to read one to you." Amy assured Amanda that her father wouldn't mind. She wheeled the child out on the porch to the sunlight to begin remedying the effects of months of hospitalization away from fresh air and sunshine.

Marcus walked out on the porch through his bedroom door and found them sitting beside each other holding hands. He couldn't help the sensation he experienced in the region of his heart at the sight of this woman chatting with his child and holding her hand as if they were two adults.

He didn't begrudge his daughter the love he knew Amanda would give her, because she had never known a mother's love and selfless devotion. Amanda offered her that and more, and Amy needed it. And from what he saw of the bond that had already developed between them, it was inevitable that Amy would become deeply attached to Amanda. Then, he'd be even deeper in Amanda's debt. He couldn't bear to think of it. Yes, theirs was a contract in which each gave something to the other, but he brought nothing to the relationship except his presence, a shield for her reputation. Her material contribution was enormous, yet it paled in importance compared to what she gave of herself. He'd thought he wanted to keep them apart for Amy's sake alone; how wrong he'd been. With every passing day, Amanda settled more comfortably inside of him, toying with his resolve, firing his desire and nurturing his soul. He ducked back in, not wanting Amanda to see him.

Late in the afternoon, Amanda put Amy in bed for a nap and started preparing dinner. When she noticed Marcus' preoccupation with his work, she ran a tub of warm water and put Amy in it along with an assortment of rubber ducks, frogs and pigs. While the bubbling Amy repeated the alphabet up to the letter *Q* and counted to twenty-five, sloshing water delightedly for the first time in many months, Amanda exercised her legs in the warm water. She hadn't realized that Marcus had been watching unobtrusively from the door when she attempted to take Amy out of the tub, lay her on a towel and dry her. He rushed to help as she struggled with the child's weight while on her knees facing the tub. Amanda looked up at him, relieved not to see obvious disapproval. Amy giggled when Marcus rolled her over on her stomach.

"That's cold, Daddy." Then she twisted and looked up at Amanda, eyes twinkling with merriment as her father's often did.

"Lady, is your name Lady, or something else? My daddy has a name, and it's Marcus Hickson, isn't it, Daddy? What's yours, Lady?"

Swept up in the child's charm, Amanda smiled, adoring her. "My name is Amanda."

"Is that all? Don't you have any more?"

Marcus answered for her. "Her name is Amanda Ross Hickson." Amy frowned at that, but neither adult bothered to explain it.

Amanda asked Marcus to bring Amy downstairs to dinner, and he hesitated, but did as she asked when she argued that it would be poor psychology to feed her in bed. The three of them ate their first meal together, to Amy's delight. She demanded that they both put her to bed and that Amanda read her the story of "Winnie the little poop."

Amanda and Marcus cleaned the kitchen together in silence. But Amanda knew it was only a temporary reprieve. She dressed for bed and walked out on the upstairs porch, using the hall entrance in order not to disturb Amy. It made her uncomfortable to find Marcus standing there, a solitary, seemingly lonely figure. They didn't speak; their attention was on the slowly rising moon. She marveled at the awesome sight, as the brilliant disk seemed to climb against its will out of the wicked Atlantic. They could see the waves undulating seductively beneath it, as if attempting to lure it back into the ocean's cradle.

"It's breathtaking." Amanda was too affected by the sight to remain silent, knowing that he was there.

"Yes. As seductive as you." The comment sounded like an insult, as it was meant to be, and Amanda accepted it as one.

"I'm truly sorry, Marcus."

"Save it, Amanda. The damage is done. I will remember this for a long, long time."

"I know. But I wish you would hear me out." She turned to face him, but he refused to look at her and focused instead upon the ocean in the distance.

"You pulled off one of the slickest con games on record. Tell me, how could you know that learning is a great game to Amy? Oh, yes, I forgot. You're a teacher. But how did you happen to create 'Daddy Goose' for her? It's become her favorite story, and you're the only one who can tell it to her. You should be ashamed of yourself. I trusted you, Amanda." His voice had lowered and his speech had become slower and increasingly deliberate. She knew he was on the verge of losing his temper.

"Marcus, you have already decided not to believe me. But before you hang me, let me have my say." Noticing that he had fallen silent, she continued. "I volunteer at the hospital regularly four hours each week. I read to the blind and to older patients who don't read, and on occasion, I tell stories to children. I didn't go to see Amy on impulse. I thought about it. Here I was easing the lot of others in that hospital, but I wasn't allowed to give comfort to the one person for whom you care so much. I was on the children's ward, so I went to look for her. She was so warm and friendly with me, so accepting. But most of all, when I looked down at her, it was almost like seeing you, a mirror image of one for whom I care so…" Dear Lord, what had she said? She wanted to vanish through the floor. *I can't walk away now,* she told herself, *it may be my only chance.*

She squared her shoulders and continued. "I read a story to her, and then I started to leave, but she begged me to stay. And when I told her that I didn't have any more stories with me, she said it would be all right if I just talked to her. So I stayed and invented Daddy Goose. She begged me to come back. I'm human, Marcus, and she is your flesh and blood. She was so easy to love. You're angry with me, but shouldn't I be angry with you, Marcus? You're on a slippery slope, yourself. No matter how you define our marriage, Amy Hickson is my stepdaughter, and you refused to honor me by introducing her to me. You didn't honor me as your wife, but you wanted me to honor you as my husband and to obey your wish, even though you must have known that it was unreasonable. Maybe you think a marriage like ours doesn't demand that you honor it.

"I know I've displeased you, gone against your will, and I can't tell you how sorry I am. And I'm doubly sorry that you had to learn about it the way you did. I tried to tell you, though I admit that my efforts were very feeble. My fear of your leaving me was so great that I couldn't bring myself to tell you after I had done it. No matter the reason, you're giving my child your name, giving it the ticket to the dignity that it might not have otherwise. And you're helping me to preserve mine. Do you honestly think there's anything I wouldn't do for Amy?" His silence weighed on her, and she stepped toward the door.

"Good night, Marcus."

Marcus had been silent, but he had been listening. And he'd heard Luke's words all over again. *You mean you haven't taken Amanda to meet her stepdaughter? Are you out of your mind?* Marcus could be explosive when he knew he was right, but not when he was wrong. And suddenly, he wasn't so sure.

He turned toward her. "Let's talk about this again in a day or so. Right now, I can't deal with it." His distress at the awkwardness of his relationship with Amanda hadn't abated, and he wasn't going to pretend that it had. He told her, "I do want to thank you for making Amy's homecoming so wonderful. It was like a dose of good medicine. Sleep well."

The next evening after dinner, Marcus stood in front of the house, contemplating his situation. Too often in the African-American community, women had to support their families, because jobs were denied their men. He'd always been the provider, the protector, until fate dealt him this nearly lethal blow. True, he was giving Amanda something in exchange, but he hated the role into which he'd been cast. If it took the rest of his life, he'd repay her every cent. Absentmindedly, he started walking and, nearly an hour later, found himself on Port Street going in the direction of the Sound. He often walked alone in the evenings for pleasure, but on this night he was attempting to deal with his conflicting emotions, to sort out the truth and to force himself to see things from Amanda's perspective. Luke's words wouldn't leave him. His brother had an uncanny ability to understand people, to decipher motives, and Marcus respected that. He walked down to the pier and looked out. The night shone clear and bright and his gaze wandered to the cloudless sky as a big jet thundered on its way. His feeling of loneliness intensified. The despair he had known during the months before Amy's last operation had vanished, but his life lacked something important. Something vital. And it was an incompleteness that he knew he hadn't felt in years.

He leaned against a hitching post used to anchor small boats and thought about Amanda. She was a good woman, a loving, caring woman and, God help him, he wanted her.

He had always taken pride in being completely honest, and he forced himself to be now. More than his status in her home worried him and more than the deception about Amy unsettled him. It was this in addition to his all-consuming physical attraction for Amanda that he knew she reciprocated, along with his growing hunger for more than a physical expression of what they seemed to feel. He had begun to walk rapidly, but stopped suddenly. What was it that she had said about not being allowed to give comfort to the person closest to someone "for whom I care so much"? He wanted to run back home, but he controlled it; he was not going to have a marriage with Amanda Ross or any other woman, and that was that.

The ocean breeze whipped around his broad shoulders, invigorating him. He loved his solitary evening walks, a habit he'd developed after Amy's accident, when she was safely in the care of hospital authorities. His pace quickened. He had gone off without remembering that Amy might awaken in the strange environment and need him.

He stepped quietly into his daughter's room, and a sense of well-being enveloped him; Amy was at last sleeping under the same roof as he. He glanced toward her bed, saw that it was empty, and looked around anxiously. He didn't believe that anything could have prepared him for the sight that greeted his eyes in the shadowed room; his heart soared. There on the chaise lounge lay his wife-in-name-only with Amy sprawled facedown on top of her, secure in Amanda's arms. The child's head rested on the gentle woman's shoulder, arms around her neck and her weak little legs straddled Amanda's protruding belly. He couldn't suppress his loud gasp at the tender scene.

A tremor passed through him as he stood there, his heart pounding, imagining what could be and not daring to want it. When he could, he moved over to his child and the woman who cradled her, reaching them just as Amy buried her face in the curve of Amanda's shoulder and received a comforting, loving pat from the still sleeping woman who held her. There was more mothering in that protective, love-giving gesture than Amy had had in her lifetime. Amanda's hand came up to stroke Amy's hair, and he clenched his fists as he fought a spiraling sensual awareness.

"Amanda." It was barely a whisper, little more than the heated caress of his breath. Her eyes fluttered open, then closed and, though she was almost asleep, a smile illumined her face. Was that smile for him?

"Marcus." She said it dreamily, softly and intimately, answering his unspoken question.

"Marcus." She drifted toward sleep but, captivated, he leaned over them, brushed his lips across her mouth, and her eyes flew open. His breath came fast and shallow, and her uncensored gaze swept over him, brilliant with unguarded love. Sensations of desire surged through him, and he kissed her. Kissed her with the want that threatened to strangle him, with the need that nearly overwhelmed him and with the love that he refused to acknowledge. He felt her soft, delectable fingers moving lightly over his face in a shattering caress, and watched, mesmerized, as she parted her lips for his tongue and smiled sleepily when he gave it to her.

Marcus broke away and stared at her, feeling poleaxed, his passion warring with his common sense. He'd had plenty of experience at ruling his emotions, and he hadn't lost control, he assured himself; he had simply done what he hadn't wanted to avoid. Had taken what he needed. He couldn't deny what he felt and didn't try.

"Amanda, honey, what have you done to me?"

Fully awake now, Amanda murmured, "That's what I ought to be asking you."

He smiled, resting on his haunches. "What happened? Was she in pain, or just restless?"

Amanda couldn't climb down so easily from the cloud on which Marcus had thrust her and, for a moment, was at a loss as to what he meant. Then she looked down at the head full of curly black hair resting at her collarbone, looked up at him and wrinkled her nose. "She called me, and I woke up. I'm not usually a light sleeper but, tonight, well I could hardly get to sleep at all. I think she was a little afraid awakening in a strange place, and it took her a while to remember where she was. When I got to her, I saw that she'd been crying. That's why I put the chaise in here, Marcus. Either one of us can go to her, get her accustomed to her room."

Marcus nodded, and she knew he was not in the least fooled by her rambling. She was as disconcerted by their kiss as she imagined he was. He took the still-sleeping Amy out of her arms, put the child back in bed and turned to her.

"Amy is too heavy for you to lift. When I'm here, of course, I'll lift her, but when I'm not and it's absolutely necessary for you to move her, please be careful."

Amanda observed him closely, not wanting to misunderstand what he was telling her. And what she heard was that he was going to let her help him take care of Amy. He didn't really want her to know that he cared for her, maybe he didn't even know it himself, she decided, but he'd told her anyway. And for now, it was enough.

Chapter 5

Amanda awakened shortly after sunrise the next morning, dressed and went to Amy's room, anticipating the pleasure of their first full day together, and found her sitting up in bed teaching the bunny how to count. She marveled at the ease with which Amy accepted her into her life and as a mother figure. *She takes to me like a duck to water,* Amanda thought, as she gave the child a sponge bath and dressed her. *I mustn't get too attached to her,* she cautioned herself, *because he's bent on taking her back to Portsmouth when this is over.* But from the day she met Marcus, she had felt as if fate had intervened in her life. Great-Aunt Meredith, who claimed the Lord planned everything from start to finish, would have laughed at the idea. She'd have said that Amanda's meeting Marcus had been the work of Providence. Amanda straightened from her pleasant task, the discomfort of pregnancy already beginning to wear on her, cheered Amy with hugs and kisses and went down to start breakfast.

Amanda enjoyed mornings, and breakfast was her favorite meal. After setting the table for three, she began preparing the food, thinking back to the evening before, and almost dreaded the moment when Marcus would walk into the kitchen. Maybe she was being foolish, but he had drummed it into her head that there was no future for them. "If he acts cool and distant after what he did to me last night," she muttered to herself, "I won't be one bit friendly. I may just shackle him." She bent over the sink, annoyed with herself and angry at Marcus. *How could I give a man so much power over me,* she fumed silently, *when I'm living with proof that I should know better? And why the devil can't he be consistent? If he doesn't want me, he shouldn't touch me.*

She remembered how she had trembled when his marauding mouth and tongue had taken possession of her, knocking her senses out of order, destroying her willpower. With just that kiss; without touching her anywhere else. She clutched the edge of the sink and crossed her thighs tightly in frustration.

"Good morning. You're up early." His voice must have startled her, he realized, when she jerked her head up, and her face ashened. His gaze swept over her, and he knew at once that thoughts of him had aroused her, that he had caught her in a moment of intense privacy, and that she had been thinking about what they had shared the evening before. He had planned to talk to her about it, but if he did that now, she might be embarrassed. He squelched his response to her wanting him and grinned disarmingly. "What's for breakfast? I was going to cook this morning."

"We're having blueberry pancakes."

He frowned, uncertain. "I'm not sure Amy has ever had pancakes. I don't know how to make them."

So he wasn't going to be aloof. And so far, at least, he hadn't told her to forget the evening before. The tension eased from her shoulders, and she felt herself relax. "Amy got to choose the breakfast, and she wants a pancake and some bacon. I can cook you some eggs."

"No way. I love any kind of pancakes, as long as they're oozing with maple syrup and butter."

"What about your arteries?"

His raised eyebrows suggested that her sanity might be in

question. Then, he laughed, his white teeth gleaming against his brown face. "I don't let anything rule me, arteries included." He was a living advertisement for beguiling, virile grace and masculinity, she thought, but when he laughed, really laughed, he was devastatingly handsome.

She turned to the stove, then looked at him over her shoulder. "'It is in the ability to deceive oneself that the greatest talent is shown.'"

He was impressed, but evidently not outdone, she discovered, when he smoothly retorted, "Anatole France was never one of my favorite writers. And who says I'm deceiving myself? Anyway, 'Lying to ourselves is more deeply ingrained than lying to others.'" He waited, while she supported her thick waist with both hands and looked upward, trying to recall the author of that phrase.

"Give up?"

She pretended annoyance. "Never. It sounds Russian, but Russian literature isn't something I ever got a bang out of reading."

"Not a bad guess," he allowed, haughtily, with an amused glint in his eyes. "Dostoyevsky is your man," he told her.

"Well, now that your genius is a matter of record, would you please bring Amy down?" she retorted, swatting him playfully on the buttocks as he passed her. Swift as a coiled snake, he had his hands on her, gripping her shoulders, as his gaze scorched her. She stood there motionless, mesmerized by the pure unadulterated hot man in him and by what his desire-filled eyes told her he wanted. Neither of them could have said what would have happened next, if her eyes hadn't suddenly grown large with wonder, breaking the tension.

He recovered quickly. "What is it, Amanda?" he asked, anxiously. "What's the matter? Are you all right?"

Marcus realized she was speechless when, wordlessly, she took his hand and placed it on her belly. He felt the motion and watched her face with its awed expression. "Is this the first time it's moved?"

"Yes. Unless I was asleep and didn't notice."

He probably knew more about what to expect during a pregnancy than Amanda did. Careful not to move his hand too quickly, lest he hurt or offend her, he assured her that she would have awakened.

"Really?" She seemed as worried as she was curious. He made a mental note to talk with her about maternity care and to make certain that she followed her doctor's advice. He remembered her question.

"Yeah. The little rascals can raise hell. After a while, you'll be able to feel their little toes and fingers punching at you. Keep you awake half the night." He wasn't speaking from personal knowledge, but from what he'd read. The experience of Helena's unwanted pregnancy with Amy was suddenly fresh in his memory and with the thoughts came the bitter sadness he felt each time he thought of the one that he would never know, never see.

He hadn't meant for thoughts of Helena to spoil their good mood, but Amanda had sensed it immediately. He looked down at her when she wrapped her arms around him and tried to comfort him, to rock him as she would a baby, to give him peace. And for the first time in his life, he knew what a woman's caring could do for a man. His pounding heart wanted to reciprocate, to let go and love, but he wouldn't give in to it. He held her to him for a while, selfishly enjoyed what she offered.

"Daaaaaddy! Laaaaady! I'm hungry. I wanna come down and eat." They looked at each other, both nearly stupefied, but thankful that another crisis had passed.

"Pretty good chaperon, isn't she?" He wasn't amused and tried, but couldn't force a smile. "I'll be right back."

Amanda didn't lull herself into viewing Marcus' warm and genial manner during breakfast as evidence that he'd come to terms with the three of them as a family. She had learned that his good manners often camouflaged his discontent and obscured his impatience. To her mind, some of the great actors of the English-speaking stage could take lessons from him. "Well," she decided, "I'll deal with what he shows me, not what I *think* he feels."

She reminded herself to order a stroller so that she could move Amy around more easily downstairs and take her for walks in the garden. She watched for evidence of Marcus' turn of mind while he straightened the kitchen after breakfast and prepared their shopping list. When he returned from the market, he and Amy left immediately for the child's therapy session, and she still had no idea of his reaction to their first morning as a family.

Even in her excitement about the baby moving, Amanda had sensed the torment in Marcus. He would rather do anything than face what had almost happened between them that morning. Not that he was a coward; he wasn't. He simply didn't want to be married, and she had better not forget that fact. She had wanted to go with them, to see what was involved in the therapy so she could follow through at home, but Marcus hadn't offered her the chance. Whatever progress they made would come inch by inch, she knew. At least he wasn't trying to place distance between Amy and herself. And that was more than she could have hoped for only a week earlier.

After the therapy session, Marcus brought Amy back home, settled her in her chair and glanced at his watch. Just time to make the eleven-thirty-eight to Portsmouth, a trip that he no longer dreaded. Later, at the buzz of the factory's front doorbell, he stepped quickly away from his desk, where he'd just begun writing a procedures manual for a Boston-based company that trained piano technicians. He had accepted the offer to write it, because he couldn't afford to ignore the substantial income. He walked toward the man who strolled around the showroom, fingering various instruments.

"What can I do for you?" He looked around, wondering where his workers were until he realized the time; they'd gone to lunch.

"May I help you?" he asked again when the man didn't respond. "Do you have a string instrument that needs overhauling? That's what we do here." When the man glanced at him and continued to move around the store, Marcus told him, "I'm very busy. If you just want to look around, come back around three, and be prepared to tell me why you're here, otherwise I'll have to conclude that you're trespassing." As though coming out of a trance, the man looked up from a piano he'd been inspecting and spared Marcus a nod.

"I'm thinking of taking an option on this place, so I get first chance when the bank's ready to unload it." Stunned, Marcus reached deep within himself to summon the composure he needed right then. How could the same institution on whose counters he had emptied his first piggy bank write him off without a word?

"That doesn't give you the right to walk around here as if you're already the owner. Don't slam the door when you leave," he told the stranger. The man's shrug suggested that it was only a question of time before their roles would be reversed. Marcus went back to his desk and tried to pick up where he'd left off, but he couldn't concentrate. Every day, an incident occurred, some unexpected thing that made him wonder whether his efforts were futile. He looked out of his office window at a red-breasted robin that chirped happily from his perch on an evergreen shrub, and it occurred to him that birds sang for their own enjoyment; they didn't care whether anyone or anything heard them. He went back to work, and he concentrated. He'd give it everything he had for the satisfaction of doing it and, if he defaulted on his loans, he wouldn't beat himself to death over it. When he got home that night, he couldn't figure out why he felt less depressed than he had in recent days. He merely welcomed the change in himself.

Amanda and Marcus tiptoed around each other for the next three weeks without incident. By some unspoken agreement, each withheld from the other thoughts and concerns that would have upset their peace. A fragile peace, Marcus thought. Each day, the bonds between Amanda and Amy became stronger, irrevocably sealed, he now knew. And each day, his certainty increased that the tension between Amanda and himself would soon ignite and flame out of control. But they didn't discuss either their relationship or their differences and, instead, concentrated on what united them—Amy. And that suited him. He kept his promise to help her, preparing breakfast, taking Amy for therapy, running errands and sharing the housework.

"You must have been a wonderful husband." Amanda told him one morning, alluding to his activities around the house and his devotion to Amy.

He frowned with displeasure. "I might have been, if I'd ever had the chance." Amanda didn't have to be told that they were on shaky turf, and she quickly changed the subject.

"Amy's so much stronger now. Do you mind if I go walking with her in her stroller and if I take her out in the garden with me in the afternoons? She needs the sun. I won't keep her out too long."

Marcus stopped eating and looked at her in a way that suggested he might be seeking the solution to a difficult puzzle, as if by asking permission she had raised a prickly issue. "Why do you feel you have to ask me?"

"I've never taken her away from the house, and I wouldn't unless you agreed." He nodded, seemingly still perplexed. She wished she hadn't mentioned it.

She reached across the table and took his hand. Touching him felt so good and so natural. At times she longed for him just to graze her cheek with his fingertips, to pat her on the shoulder, anything, just touch her. It had been weeks since he'd put his hands on her. Not since that morning when surely they'd almost... She corralled her wayward thoughts and forced herself to look straight at him.

"Marcus, I know that things aren't...well...aren't settled between us. But I need to tell you something, and I hope it won't make you angry." He must have sensed her nervous anxiety; seemingly thoughtful, he looked down at Amy, then at her.

"Can it wait until I get her settled? I'll only be a few minutes."
He was right, she realized. Amy repeated everything she heard
and remembered most of it. True to his word, he returned shortly
and stood beside her chair, obviously weighing a decision. Then,
taking her hand, he walked them out on the porch in the still fresh
morning air and sat down.

"All right, now. What is it?"

"When I went to visit Amy in the hospital that first time, I
wasn't thinking of you or of me. I was thinking of her. I admit
that my feelings for you had something to do with it. But I've
been lonely in my life, Marcus, lonelier than anyone could guess,
and if it hadn't been for my aunt Meredith, I don't know what
would have become of me. Neither you nor I can foresee the
future, Marcus. And I had been thinking that if you should die
or become incapacitated this year, who would raise Amy? I
would. And how would I explain to her my failure to visit her, a
sick child, even once? Tell her that her mean old daddy forbade
it? I understood all of your reasons, including the ones you
haven't given me, and I don't blame you. I want you to know that
I felt wretched deceiving you. I felt as if I'd dishonored my
husband, and it hurt. Please try to find it in your heart to understand." She fought back the tears that glistened unshed in her
eyes. She didn't want his sympathy, but his understanding.

Marcus had known instinctively what the topic would be, but
he hadn't expected either her candidness or her humility, and he
was unprepared to respond. He squeezed her hand absentmindedly in reassurance, leaned back in the porch swing and closed
his eyes. Yes, he acknowledged to himself, the issue had been like
a festering sore between them. They had managed by pretending that it didn't exist, and now she wanted the slate cleaned. He
sat forward, rubbing his brow with his left hand.

"I was angry with you, Amanda, and you know it. I felt
betrayed, deceived and numerous other tags that I righteously
attached to your behavior. You said I failed to honor you when I

refused to introduce you and Amy. So it appears we were both wrong. Anyway, I don't know how I feel about it now; it just doesn't seem to matter so much. I admit that, by visiting her in the hospital, you eased her adjustment here."

"Think, Marcus. Had you planned for her to remain in the hospital until April eleventh, when the year is up? Had you? It wasn't going to be possible to avoid our being together. And I'm glad. I love her. She's a wonderful child and, if I have her just for these few months, I'll always be grateful."

He looked into the distance. "You've been good for her." *And for me,* he thought. "I wonder if either of us would have gone into this knowing what we know now."

Her answer was immediate. "I would have. Oh, yes. Definitely. In a New York minute."

Carelessly, Marcus patted her thigh. "You're a good woman, and I don't think there's anything to forgive." He noticed the position of his hand high on her thigh, and it occurred to him that they both behaved occasionally like two people in an intimate marriage. He smiled ruefully. Amanda was quicksand. He looked at the heavy cotton smock she wore in the oppressive July heat. Why did she wear those hot, ungainly things? They certainly didn't obscure her protruding belly.

It was not Marcus, but Luke who brought Amy home after her therapy session that Saturday morning. Amanda greeted him warmly, having developed an affection for her brother-in-law. Luke always behaved as if his brother's marriage to her was like any other, and she knew he wanted the two of them to make a go of it.

"Where's Marcus?" Conscious of her obvious pregnancy, she looked away when his gaze examined her from head to foot. She had learned that Luke got as much information as he could by observing and didn't ask a question unless he had no alternative.

"I met him at the hospital and sent him on to Portsmouth to check on things at the factory. I've got the weekend off, and I wanted to see you folks. He'll be here around five or six."

Amanda got the stroller, and they settled Amy in it. The three sat on the back porch with the awnings down to protect them from the scorching sun, and sipped iced tea, that universal Southern elixir. She gave them the choice of crab salad and corn-on-the-cob or hamburgers for lunch, and both wanted the hamburgers. "I'll fix them," Luke stated and got busy in the kitchen. They ate on the porch, because Amy wanted to watch the butterflies.

"Do you like Uncle Luke, Lady?" When Amanda assured her that she did, Amy wanted to know, "Better than my daddy?"

Amanda tweaked the child's nose playfully. "I don't like anybody better than your daddy, except maybe you." That brought a happy giggle from Amy and a narrow-eyed appraisal from Luke.

"You two getting along all right?" he asked, lowering his voice. When it seemed that she wasn't going to answer, he changed the question. "How are you getting along?"

He was crowding her and it irritated her, but she knew that he wasn't satisfying a curiosity, that he wanted to know because he cared.

"Fine and awful" was her enigmatic reply.

"You're going to explain that, I gather." He raised his voice above Amy's serious reprimands to the bad little bunny who had eaten all of her hamburger.

She glanced downward, fighting to hide her sensitivity to the topic, leading him to reach out and pat her shoulder. "It's all right if you can't talk about it."

But she had a need to talk, to tell someone about the longing that churned inside of her. "I've done a foolish thing, Luke. I've fallen in love with Marcus." She heard his sharply indrawn breath, but she plodded on with words that had been pressing for release. "Even at my best, I know I could never get a man like him, but in this state, I'm way out of my depth, out of my league. After April eleventh, he'll go his way, and I'll go mine and he'll take this precious little one with him. Being here with him like this leads to dangerous make-believe, but I wouldn't change it. I'm happier than I've ever been in my life."

* * *

Luke gazed across the garden and ground his teeth. Amanda knew that he sheltered his thoughts, that his high-powered grin, so much like his brother's, belied his mood. "That's the bad news, I take it. What's been happening that's 'fine'?"

"There's peace between us," she said simply. "There's tension, too, but nothing can be done about that. And he doesn't interfere with our relationship anymore." She pointed to herself and Amy, hooked her toes under the stroller and pulled Amy back into their midst. "That's more than I dared hope for."

She knew that he respected his brother and wasn't comfortable discussing her relationship with Marcus in his brother's absence. He spoke with seeming reluctance. "So you think you're hanging out here all by yourself, do you? Take my word for it. Nothing could be further from the truth." There was no chance for a reply.

Amy had stopped talking to her bunny and was watching the two adults attentively. "Where is Lady hanging out all by herself, Uncle Luke? Is she gonna get hurt?" Amanda laughed. It was impossible not to. Maybe God spoke through the mouths of children. She didn't know, but Amy's question made her spine tingle.

Luke soothed the child's fear. "Sweetheart, your daddy and I would never let anything happen to…her." He had almost said "Lady." "Why do you call her Lady? Her name is Amanda."

Amy looked mutinous, something rare for her. "I know what her name is, Uncle Luke. Daddy always reminds me, too, but I'm going to call her Lady. I don't want to call her Amanda. She's Lady," Amy explained and got an indulgent smile from Luke. "You've shown a lot of guts, Amanda, and I admire you for it. You did exactly the right thing."

Marcus greeted Luke, whom he found clipping shrubs around the front steps, but he barely paused before continuing around the side of the house to the back porch where he knew he'd find Amanda and Amy. He felt a stirring shoot through his middle in anticipation of…he didn't ask himself what. Neither did he ask himself why his heartbeat had accelerated. He told himself he didn't give a hoot and increased his pace. He reached for the knob of the screen door and paused at the sight of them sitting together on the porch lounge, bowed heads almost touching, while Amy held a bird and Amanda appeared to be putting a splint on its leg.

A powerful stirring possessed him, and he knew a tenderness, and an almost overwhelming need to be cared for. The feeling was almost immediately replaced by one of dismay, of apprehension that things were getting out of control. He stepped back a few paces, tempted to get away, to walk and walk until he winded himself. Then Amy's words brought him up short.

"Lady, you're fixing up the bird just like the doctor is fixing up my legs, aren't you?" He watched as Amanda hugged and kissed her, telling her, "Yes, sweetheart. And it's going to walk again, just like you are."

Shaken, he grabbed the door, threw it open and startled them when he walked rapidly across the porch and pulled them both to him.

"Daddy, you're squeezing the bird. It's hurt bad, and you're squeezing it, Daddy." She covered his face with kisses. Marcus kissed her back. Then he looked inquiringly at Amanda, silently demanding, "What about you?" Obviously flustered, she lowered her gaze when he looked at her again. Her black eyes widened, and a smile creased her face as she took the package he handed her and opened it with shaky fingers.

Amanda couldn't believe what she saw, the first gift he'd ever given her. Three pairs of wildly patterned, brightly colored maternity shorts and matching halter tops. She would keep them as long as she lived. She stared at him in astonishment, nonplussed, and then told him, "Thank you. It's such a thoughtful thing, but I'm awfully large for these, aren't I? Aunt Meredith always said expectant mothers shouldn't wear anything that calls attention to themselves."

"Nuts to Aunt Meredith," he growled. "If you can't hide it, decorate it. And that's from Hickson." She rewarded his irreverence with a howl of laughter as did Amy, who had developed the habit of imitating her.

Marcus looked from one to the other. *I'm getting to be duplicitous,* he acknowledged to himself, *and I hate that in anybody.* He rubbed the back of his neck and leaned back. She was getting next to him, and he had to do something about it without hurting her or his child. It wouldn't be easy.

Luke turned around and walked back to the front of the house; he could wait until later to call the Portsmouth police station in answer to his beeper. It would have been near criminal, he figured, to interrupt their bonding. He just hoped that Marcus wouldn't be the fool and walk away from that gentle, caring woman.

Amanda moved a ficus plant from the foyer out to the porch and let the bird nest in it after she and Amy fed it. The little creature hadn't seemed to want to leave Amy's warm little hands, but appeared content in a tree. Marcus observed them, something akin to apprehension stealing over him as he stood there. Amy would get attached to that bird and, as soon as its leg healed, it would be gone. He said as much at dinner that night, but Amy surprised them all.

"I know that, Daddy. Birds are supposed to fly away, but they can't fly if their legs are hurt, can they? If they get tired and have to stop flying? Is that right, Daddy?" He pondered his daughter's words. How could a four-year-old be so fearless and have so much sense?

"Coffee, Luke?" Marcus stood at the stove, pouring a cup for himself. "Amanda isn't drinking it. Not good for the baby." Luke's penetrating look didn't disturb him. He didn't discuss Amanda's pregnancy with his brother; he tried to ignore it. Not that he succeeded, considering how she looked. Luke accepted the coffee and sipped it slowly, watching his brother settle comfortably at the table.

"I'll have some coffee, Daddy."

Marcus studied his adorable, precocious daughter. "Sorry, baby. Coffee is for grown-ups."

Showing some of the charisma she'd inherited from her father, she smiled flirtatiously, then broke it off and told him deadpan, "I'm going to be a grown-up soon. The doctor's giving me leg braces."

Marcus nearly strangled as the coffee entered his windpipe. When he could stop coughing, he asked her, "When did the doctor say that?" The child seemed unperturbed, as the startled adults awaited her answer.

"At the hospital when Uncle Luke was getting the wheelchair for me. He said it's our secret, 'cause I been so good."

Marcus tried to stave off the scepticism and just be happy, but he was afraid to believe it. Why hadn't the doctor told Luke? He looked at Amy, who was busy giving her bunny an imaginary glass of milk.

"Did he say you could tell your daddy?" Amy had lost interest in the subject. He went upstairs, got his address book and called Amy's therapist. It was true, and the doctor planned to give him the particulars on Monday. He sat on the edge of his bed, his elbows resting on his knees, and buried his face in his hands. At long last, he was beginning to see the light. He said a word of thanks, got up and was midway down the stairs when the telephone rang. Luke answered it.

Marcus stopped on the bottom step. "What is it?" he asked, something akin to terror curdling his insides as he took in the expression on Luke's face.

"Thanks. We'll get right over there." Luke replaced the receiver and turned to his brother. Why, he wondered, was light always followed by darkness? For the past five years, Marcus had been beleaguered with one catastrophe after another. He had finally gotten some long-awaited good news about Amy. And now *this*. Well, there was no way to say it, but to say it.

"A water main bursted on South and Jefferson; the factory's flooded."

Marcus stood with Luke at the front door, preparing to leave for Portsmouth. He and Amanda had gotten Amy to bed, read her a story and kissed her good-night. It had been established that Amy expected the nightly ritual to include both of them. He wanted to impress upon Amanda that he would have preferred not to leave her with the burden of Amy. His hand lightly caressed her upper arm.

"I don't know what we'll find, so I don't know when I'll get back. Amy is too heavy for you to lift. I…"

She interrupted him. "Marcus, I can manage. Please don't worry. Amy has already learned ways to make things easier for me, and she tries. I'll take good care of her."

He didn't move his hand from her arm and continued to look at her intently, but kept his eyes unfathomable, his expression unreadable. He turned to leave, stopped and walked back to her.

"Amanda, the factory is very important to me. It's my livelihood, the place where I practice my craft. It's also mortgaged to the hilt, and I have to save what I can. But if either you or Amy needs me for anything at all, even for one minute, Amanda. Call me. I'll come home." He walked off without looking back.

Luke put an arm around her shoulder and kissed her on the cheek. "What did I tell you?" he whispered.

I know what you told me, she thought, *but he's vulnerable right now, and I can't hold him accountable for those words, as much as I'd like to.*

She watched until Luke's car disappeared from view. How much could a man bear without breaking? She'd seen Marcus strong, had witnessed his courage. And she knew that every day was a trial for him, an ordeal that he did not permit to blemish his dignity nor daunt his resoluteness. And now this. She couldn't imagine how he could shoulder yet another load. Nothing in his demeanor as he left for Portsmouth suggested that his burden had gotten heavier, though it had. The only indication that he felt his struggle had become more onerous, she realized, was his revelation, perhaps unintentional, that though he needed the work he loved, he would sacrifice it for Amy and for her, a schism that the anguish in his eyes told her he found painful. He had all but said she was important to him, almost told her that he cared.

Tremors darted through her and a cold sensation settled in the region of her heart. He needed help, and she would give him anything she had, but she knew he had taken as much from her as he ever would, that if she mentioned giving more, she risked deflating his ego. Everywhere an African-American man turned, someone or something aimed an arrow at his masculinity, attempted to puncture his pride and smash his dignity. Stalwart though Marcus was, she'd still have to work carefully to avoid bruising him more. She locked the doors, went upstairs and looked in on Amy. The child would be disappointed when she awoke to find that Marcus had gone to Portsmouth. Amanda got ready for bed and decided to sleep on the chaise lounge in order to be near Amy if she awakened and called her father. The next morning, Amanda awoke to Amy's cheerful voice, and her first thought was how she would get the child downstairs.

At eight-thirty, Amanda telephoned a private employment agency and specified her needs in a mother's helper. One hour and a half later, she opened the door and greeted Ellen Whitfield, a tall, attractive young African-American woman with a brilliant smile and hard-to-miss dignity. At twenty-two, she had just completed college and wanted to earn some money before starting graduate school on a fellowship at Berkeley in January. She had taken the job because the salary was better than any she had hoped to get in Caution Point, and she met all of Amanda's criteria. They talked, and Amanda decided she liked her and that, if Amy did, too, she would hire her. She took Ellen upstairs to meet the child, who greeted her warmly.

"Do you have any children to play with me?"

Ellen told her that she didn't, but that she had a nephew Amy's age. Amanda observed their exchange. More than satisfied, she telephoned Marcus to let him know what she'd done. He was relieved, but she could not miss the concern in his voice.

Taking a guess, she told him, "If you're concerned about the expense, Marcus, I had always intended to hire someone for housework after my fourth month, and I would already have done so, if you hadn't been here helping me." That didn't satisfy him, she knew, but she'd told him the truth and he would have to accept it. She wondered for a moment what their relationship would have been like if it had been *she* rather than he who needed the money. Never tamper with a man's pride, Aunt Meredith had said. She might have added, *do it at your own risk.*

Ellen drove her own car to work and used it to take Amy for therapy. Amanda wasn't comfortable sending Amy off with a stranger, and she knew that there was no cause for alarm, but she decided to accompany them that first time and was glad that she had, because the doctor was waiting to speak with Marcus about Amy's braces. Amy informed him blithely that her daddy had too much water, adding that "Lady lives with us." Amanda had to introduce herself properly, and she knew that Amy would be asking Marcus about it.

Marcus called Amanda before eating lunch and, when he got to Luke's apartment that night, he called her again and attempted to explain the damage without alarming her. He was tired, and he was far behind, but he had good people working for him, and they'd promised to stick with him. The four men had put in more than twelve hours that day, and had said they didn't want overtime for it. Still, he was in trouble, and the insurance would pay a mere pittance compared to what he would lose. Six months of work had to be redone. Six months of salaries and other expenses with no money coming in. Grand pianos that had been ready for packing and shipping now had to be re-overhauled. One concert grand was due in New York's Carnegie Hall in ten days, and he'd have no choice but to put it outside to dry tomorrow, so he could get to work on it immediately. He sighed just thinking of what he faced. He would have to partially rebuild the body of a priceless seventeenth-century harpsichord that he had kept locked in the back room for security reasons. Unfortunately, that was the area most heavily flooded. But in spite of the damage, he considered himself fortunate; everything could be repaired.

Marcus and Luke had a big "everything" pizza delivered for their supper and washed it down with cold beer. Marcus tried to ward off Luke's curiosity. Since their childhood, his brother had known that when he didn't talk at all, something bore heavily on him. Luke asked, "You want to talk about it, Marcus?"

Marcus leaned back in the most comfortable dining chair he had ever sat in and shook his head. "It's been years since we lived together, so I tend to forget that you're either a psychic or you've got an uncanny ability to read *me*. I always thought I had a poker face."

"You have. But I practically raised you, and six years is a hell of an advantage. What is it?"

"Amanda has hired a mother's helper, and it's just one more expense for her because of me. She decorated and furnished Amy's room, bought the wheelchair and stroller, and now this. Luke, she had it written into the contract that she maintains the household. It's killing me. I… It seems to me that every move she makes says, 'Marcus, I don't need you, just your name.' It's humiliating."

"You want to take care of her. It's not just Amy. Why can't you be honest and admit that? You always were honest with yourself and blunt with everybody else. What's happened with you?"

Marcus knew from Luke's reaction that the torture he felt was mirrored in his eyes. He disliked being exposed and covered it with a shrug. "Would you be content to let a woman, any woman, take care of you and your child? A child that wasn't even hers?"

Luke spoke as if exasperated. "You have a contractual agreement, and I've told you and told you: your honor isn't involved. Your masculinity isn't involved. Each of you is living up to the terms of the agreement."

"She's doing more than that, but the better I know her, the better I understand that she can't be any other way. Did you see her and Amy patching up that bird? That spoke more eloquently of the person Amanda is than any words I could use."

"And you're still planning to leave her when the contract expires?"

Marcus supposed that his cynical laugh was more than enough of an answer for Luke; a man shouldn't be faced with momentous decisions at a time when his head wasn't above water, and he didn't know whether he'd sink or swim.

"If you think you're schizoid about it now, wait until she has another crisis and needs you; believe me, you haven't even begun to have mixed feelings about Amanda," Luke told him, voicing a truth that Marcus knew well. He got up and paced the floor, mulling over his brother's words, when he remembered something that he had intended to remind Luke about. He stopped.

"Yeah. You may be proved right. She's got a teacher on her staff who dislikes her intensely and had the temerity to express her distaste and disrespect to me. Remember? I expect Amanda can handle that, but the woman claimed to be a close friend of the Lamonts, and that's a potential bomb." Luke reacted with a sharp whistle.

"You still haven't told Amanda?"

"Not yet. School's out for the summer, and it's not likely to be a problem for her until September. No point in worrying her needlessly. Still, not many people would express distaste for their boss in a conversation with her husband, unless he or she had plenty of clout. I wish I knew *why* she's buddy-buddy with the Lamonts, because she isn't any socialite I've ever met."

"Yeah. I'll look into it. And Marcus. Stop worrying about how much Amanda gives to your relationship and try to face the truth about your feelings for her."

Marcus had to struggle to conceal his emotions. Frowning, he went to his room without answering and stood by the window, a towel thrown across his shoulder in preparation for his shower, trying to understand why he seemed unable to live with the terms of that legal agreement. Luke thought Amanda's behavior reasonable, but then Luke wasn't involved, and he wasn't dealing with a hunger for her that was close to being debilitating. Maybe if he'd just… No! He wasn't going to consummate that marriage. He had accepted that he wanted Amanda to need him, and he knew that she would—perhaps more than she had ever needed anyone—if she had a custody battle with Pearce Lamont, Sr., something that he gave a fifty-percent chance of happening. He looked over at the telephone on the table beside the bed. Maybe he should call her and ask about Amy. He moved toward it and stopped. "Don't lie to yourself, Hickson. You want to talk to her." He reached for the phone, dropped his hand and stood here. What on earth was going on? He went into the shower and stayed there for half an hour cooling his desire with a torrent of cold water. "I don't want to stay married," he told himself aloud. "After what I went through before, I'd be stupid to do it again. I know she's special, and she's sweet, but I just can't do it."

Chapter 6

Amanda sat at the computer in Marcus' bedroom working out personnel changes for the coming school year. She would be seven months pregnant when school started, so she planned to open school, put her program into effect and, after two weeks, turn the operations over to the assistant principal. The rapport that had developed between Ellen and Amy after only three days pleased her, but she found that she hated having free time. She didn't want to think too far ahead. Marcus' absence during the past few days had made her lonely for him, and she had already begun to dread the day when he would leave her for good.

She reached across the desk for a writing tablet and accidentally scattered the papers beside it. Her glance fell on an inventory that Marcus had made of his outstanding debts, the payment dates and his estimation of his ability to honor the obligations at that time. She hadn't realized the extent of his indebtedness, though she'd known he'd borrowed large amounts on his credit cards in addition to the mortgage. Reading on, she gasped, horrified; two years earlier, he had been wealthy. Amy's five operations and her one year in an intensive care room had destroyed his financial position. She didn't wonder at his occasional testiness and found it amazing that he didn't show more bitterness.

She started to put the papers back in order and noticed a sheet of notations in red ink. Her heart pounded wildly and perspiration beaded her forehead. A forty- to sixty-percent chance of keeping his business, he'd written, and a fifty-percent chance of keeping his home. She wiped away the tears and resisted the urge to call him.

She heard the front door open, turned off the computer and started downstairs, but she hesitated at the unusual quiet; Amy always entered the house chattering and calling for her. When she reached the foyer, she heard and saw Amy at the same time.

"Surprise, Lady! Surprise! I got my braces. See?" Amanda rushed to Amy and hugged her, tears filling her eyes. "Why are you crying, Lady?" a suddenly subdued Amy wanted to know.

"Oh, sweetheart, I'm crying because I'm so happy. I'm so happy."

"Why? 'Cause I'm going to walk? They don't feel so good, Lady. They're heavy. But the doctor says I'll learn faster if I wear them." Amanda decided that her euphoria might have been premature when Ellen explained that Amy had to wear the braces always except when in bed and that she had to practice walking two hours every day.

"She had difficulty walking with them even for a couple of minutes," Ellen explained, "but she tried."

While Amy had a nap, Ellen suggested to Amanda that it might be helpful if her five-year-old nephew played with Amy for about an hour several times a week. She reasoned that Amy would be encouraged if she were around a child her age who walked.

"Don't worry," Ellen explained, "Robert is very smart and he is even more protective of his two-year old sister than his father is, if that's possible." Amanda decided that they might try it one day at a time.

They bathed Amy, got her into her shorty pajamas and ready for supper. Then they went into Marcus' room, because Amy loved going in there, and Amanda sat the child on her knee and dialed Luke's number.

"Luke Hickson speaking."

"Luke, this is Amanda. How are things?"

"About as good as could be expected." They exchanged pleasantries, and he called Marcus. Her heart kicked over in anticipation of his voice. She loved his rich baritone and its dusty edge that made it different from any other voice she'd ever heard. Different and seductive.

"Hi." Feeling as if she were beginning to come apart, she took a deep breath and calmed herself.

"Hi. Amy wants to talk to you. We can speak later." She handed the phone to Amy, who giggled excitedly.

"Hi, Daddy. Guess who this is." She laughed some more. "Daddy, you won't know who I am when you come home. I got my braces today." There was a pause. "Daddy, what's the matter? Don't be silly, Daddy, 'course I miss you. When are you coming home? Soon? I love you, too. Bye."

Amanda and Marcus talked without really saying anything. She didn't tell him how much she missed him, how worried she was about his business and whether he would lose it, or how she dreaded the day when he would take his precious child and leave her. When the conversation ended, she felt empty and dissatisfied. Afterward, she remembered that she hadn't broached the subject of Robert playing with Amy. Surely he wouldn't mind.

Robert was not what Amanda had expected. After shaking hands with Amy as an adult would, he asked her, "You want to play, Amy?"

She gave him a rather dark look, reminding Amanda how much the child resembled her father and as bluntly as Marcus would have said it, she declared, "I don't walk, Robert."

Seemingly unflappable, he showed white teeth that sparkled against his dark face when he smiled. "We can play sitting down, Amy. When you start walking, we can play ball. Okay?" He turned to Ellen.

"Auntie Ellen, can we sit at the table here?" As soon as they seated Amy, Robert sat down and emptied the bag that he had brought with him. He looked sceptical for a minute before asking, "Can you count, Amy?" At her positive response, he probed, "How far?"

"A hundred," she proudly informed him. But she couldn't add, he learned, and he set about teaching her one of his favorite games. He placed the blocks before her. One block, a plus sign, another block, an equal sign and two blocks. Soon, they were up to two digits. After an hour, Ellen said she'd drive Robert home and that Amy could come along. Amy didn't want Robert to leave, because she didn't want to stop adding, and she showed her displeasure. The boy patted her on the shoulder.

"It's okay, Amy. I'll come back. Next time, I can watch you walk."

When Ellen returned, Amanda questioned her about Robert and learned that his father headed the math department at the regional junior college and that his mother did a thriving business as a psychotherapist. She also learned that Robert could multiply as well as add. For the remainder of the day, Amy added everything in sight. When Marcus called that evening, the child shouted for the phone.

"Hi, Daddy. Can you add?" Of course he could add, he told her.

"I can, too, Daddy." And she proceeded to prove it. He asked how she'd learned, and she informed him joyfully that Robert had taught her.

When he got Amanda back on the phone, his first words were, "Who the devil is Robert?" To her amazement and enormous relief, Marcus not only didn't mind about Robert, but actually welcomed the opportunity for Amy to play with a sympathetic child her age.

Marcus related Amy's adventure to Luke, who asked him, "Do I suspect you of having been jealous of a five-year-old?" Marcus denied it vehemently.

"Oh, really?" Luke teased. "Then why were you so hostile when you asked Amanda who Robert was?"

"I have a right to know who's teaching my daughter to add," Marcus grumbled, defensively.

"Yeah. Especially if the teacher is male."

Marcus couldn't shake the feeling that he had been excluded from something important, and he had to admit his need to be at home with Amanda and Amy. To share their experiences. Yes. And to protect and care for them. He wanted them to need him. He'd been split in two pieces, with a part of himself in Portsmouth and the other part in Caution Point. He shook his head, as if to clear it, and told Luke, "It'll be months and months before I get the factory back to normal. I'm going to start commuting."

"I've been wondering when you would decide to do that. It's the right decision. You can use my car if you like, and you won't have to worry about making train schedules. I'm entitled to keep a squad car with me, so I can get along with it."

"Yeah. I know. And I wouldn't have the expense of train tickets, just the gas. Thanks. I'll think about it." Marcus appreciated his brother's offer, but he was tired of being on the receiving end of people's largess. It wasn't right to think of Amanda and Luke in that way, but his pride had been battered enough, especially where Amanda was concerned. His smile was forced. "We'll see." He went to his room and called his wife.

"I'll be home tomorrow night. Do you need anything here?"

"Just y... No, I guess not. We'll be glad that you're here. I won't tell Amy, because she won't be able to sleep, she'll be so happy."

Marcus hung up, dissatisfied. Why, he wondered, did adults find it so difficult to be honest about their feelings? And that included him. Amanda had almost told him that she needed only him, but she'd stopped herself. Didn't she know how badly he needed for her to need him? He went into the kitchen and got a beer from the refrigerator, propped his foot on the rung of a chair, rested his right elbow on his knee and opened the can. He sipped slowly, idly rolling the can between his hands. He hardly recognized the man he had become. How different he was from his days of dining on sixty-dollar dinners with French wine at an added thirty dollars a bottle. He laughed. He didn't miss it one bit. So many little things gave him pleasure now: a solitary walk after dinner, Merle Haggard or Buddy Guy on the radio, a breeze from the Albemarle Sound caressing his naked body while he stood on Amanda's upstairs porch watching the moon rise, Amy's happy giggle, Amanda's soothing voice. It all came back to Amanda, because five months earlier, nothing had given him pleasure.

Amanda trudged up the stairs, wishing she could stop thinking about Marcus, and began preparing for bed. Thank God, he would be home at night. *Home!* Marcus had said he was coming home. Had it been a slip, or did he really regard the place where they lived as his home? She wouldn't dwell on it, because no matter how or what he felt, he was going to end it in April. Her mirrored reflection amused her, and she made a face. What could she expect? She was thirty-nine years old, pregnant, married in name only, and never in her life had a man loved her. She laughed at herself. With her rapidly expanding belly, she didn't have much going for her now. Certainly not enough to attract a man. And Marcus Hickson would represent a challenge for a beauty queen. She got in bed and read until she went to sleep.

Amanda had told herself the night before that she would learn how to be content, if not happy, without the love and caring of a man, but she couldn't help responding like a teenager to the brief kiss that Marcus dropped on her mouth when he entered the door for the first time in more than a week. How was she supposed to be content without him?

"Hi. You're a sight for sore eyes. We missed you around here." Why couldn't she suppress her feverish excitement? She was already at a disadvantage. But she felt her heart dancing in her chest, overjoyed at the sight of him, and she couldn't contain a smile. He was there. He was home.

* * *

Marcus was too busy camouflaging his own feelings to notice her subdued greeting. "Yeah. You look good, too. Still growing, I see. Everything okay?" He wanted to crush her to him, but he settled for a light pat on her shoulder. She was so soft, so gentle and yet so strong. He needed to forget about the factory, the mortgages, everything, and just get lost in her, but, he shook himself out of his reverie and looked around, gaining psychological distance. He shifted his weight from one foot to the other, uncomfortable; the entire scene smacked too strongly of the husband coming home to his loving wife and child. But he had kissed her because he needed to. He knew she needed to know what progress he'd made at the factory, but he didn't want to talk about that. He wanted to get his mind off of how little he and his workers had accomplished and how far behind he was, and he wanted to do that in her arms.

They walked down the hall to the kitchen where Amy sat telling the bunny about her day. He draped his arm casually around his wife's neck, needing the contact, but sensed a chilliness in her as she eased away from him. She didn't leave him guessing.

"Are you going to hug me when you come home tomorrow? Or will you be your usual self?" Thanks to Amy, he didn't have to respond. The child screamed in delight, overjoyed at seeing her daddy, so much so that he felt a twinge of guilt for having been away from her and hugged her tightly, while she spread kisses all over his face.

"Daddy, I been walking. Lady and Robert and Ellen are helping me. Lady gives me exercises, too. And Lady gives me ice cream after I walk. But Lady can't lift me much anymore, so Ellen lifts me. Now you can lift me, Daddy." The more she chattered, the more he realized that the bond between her and Amanda had become tight. Watching them, he wondered if he should see a shrink: in spite of his pleasure at seeing Amanda, the tie between her and his daughter gave him a sense of… The thought brought him up short. Could he be jealous?

After dinner, they got Amy to bed and met her demand for stories. "She winds us both around her fingers," he said under his breath and added to himself that he didn't care that she got her way; she overflowed with joy, and that was enough for him. He glanced at Amanda and happiness flooded his heart.

"What did you say, baby?" he asked Amy. The child's eyes drooped and she fell asleep telling him about her adventures in his absence.

"I wanna go to that place where Lady decided to live with us, and I wanna eat a hamburger there," were the last words she managed before falling asleep.

He tried to keep a look of censorship out of his eyes as he gazed steadily at the woman he married. "What have you been telling her?" He hadn't come back to Caution Point to fight with Amanda; he was there because he needed the peace that she unknowingly gave him. "How does she know about that?" he persisted.

Amanda knew he was concerned about her relationship with Amy, but she figured he ought to know she would use discretion in talking with her. Her studied look was intended as a mild reprimand.

"Marcus, Amy loves stories, especially stories about you. So I told her where you were and what you were wearing the first time I saw you and where we were when we introduced ourselves. I'm trying to teach her what kind of father she has. Somebody has to do it." His tolerant smile suggested amusement at her mild flare of temper.

Her gaze roamed over him as she waited for his rejoinder, knowing it would never occur to him to back away from a good fight. "What kind of father does she have, Amanda?" He might not have intended it, but his voice had become lower than usual, husky and seductive.

She had been sitting on the edge of the chaise lounge in Amy's room while he leaned against the doorjamb. She moved to stand, but had to brace herself, hands on her knees, and make a second attempt. He rushed over to help her and, as they stood close enough to kiss, he repeated the question, almost tauntingly.

She stepped sideways away from him and informed him hotly, "I told her that you're one good-looking, downright, drop-dead gorgeous sexy hunk that every woman ought to get to sample at least once in her life." *That ought to fix him,* she thought.

She enjoyed the satisfaction of seeing Marcus gaze at her, mouth agape in obvious astonishment. But she had to swallow her revenge, and her heart skidded in her chest at his impudent challenge after he pleasured her with his A-one smile, his dimples in full view.

"No kidding. You, too? Well don't give up, honey," he soothed. "'A man's reach should exceed his grasp, or what's a heaven for?'"

Exasperated, she grabbed the pillows from the chaise lounge and tossed them at him. "Browning. And you omitted the first two words from that quote."

"They weren't relevant," he countered. "But you can have a shot at me anytime you want it. As many samples as you'd like."

She arched an eyebrow. "Mmm. Frisky, aren't we? How bravely we speak, since there's no possibility of following through on that promise!"

His disbelieving stare confused her, as did his words. "You're kidding, right? Don't you believe that for one second."

Wearing an expression between a smile and a smirk, she countered, "Please! I'm going on six months pregnant. There wouldn't be anything in it for either one of us."

The ease with which he was able to read her surprised him. Embarrassed at the turn of conversation, she lowered her eyes, blushing, and licked her lips innocently but with a seductiveness that would have befitted a courtesan.

He knew with certainty then that she had thought about making love with him. It was like a shot of adrenaline to his groin, as the heat of desire filtered throughout his body. He tried to shake it off. He didn't want to dig into his feelings right then; it bothered him enough that he had them. But he had never permitted any woman to call him on the carpet and do it with impunity while she dangled sex and sensuality in front of him. He glared at her.

"Don't make the mistake of issuing me this kind of challenge, baby. You'll get tossed in my bed so fast you won't know how it happened." The knotting of desire shot through him. "I've seen the day when I'd make a woman eat those words."

She wrinkled her nose. "That was then. 'Don't look back, something might be gaining on you.'"

His left eyebrow shot up. "So you're a baseball fan. I wouldn't have expected you to quote Satchel Paige. Not bad. Especially since you're too young to know anything about baseball's Negro League."

She glanced at him through lowered lashes, her head slanted to the side, unwittingly sending him an invitation. "I can quote Frederick Douglass, and I wasn't alive in his era, either." He took a step toward her, swallowed hard and opened his face to her. Desire lit it with the brilliance of a neon sign.

I'm out of my depth, Amanda thought, as she watched him, mesmerized. His stance shifted, and she could see the aggression in him, could almost smell the male in him trying to break loose. *I don't know this man well enough to play with him like this,* she told herself, realizing that she had better back off. But she didn't consider herself timid and had little tolerance for cowards, so she resorted to brazenness. With her head high and chin jutted out, she informed him, "Our contract doesn't call for…"

"It doesn't preclude it, either. It just doesn't mention it." He regarded her intently, taking in her softness, the delicate feminine air that always enveloped her, her innate vulnerability. She was scared, too, he realized, and the protectiveness he felt for her overrode his desire. He took a deep breath and grinned, knocking her off balance and enjoying it.

"Come on, let's go downstairs and get something to drink. I

could use a beer, and you can have some mint tea." At her inquiring look, he explained, "I brought you some. You can't have alcohol, soft drinks, coffee or regular tea, but you can have mint tea. Hot or iced."

He had come home for her warm, loving smile and, when she smiled her thanks, he wanted to give her the world. Her smile was more than the baring of teeth and the easing of lips; it changed her face and brought an added softness to her demeanor, a glow to her skin, sparkles to her eyes and a wild pounding to Marcus Hickson's heart. It was enough for him; he had found that he liked to please her.

They settled in the living room, he with a beer and she with a cup of the mint tea, both of them suddenly self-conscious. She wanted to ask him how things were at the factory. And she wanted the truth, not a perfunctory reply that everything was fine, when she knew that wasn't the case. Then she remembered. "Oh, Marcus, I forgot to tell you that I spoke with Judge McCullen." Marcus leaned forward. She noticed his tension and told him, "Relax. He'll be hearing the case. Said it should be on the docket within four months at the latest." She heard his deep sigh of relief.

"Thanks. I appreciate your speaking with him. I need the money from that settlement." She studied his facial expression, trying to determine how much she could say, whether she should tell him she knew how far he'd extended himself financially, that he might lose his beloved factory. After thinking about it, she decided that he wouldn't welcome a discussion of his affairs right then. Maybe never.

"Was that the front door? Who'd be ringing after supper?" Marcus looked at Amanda, but she settled back, giving no indication that she intended to answer the door. She nodded in the direction of the foyer.

"See who it is."

"See who..." Marcus felt the blood heat his face. He was behaving as if he didn't live there and, for those few minutes, he hadn't remembered that he headed that household. He glanced at Amanda.

"You're not expecting anybody?" When she shook her head, he went to the door and flicked on the porch light. What the…?

"Jack! This is certainly a surprise. What's up?" Marcus didn't examine his thoughts or his reaction at seeing his close friend standing before Amanda's front door. A peculiar emptiness, a hollowness inside of him had replaced the contentment, the rightness with things that he'd felt since walking through that same door earlier in the evening. The last time he'd greeted Jack at a front door, he had welcomed him into his Portsmouth, Virginia, home that had been built to his own specifications, an elegant abode in which he took great pride. Something of his own. He fidgeted with the doorknob, surprised at his tenseness.

"Come in, Jack," he heard Amanda say from where she stood just behind him. He watched in disapproval as Jack stepped past him and hugged Amanda.

"You've got a nice place here. How's Amy?" Jack asked Amanda.

"She's progressing more rapidly than we had dared hope. Come on in the living room; I was just about to get Marcus and me some dessert." A luminous smile blanketed her face as she looked up at her husband and took his arm. Marcus knew that Amanda was trying to put him at ease, to banish the awkwardness that his own reticence had created. Jack seated himself in a comfortable wing chair, looked around the room and asked Amanda questions about the family pictures and assorted memorabilia as though there was nothing out of the ordinary about his being there. Marcus wanted to know the reason for Jack's visit, but he wouldn't ask him. Rudeness wasn't a part of his nature, and he figured that Jack would let them know why he'd come. Guilt washed through him at the memory of the many kindnesses he'd received from Jack and Myrna and the thought that there never seemed to be anything he could do for them. And it shamed him that he hadn't encouraged their visits when he lived within five blocks of them. He'd seen more of the couple when eighty miles separated their homes.

Amanda attempted to rise from the softly cushioned sofa, a seat she took only because Jack had sat in her chair, but the effort defeated her and she flopped back down, holding her back as she did so. Both men rushed to her aid, clearing the air as they all laughed when Marcus and Jack collided. She stood with their help and padded out to the kitchen.

"I hope I didn't interrupt anything, Marcus, but I read about that water-main break, and we didn't know how things were here with Amy and Amanda. Just stopped by to make certain they were all right, since we knew you had to be in Portsmouth. How bad is it there?" Marcus knew that his coolness had embarrassed his friend, and he leaned forward, hoping to put him at ease.

"Every instrument suffered some damage, Jack. Water soaked a lot of them; the rest got too much humidity. And it's still damp there, because the walls got wet and the floors are a mess. I had a new, hardwood floor laid in the showroom about two years ago but, man, those boards buckled so badly that you risk your neck walking over them. I appreciate your stopping by. I've been in Portsmouth all week, but Amy is too much for Amanda to handle now, and I've decided to commute." Amanda's arrival with a tray of pie à la mode and coffee brought an end to the discussion. Marcus took the tray from her and served the dessert.

"Sit down, Amanda. Jack, would you mind switching places with her? That's about the only one of these chairs she's comfortable in now." If Amanda noticed the smile on Jack's face, she didn't let on, but Marcus knew that Jack liked his protectiveness of her. His friend finished the pie and ice cream, declined more coffee and stood to leave.

"I wish I could eat that kind of apple pie in my house. Myrna can cook a lot of things, but desserts aren't among them. Where do you get the apples this time of year?" Marcus rose and began walking toward the front door. His jealousy at Jack's cozy familiarity with Amanda and his compliments surprised him. Amanda said she'd frozen the apples the previous autumn and asked Jack to come back and bring Myrna, but Marcus didn't sanction her request and he knew that Jack realized it. Amanda let him know that she also realized it when she told Jack good-night, walked past Marcus without looking at him and went upstairs to her room.

Marcus knew he'd hurt Amanda, knew she was aware that he hadn't wanted to entertain his friend in her home. He stood at the bottom of the stairs with his right foot propped on the first step and his hands in his pockets and looked toward the second floor. If another man did anything to hurt her, he'd bring him down. Yet he regularly did it himself. He started up the steps wondering what he could say that would pacify her and blunt the effect of what even he regarded as a snub. She met him on the stairs and when he reached for her hand as he turned to walk down with her, she held back.

"Marcus, it's time you let me off of this seesaw. You walked in here this evening and kissed me, surrounded me with warmth and kindness. Two hours later, you were ashamed to have your friend enter this house. If you live here for the next nine months and don't say a word to me, it will hurt, but I can tolerate it. What I can't bear is your inability to accept this marriage for what it is and make the best of it. I know there's something going on between us, and I also know that you're fighting it tooth and nail. I can't blame you for it; you see yourself as a victim, but don't you think I'm a victim, too? You have no more to be ashamed of than I have; maybe less." They arrived at the bottom step, and he reached again for her hand. She let him take it, but she didn't close her fingers around his.

"Bear with me, Amanda. I've never been beholden to anyone, never had to envy another man's financial position nor his status in his home, on his job and among his friends. I've never before been on the bottom, Amanda, and I don't know how to act down here. I've learned some things about life and about myself, and I know I'm a better person for that, but I've taken one hell of a tumble. As a kid, I never had to begrudge my playmates anything;

I made any team that I tried out for, graduated at the top of my class in high school and in college and, eighteen months after I opened my business, musicians from around the country began sending their work to my shop. You could say I'd led a charmed life and needed a dose of humility, but I don't think so, because I worked hard for what I got. And I've had my recesses, as you know, especially in my personal life. I'm telling you this, so you'll understand that I'm not ashamed of you, Amanda; it's what I've come to that bothers me. My respect and admiration for you are practically boundless."

Marcus felt the tension slip away from him when her fingers closed around his own. He walked with her to her favorite chair, eased her into it and assured himself that she was comfortable. Then he kicked a footstool over to where she sat and took a seat beside her. He smiled to himself when he felt her hand soft on his head, absently caressing him, but if he moved a muscle, she'd realize what she was doing and stop it immediately. When she spoke, her voice trembled with compassion.

"Our confrontations and misunderstandings have their uses, don't they? Every time we weather one of them, we know more about each other. More than meets the eye or ear." He relaxed and let himself enjoy her hand smoothing his hair.

"What do you know that I didn't tell you?" Her soft laughter thrilled him, and when she leaned back in the chair and closed her eyes, comfortable with him, seemingly contented, he waited for what he knew would be her sassy reply.

"'The secret of being a bore is to tell everything,'" she said in an imperious tone. He slapped her thigh playfully, in triumph.

"My old buddy, Voltaire. You can do better than that," he said of her quote and added, "Go ahead. You can tell me what a great guy I am. 'Flattery was never lost on a poet's ear.'" He felt her tug on his hair and regretted that she quickly withdrew her hand when she realized what she'd done. He had enjoyed a strange comfort from the unfamiliar feeling of her idle caresses. "What's the matter?" he asked her. "Did I stump you with that one?"

"Something from that Scotsman, Sir Walter Raleigh, I think.
I'd have gotten it sooner, if you hadn't misquoted him."

"Excuses. Excuses." He patted her shoulder and got up. "I'm
going to get myself a beer. Do you want something?" She shook
her head and smiled at him without opening her eyes.

Marcus took a slug of the cold beer, set the bottle on the
coffee table and looked at Amanda Ross Hickson. He wasn't
staring; he was just looking. There was so much about her that
he didn't understand, probably didn't even have the right to
know, he mused. He suddenly wanted, needed to know everything about her, but he fought the yearning. He didn't want to be
any more susceptible to her than he was and, as long as he didn't
dig into her, he'd be free to use his own judgment and arrive at
his own conclusions. Not fair, maybe, but a lot safer was his silent
conclusion. His long and thorough appraisal must have unsettled
her, because she began to fidget, her composure of minutes earlier
having seemingly deserted her. It occurred to him that, where he
was concerned, her self-confidence was tenuous at best.

He swore at himself for having gotten her perturbed and
grasped at the first conversation opener that came to his mind.
"Luke's loaned me his car for as long as I need it. I thought I'd
commute daily between here and Portsmouth." When he noticed
her evident pleasure at the news, he hastened to add, "I have to
be at the factory these days, and I want to live up to my part of
our contract. Also, I don't like being away from Amy so much,
especially now that it's getting more and more difficult for you
to manage her after Ellen goes home."

Amanda gazed at her hands. What had happened to the close-
ness and camaraderie that they had enjoyed only minutes earlier?
She didn't dare look at him, couldn't bear to have him see what
his unnecessary explanation had done to her. She knew that her
face had literally crumpled, because it was what she felt. She
plastered her face with what she knew was a plastic smile and
asked him, "Would you like another beer?"

As if unaware of her discomfort, he replied amiably, "Thanks.

You stay put. I'll get it." She used his absence to regain her composure and to remind herself that she wasn't to expect anything from him except fulfillment of their contract; all he owed her was one year of marriage during which time he stayed in her house. But oh, she wanted more, fool that she was. She wanted, needed so much more.

Marcus braced himself against the refrigerator. He'd made two mistakes with her in less than an hour. She had gotten cozy and familiar with him only because he'd showed his hand. And whether she knew it or not, that's what she had responded to. What on earth had he been thinking about, telling her that he would take her to bed, letting her know that he was tempted to make love to her? And he had been. If he had ever thought that her advanced pregnancy would have a calming influence on his hormones, he'd been kidding himself. He wanted her as much as he had ever wanted any woman, and he had sense enough to see the danger in that: it wasn't his senses, but his heart that was dictating his feelings toward her. He desired her because… He wouldn't let the thought complete itself. The women to whom he had been previously attracted had been tall, willowy, light skinned and fashionable. She was none of those, but there was a tenderness, a sweetness and a gentleness about her that he'd never found in any other woman and that drew him like a magnet. He sipped the beer while he mentally berated himself. He'd let her know he wanted her, and then he'd shored up his defenses by deflating her.

He walked back into the living room with his beer just as she passed her hand over the lower part of her abdomen, as if favoring the area. "Are you having cramps?" he asked her, trying to hide his anxiety. He sat at an angle on the edge of the sofa, his right knee touching her left one. "Are you?" he asked again.

"I don't think so. Sometimes I have a little discomfort."

"How often do you see the doctor?" He put the beer down

without tasting more of it, lifted her feet and put them on the coffee table.

"I go once a month because of my age and this is my first pregnancy." Her eyes questioned him. "Why did you do that?"

"Your ankles are swollen, and it might help to raise them." She seemed touched, but was silent for a while, then spoke hesitantly.

"Do you have any more tips like this one?"

"Yeah. I suppose I do." He changed the subject. She could so easily draw him into intimate conversation, and he didn't want that.

"Are you having a girl or a boy?" He released his breath and realized that he had been holding it while he waited for her answer. He hadn't thought to ask her earlier. He walked to the window, turned around and faced her. Why did he care now whether her child was a girl or a boy? He wasn't supposed to care one way or the other. But what if she had a boy and Lamont, Sr., found out?

She patted her belly. Proudly, he thought, and wondered if he was watching maternal instinct at work, because he hadn't seen it in Helena. "I don't know which," she answered. "I wouldn't let the doctor tell me."

"I'm surprised. I thought you the type who likes to plan for everything."

Her eyes clouded up and she told him in a shaky voice, "If I don't know and if anything happens…you know…I mean if things don't work out, I'll be less attached to it. I am already, but not like I was thinking of it by name." Marcus cursed the man responsible for the pain and anxiety that she suffered, cursed fate for throwing her into his path even while he thanked God for it. And he cursed his ambivalence about her. Never once had his ex-wife discussed her pregnancy with him, except to blame him for every discomfort that she suffered and to accuse him of disfiguring her to ruin her career and to make certain that other men didn't notice her. Yet this woman professed love for the child she carried, a child that had been conceived in pain and humiliation by a man who had only pretended that he cared for her.

* * *

Amanda didn't understand the conflict mirrored in his eyes. Was he repulsed, or was it pity that she saw? When his eyes darkened until they were almost black, she wondered if it was desire that he felt. But how could he? She realized she was way off the mark when he asked her, "Are you going to have natural childbirth?" Helena had opted for cesarean, he told Amanda, because she didn't want the discomfort of normal birth.

She closed her eyes to shelter her thoughts. She had gotten far more out of her marriage to Marcus than she had dared to hope, and she was grateful. But if it were a real marriage... She would give anything if she could have natural childbirth. But without a partner to help her...

"What is it?"

"I want to, but the doctor said I would have to take Lamaze classes, and I don't have a partner."

For the first time, Marcus considered the enormous difficulties faced by women who go through pregnancy and childbirth alone. He wondered how she could accept it so calmly; to his knowledge she had never once complained.

She attempted to change the conversation, but he sensed that not being able to give her baby the advantages of natural childbirth worried her.

"It's getting late," she told him, with obviously feigned brightness. "I should get to bed." Her nervousness was apparent as they walked up the stairs together, only to separate at the doors of their respective bedrooms. They reached her door first and she turned to him with what he recognized as her "I'm just fine, Marcus" smile.

"I can't tell you how nice it was just talking with you tonight. I enjoyed your company so much, Marcus. Good night." She didn't wait for his answer, and he was still standing at her door when she closed it. He smiled ruefully, rubbed his chin with his left hand and thanked God for small favors. He had been trying to figure out how to kiss her good-night without risking the danger of really kissing her. Kissing her and nurturing his soul with her fire, sweetness and warmth. He spent the remainder of the night tossing the covers around as he wrestled with his desire and his conscience. She was a rare treasure, one that he wished he'd encountered when he was still innocent enough to believe that a man's greatest joy was to be found with the woman that he loved and who loved him. She needed him. What was he going to do about it?

Shortly after six o'clock the next morning, Marcus gave up the effort to sleep and staggered out of bed. Wearing only his bikini undershorts, he walked out on the balcony and let the crisp morning air play against his skin. He looked over toward Amy's room and felt good, contented, happy in spite of the cost, because he could go to bed and get up with her nearby. He had known fourteen months of hell commuting daily between Portsmouth and Caution Point to visit her in the hospital, trying to work and nearly losing everything he owned. Without thinking about his near nudity, he opened the porch door to Amy's room, and his heart kicked over as he watched her lecturing the bunny for failing to give her the right answer to five plus five. He backed out quickly to prevent her seeing his terrible battle for self-control, and turned into Amanda, his abrupt movement nearly knocking her off balance.

He reached out to her and forgot the reason why, when her hands went to his face.

"Marcus, darling, what is it? What's the matter? Tell me. Is it Amy? Why are you...?" He looked down into the tender, loving face of the woman he craved. The woman whose unguarded look of love told him that she would give him the moon if it were hers and he needed it. With a hoarse, animal cry of surrender, he buried his face in the curve of her neck and moaned her name.

"Amanda...oh, Amanda, I need you. I need you so!" She squeezed him to her, caressing his broad shoulders, his iron-hard biceps. He forgot about staying away from her, playing it safe. Forgot everything but his need for her to hold him as no woman had ever held him. To love him as he had never been loved. Unselfishly and without reservation. To fulfill a need he'd never known he had. When she pulled his head down, inviting his kiss, he bent to her and ravished her parted lips as if he teetered on the brink of starvation. She opened up to him, seeming to sense his need, as though willing to give him whatever he wanted, whatever he needed. He thrust his tongue into her mouth, darting here and there until every sweet centimeter of it knew him. When she held his head to increase the pressure of his kiss, his hands went to her full breasts.

"Marcus, I need… Oh, God, do something…"

He arched her over his left arm and licked a taut nipple until she cried out. Then he circled it with his eager lips, pulled it into his mouth and sucked it vigorously while she dug her fingers into his naked back. She tried to lift her leg around his thigh, and it occurred to him that he should stop, that they were standing on the porch with only the screens for privacy.

He picked her up, strode into his room and lay her on his bed, never taking his mouth from her breast. He knelt beside her, and she looked up at him, her eyes pleading. It was too late. Drowning in the sensual pull of her unsheltered gaze, he sucked in his breath. He was human, and he needed what she offered. It was far too late.

Even in her innocence, she realized that she had to make a move or lose. Lose this. Lose all. Her hands went to his tight buttocks, and he almost jerked away from her.

"What is it?" She feared suddenly that he would push her away again.

His smile seemed forced, as he told her in a hoarse voice, "Honey, if you touch me anywhere below my shoulders right now, I may embarrass both of us."

"Will it make you feel good?" She reached up to touch the hair on his chest. It fascinated her, as she realized for the first time that Marcus' rich brown body was almost completely exposed to her. Naked. Her hand brushed his nipple, and he groaned. Afraid that she'd hurt him, she moved the hand, but he grasped her wrist, put her hand back there and stretched out beside her.

"Touch me there. It's been so long. Honey, touch me." She found the little nubs and gently grazed them with her flat palms. When he began to writhe in agony, she was emboldened by the knowledge that she could move him and, without giving him any warning, she let her searching hand find its way into his skimpy bikini. He shouted aloud, warning her of the consequences, but she continued her unschooled fumbling. And when, nearing completion, he rubbed helplessly against her hand, she realized what he needed and gave it to him lovingly. He splintered in her arms, calling her name, gripped in the powerful surge of ecstasy.

They lay there quietly. He seemed totally spent, but she knew a greater, more precious fulfillment; she had given him the love that he needed, and she was satisfied. Yet, she knew he wouldn't be pleased with what had just transpired between them and braced herself for his rejection.

Marcus closed his eyes, astonished at his total loss of control for the first time in his life. Never had he let a woman do that to him. He wanted to get up and walk until he was exhausted, but he knew he had to move with care, that her feelings were fragile right then. He turned on his side, facing her and saw that small beads of perspiration dotted her cheeks. He reached over and caressed her face, silently urging her to look at him.

"Amanda. I…" Unable to say the words, he leaned down and kissed her lips, first gently and then, surprising himself with the urgency he felt, he kissed her passionately. Be truthful. Be honest, his heart told him, but he refused to obey. Instead, he pulled her into his arms and told her, "Thank you."

Evidently unsure as to how to take that, she asked him, "For what?"

"For being here for me when I needed you."

Her hot flesh nearly burned his fingers, and she didn't look at him. He felt the shivers of delight that shot through her when he stroked her arm, and turned her face toward his.

"Look at me, Amanda. Open your eyes." She forced herself to comply, shocked at the tenderness, the sweet caring that shone from his hypnotic gaze. Her eyes must have darkened with desire, reflecting her terrible need, because his gaze became hot fire, and he bent to her, covering her face with kisses until, in frustration, she claimed his mouth with parted lips. When she tried to touch him intimately, he grabbed her hands with one of his own and pinned them above her head. Flames roared in the seat of her passion when he suckled her until, helpless with want, she moaned and begged him for relief.

"Marcus, please, I'm aching deep inside."

He sucked her deeply into his mouth and, as if crossing a bridge that he had long feared, he let his trembling hand slide over her distended belly and down to the apex of her thighs. He knew that his next act would bind him to her, but he couldn't give her less than she'd given him, nor did he want to. He touched her gently at first, testing her reaction.

"Do you want this?" he whispered, caressing her tentatively. She trapped his hand reflexively, giving him her answer.

He knew he would give her something she'd never had and, suddenly, he wanted to be the man to introduce her to her body's potential. He'd hardly begun the gentle strokes before her response told him that she was on the edge. He increased the pressure, all the while murmuring sweet words of encouragement. Then he raised his head from his feast at her breast and looked into her eyes as he carried her to a shattering climax.

Helplessly, her body bucked and surged as ecstasy claimed her. "Marcus," she cried. "Oh, Marcus. Oh, love," and went limp in his protective arms. He'd never seen anything so beautiful in his life. A woman who had let herself go and enjoyed what he gave her with no thought as to what she looked like, just what she felt. A woman who hadn't faked, who hadn't needed to, who had simply given herself up to his ministrations. He gathered her to him and held her as close as her advancing pregnancy would allow.

She hid her face in his shoulder. "Not that," he told her gruffly. "I won't have it. We're…we're two consenting adults." He'd almost reminded her that they were married and had stopped himself, knowing the consequences. "I guess it was inevitable, but I'll try to keep my hands off you in the future."

She kissed his salty, damp flesh. "I understand. It's all right. But, dar…Marcus, it was wonderful. Thank you. I had no idea that a man could make a woman feel like that. I'll cherish it."

He brushed a handful of hair away from her face and stroked her glowing cheek. "There's more, Amanda. So much more. In the scheme of things that can happen between a man and a woman, that was minuscule."

"Tell me about it." She tried to snuggle closer, but nature didn't cooperate.

Marcus wasn't so foolish as to describe the elements of love-making to the woman in his arms. He was already aroused, and after the way she had responded to him, he knew that if she caught him on the blind side again the way she'd done before, she'd have her next experience with him buried deep inside of her. And he'd be married in more than name. Refusing to examine that thought, he chose levity as the best escape route. "Be careful what you ask. Sex talk is…well, 'verbal seduction is the surest road to actual seduction.'"

She punched him playfully in his hard midsection. "How much of that was from Mannes?"

She wasn't surprised at his long, heavy sigh. He had to be relieved to have avoided a potentially embarrassing and hurtful situation, and he probably wanted to forget what they'd done. She didn't.

"Just the last part," he replied. "We'd better get up. I'm starving."

She didn't want to move. She wanted to be in his arms forever. But she wasn't used to having everything she wanted; very little of it, in fact. So she eased slowly away from him, not wanting to feel him move away from her. They'd just breached a chasm, but she didn't know whether that was good or bad.

She'd told him that she understood when he said he wouldn't touch her again, but she hadn't understood at all. And it hurt that he didn't feel for her what she felt for him, that he didn't want her the way she wanted him.

Chapter 7

It had taken her a mere twenty minutes to shower and dress herself and Amy. But when she walked into the quiet, empty kitchen, she sensed that Marcus was not in the house. She trudged toward the garage and paused, afraid of what she knew that she would find, finally forcing herself to open the door that connected the garage with the house. Luke's car was gone. In the short time since she had eased out of his bed, Marcus had dressed and left the house without a word to her, and without bringing Amy downstairs or telling the child goodbye. He hadn't mentioned plans to work during the weekend. She stood there, fighting panic. What had driven him to flee in such desperate haste? In the months that she had known him, that they had shared her house, he had always behaved honorably. But *this!*

Amanda padded slowly back into the kitchen and sat down, ashamed. Mortified. He had run from her, because he hadn't wanted to face her. Hadn't wanted a reminder of what they had shared. She cringed when she thought of her willing participation in it. Her willingness, her desire to give him anything he wanted. Whatever he desired. "Won't I ever learn?" she asked herself. Marcus had promised her nothing, and she could stop hoping, because *nothing* was what he was offering her. After setting the table, she telephoned Ellen and waited for her to arrive and bring Amy down for breakfast. Had Marcus forgotten that Ellen didn't work on weekends?

Late in the evening, she closed her book. Amy slept peacefully, but the child had been cantankerous all day, and Amanda knew it was because the little girl missed her father and sensed something amiss. She turned out the light, went downstairs for a glass of iced mint tea, sat on the porch sipping it and tried to bank her seething anger. Should she have behaved differently and ignored his needs and hers? Or should she have given her lawful husband, whom she loved, what he had begged for? No, she wasn't ashamed, and she wasn't going to feel guilty. He had mistreated her by walking out, and she intended to let him know it. How dare he leave without a word, without saying where he was going or when he'd be back? How had he expected her to manage with Amy? And did he have any idea what he had done to her soul? She heard the front door open and got madder still.

Marcus walked into the factory and locked the door behind him. He wanted to call her, but he couldn't force himself to do it. He needed to sort out his feelings, to try and understand what had happened to him in that bed. He wasn't in love with her, he reminded himself, and he wasn't ever going to be. But when he let himself remember how she had made him feel, his temperature shot up and sweat poured from him. Seeking diversion, he sat down at a grand piano, but he had no interest in playing. He was displeased with himself; he had hurt Amanda badly, but he didn't want to go into a real marriage with her or anybody else. He was going to leave her on April eleventh and let their agreement expire, and that was final!

He answered the phone on its sixth ring, praying that the caller wasn't his wife.

"Hickson."

"Luke. When I called you at home, Amanda didn't know where you were. Is anything wrong?"

"No. I just had to work out a few things." Marcus took the long pause for the silent censure that Luke no doubt intended it to be.

"I guess you know what you're doing."

Marcus bristled at the intrusion into his privacy, however well meant. "You guess wrong," he growled. "I'll see you Monday." Gently, he replaced the receiver and began pacing the floor, torn up inside. Struggling with himself.

He ought to buy her some flowers, he mused. No. Flowers weren't what Amanda would want and not what she needed. She needed for him to get back there and tell her that he'd been a jerk. That she meant something to him. That what they had done there that morning had been the most shockingly sweet thing he'd ever experienced. That it had been an act of love on both their parts. *And if he told her that…?* He looked out at the bright, early September morning, at the trees swaying seductively in the gentle wind and gave his thoughts free rein. Amanda wasn't experienced, but she was a quick study, and she'd learned enough about him that morning to bring him to heel if she chose to and if she remembered what *he* remembered.

"I'm not about to dig my own grave," he told the silence that surrounded him as he walked back to his office and sat down to work. "'I am the master of my fate. I am the captain of my soul,'" he admonished himself, quoting one of his favorite authors, and began to chant it like a karma. "The damned thing doesn't work," he protested in frustration and self-derision an hour later. An hour in which he'd done nothing but stare into space thinking of Amanda and how sweet and loving she was. He got up. He had to do what he could to heal the wound he knew he'd inflicted.

Marcus slowed down below the speed limit as he neared Caution Point. He had spent most of the day sitting in the park watching the waterbirds and wrestling with his terrifying response to Amanda. Time after time, he'd told himself to go home and talk with her, but his heart and head were at war, and he couldn't force himself to move. She was nearly seven months pregnant with another man's child, for heaven's sake. Still, he wanted her. He was aching for her. But he'd had enough of marriage, and he respected her too much to offer her less.

He drove into the garage, his mood lighter, and raced jauntily up the steps, but as he opened the door, the magnitude of what he had done stung him. How had she managed with Amy? In his tortured mental state, he had forgotten that Amanda couldn't handle the child alone. He went in search of her.

"Hello, Amanda." She didn't turn to face him. Nor did she bother to return his greeting.

"How did you think I was going to bring Amy downstairs?" It surprised him that she focused on what she knew was the one thing for which he did not want her to have responsibility. Amy. He figured that was a screen. Oh, she was upset, all right, but for a very different reason.

"I'm sorry. I realize that I blew it in more ways than one." She moved as if to rise, and he reached out to help her.

"Don't touch me, Marcus. Just don't touch me."

"Amanda!" It was a cry of pain.

Let him hurt, she thought. *Let him feel what I've been feeling all day.* As she started past him, he reached out to touch her, and she reeled backward, almost stumbling. When, in spite of her protest, he grasped her to prevent what surely would have been a fall, she let her temper have full rein and threw the remainder of her tea at him. Marcus stared hard at her, but she didn't let that influence her. Let him give the lie to what his eyes had seen and his body felt, if he wanted to fool himself. Too bad the glass hadn't been bigger and full to the brim.

"The next time you get as hot as you got this morning, head for the shower," she told him through clenched teeth. But knowing that she'd hurt him didn't make her feel better. Nor was

she proud of having drenched his face with her tea. Still, she
didn't feel remorseful, or that she ought to apologize. She mused
over the day's events, not wanting to think that Marcus might be
as selfish as Pearce Lamont, Jr. She wasn't angry enough to
believe that.

Amanda had tossed fitfully in bed for hours, barely asleep,
when she realized that Amy was awake and calling her. She
turned on the light beside her bed. Two o'clock. She got up with
care—getting in and out of bed took a lot more effort now—
entered Amy's room just as Marcus walked in from the other
door. They stood gaping at each other, she wearing only her maternity teddy and he in the briefest of shorts. Amy had already
gone back to sleep, and Amanda knew she should get back into
her room fast and lock the door, but she stood rooted to the floor.
He stood there in all his glorious maleness, like a Michelangelo
black masterpiece. Spellbound. Mesmerized, Amanda found
herself walking toward him. Bewitched by him, as though the
previous day's events had never occurred. But they had, and she
didn't plan to forget it. In her rush to get away from him, she
found herself on the porch rather than in her room.

"Amanda." He felt the cool night air soothe the fire of his
loins, and he was glad. He couldn't make a mistake with her now.
"Amanda." When she didn't answer, he wrapped her in arms
of steel and turned her around to face him. "Forgive me, Amanda,
if you can. I walked out of here this morning because you had
gotten into my head and messed up my mind. I have to tell you
honestly that I didn't think about you or Amy." He drew a deep
breath and plodded on. Since she wasn't fighting him, perhaps
he had her attention.

"When you left me alone in my bed and I wanted to haul you
back and finish what we'd started, I knew I'd gone too far." He
had no intention of telling her what he'd truly felt, but he couldn't

let her feel that he'd merely used her. "I had to put some distance between us and do it fast, or I would have broken my promise and ignored my responsibility to behave honorably with you."

"And this is your excuse for what you put me through today? I don't suppose there were any telephones where you went." She didn't approve of spitefulness, but she suddenly had an intense desire to get some of her own. Without warning, she turned sideways in order to get closer to him, reached up and tugged his face down until she could reach his lips. After his initial surprise, he helped her. She kissed him. Mouth open and tongue twirling. And to get her point over properly, she sucked his tongue into her mouth and fed on it while she squeezed his buttocks. When he was fully aroused and had begun to tremble, she abruptly stepped away, herself unsteady but thoroughly gratified.

"I'm sorry, Marcus," she parroted, "I've gone too far. Forgive me." She went into her room and closed the door without looking back, nervous and unsteady, but no longer angry and certain now that she had a chance to win him.

Stunned, Marcus stood there for minutes before returning to his own room. He stood by a window for a short while thinking about what she'd done and how mean she had been. Suddenly, he laughed. She couldn't possibly be mad at him after that. To spend the remainder of the night and possibly longer aroused and wanting what he couldn't have was a small price to pay.

Late Sunday afternoon, Amanda walked out into the back garden and handed Marcus a glass of lemonade and a towel. They had enjoyed a fragile peace since she'd teased him on the upstairs porch early that morning. He reached first for the cold drink, drank it down and extended his hand for the towel. Her smile broadened, and when he reciprocated it, her hope rose that he would let them have a warmer relationship.

"Don't rub," she cautioned. "Your back is probably going to peel if you do, because you've been working in this scorching sun for three hours. I was wondering if we couldn't take Amy somewhere. She goes out, but only to the hospital, and I think we ought to change that." He wrapped the towel around his shoulders and chest, soaking up the perspiration, and she was pleased that he'd accepted her caution. He took his time answering, and it occurred to her that he might think her suggestion presumptuous. He moved closer and handed her the glass.

"Thanks. That was exactly what I needed." He pointed to the towel around his naked back and shoulders. "This, too."

She looked up at him, not trying to hide the hope that she knew he had seen in her eyes.

"About Amy, Marcus. Do you think we could…?" She let the sentence drift unfinished.

"What did you have in mind?" Amanda girded herself as if for battle, ready to stand him down.

"Robert and his daddy go fishing around sunset, and Amy wants to know what fishing is like. Of course, if you'd prefer to take her by yourself, I wouldn't mind. I just thought…"

"We'll all go. I suppose we ought to take her stroller. Today's Sunday. Where do we get the rod, reel, bait and…" He ran his thumb and forefinger across his chin and gazed intently at her. "Whatever." Amanda couldn't determine his mood. He had drawn a curtain over his emotions, and she wasn't sure whether he'd decided to maintain their fragile peace and do as she asked at the expense of anything else he might want, or if he welcomed the idea.

"We don't have to go if you'd rather not," she offered, hoping that he wouldn't accept the easy out she'd given him.

"We're going. Why don't you get Robert's father on the phone and ask if he'd like to join us." He took the towel off his back, slung it over one shoulder and started pushing the container of leaves and grass clippings toward the garage.

"Scratch that; I'll call him myself," he said as he walked away. Amanda hurried in the house to awaken and dress Amy. She found a pair of green cotton overalls printed with yellow rabbits, Amy's favorite, a yellow T-shirt and the little straw hat she'd bought in anticipation of the outing. The sound of the child's squeals of delight at the prospect of fishing in the Albemarle sent Amanda's spirit soaring, and she hugged Amy and whispered words of love and encouragement to her. Amy wrapped her arms around Amanda's neck.

"I love you, Lady. I love you and Daddy and Robert and Uncle Luke, and when I start walking, I'm going to walk a little bit for you, a little bit for Daddy, and a little for Robert and Uncle Luke. I'm going to walk and walk all the time." Amanda tried to stop the tears that rolled down her cheeks as she hugged the precious little girl.

"We have to get you dressed," she told her, brushing the tears with the back of her hand. She ducked her head to prevent Amy from seeing them and looked directly into Marcus' naked gaze. But he lowered his eyelids immediately, leaving her to wonder if she had seen love in his eyes, or if she had imagined it.

"Robert's folks have guests," he said, "but Robert is all fired up to come, and I can't wait to see him. His father agreed and said we can use their tackle. Naturally, Robert has worms. Seems he cultivates them in his parents' backyard. Wonder where they got this kid?"

Amanda rested on a stool beside Amy and Robert near the end of the long pier while Marcus enjoyed a swim. She hadn't considered how pleasant the outing might be for her; she'd thought only of Amy and the child's desire to fish because Robert did it. She listened to Amy denounce Robert's worms as ugly and was amazed at his patience, volunteering to thread the worm on the hook for her. She had learned that they had a perfect understanding. Amy loved Robert and expected him to accept her as she was without criticism or censure. Robert loved Amy and knew that she loved him without reservation. And because of that, he would do anything for her. When Amy hooked a fish, Robert told Amanda that the fish was too big for the little girl to land, but Amy wanted to bring it in herself and insisted on doing so. They argued about it until Marcus swam over to investigate.

"Why didn't you call me, if you can't settle this?" he asked Amanda, jumping up on the pier. She raised her hand slightly, palm up, and smiled.

"Marcus, they don't fight; they don't even get angry with each other."

"What do you call what they're doing now, if they're not bickering?" Droplets of water glistened on his body hair from his chest to the top of his bikini swimsuit. Amanda licked her lips and shifted her gaze away from him to the children.

"Go over there and interfere, and you'll see who's the odd person." Marcus rested his hands on his slim hips and looked toward his daughter who sat gaping in delight as Robert pulled the little fish out of the water.

"What happened?" Marcus wanted to know, his demeanor suggesting that he didn't trust what he'd seen. Amanda shrugged.

"Robert wants Amy to be happy, and he does everything he can to make certain that she is. Amy knows that, and she cooperates with him. Does that tell you anything?" Her intent gaze must have had the desired effect, because he looked away.

"I suppose there's a lesson in that," he said after a while. Robert came over to them with the fish hanging on the end of the pole.

"See what Amy caught?"

"Great guns," Marcus exclaimed, alluding to Robert's willing deprecation of what he'd done, giving the credit to Amy. "And to think she's only four years old."

"But she'll soon be five," Robert boasted as he took the fish back to Amy. Marcus threw up both hands, grinning at Amanda. Robert didn't know what he'd meant, but the boy would soon learn.

"Sometimes I forget that life can be that sweet," he murmured, but she heard him. He cast a cool, impersonal glance her way, but she didn't allow that to mislead her and let everything about herself—from the tilt of her head to the casual way she crossed her ankles—challenge him to find that sweetness again. *With her.*

Early the next morning, Monday, when Amanda entered the kitchen fully dressed, Marcus stood at the stove preparing breakfast.

"Good morning. You're all dressed. Going out?" Marcus was reluctant to ask where she was going, because he wasn't sure he had that right. And he began to feel uncomfortable, when he remembered his precarious position in that household. He looked up from the eggs he was scrambling, his lips thinned in an expression of exasperation at himself, and saw her wilt right before him. She had known him only a few months, and already she sensed his moods. With sudden empathy for her, he let a smile curve his lips upward and glanced at her. She looked uncomfortable, too, he thought, sensing that she hadn't yet come to terms with what they went through on Saturday. Oh, the hell with it! "Where are you going?"

"I get my checkup while Amy is in therapy," she answered in a tone that said the question was a natural one. "Ellen will take us. Would you please bring Amy down so she can have breakfast with us?"

He stared at her. "Isn't it a bit early for her to have breakfast? She'll be hungry long before lunchtime."

"No. She can eat whenever she gets hungry. She told me that she wants to eat breakfast when you eat yours, and I think it's a reasonable request. Don't you?"

He nodded. "Yeah. I'll get her in a minute. Could you pour the milk and juice?" He passed her carrying a platter of eggs and sausage to the table, and she reached up, pinched him playfully on the cheek and winked at him. He knew that fire must have shot from his eyes when she stepped backward quickly, as if he had burned her, and lost her balance. He grasped her waist with one arm, settling her, while holding the platter in the other hand. And they stood there looking at each other. He was off guard, exposed, and he saw the same in her. Her rapid breathing and heated look sent desire plowing through him. He wanted her. And when she bathed her parted lips with her tongue and moved, zombie-like toward him, he reached complete readiness.

"Sweet Jesus!" he muttered, bitterly, as he set the platter on the table and bolted from the kitchen. Amanda relived the scene throughout the morning, finding reason first for joy and then for gloom.

Her checkup completed, Amanda sat in the parents' waiting room while Amy completed her therapy and Ellen went to the nearby supermarket. It occurred to her that all of the teachers at her school had returned her questionnaire about their preferences for homeroom activities except Iris Elms. On impulse and because she wanted better relations with the woman, she telephoned Iris from a nearby pay phone and asked when she could expect her reply.

"I don't know where the thing is. In my twelve years at that school, I've always had seventh graders' study hour. You're not going to get anywhere giving people new assignments and turning things around. We're all satisfied with the things the way they are. If I were you, I'd be worrying about my own business and, honey, you've got something to worry about."

"What does that mean?"

"That's good advice for anybody, wouldn't you say?" the woman parried in obvious evasiveness. Amanda admonished her to send back the questionnaire within a week if she didn't want daily corridor-watch duties and hung up. She wondered what gave Iris such assurance that she had the upper hand with her boss? Tendrils of fear skittered from her neck to her fingertips as she recalled the woman's bitter, icy tones. She doubted that professional rivalry alone would generate such animosity. She wanted to discuss it with Marcus, but his own problems with the factory were nearly overwhelming, and she didn't want to burden him more.

* * *

When they returned from the hospital, Ellen asked her about preschool for Amy.

"I've been planning to speak to Marcus about it, but he isn't going to like it. He is extremely protective about Amy, and that's understandable. But this can't be avoided."

"If he objects to her attending Caution Point's kindergarten," Ellen offered, "we could organize our own with, say, three or four well-chosen youngsters. We're both qualified to teach them. What do you think?"

"That's an excellent alternative, if we need it." She glanced sharply at Amy, who had placed her hand on Amanda's belly after watching the movement under her maternity shorts.

"Look, Lady," the child squealed. "Something's jiggling in your tummy. It's poking out. Look." Amanda laughed and hugged Amy, careful not to remove her little hand.

Ellen watched the tender scene. "She needs a simple lesson in the birds and bees, Amanda. Otherwise you may have a real trauma on your hands. She'll adjust better to sharing her parents if she understands why she must."

"I'm not her parent, Ellen," Amanda corrected wistfully.

Amanda didn't miss the sympathy in Ellen's smile. "We all know that, but her little heart doesn't understand the difference." Amanda nodded. One more bridge to cross, she told herself.

Amanda opened the door before Marcus could use his key, surprising him. He looked inquiringly when she beckoned and followed her to the back porch where he got a riveting jolt: Amy stood at a chair, leaning against the seat and using her forearms for support. As he arrived, she stood alone without any help, leaned on the chair for a second, and then practiced standing unsupported again. Marcus thought that his heart would run away. He started forward, but Amanda restrained him. Finally, Amy saw them and giggled.

"Daddy, you're not supposed to be here. I'm practicing my surprise for you. The doctor took off my braces. And he says I can stand by myself a little bit. Didn't he, Lady?" Marcus opened his mouth, but words wouldn't come. Reaching for Amanda's hand, he moved toward his daughter who immediately scolded, "You're not supposed to help me, Daddy. I have to start walking by myself so I can help Lady take care of the baby."

"What?" He hadn't heard her correctly. He looked at Amanda, whose face was suddenly without expression. "What does she know about that?"

Amy answered for her. "I saw the baby jiggling her tummy. When I put my hand there, it even pushed my hand. Try it, Daddy. It's fun. Is it jiggling now, Lady?" Amy giggled, happily. "You ought to see it, Daddy." Marcus picked his daughter up and got his welcome-home hug. But it surprised him that she wanted to be put down so that she could continue practicing. "I have to practice, Daddy. I won't be the baby anymore." Still holding his daughter, he glanced at Amanda and caught an unsheltered look that said she adored him. In spite of himself, heat seared his face as their eyes locked and held.

"Put me down, Daddy. I have to practice." He took Amy to the chair, where she leaned against it for a second and then stood alone. He watched as she alternated the two positions, her little face serious and proud. Marcus wanted to watch Amy in case she stumbled or fell, but he also needed to look at Amanda. He needed to touch her. He was almost happy, and it practically terrified him, because he didn't trust it.

His emotions shot, he asked her, "Can you handle this? I want to change into something cooler. I'll be right back."

What was happening to him? He needed a long walk to clear his head. Marcus sighed and raced up the stairs. Who was he fooling? It would take more than a walk, no matter how long. He showered and changed into white shorts and a yellow T-shirt that opened at the neck to display dark masculine curls. Bounding down the stairs, he stopped halfway. The knowledge came like a shining revelation. Amanda was honorable and she was a warm, gentle and loving woman, but she was no Pollyanna; she stood up for what she thought was right. And she gave him something that he had never had. To her, he was a special man, ten feet tall, and she let him know it. She made him feel all-powerful, and she wanted him and wasn't afraid to show it. He amended that. She didn't know how to hide it. He didn't wonder at his dogged inability to dismiss this wonderful woman as an inconvenience, a bothersome year out of his life. The thought was a dangerous one. He took the stairs down a little more slowly.

They sat together on the porch lounge, Amy between them, as the late-day sun rays filtered through the tree leaves, tracing patterns across their bodies. The wind gained force, and a refreshing breeze off the Albemarle brought relief from the sweltering heat. It was the time of day when Amanda enjoyed the back porch most. She wanted to talk to Marcus, but she hated to shatter the moment.

Finally, she did speak. "I'm glad you aren't angry because I told her about the baby, but I figured that a complete surprise might be traumatic."

He seemed to muse over her words, resting his elbows on his knees and his chin on his clasped hands. "Yes. Of course, you're right. It would have been, and I hadn't thought of it. That she took it so well shows that you handled it properly. Truth is, it had a good effect all around, because it made her strive even harder to walk on her own." He reached for Amanda's hand and squeezed it gently.

"What does Robert think of all this?" he asked, jokingly.

Amanda laughed. "I don't know, and I'm afraid even to contemplate his thoughts on the matter. Robert is five going on ninety; you know that." He grinned, accelerating her heartbeat as he stroked her arm and gently caressed her shoulder.

Here he goes giving me mixed signals again, she thought waspishly. Frowning to show her displeasure, she asked him,

"Have you ever had the water suddenly run hot while you were taking a cold shower, or suddenly change to cold when you were taking a warm one?"

He rested his right ankle on his left knee, clasped his hands behind his head and leaned back. "If so, I don't remember it. Why?"

"It's an awful shock to the body," she told him, tossing back her head and eyeing him speculatively. "Let's go in the kitchen and start dinner."

Marcus studied her for a moment. He didn't figure he'd describe her as sweet right then, and wondered about the sudden change. She could be maddening sometime, he had observed of late. Maybe it was his effect on her personality. He hoped not. She was unique, precious and he didn't want to spoil that. He followed her into the kitchen thinking that many men would envy him.

They got Amy to bed quickly that evening, since she was too sleepy to demand her usual quota of stories. Amanda had been sitting on the edge of Amy's bed saying the child's nightly prayers along with her and, when she attempted to stand, she clutched her back. Marcus moved quickly to her to lend support. "What's wrong? Are you having pain or cramps? What is it?" She explained that she had occasional back discomfort, but that it wasn't a problem.

"I think I'll freshen up. It's so humid. Meet you on the balcony for a spell, if you'd like," she offered.

She ran water in the tub, tossed in some bubble bath, one of her favorite luxuries, and climbed in. She'd had to forego the pleasure of warm baths during the weeks that Marcus had stayed in Portsmouth with Luke. Now that he was at home, she could enjoy the soothing water without worry. Her thoughts went to Marcus' inconsistent behavior. He didn't intend for her to have a place in his life permanently, but inadvertently and frequently he did things to bind himself to her, destroying any chance she might have for happiness after he left her. Maybe her own baby would fill the gaping hole that he and Amy would leave. Sure. *And I'm the First Lady, too,* she told herself, giving in to a brief moment of self-pity. She grasped the side of the tub to pull herself up and realized that she couldn't. She tried repeatedly, but without success. "Thank God, I didn't lock that door," she told herself and made a mental note to teach Amy how to use the telephone. Now what? Marcus was unlikely to hear her through three closed doors. And even if he did, she didn't want him to see her in that state. The latter was something that she needn't have wasted time worrying about.

Marcus waited for what he considered to be a reasonable length of time for Amanda before becoming concerned. He paced the floor for some minutes, and then decided to investigate. She had been favoring her back. Alarmed by that memory, he raced through Amy's room and, seeing Amanda's room empty, yanked open her bathroom door. He found her struggling to get out of the tub, unable to raise herself upright and near panic from fear of slipping. Why hadn't she called him? He opened the drain, threw a bath sheet around her, lifted her from the tub and placed her on her feet.

"Thanks. It's so good that you're home." Her embarrassment annoyed him. Hadn't they already seen every inch of each other? He wanted to shake her.

"You wouldn't have been in that tub, if I hadn't been home," he growled. "I'm sure I told you to stay out of that tub. Use the shower stall; I secured it for your protection. Don't you remember what happened when you slipped?" Irate, he shook his finger in her face, warming up to his anger. If she didn't want to be told what to do, that was too bad. He felt responsible for her.

She observed in his fierce scowl, the sparks flying from his beautiful eyes and giggled. Unable to suppress it, she began to howl with laughter.

"What is so funny?" he demanded, and she could see that he was perplexed.

"After all we're going through here, do you think I want to see you lose this baby or, God forbid, hurt yourself or worse? Do you?"

She shook her head and tried without success to suppress a grin.

"What is it now?" If he was amused, he refused to give in to it.

"I've heard that men have been known to tell women, on occasion, that they're beautiful when they're angry. I suppose you'd go into a rage, if I said that to you, wouldn't you?"

He frowned and shook his head as though to clear it. Then he grinned, his eyes flashing with mischief, erasing even the possibility that he didn't like compliments.

"Perish the thought. I like sweet talk as well as the next guy. And believe me, lady, you can't overfeed my ego, no matter how many nice things you say to me. I'll go down and get a pitcher of lemonade and a couple of glasses." He turned to leave and threw over his shoulder, "Put some clothes on. Not that you aren't beautiful just as you are."

Marcus returned with the drinks and found Amanda sitting in a chair on the balcony holding the sneakers she'd begun to wear at home to ease the pressure on her back. He guessed her problem at once, set the drinks on a small table beside her chair and knelt before her, put her feet in the sneakers and tied them. Resting on his haunches, he put a hand on her knee. "You don't need me for much," he told her quietly, "but you do need me for things like this. So just ask me."

She folded her hands in her lap, blinked her eyes rapidly and, with a few simple words, let him know the futility of his efforts to keep their relationship platonic.

"If you think I don't need you, you're nowhere near as smart as I thought. When you leave here, I'm going to be like a bow without an arrow."

He shook his head, denying the implications of her words. "You'll miss the company, maybe. And that, only for a while. When 'we do not succeed in changing things according to our desires,' Amanda, 'gradually our desires change.'"

She closed her eyes tightly. "Speak for yourself. Anyway, I always thought Proust and his philosophies were overrated." Perhaps it was too serious a conversation, he decided; she didn't appear to be enjoying their jesting with quotations as usual.

"'To eat bread without hope is still…'" He cut her off. It had been her heart speaking, and he wasn't ready to hear the words from her lips.

"Yes, I know… *'slowly to starve to death.'* No one could express pain as Buck could." He suppressed his anxiety when she shifted in the chair, trying not to let her hand go to her back. He knew she hated pity, but he couldn't help feeling for her; she was uncomfortable. So much discomfort. How could she be so noble? So cheerful and optimistic? Amazing. Still on his haunches before her, he took her hand.

"I'm going to your Lamaze classes with you." For days, he had wrestled with the consequences of such a decision. But he knew he couldn't do less. Amy was taking small steps alone, and he had Amanda to thank. Not merely because of their contract, but for what she had done that wasn't included in the agreement. He felt her hand tremble as it covered his.

"You're going to coach me? Is that what you said?" She seemed afraid to believe it.

"Yep. And you're going to do as I tell you. What night are the classes?" She told him that she would have to go twice weekly, and he readily agreed. Suddenly, she began to cry, and her whole body shook. Marcus put his arms around her and, after a long while, she was quiet. He picked her up, took her into her room and lay her on her bed. "Good night," he whispered softly and left her.

Amanda lay awake most of the night. She had to draw heavily on her inner strength in order to contain her emotions. He treated her so gently, with such tenderness. What would he be like if he loved her? Each time after she dozed off, she awakened with the thought that he hadn't asked why she was crying. Perhaps he knew. Or, perhaps he didn't want to know. And she was glad that he hadn't asked; in her state of mind, she would have told him how much she wished that it was his child she carried.

Marcus stood on the upstairs porch, his right foot propped on the wooden tub that held Amanda's prized evergreen shrub, wishing foolishly that he could know what his life would be like on April twelfth. He wouldn't hazard a guess. His business wasn't moving as he'd hoped. He was hounded by vultures, brokers who wanted to buy his business from the bank for a pittance of its worth. And each day seemed to sink him more deeply. Amy would probably be walking normally, but she would be heartbroken for having left Amanda. And she'd be missing Robert, who had proved to be the perfect playmate for her. The boy challenged her mind, and Amy loved it. The breeze had a slight nip, and it cooled his nude body, but he savored it. A niggling thought lingered that he tried to suppress. He didn't want to think of the time when he would have to face the consequences that leaving Amanda would have for him personally, but pushed it from his mind as he clung tenaciously to his passionate vow that he had finished with marriage for all time. Yet he knew that marriage was what Amanda wanted and what she needed.

A cloud raced over the full moon, momentarily obscuring it. He watched it with growing awareness that he had been playing games with himself. He didn't see the moon, but he knew it was there. He could pretend as much as he liked, but in a second or two, the moon would emerge full and proud in a clear, star-filled sky. He'd always tried to be honest with himself and with others, and he had a strange feeling that he had begun to mislead himself. Ignoring a problem or covering it up did not make it go away. He had to admit that, unless he won the suit over Amy's injuries, he could say goodbye to his home and his business and still be in debt, and he'd better not forget it. Then,

Amanda wouldn't even be an option for him. If he didn't slow down and back off, he was going to miss her more than Amy ever would, and he had better not mislead himself into thinking otherwise.

School opened on the Tuesday after Labor Day, and Marcus announced that he would take the morning off from his business—a sacrifice the importance of which Amanda could only imagine—and drive her to school.

"Ellen can take me," she told him, wondering why he persisted so adamantly. She was learning the many ways in which Marcus' protective streak could manifest itself.

"I want everybody there to see that you have a husband, because it's important to thwart gossip and speculation before it takes root."

Amanda studied his stubborn, handsome face as he looked down at her, scowling. She felt protected and cared for, and her trust must have shone in her guileless adoration. Marcus took a step backward, away from her, making it impossible for either of them to touch the other.

His comment brought a droll reply. "If they see you, they're less likely to believe I'm married than if I just go there and announce it."

He stared at her, eyes narrowed, as if he were slightly dense. "Marcus, everybody at that school considers me a dull, boring spinster. Such women do not marry men who look like you. Admit it. You would never have given me a second glance, would you?"

His honey-brown eyes seemed to bore into her, as he ran his fingers over his tight curls in frustration. "I don't like being reminded that I've been a sucker for skinny, light-skinned women with forever legs. And no, I probably wouldn't have given you a second look. But believe me, sweetheart, my eyesight must have improved, because I can see you now, through and through." He hesitated, as what he'd just said sank in. "Amanda, get your stuff together, and let's go. You don't want to be late on opening day. Do you?" Marcus put Amy into Ellen's car and waved them off to Amy's therapy session. Then he turned around to find that Amanda was having difficulty getting into Luke's big sedan.

"I don't think you should sit in the front anymore," he told her, as he opened the back door on the driver's side, seated her and attempted to strap her in. That effort brought a laugh from both of them, as he gave up, got in the driver's seat and drove off. Then he laughed uproariously, asking her, "What is it the Bible says about getting a camel through a needle's eye?"

Amanda feigned annoyance. "I'm smaller than most camels." She let herself enjoy his deep resonant laughter and asked him, "Are you always so bossy?"

"I'm not bossy. But when something is as plain as your face, there's no room for argument. Why? You got something against my offering you advice? I'm just telling you what seems right and logical to me. If I stopped suddenly, you might be injured, or worse. So no back talk." Amanda was too comfortable and too happy to argue. His last remark was apparently intended to lighten the matter, and she accepted it that way.

"Whatever you say. I'm not one to dash water on a good fire in the dead of winter."

"Another one of Aunt Meredith's bits of wisdom?" he asked facetiously, as he drove in the principal's allotted spot.

"Why are you parking here? This is reserved for the—"

"Principal," he finished for her. "And you're the principal as of this morning."

Amanda knew at once that Marcus' effort wasn't wasted. The whispering during the opening assembly while she spoke from the dais wasn't confined to students. Marcus made it so obvious that he was her significant other, walking her to the front of the room and assisting her in sitting, that she had to introduce him as her husband. Later, teachers and students, especially the older girls, managed to get close enough for a good look. And most of the teachers succeeded in having a few words with him. Amanda was surprised at Marcus' cool facade. He had assumed an air of elegance and authority, and she realized that she'd never seen him dressed so fashionably or expensively, not even at their wedding. So this was Marcus as he'd been in his more prosperous days before Amy's accident, she mused, as she realized why he'd brought the small suitcase home the week before. "Something he'd collected from things stored at Luke's place," he'd explained. The fierce pride that she felt in him was punctured, temporarily, when Iris Elms, the modern dance teacher, sauntered up to them as Marcus was preparing to leave.

"Well, Mr. Hickson, I see you're still around. I'm having my debut dance performance in Norfolk on December eighteenth, and I'd love for you to come." She held out one ticket to him.

Marcus recognized the woman as the one who'd suggested to him last May that he'd married Amanda because he'd made her pregnant and who had boasted friendship with the Lamont family in Portsmouth. He curled his upper lip into a snarl, let his eyes sear her rudely from her head to her toes and back again and then, as if he'd seen nothing whatever, turned to Amanda.

"I'll see you tonight, baby." With a slight nod toward the offending teacher, he added, "I wouldn't expect to find anything unsavory among these young innocents, but it's here, so be careful." He kissed her soundly and walked away leaving a shocked Iris Elms holding her ticket and sputtering indignantly.

Amanda smiled at her as though she was to be pitied. "Sorry, Iris, but not every man is flattered by such an obvious pass, and especially not when it's a flagrant act of rudeness to his wife. Better luck next time, girl. And beginning tomorrow," she added, pointedly exerting her authority, "every female teacher in this school will wear dresses that are no shorter than five inches above the knee." Amanda left the woman standing there. She was certain that the only time in her life that she'd ever felt so good was the morning that Marcus had put her into his bed. She was certain she had an enemy in Iris but, right then, she didn't care; she would no longer be the butt of Iris Elms' cruel jokes about her lack of attractiveness to men.

She arranged a conference with her assistant principal, agreed with the young man that he would take over in two weeks and act as principal until after the Christmas holidays when she would return to work. She scheduled meetings with the teachers, posted exam schedules and homeroom assignments—amused that Iris had returned her preference within the deadline—and got down to the business of being principal. Amanda found it exhilarating. The time went so quickly that, when the bell rang, she couldn't believe she'd completed her first day on the job and that it had gone so smoothly, thanks partly to Marcus. She reflected on the encounter with Iris Elms. When the woman first joined the staff, she hadn't been friendly, but neither had she been mean. Amanda rested her elbows on the impressive mahogany desk and twirled a pencil. What had caused Iris to become hostile and, at times, abusive? For more than a year, she had been the butt of Iris' derisive remarks about her status as a spinster. "Well, I got some of my own today," Amanda concluded with a great deal of satisfaction. She looked up, surprised when, at three-thirty, her secretary announced Ellen and Amy.

The child could hardly contain her excitement. She hadn't visited a school before, and she wanted to know if any little children went there. That served as a reminder to Amanda that she would have to face Marcus that evening with the question of preschool. She dreaded it.

Marcus let himself in the house, closed the door and walked slowly through the long hallway toward the back porch, where he knew he'd find Amanda and Amy. He had to put on his best face, and he was too tired, too worried for farce. He let the back door bang to announce his presence. Amy greeted him with a casual "Hi, Daddy," and didn't break her rhythm as she continued her halting reading aloud of *Baa, Baa, Black Sheep*.

Marcus knew he should be happy that his daughter was reading before her fifth birthday, but what he felt was neglect. It didn't surprise him that Amanda sensed his foolish hurt at Amy's slight and knew it was because he'd come home seeking respite from his troubles at work in the warm and loving welcome he always received from his wife and daughter.

She grasped his hand and walked him over to Amy. "Amy, darling, you haven't greeted Daddy properly. He's tired, and he deserves a big kiss."

Amy read some more, stopped and looked up at them. "Want a kiss, Daddy?" She held out her arms to him, kissed him smacking wet kisses and turned to Amanda, giggling. "Now, you kiss him." She went back to her book.

Amanda saw in him the raw, exposed man, and something that she couldn't identify. It seemed as if pain, loneliness, need—she wasn't sure which—flickered ever so briefly in his eyes before his mask was firmly in place. They stood there not speaking or touching. And then he said in barely audible tones, "Amanda, I... Oh, Amanda." She heard him, and folded him into her arms. Somehow, she understood that he didn't want or need passion. He just needed to know that someone was there for him, and Amy had chosen that time to assert her independence. Amanda reached up, grasped his shirt collar, tugged his head down and gave him a tender, loving kiss that was devoid of passion.

"Why don't you sit here, while I get us something to drink?" She brought lemonade for Amy and herself, and a gin and tonic for Marcus.

"How did you know what I wanted?" He sat with his long muscular legs stretched out in front of him and his head resting on the back of the swing. "Thanks. You know, you've got an uncanny knack of reading my mind sometimes." She knew that, if it were true, he wouldn't like it.

"I can't read your mind and I'm glad of that," she told him, pointedly, "but you're down, and your smile doesn't hide it." Looking into the distance, he gulped down his drink and announced that he was going upstairs to change. Then he attempted to soften it by ruffling her hair as he passed her, but Amanda wasn't misled by his gesture. She watched him walk away and thought, *In spite of all that's gone on between us, he's no closer to accepting me as part of his life than he was the day I met him.*

Marcus got out of his business suit as quickly as possible. He preferred casual clothes, but he had realized the importance of making a good impression that morning for Amanda's sake and had dressed to accompany her to school. Amanda. He had needed her. When he had reached the front door, the weight he carried had seemed unbearable. She had sensed it and, though he hadn't even known that he needed her, she'd come through for him with her sweetness and tenderness. How was it possible that she could look at him, put her arms around him and make him feel he could fix anything that was broken? He stopped pulling on his white Bermuda shorts, suddenly alert and on edge. He should put some distance between Amanda and himself, for both their sakes. But how could he when, without even trying, she knocked down every barrier that he put up?

She saw no point in postponing what she knew would be a confrontation about Amy going to preschool. Yet she was loath to present him with that or any other problem, when she realized that he was heavily burdened, that conditions over which he had no control were tightening their choking hold on him. She wondered for the nth time why he couldn't bring himself to tell her about it. *Because a man shares his problems with his wife, and you're not a bona fide wife* was the answer that her instincts gave her. She had thought of calling Luke but had refrained; she couldn't be disloyal to Marcus, and going behind his back to get information about him was exactly that. She pulled herself up from the straight back chair that Marcus had placed beside her bed and went into Amy's room to make certain that the child was comfortable. The air from the Albemarle often made the September nights chilly and, as Amy's legs became stronger, she tended to kick off the covers. Amanda threw a light cotton blanket over the child, leaned down and kissed her. When she straightened up, she looked directly into Marcus' turbulent eyes.

She didn't know what to say but, if she had known, she wouldn't have trusted herself to say it, so she padded self-consciously back to her room and sat on the edge of her bed. She hoped he'd go directly to his room. One touch, and she'd go up in flames. She didn't want to respond to him, only later to come crushing back to reality; she wanted him to leave her with her pride. If he cared for her, he should act like it and be consistent. If he knew that she needed him, he became the loving, caring, protective husband of every woman's dreams—the way he'd been at school that morning. But when he needed *her,* he made certain that she didn't get the chance to behave as if she was his loving wife. Well, he was the one calling the shots, and he had been from the beginning, she reminded herself, as she heard him tap lightly on her door.

She opened the conversation, not wanting him to have the advantage of choosing their topic. "I've been intending to speak to you," she told him, keeping her voice businesslike. "Amy should be registered in preschool. Otherwise, she'll be behind in her kindergarten class in January and probably first grade as well. And what is most important, she may have difficulty relating to other children."

Marcus grazed his chin with his left hand as though deep in thought, released a long sigh and sat down beside her on the edge of her bed. "I'm not sure it's wise to put her among a group of active children who'll romp all over her and undermine her self-confidence. Besides, she'd probably out-read every one of them, thanks to you. And another thing, Amanda, how is she going to get to the bathroom? What if they want to play ball? Is she supposed to ask some other kid for help, or be a nuisance to the teacher? I don't like it."

Amanda knew his objection stemmed from his need to protect Amy, but she also knew that Amy would adjust to any situation in which she found herself. But this wasn't the time to take a stand, she decided, not when she suspected that he had just received another blow. Aunt Meredith used to say that there was more than one way to ripen fruit; if the sun didn't shine, half an apple in a brown bag filled with the fruit would do the trick. She rested a hand on his knee, then patted him gently.

"If you don't like that idea, would you agree to my having a preschool class here with Amy and three or four other children? Both Ellen and I are qualified to teach the class. Robert is going to first grade, and Amy needs to interact with other children her age. I would choose the children very carefully. What do you say?"

Even as she spoke quietly and soothingly, as if he needed comforting, Marcus had marveled at her capacity for understanding and gentleness. Still, he couldn't dismiss the feeling that everything had begun to slip away from him. No matter how hard he and his crew worked, he couldn't seem to get a penny clear. In two months, he wouldn't be able to meet his mortgages, and the banks would own everything he had worked for, or they'd sell his property to a crafty speculator. He ran the fingers of his left hand through his hair and regretted it, for Amanda would recognize it as frustration.

"Are you sure you're up to it?" He looked down at her sitting there looking lost with her hands lying loosely in her lap. And it occurred to him that, in the whole world, he was all she had.

He took both her hands in his own and squeezed them gently in an attempt to communicate the depth of his feeling for her, though he was loath to gauge them himself. "Bear with me, Amanda. Life's a real screwdriver right now. What are you suggesting?"

She outlined the plan that she and Ellen had devised as an alternative to Amy's attendance at school, adding that the children she chose would not have to pay.

"I'll install the glass storm panels on the porch and move the porch furniture around to create a classroom atmosphere," he said, mostly to himself. Amanda nodded. She had planned to have someone do the work, but she said nothing, realizing that he needed to do it for the sake of his pride.

Ellen conducted the afternoon classes with Amy, two boys and one other girl, leaving the mornings free for Amy's therapy. She and Amanda had chosen children who were advanced for their ages and who enjoyed learning. After two weeks, Amanda began maternity leave and was able to assist with the children.

Amanda couldn't help being glad that her maternity leave had begun, but she couldn't dismiss her concern and the trouble she sensed festering below the surface, trouble that could intensify in her absence. In the short while that school had been in session, Iris Elms had succeeded in drawing around herself a coterie of troublemakers who disapproved of every change their principal made, beginning with the new homeroom assignments. The group—the gang of seven as she'd come to think of them—had stood apart at her going-away party, deliberately making their non-participation conspicuous. Amanda knew that many of her staff thought her too gentle for sharp and decisive action, but they were in for a surprise. Her first act when she returned to school in January was going to be Iris Elms' transfer to another school in the district. Having decided that, she put school and its problems out of her mind and looked forward to enjoying the remainder of the time that she would have Amy and Marcus with her.

Amy blossomed in the preschool program that Amanda and Ellen held during weekdays, and she and Robert played together on Saturday afternoons. One Saturday in mid-October, Marcus had planned to take them for ice cream but, as he reached the porch where they played he stopped, unable to move. He watched, horrified, when Robert threw the ball to a far corner and told Amy, "Since you're so smart, walk over there and get your ball. I'm not going to get it for you."

Glad that he hadn't expressed disapproval, Marcus quickly realized from the boy's obvious anxiety that he was not being cruel. But he waited anxiously for Amy's reaction and was rewarded beyond his dreams by her sharp retort.

"All right. I'll get it myself." She stood alone for a minute, gathered her courage and started toward the ball. When she faltered, Robert encouraged her.

"Go ahead, Amy. You can walk. You see? You can. Go on." Amy giggled happily at Robert, no longer annoyed with him. Then she took a deep breath and made a dash for it.

"I got it," she yelled. "Daddy! Lady! I walked and got the ball." Hearing the excitement, Amanda padded toward the porch as quickly as her burden would allow and found Marcus standing by the door, speechless, with tears streaming down his face. The thrill of seeing the children hugging each other in celebration of Amy's triumph nearly overwhelmed her.

"What happened?" He turned, pulled her to him and buried his face in her hair.

"What is it? Tell me."

He loosened his grip on her and shook his head, hardly believing what he'd seen. He said simply, "She walked. All alone, she walked." He kissed Amanda then, and it was a special, bonding kiss. A salve for him. And for Amanda. "Thank you for giving my child her health. A normal life."

"I didn't do that," she told him. "You did. You've given her everything you had—your wealth, your time, your privacy, your independence and your love—and you would have given your life for her. Don't you ever underrate what you've done." They walked toward the happy children.

Amy looked up and, with simple eloquence, told them, "I can walk now." Marcus moved closer and held out his arms to her. She took the remaining half a dozen steps and, with barely steady arms, he folded her to him. Amanda went over to Robert and asked him what happened.

"My mother told me to do it," he boasted. "I did what she told me, and Amy walked." Amanda remembered that Robert's mother was a psychotherapist.

The excitement eventually waned, and Marcus put the children in Luke's car and drove Robert home before taking Amy to visit Ellen with the good news. Clearly overjoyed, Ellen hugged Amy and told her to go slowly at first, but the child told her proudly, "I'm going to walk all the time. Then, I'll be running."

As soon as they reached home, Marcus telephoned Luke with the news. "You needed it," his brother told him. "If anybody ever deserved a break, you do. Amanda must be ecstatic."

"Oh, she is" was the quiet reply.

"Now, don't tell me you're already planning how you'll self-destruct," Luke shot back, reading his brother with consummate ease as usual. Then he added with acerbic bite, "I've got a criminal case involving a tall, sloe-eyed willowy café au lait dame, self-centered as she can be and just as beautiful. She doesn't do a thing for me, but she's probably just what you're looking for. Want to meet her?"

Marcus got the message and didn't care for its implications. "Back off, Luke. I don't interfere with your mistakes; leave me to mine."

"Since you're hell-bent on trashing both your life and Amy's I don't have a choice. I'll be down there tomorrow to see my niece walk."

Chapter 8

Marcus swore under his breath. He'd just snapped a string on a concert Steinway and, an hour before, he'd ruined a hammer. He looked over at Jerzy Heiner, and declared that he was leaving for the day.

"Man, you can't work twelve hours straight on jobs like that one without making mistakes. When you're tired, anything can happen. Go ahead," Jerzy told him. "I'll lock up." Marcus thanked him and walked back to his office to secure his tools and straighten up his desk. Since he'd started the business, he'd never left his desk untidy and had never walked away from a job that he'd planned to complete that day. He hated to leave that grand half-finished, but he was tired and, he admitted, he needed to get home. Weary, he sat down and turned on the radio. He'd left home around five-thirty that morning and hadn't stopped for more than half an hour since seven o'clock. He looked at his watch and grimaced. He should have been home an hour ago.

He reached out to lock his desk, and his hand stilled. The weather forecasters had predicted that a much-heralded storm would veer out to the Atlantic somewhere below Wilmington near the South Carolina border, and he hadn't given any more thought to it. But if he was hearing right, that storm had just touched land somewhere between Cape Hatteras and Nags Head, almost on top of Caution Point. He slammed his office door shut, yelled something to Jerzy and headed to Luke's car. He jumped in, turned on the radio and listened. The storm was barreling up the coast, and the interstate was closed from Suffolk, Virginia, to New Bern, North Carolina. He slumped in the seat, cursing himself for not having paid more attention to the weather. He had to get home to Amanda and Amy.

He sat there, considering his chances of getting home if he took a back road until he remembered that trees in his garden had fallen across his driveway in winds of less than hurricane force. A back road might well be strewn with trees and debris, and he could be stranded for days. He backed up, barely avoided a minivan, and drove to Luke's apartment building.

"We're expecting it full force," the young doorman proclaimed cheerfully. "With good luck, I won't have to come in to work tomorrow."

"If you can't find your house when you get to the place where it used to be, I hope you have a good laugh," Marcus said, without looking the man's way. He dug in his pocket for Luke's key and walked into the empty apartment. He got a busy signal when he called Amanda and another one when he telephoned Jack Culpepper. So the lines were down. He paced the floor, berating himself for his tunnel vision. If he hadn't been determined to finish that grand, he might have paid more attention to the weather. *If!* He telephoned his brother at the precinct, but Luke was on call, and the captain declined to say where.

Marcus paced the floor in desperation until the open kitchen window alerted him to the rising wind. He bolted back to the telephone and called Luke's precinct captain.

"You've got to help," he said after identifying himself and explaining the problem. "My wife and child are in a house less than a mile from the Sound in Caution Point and they're by themselves. My wife can't even close a window, because she's about eight months pregnant. Can't you get in touch with the police there and ask them to send a man out to help her? One eighty-seven Ocean Avenue."

"All right," the captain told him. "I'll see what I can manage and call you back."

Marcus raced for the front door when he heard the key turn. His face must have told Luke the story, because his brother didn't bother with a greeting; he pulled out his beeper and cellular phone. "If I can't get through to them with this, I'll go down to the basement and try my call box or the CB in the squad car." Relief washed over Marcus; if anyone could help, Luke would manage it.

"Who are you calling, Luke?" Luke sat on the arm of the sofa and began pushing buttons.

"The police in Caution Point. I know it's hard, Marcus, but you might as well sit down. Neither you, the trains nor the buses can get to Caution from here." Marcus let the wall take his weight. His stomach burned, and a rawness ate at his insides. Desperation overcame him, and he didn't want his brother or anyone else to see him that way. He walked down the hallway to Luke's guest room and closed the door. He hadn't prayed since the paramedics had pulled Amy from the smashed automobile in which the two of them had been riding when a building crane crashed the roof of his car. But he prayed then. And he faced the fact that he would have been equally as concerned for Amanda alone. He started back to the living room, pushing the latter thought out of his consciousness; he'd deal with that some other time.

The static faded after some minutes, and Luke connected with the Caution Point police station. Marcus had to struggle with his fears. Foolish though it would be, he knew he'd have to start walking to Caution if he didn't know something soon. Luke handed him a can of beer and regarded him sympathetically, but Marcus took the can and put it on a nearby table without tasting its contents. He waited in silence for word of his wife and child's safety, and he'd never realized that a minute could last so long.

* * *

Amanda sat on the chaise lounge in Amy's room with the little girl huddled between her legs, refusing to lie down.

"Honey, it's your bedtime. I'll read *Puss 'n Boots,* and when Daddy gets home tomorrow morning, you'll be able to surprise him with a new story."

"I don't wanna read anything, and I don't wanna go to bed. I wanna stay right here with you until my daddy gets home." Amanda was familiar with the child's stubborn streak, and she knew how to handle it, but discipline wasn't what either of them needed. She hoped Marcus hadn't tried to drive home, but if he wasn't stranded on the road somewhere, where was he? Why didn't he call? Her eyes closed tight, and she inhaled and exhaled deeply; she couldn't break down and frighten Amy.

"Lady, are you going to cry?" the plaintive voice demanded.

"No, darling. There's no reason for me to cry." Amanda shook herself. Where was her common sense? She took Amy by the hand and went into Marcus' room to dial Luke's number. Alarm streaked through her when she couldn't get a dial tone. Suppose the baby decided to come a month early? She went into the bathroom, got a glass of water and sipped it while Amy clutched her thigh, still refusing to be separated from her. She thought one of the windows in Amy's room would be ripped from its sash. The shaking finally eased and she relaxed, but only for a minute, as she had to pretend not to hear a loud clanging noise that she suspected came from the garage. And shudders passed through her as the wind lifted objects and hurled them against what had to be trees, buildings and posts. In her mind's eye, she conjured up the chaos she knew she'd find in the morning if they survived the storm. Caution Point got at least three good storms every autumn, but she couldn't remember having witnessed one so severe. She decided to go into her own room and let Amy sleep with her, but just as she entered the hallway, the lights went out. She fumbled in her pocket for the book of matches she'd put there when the storm struck, found her way into her room and lit a candle.

Her breath caught in her throat and her heart pounded rapidly when she heard the loud banging on the front door. She held the candle high as she picked her way down the stairs, holding Amy's hand, but her initial relief turned into anxiety and the fear of bad news. That wasn't Marcus at the door; he would use his key.

She tried to still her trembling fingers as she reached for the knob. She opened the door and, when she saw Clay Adams, she grabbed her chest, certain that her heart had fallen to her toes.

"He's all right, Miss Amanda. Everything okay here?" She nodded, unable to say a word.

"I'm going to let you speak to him in a minute." She waited with Amy by the door while the man checked in all the rooms with his flashlight and assured himself that the house hadn't sustained any damage. Then he came back downstairs and called Luke's cellular phone number.

They heard the scratchy sound from the phone and Marcus jumped and grabbed it from Luke's hand.

"Sergeant Adams on Ocean Avenue in Caution. I've got Mrs. and Miss Hickson here. A couple of trees down out front, and the garage door is missing, but other than that, no damage that I can see. I'll stay with them until there's no longer any danger. Here's your wife, Mr. Hickson." Marcus thanked the officer and leaned against the wall, weak with relief.

"You're all right? Both of you? I worked late on a grand that has to be shipped next week. When I heard the weather report, I tried to get home, but the interstate had been closed. Then, I couldn't reach you, and I tried to get Jack to go and see about you, but I couldn't reach him, either. Look, I don't know what I'm saying here, Amanda. You can't imagine what I went through not knowing whether the two of you were safe or…" He sat down, but a second later, he stood up. "I'll get home as soon as I can." She reassured him, but he barely heard her. "Let me say a word to Amy." He clutched the back of his neck, feeling as though he'd had the wind knocked out of him.

"Yes, baby, I'm all right. I'm with Uncle Luke, and I'll get home as soon as I can." She hadn't been that solemn during the worst days of her illness, and he realized that she'd had a terrible scare.

"No, baby, the house won't fall down, and I'm fine. I love you, too." He handed the phone to his brother. Luke put it back in its case, dropped it on the sofa and went to the kitchen. He returned a few minutes later with ham sandwiches and two cans of beer.

Marcus rested his elbow on his thigh and propped up his chin with the heel of his hand. "I'm wrung out, Luke. Maybe later. Right now, I couldn't eat a thing. You know, this is the first time I wasn't there for Amanda when she needed me. Suppose she'd gone into labor."

"She didn't. Marcus…"

"I appreciate what you did, Luke. You know that. But please don't lecture me. I know I would probably have gone berserk if anything had happened to either Amanda or Amy, and I know I responded to this thing the way any husband and family man would. But don't get on my case about Amanda and me; I've had about as much as I can take for one night." Marcus' head snapped up at his brother's raucous laughter.

"You said it, Marcus. I didn't open my mouth."

"Said what?" He wanted to wipe the smirk from Luke's face, but not badly enough to try it.

"That you responded like a husband and father. How else would you act? That's what I've been telling you. You *are* a husband, and you feel like one."

The interstate opened at about two o'clock in the morning, and Marcus was on it by two-fifteen. An on-duty fellow officer had telephoned Luke with the information. Having a policeman for a brother had its advantages, Marcus decided, not for the first time. But when he neared Caution Point, a fit of ambivalence caused him to slow down below the speed limit. How was he going to greet Amanda? He wanted to take her to him, to hold her and love her, to let her know how he'd suffered thinking he might never see her alive again. Or that she might have been injured. Or that she might have lost her child. But what would that communicate to her? His foot relaxed on the accelerator, and the car jumped forward. *I'd better watch it,* he cautioned himself. In the end, the late-night hour solved his dilemma.

He let himself into the quiet house. Why hadn't he realized that after they spoke with him, they'd be able to sleep? He'd envisioned them huddled together, waiting. He looked into Amy's room and saw that she slept soundly. Then he opened Amanda's bedroom door, the first time he'd done that without knocking, and looked in. Did she always sleep with a light on? He walked over to the bed, looked down at her and gave thanks. He didn't ask himself thanks for what as he knelt beside the bed and kissed her lightly on her lips. A sense of contentment, of rightness pervaded him when she opened her eyes, recognized him and smiled.

"What time is it?" Her hand reached out and touched his unshaven jaw.

"Twenty minutes to four. I just wanted you to know that I'm home." He felt her hand clasp the back of his head as she raised toward him. And he took the soul-satisfying kiss she gave him without guilt or shame, because he needed it, and he knew that she needed to give it.

After breakfast the next morning, Amanda walked around the garden with Amy holding her hand. The child didn't want to be separated from her even for a minute, something unusual for Amy who liked to show independence. It was another indication that she'd been sorely frightened the night before.

"When is my daddy coming back?" Amy had asked that question at approximately five-minute intervals ever since Marcus left the house to help Jack Culpepper clear a tree from his driveway.

"Pretty soon now, and Mr. Culpepper will come, too, and help Daddy remove our trees and reattach the garage door."

"A tree fell on Robert's daddy's car."

"How do you know that?" Sometimes she thought Amy and Robert communicated by telepathy.

"Robert called me. He wanted to know if I was all right." Amanda couldn't help laughing. The fear that had tied her in knots the night before and the heat she'd harbored ever since she'd welcomed Marcus home with that kiss rolled out of her in a powerful release of energy, and her laughter escalated until tears drenched her cheeks. Amy joined her in it.

Marcus walked around the side of the house with Jack checking for damage and stopped short at what he saw.

"Amanda! Amy! What is it? What's the matter?" Neither of them could stop laughing until he gave Amanda a gentle shake and laid a heavy hand on Amy's shoulder.

"They're having a reaction to that hurricane, I expect," Jack said and knelt down to look closely at Amy.

"I was laughing at Amy, and she copied me. It got out of hand." Amanda didn't add that her tears had suddenly become real, and she needn't have. Marcus knew the difference between happiness and what he'd seen in her face. He splayed a hand at her back when she turned and waddled toward the house with Amy still holding her hand. He closed the door behind her, walked back toward Jack and picked up the chain saw that he'd dropped when he saw his wife and daughter.

"Do you think both of them were hysterical?" Jack asked.

Marcus didn't answer for a while, and anyone would have thought that sawing the thick tree trunk required his full concentration. The tree split from its stump, and he said, "No. Just Amy. Amanda was brokenhearted." He checked himself. He didn't make revealing remarks about Amanda, not even to Luke, and he was glad Jack had the good taste to refrain from comment.

They cut up the two trees and stacked the wood in a corner of the garden. Marcus didn't know what to do with it, since

Amanda used oil heat. "You won't have any trouble getting rid of it," Jack assured him. "Half of this town uses wood for heat all winter." Marcus tried to force a good mood, but when he'd almost said that he'd have to ask Amanda about it, a feeling of sadness and frustration and his sensitivity about his status with her had surfaced that he hadn't felt in weeks.

Luke arrived unexpectedly to help with the cleanup, and the three men got the garage door back on its hinges and cut and stacked the broken branches that the sanitation department would cart away. Jack went home, and Marcus went to the far end of the garden, glued together broken spindles of the trellis that Amanda loved so dearly and sat down on the stone bench that rested beneath it. He couldn't remember when he'd had such a good workout; every muscle ached, and he welcomed it. But it didn't reduce his frustration. Six more months of this merry-go-round and he'd be fit for an asylum.

He didn't begrudge having passed the day clearing away effects of the hurricane when he needed to spend every possible minute at the factory. It had to be done, and he didn't want Amanda and Amy to have those reminders of a night that had terrified them. But he didn't see how he could tolerate another infraction of his masculinity such as he'd experienced earlier. He hadn't felt free to make a simple decision about where to put a few pieces of wood, and he was sure that Jack sensed it. He didn't want to go in the house, but he didn't want to sit out there fretting about it, either. After what she'd been through the night before, Amanda needed the comfort and assurance of him beside her. He got up slowly, knowing that he probably wouldn't be able to fool her; she had a special sense about him and could divine his moods as quickly as he could. He put the tools in the garage and entered the house through the front door, prolonging his solitude.

Amanda met him in the foyer, took his hand and walked him toward the kitchen. "Luke and Amy are playing Chinese checkers. I thought you might like a cold beer and a little quiet." She took a can from the refrigerator and handed it to him. "I know you needed to be at the factory today, and I'm not going to insult you by thanking you for what you did around here. What do you think we should do with that wood? A lot of people don't have central heating, and we don't need it."

Marcus stared at her, unwilling to believe what he'd heard. He leaned against the banister, hands in his pants' pockets.

"Run that past me again," he said. She rubbed her cheek with the palm of her hand, something he'd noticed she'd begun to do frequently.

"What?" she asked, squinting as though to emphasize her puzzlement.

"That part about the wood. I didn't get it."

Her frown deepened. "What will we do about that wood?" His intent gaze seemed to disarm her, but he couldn't help it. He had spent the better part of the day fuming because he'd thought he hadn't the right to decide what to do with the blasted wood, and now Amanda was demanding that he tell her how to dispose of it. He laughed. He didn't know why, but peals of it bubbled up in his chest and demanded release. He gave in to it, and let the catharsis begin. Her face bloomed in a smile that said his happiness was all she could want. *She's an open book,* he thought and couldn't laugh anymore; a pain around his heart wouldn't let him. He wanted to kiss her, but he'd told himself as he got in bed that morning that he was going to stop giving in to his feelings and leading her to expect what could never be. Her sparkling eyes tempted him. Damn the luck. He took her face in his palms, bent to her and rubbed her nose with his own.

"The wood," she repeated, though she smiled her pleasure at his gesture of tenderness.

"I'll put in a call to the pastor of that little storefront church over on Michael Jordan Avenue. He'll know what to do with it."

He admitted to himself that the feel of her fingers squeezing his hand made up for the misery that he'd forced on himself all day. Luke glanced up when they walked into the living room, and Marcus couldn't ignore the look of satisfaction on his brother's face. It was the same feeling that drifted through him right then. Marcus' wink brought a grin from Luke, and he pushed back the notion that what he did affected too many people. He shrugged, draped an arm across Amanda's shoulder and enjoyed the way she quickly snuggled to him. Marcus knew that Luke continued to observe them, though he didn't make it obvious and gave the impression of focusing his attention on Amy. And he also knew that when Luke was ready, he'd hand down his judgment on what he'd seen. Marcus smiled. Luke would pontificate about him and Amanda, but he knew where to stop.

"I was hoping to get some of my sister-in-law's buttermilk biscuits and apple pie, but if we don't eat soon, I'll have to leave."

"Today's Saturday," Marcus reminded him. "You've got until midnight." He mused over that for a bit, remembering when he hadn't wanted Luke to come to Amanda's home with him. He walked over to the card table at which Luke and Amy were playing checkers and looked down at his daughter.

"Who's winning?"

"Uncle Luke won't let me win, Daddy. He says I'm already too precodious." Marcus laughed. For a little while, he could be happy.

"You mean precocious." She looked at Luke for confirmation that he'd said that, and he nodded.

Luke helped Marcus set the table and put the food on it, and the four sat down to the meal.

"Do you eat like this every day?" Luke asked Marcus. "Believe me…" Luke must have taken his brother's glare as a warning not to meddle, because he changed both the topic and his demeanor.

"Can I have ice cream with my pie?" Amy asked.

"Is that what we're having?" Marcus asked her.

"Yes," Amy confirmed. "Lady said you wasn't too happy and you needed some apple pie." Marcus looked at his wife, his gaze piercing her. Why hadn't he met her before he'd soured on love and marriage?

Amanda finished her version of a sunset coloring the sky

above the Albemarle, put away her paints and washed her hands. The watercolor was a modest effort, but she hadn't painted for years and needed practice. With Marcus in Portsmouth and Amy away at her morning therapy sessions, she'd returned to her old hobby. She intended to give it to Robert's mother, whom she'd met briefly several times and had liked. She felt the need to talk with a mother, and she thought the painting would give her an opening with Barbara Whitfield. The Lamaze classes had taught her a lot, but she felt the need of more personal information about having a baby. She wanted to be friends with Myrna Culpepper, but Marcus hadn't encouraged it; Jack had been to their home twice, and each time he'd come alone. To her surprise, Robert's mother welcomed the chance for them to talk and said she could come over around noon.

They talked about Amanda's pregnancy and Barbara's experiences giving birth. Finally, Barbara said, "When you have your next one, you'll need to add on to this house or get a bigger one. I know you'd hate to give this up; it's beautiful, and you have such a big garden."

Amanda couldn't make herself tell the woman that she didn't expect to have another child. "You're right. I don't see how I could give it up." Barbara took a small package from her purse and handed it to Amanda.

"Honey, I didn't have time to look for anything for the baby, so I brought this for you. Soon as the baby's born, you get right into shape and start dazzling that hunk of yours. For some men, the late stages of pregnancy can put the seal of doom on romance, so child, you get busy." Amanda decided Barbara didn't need to know that her pregnancy hadn't cooled Marcus' libido.

"Get busy doing what?" She sat forward, intent on learning as much as she could that would keep Marcus with her. Several times recently, she'd seen something in him that told her it was possible.

"Well, I guess you already own the bedroom stuff—you know, the garters, sheer red bikini undies, lace nighties, that kind of thing. Make sure he sees them on you."

She must have noticed that she had Amanda's rapt attention, because she added, "Amanda, honey, sometime you have to be reckless. Bold. I once stuck a note on the front door, and told Jeff to follow the instructions until he found me. As soon as he'd obeyed one sign, he had to follow another one. You wouldn't believe what I put him through, including a shower and a martini. I'd put a cold pitcher of that on a stool beside the bathtub. A hot shower followed by a couple of those had him in just the right mood when he found me, lolling on our bed in a tiger striped, sheer teddy. He went nuts." And as if she sensed that her lecture had been sorely needed, she grinned and said, "Go for broke, girl. You may even embarrass yourself a little, but I'm here to tell you, you'll get what you want."

Amanda mused over the woman's words long after she'd left. She didn't think she had enough self-confidence with Marcus to pull a trick such as Barbara had, but if he was susceptible to her when she looked and felt like a baby elephant, well…it was worth a try. She wasn't a femme fatale, and she knew him well enough to realize that if she waved sex at him, he'd take it and she wouldn't have gained an inch with him. Anyway, she figured there was something about her that Marcus liked, and she intended to find out what that was and exploit it to the hilt. Where there was a will, there was a way, Aunt Meredith had always said. She rested her hands on her hips.

"I'm married to him, and I'm going to stay that way."

Marcus was not of the same mind. She'd packed a lunch for him that morning, and he'd been tempted to leave it right there on the table; husbands carried their lunch to work. But if he hadn't brought it with him, he would have hurt her, and he didn't want to do that. He tightened the metal string on a console piano, and could have considered the job finished, if he'd had a replacement pedal. But he'd have to order that. He threw his hands up in disgust and started to his office just as the telephone rang.

"Hickson."

"Luke. Can you spare time for lunch?"

"Yeah. Come on over here. Amanda fixed my lunch and, from the look of it, she expected you to join me."

They finished the elaborate lunch and Marcus was tempted to ask his brother why he hadn't commented on Amanda's gesture. He'd almost begun the question when it occurred to him that Luke didn't consider it worthy of mention; a lot of wives packed a lunch for their husbands. He used his napkin to wipe a tiny shrimp off his desk.

"What did you find out about that teacher?" Luke leaned back in his chair. Pensive, Marcus thought.

"Nothing solid. The word at the precinct is that Pearce, Sr., was caught collecting his due from a woman who'd just sold him her favors, and one of his bodyguards, a Joe Elms, took the rap. Swore he was the one in the backseat with that woman. After that, Pearce, Sr., stopped trying to break up his son's affair with Joe's sister. No telling what would have happened if Pearce, Jr., hadn't gotten killed. I don't know whether this Elms woman is the same as that teacher at Amanda's school, though from the information I could get, I suspect she is. But like I said, no hard facts."

"That's plenty."

"Maybe. When is Amanda due? Oh, yes. I remember she said the seventh of this month. Are you ready for it?" Marcus felt a chill sink into his pores.

"Ready? I can't say that I'll ever be ready." He drew a deep breath and continued, though he would have welcomed a different topic. "I've thought of little else for days. I'm worried about her chances of getting through it safely with a healthy baby. She isn't young, and she hasn't had an easy pregnancy."

"How old is she?"

"She's four years my senior, and that's stretching it for a first birth." Luke's long whistle was not reassuring.

"I'd hate to think she went through all this and… Look. I'll let you know when I take her to the hospital." Luke strummed the desk with his fingers, and Marcus was aware that he formulated his thoughts with care.

"I suppose you realize how important this is to you. You're not going to come out of this relationship unscathed, Marcus. Amanda means a lot to me, and I know she means so much more to you. She's the sister I never had, and I care about her. I'm going to tell you right now that I'll always think of her as my sister-in-law. I can't tell you what to do, but I hope you'll be careful of every move you make from now on." Marcus emptied the refuse from their meal into the garbage receptacle and got two cans of beer from the small refrigerator on the shelf above his desk. He popped his own can.

"No contest. Tell me about it!"

Marcus had wanted to get home before dark, because Amy had reacted nervously to darkness ever since the hurricane. But when he finally left the shop, frustrated because he didn't have what he needed to repair the one instrument that could put him in the black, he had no desire to go home. He drove toward the interstate and stopped. He couldn't walk into that house looking like the man he knew he was—competent, successful, a man with a golden future—because the day he'd just gone through made him doubt all of that.

He started the motor, glanced up and saw that the car sat across from Shakespeare's Tavern. He cut the motor, sat there and struggled with his conscience. He didn't want a drink, because he didn't drink so close to the time he had to drive. But he didn't want to go home with his raw insides exposed, and he'd had as much of Luke's wise counsel as he could handle in any one day. He walked in. If any of those would-be actors past their prime staggered up on the stage and began reading sonnets between slugs of draft, he'd take that as his cue to move on.

"What'll it be, sir?" Neither her speech nor her manners were that of any cocktail waitress he'd ever seen. He leaned back in the corner of the booth and swept her with an impersonal glance.

"Tonic without the gin. No ice, please." She put the pencil behind her ear and looked steadily at him.

"Anything else?" He stared back at her.

"Yeah. A double shot of privacy."

"In *this* place?" She shrugged, walked off and was back in minutes with a glass of tonic and a napkin.

"Why don't you go home? You look like the type of guy who'd have a nice, understanding wife, and here you are trying to get into trouble." He tried to suppress the laughter that began to rumble in his chest, but it surfaced and he gave rein to it.

"What's so amusing? If you told me you didn't have a wife, I wouldn't believe you." Marcus didn't want to invite the woman's conversation nor her continued presence.

"You don't want to know" was his cryptic reply.

She raised an eyebrow and handed him the bill. "When you've been hurting badly enough and long enough, you'll talk, and when that time comes, anybody will do," she told him, as one who'd had the experience.

Somebody went to the jukebox and spent a quarter on John Berry's "Your Love Amazes Me," and Marcus' thoughts went to Amanda. She loved him. He couldn't count the women who had wanted him, but he knew with certainty that, other than his mother, Amanda was the only woman who had loved him. And until she loved him, he'd thought that several women had. But he had no doubt now that he'd never before known a woman's love. The waitress returned with another bottle of tonic and suggested again that he ought to consider going home.

"I won't ask why you care, because I'm not sure you do. Who are you and what are you up to? You're not a waitress."

"Right. I'm gathering material for a study of social behavior. I'm a university professor. If you want to talk, I get off in two hours."

"What about the advice you gave me a few minutes ago?"

"You didn't take it; my conscience is clear." His gaze took in her flawless brown skin, long, thick lashes, almond-shaped eyes and willowy body. Seven months ago, she'd have been just his type, but that was before he met Amanda, before he'd known what it was to have a woman give herself to him. Totally. Without artifice. With love. With no thought of anything but how he made her feel. The image of Amanda in a shimmering ecstasy the morning he'd almost consummated their marriage burned in his memory. Yes. He might have been susceptible before that, and before the gentle squeeze of a woman's fingers could make him forget his cares, if only for a while.

He needed physical release, needed it badly, but not with this stranger. He hadn't resorted to that in the darkest days of his marriage to Helena. He might wake up bankrupt, but he didn't expect ever to look in a mirror and see an adulterer. He picked up the bill.

"Take your own advice and go home. That's where I'm going."

Amanda watched from the living room window as Marcus parked the car, stepped out of it and looked up at the starry, moonlit sky. He'd said he'd be home before dark, and she'd been worried for his safety. A sensation of relief washed over her as he strode up the walkway. She flicked on the porch light and opened the door before he knocked.

"I hope today was better than yesterday," she told him and brushed a kiss over his cheek. Marcus stopped and looked down at her. She couldn't fathom his expression and decided it best to let him set the mood. He didn't move, and she began to squirm under the impact of his fiery gaze.

"Are you all right?" she asked after she'd convinced herself that he wasn't.

"I am now. I'm fine. Nothing new with you, I see." She let the expression on her face tell him she knew he was covering his true feelings, but she didn't speak the knowing words that would have meant a violation of his privacy. Instead, she smiled the welcome that she truly felt. He glanced down at her stomach and gave her a rueful look.

"You're one terrific gal, Amanda." She accepted his pinch on her nose as the gesture of affection he'd meant it to be, took his hand and started walking them to the kitchen.

"Got anything to eat? Any pie, I mean." Amanda thought her heart would burst with joy when he sat down, put his hands behind his head and grinned at her. He didn't have to tell her where he'd been during the four hours since he left the office. It didn't matter. She knew that he'd faced temptation, put it behind him and come home to her. And he was proud that he'd done it.

Chapter 9

Amanda sighed with relief; it was her last Lamaze class. During the classes Marcus touched her, coached, teased and stroked her, creating such a level of intimacy that she almost forgot they were surrounded by other people. But even before they reached home, he managed to erect what seemed like a barrier between them. He was gentle and thoughtful, waiting until she was ready for bed so that he could help her lie down. Propping up her feet to relieve the swelling. Rubbing her back and putting pillows beneath it so that she could rest. And he did it all with seeming dispassion. Knowing that his caring didn't mean what she wanted it to was becoming unbearable. She'd heard that when a woman was pregnant, her hormones played tricks with her emotions. Maybe once the baby came, she'd stop loving him.

The instructor got Amanda's wavering attention when she began to tell the men about delivery procedures. That, she told them, was because babies sometimes refused to wait until the mother was safely in the hospital.

Alarmed, Amanda asked Marcus, "What would you do if the baby started to arrive at home?"

"Push it back, of course," he told her with dry amusement.

* * *

The lecture alerted Marcus to the need for precaution. He had not forgotten that Amanda would be forty years old in a few weeks and was well past the ages considered safe for a first birth. Preparing himself for any emergency, he arranged for Amy to stay with Jack and Myrna Culpepper when the time came for Amanda's confinement. And he decided to bring a few small stringed instruments home and work there for the two weeks prior to her delivery date. He also made a note to have secure locks installed on the doors and lower windows of Amanda's house. The lutes, violins and violas that he planned to bring home were worth well over a million dollars.

Marcus locked the stringed instruments in the closet of his room and stored the case of tools beneath his desk. He looked lingeringly at the leather-lined alligator tool case, a remnant of his more prosperous days. Days before Amy's accident and the financial beating he'd taken to save her life and make her whole again. He resented his present situation—living in a home that wasn't his, in a marriage that was a business contract because he'd bonded himself to a woman. A bartered husband. He spat out a bitter curse. But even as it wore on him, he admitted that it must have been divine providence that had brought Amanda and him together. Both had been desperate and each had been able to solve the other's problem. He walked down the stairs thinking that he hadn't made the last two months since their gut-searing intimacy easy ones for her. He'd been nice, but he had maintained his distance, a distance that he neither felt nor wanted. If she only knew what it cost him, he would be lost. What was it like for her, he wondered, being with him constantly while he treated her like a sister after having taken her to bed and given her a glimpse of how he could make her feel? He wasn't proud of himself, but he wasn't going to be caught in a trap of his own making, either.

* * *

He found her in the dining room leaning against a hutch. Immediately anxious, he moved to her and wrapped his arm around her shoulder. "You okay?"

Her smile was a weak effort. "I feel all right. I just get tired so quickly." He led her to a chair and was about to seat her when he noticed the rapid movement of the shirt she wore over her maternity skirt.

"This kid really gives you a beating, doesn't he?"

She took his hand and placed it on her belly. "Do you think it's a boy?" She watched his face as he marveled at the action beneath his hand.

Grinning, he bent down and said, "Look, fellow, give your mother a break, will you? She's tired." The kicking stopped immediately, and Amanda laughed. He must have had a comical expression on his face. All right, so Steve Martin had nothing on him.

Eventually, he went to the kitchen and returned with a beer for himself and a glass of cold mint tea for her. Sitting beside her chair on an upholstered bench, he voiced a thought that had been on his mind almost since he'd met her. "This hasn't been an easy pregnancy; in fact, from my experience, I'd say it's been difficult. But I have never heard you complain about it or show impatience. You didn't ask for it and you didn't want it, but you've accommodated to it and accepted it with all its pain and problems. Explain that to me."

There he goes again, she thought, *demanding of me what he refuses to give of himself.* She measured her words carefully. "My parents, grandparents and Aunt Meredith left me wealthy. I have a good job that I struggled for, but that's all I have. I don't even have the memory of parental love; Mother and Dad basically took care of me, but they were too busy loving each other to pay more than passing attention to me. I only had Aunt Meredith.

"If I had died before this past April, all of my money and property would have gone to the state. I don't wear designer clothes or go to fancy places, so what good is the money? Now, I will have a child. I don't let myself remember *why,* only that I will and that then I will have someone who loves and accepts me and whom I can love. I know I'm too old to start having children. If I don't make it through delivery, I'm leaving everything to you and Amy. If the baby lives, I know you'll take good care of it for me. You wonder why I never complain. It does no good, Marcus. You change what you can and, what you can't change, you accept. Any other course leads to bitterness and misery. Sometimes to insanity."

Her words reached a sensitive chord deep inside of him. There had been times when he could have used that philosophy; perhaps he still could. The trick, he supposed, was knowing when to stop pushing. He was glad that he'd worked hard and sacrificed for his child, had shoved his pride aside and given Amy a chance to be whole again; and he was glad for Amanda. He could barely tolerate his role in their agreement, and now, she offered him even more. How could he accept it?

He took her hand. "You don't owe me anything. Don't feel that you have to make me your heir."

As though thoroughly miffed, she snatched her hand out of his. "Marcus, I'm not trying to pay you *anything!* You can explain it to yourself any way you like, but as far as I'm concerned, you and Amy are my family. You are closer to me and mean more to me than anyone else on this earth." *Ever has meant to me,* she might have added. Recklessly, she accused him. "To you, this is just an inconvenient, one-year arrangement, but to me..." She slapped her hand over her mouth, chagrined at what she had almost revealed, and attempted to get up.

He reached out to help her and, to his horror, his fingers grazed her breast, sending shivers through him like piercing arrows. Amanda gasped, and he started to apologize, but swallowed it when he saw the arousing effect that his touch had on her.

He had to get a hold of himself. She was barely three weeks from delivery, and he was on fire for her. The months of hunger, of suppressing his raging need for her had taken its toll. And she was no help. Her eyes locked with his and, like a puppet moving in slow motion, she licked her bottom lip and leaned toward him as if hypnotized.

"Amanda!" It was a deep guttural sound. "Don't! I...sweetheart, don't touch me." She recoiled. His words wounded her, and she let him see it. When he reached for her, she tried to elude his touch, but he wouldn't have it, stood and clasped her in his arms. "I'm trying to remember that you're almost ready to deliver. Can't you see that I want you? I'm...I need all of the help right now that you can give me. This is the damndest situation, Amanda. I promised you that I wouldn't touch you again, and I haven't. Now is certainly not the time for me to get weak." He stroked her cheek until she looked up at him.

"How about a hug for a guy who's just had his tail singed?" She laughed and they had weathered another storm.

The next morning, Marcus began to clear the breakfast table, and Amanda stopped him. "Aren't you going to work today? I can do that."

"I'm going to be working at home for a while. I want to be here in case you need me."

"Are you sure you can afford to be away from the shop? Ellen is here from noon till two, and I've taught Amy how to dial."

"What can Amy dial?"

"She knows your number in Portsmouth and how to call Luke, the doctor, police, ambulance, fire department, the Culpeppers and Robert."

Marcus stared at his wife. "Well, I'll be damned. You aren't kidding me, are you? That's wonderful, Amanda, but I've brought some instruments home with me, and I plan to work on them here. The shop's covered, and I'll be in touch with my men there as often as necessary. I appreciate what you've done with Amy. It's amazing how she's developed with your care. I wouldn't have had the time. I—"

She interrupted him. "Please don't thank me, Marcus, and there's no need to be defensive. You're needed at your factory, and I know it. Yet you're here because you believe I need you. It may be three weeks. You can't be away that long."

"I can, and I will," he replied doggedly. He avoided looking at her when he told her, "Actually, I don't think you've got three weeks. You're much lower than you were a couple of days ago and, if I remember right, that means you're due pretty soon."

"How can you...? Oh, I forget sometimes that you've been through this before."

"Yeah. I have." He didn't try to hide the bitterness that laced his speech. "But I mostly watched it from a distance. Helena moved into another room as soon as her pregnancy was confirmed and I'd talked her out of eliminating it. She didn't let me experience the changes with her. I wasn't allowed to feel it moving around, and I had no idea what it was like until you let me feel what was happening with you. I wanted to touch so badly when I'd see that rapid movement under Helena's clothes during the late stages of the pregnancy. She didn't take Lamaze classes and didn't tell me what to expect. I nearly panicked when her water broke. Amanda, she didn't even take the vitamins that the doctor prescribed for her. She didn't want it and didn't care what happened to it. That was a horrible time in my life, but in spite of Helena's negligence, Amy arrived perfectly healthy. You know, I've been so much more involved with your pregnancy than with hers. Truth is, I've actually enjoyed your pregnancy, following the stages that you've gone through."

He was thoughtful. Silent. She was right to be concerned about his absence from the factory. These days were crucial ones for his business. He couldn't spare the time, but he wouldn't risk her having to deliver alone, either. At her age, she was in double jeopardy. He hung a skillet on an overhead pot rack beside the stove, dried his hands on the back of his skintight jeans and turned toward the table to reach for the place mats.

His hand stilled. If she had been in tears, if she had worn a look of sympathy or compassion or even if she had seemed disgusted, he would have understood. But what he saw on Amanda's face was rage bordering on hatred. Her expression stunned him. He wouldn't have thought her capable of it. He walked over and laid a hand on her shoulder. "What is it? Why are you so angry?"

She knocked his beloved hand away. She had never hated anyone, not even Pearce Lamont, who had taken her affection and her innocence, considered them of meagre value and laughed at her stupidity for throwing them away on him. But at that moment, she hated Helena. Looking off into the distance and almost as if she were alone, she opened her mouth and betrayed herself.

"She had everything. You loved her. You wanted her. You needed her. *She had you!* And she had your child inside of her. She bore a child that you wanted and whom you loved. What kind of a human being is she? I would give anything, *anything,* if it was me that you love. If it were your child inside of me, I would welcome the pain of delivering it. And Amy. How could she not love that wonderful little girl? I love her as if I had given birth to her, but she won't ever be mine. Just like you won't ever be mine. I have never hated anybody, but I could hate that woman!"

Nearly shattered by the power of her quiet declaration, Marcus let the back of her chair take his weight, as his fingers gripped her shoulder. He knew that she'd begun to care for him, that she loved him, but he hadn't counted on the depth of it. The power of it. Hadn't counted on her loving him at all. And she loved him; he had no doubt of it. There couldn't be any other explanation for her words and for the toneless despair with which she had uttered them.

"Amanda. Oh, Amanda, I'm sorry. I care for you. I feel something special for you. You're not like any other woman I've ever known. But I won't open myself to that pain again. I can't. I didn't want to hurt you, but now I know that I'm going to do just that." *Heaven help me, but it's unavoidable! And you're not going to get out of this with your own heart unscathed,* a niggling voice informed him.

Amanda patted the hand that rested on her left shoulder. "You've nothing to be sorry for. You haven't promised me anything, and you haven't let me forget that we part on April eleventh. You've been honest and a good friend, and I'll always cherish these days that I've had with you and Amy."

He knew she was hurting and was appalled when she covered it with flippancy. "No problem, actually, so long as you give me a good reference to the next man I ask to marry me." Her voice broke on the weak attempt at humor.

Horrified, he gave her a gentle shake. "For goodness' sake, Amanda, don't get morbid. There's nothing here to poke fun at." *Recommend her to another man?* He stalked out of the kitchen and up to his room where he found his work and the emotional oblivion that it offered. *Recommend her to another man!* He swore bitterly. What had he ever done to deserve the constant screwing he got from life?

Amanda stood on her upstairs porch watching the turbulent sky. The ominous black clouds with their red and purple crowns were at once both threatening and exciting, and they gave her an eerie feeling. She sensed that they cradled a storm, a violent one. The evening had turned cold, too cold for early November, with strong winds whipping off the Albemarle. Not even the late afternoon sun had taken the sharp nip from the air. Marcus had joined her and Ellen that afternoon when they treated Amy's class to a cookout on the back patio in celebration of the little girl's fifth birthday. The children had been overjoyed, frolicking and playing pranks as they roasted hot dogs and marshmallows. She had seen the happiness and the incredulity on Marcus' face as he'd watched Amy playing with the other children without giving a thought to the strength of her legs. His nightmare was slowly ending, but she knew he would bear the scars of it indefinitely. What would he be like if he had his life in order and if he were at peace? she had wondered, as she watched a breathtaking smile illumine his handsome face. Amy had just banished Tommy Culpepper from a game, claiming that he'd cheated, and her doting father obviously approved of her principles. Amanda had rarely seen him so completely relaxed.

Too bad. If the time ever came when Marcus' world was the way he wanted it, she would no longer be a part of his life. Shivering as much from heartache as from the cold, she turned to go inside, entering through Amy's room. Marcus sat on the edge of Amy's bed, a storybook resting on his knee, watching his daughter's peaceful slumber. She closed the door softly, hoping to avoid disturbing him.

Her heart lurched at the thought that he might someday gaze with such love, such tenderness upon her own child. But she was a realist; she'd had to be. Life had taught her the folly of letting herself dream impossible dreams and indulge in fanciful notions, though tonight, for some reason, she seemed unable to do otherwise. She took a deep breath and began to tiptoe past them, wanting Marcus to have his trouble-free moments. He glanced up in time to see the startled expression that crossed her face.

He was immediately beside her, his left arm supporting her back. "What is it? Did you have a pain?"

With an attempt at humor, she made a comical face at him. "I'm not sure, but I think I had a cramp."

"You think it could be the beginning of labor? What did it feel like?" His tender solicitousness warmed her and made her feel protected and cared for.

She wasn't thinking about labor, but about the meaning of his facial expression. He cared deeply. She knew it, even if he didn't. *And so what!* A small inner voice cautioned her.

"What did it feel like?" he persisted.

"Like my monthly cramps used to feel. But it couldn't be the baby. I'm not due for another week."

His arm still around her, he guided her into her bedroom.

"Maybe this kid is impatient to see what's going on in the world," he joked. Then he glanced at his watch. "Let me know if it happens again. I'll be right back."

Marcus didn't want to awaken Amy from a deep sleep to take her to the Culpeppers' home, and he knew that she'd be frightened if she saw Amanda in pain. After telephoning Ellen and getting the response that he expected, he phoned Amanda's obstetrician, Dr. Lillian McCullen.

"I think I'd better get ready," she told him when he got back to her. "I just had a real pain." He went to her closet to look for a sweater and coat, and her water broke.

"Oh, my God." He turned swiftly. She covered her face in embarrassment, but he ignored it and led her to the bathroom.

"Wash up and dry off while I get you a change of clothes." He kept his voice low and soothing and was careful to speak with gentle authority. She needed neither excitement nor indecision. He helped her to dress.

"What about Amy?"

Marcus couldn't restrain a grin; Amanda was a born mother. "Ellen's coming over," he said. Then he telephoned Luke.

But Amanda seemed reluctant to leave home. It was almost as if, with the event now imminent, she wanted to postpone it. "It's too early," she protested.

"No it's not. I phoned the doctor, and she told me to bring you in." They heard the front door close as he took her bag and her arm and guided her down the stairs. "Ellen's here. Let's go." He got her into the car and himself behind the wheel seconds before the sky seemed to open, adding torrents of rain to the blustering, swirling wind.

Marcus remained with Amanda throughout her long and difficult labor. He coached her, teased her and told her jokes and, in the end, he pulled her through.

"Come on, baby, take a deep breath and push. You can do it."

She clung to his hand as pains racked her tired body, her nails scoring his flesh.

"I'm too tired to push. I want to go to sleep." He knew she was tired. Another ten minutes of this and he'd tell the doctor to put her to sleep and take the baby. He hated seeing her suffer that way.

"One more time. The head is visible now. Bear down, honey. One more time," he cooed, "and it will be over." He kept his voice low and soothing, watching anxiously as she took a deep breath to gather her strength and do as he asked. For the first time, she screamed.

Minutes later, Marcus placed a baby boy in Amanda's arms. "You have a healthy son." Overcome with emotion and humbled by the experience, he could barely say the words. And he felt cheated. Cheated because he hadn't been allowed that experience with Amy. And cheated because he'd gone through what seemed like hell with Amanda, and the child wasn't even his. He couldn't boast. He couldn't preen. He could take no pride in the incredible miracle that he had witnessed and, in the end, helped to make happen.

He leaned over and kissed her lightly on the lips. "I'm going out for a bit. I'll be back shortly."

She tugged at his hand. "Thanks. I'm not sure I'd have gotten through it without you." She smiled, and her face beamed with happiness.

Marcus caressed her jaw. "Sure you would have," he joked, his voice gruff and unsteady. "Mother Nature has a way of insisting that you follow through in matters like this. Have you decided on a name?"

Amanda lowered her eyes to the child in her arms before looking up at Marcus, her face glowing with pride. "His name is Marc Stuart Hickson." He stared at her, speechless, not believing what he'd heard.

"If that's not all right with you, then it's Stuart Marc Hickson, but that's the only compromise I'm prepared to make." Her tone told him there was absolutely no point in objecting.

He found his voice. "How do you spell the first name?"

She stuck her chin out and gave him a level look. "M-A-R-C."

Marcus laughed aloud. He couldn't help it. Amanda was the sweetest person in the world until somebody threw her a gauntlet that she figured she didn't deserve. Then, she was ready for battle.

"Marc Stuart is fine with me. Just checking to make certain you'd spelled it right. I'm sure Luke will be pleased." He felt like George Foreman's punching bag, but he covered it with a smile and a wink as he left her. Outside in the waiting room, he slumped in the nearest chair, threw his head against the backrest and tried to come to terms with what he'd felt and what he was feeling right then.

What on earth had happened in there? He couldn't shake the feeling that he'd helped Amanda deliver his own son, though he knew very well that he hadn't. Why did he feel that the child should have been his? And the name she'd given him. She had no way of knowing that had been his father's name and the name of the last four generations of his paternal grandfathers. His own father had called a halt to it, saying it was too much to name a child Marc Stuart Hickson VI. So his mother had divided the name between him and his brother Luke Stuart. She had chosen Marcus for him when his father rejected the name, Marc. And now there was another Marc Stuart Hickson. One who belonged to a different bloodline.

Tired and emotionally drained, Marcus felt that he needed to go home and tell Amy about the baby, prepare her for a change in her world. And he needed some strong coffee, a shave and a shower. He looked at his watch. It was ten o'clock in the morning. Good heavens! Amanda had had twelve hours of hard labor. He pulled himself up and stretched luxuriously in an effort to get his system back in working order. Then he saw Luke walking toward him. Until then, he hadn't known that what he needed was to see his brother, an empathetic, but dispassionate ear. They embraced warmly.

"I see you've taken a beating. How is she?" How typical of Luke to read his feelings, Marcus thought.

"She's fine, but she had a really rough time. She's got a boy, and she's named him Marc Stuart Hickson."

"She named him *what?*"

Marcus laughed. It wasn't often that he got to see Luke flabbergasted. "That was my reaction. How did she know your middle name is Stuart?"

"I gave her my card. You don't mind her giving the boy that name?"

"A lot of good it would do if I did mind. She offered Stuart Marc as the only compromise she was prepared to make. So I thought, what the hell. She wants to honor you and me both, and well…heck, I kind of like it. I was astonished though, because she doesn't know the history of that name." He looked down at Luke's hand and joked, "You brought me flowers?"

Luke feigned offense. "You flatter yourself. Do you think I can see Amanda now?"

"Yeah." Marcus walked with Luke back to Amanda's room. He refused to deal with his feelings, with his enormous pride in Amanda and, yes, in Marc Stuart. She looked anxiously toward the door as they walked in, and it occurred to him that she might feel more vulnerable now that she had her child. He warned himself to tread softly when he remembered that Helena had experienced severe depression after Amy's birth. Somehow he doubted that would happen to Amanda, but he'd be careful with her nevertheless.

Amanda hadn't slept. But it wasn't the wonder of her son that had kept her awake, but thoughts of Marcus and what he'd done. How he had treated her from the moment her labor had begun until he'd handed her baby to her.

"Luke." She stretched out both arms to him. "I'm so glad that you came. Did you get a look at my baby?"

Luke hugged her. "Not yet, but I will." He handed her a dozen white roses. "If I had known that you were going to name my nephew for me, I would have brought you orchids." He felt Marcus stiffen beside him, but paid no heed. "You've honored me, Amanda."

Unreasonably annoyed, Marcus huffed. "You've been holding her long enough, Luke. She's tired."

"Right," he needled. "And I'm increasing her fatigue by holding her."

Amanda looked at the two of them—two stunningly handsome, virile men: tall, lean and with commanding presence. She withheld the questions—what had their parents been like? Why hadn't Luke remarried? Were they going to take her child into their hearts? She turned to face Marcus and caught him off guard. Their eyes locked and they might as well have been alone.

Luke glanced from one to the other. Then he backed toward the door, knowing that they wouldn't miss him. "My God!" he muttered to himself, "Marcus loves that woman, and he's too stubborn, too big a fool to acknowledge it." When he opened the door, the silence was broken and, with it, the electricity that had sparked between them.

Amanda asked Marcus to call Albemarle Kiddies Roost and have them deliver the bassinet she'd chosen. "Put it in my room, please."

"You made a nursery, and that's where the bassinet belongs," he corrected her.

Amanda raised up on her right elbow. "Marcus, the baby is going to stay in my room in the bassinet that I selected. Don't you dare disturb Amy."

She was in for a battle, and Luke knew it. He walked closer to them. "What's the problem?"

Marcus denied that there was a problem, insisting that Amy was using the baby's room and that he was going to move her into his room.

Amanda glared at him, sparks of fury darting from her eyes. He was certain that she had never been so angry with him, not even the night when she threw her tea on him.

"Marcus, if you disturb Amy, I will never forgive you. *Never!* I love her every bit as much as I do the child that I bore this morning. Her well-being comes before yours or mine. And if you make any changes in her life because of this baby, you'll have me to deal with. As long as she's in my home, she's mine to care for, and I won't make a difference between the children, nor will I allow you to do it. Luke, if he won't take care of that bassinet, will you do it? Never mind, I can do it myself."

Marcus turned to Luke. "This is amazing. Do you know this is the first real fight we've ever had? She's mad at me, and I haven't done a thing."

"Will miracles never cease?" Amanda asked, loading her voice with as much sarcasm as Marcus had ever heard her use.

Luke laughed. "What a pair you are. A minute before, the electricity crackling between you was almost strong enough to cause a power outage. And now, you're fighting over how much you love Amy.

"What color is the bassinet?" he asked Amanda.

"White."

Marcus looked at his brother, aware that his eyes were cool and forbidding. "I'll take care of it, and I'll put it wherever she wants it." His tone said, *back off!* He looked at his mutinous wife and grinned. "I stand corrected. I know you love Amy. *Amy!* I've got to get home and explain all of this to her. I'll be back after I've had my caffeine fix and gotten cleaned up."

Luke grinned, not caring that he aggravated his brother. Marcus not only thought of Amanda's house as his home, he referred to it as such. And in spite of the financial cloud hovering over the factory, Marcus was happier than he'd seen him in years. Not that he'd ever admit it. Luke kept his thoughts to himself.

* * *

Amanda sat in a Shaker rocking chair nursing two-week-old Marc. Attentive, Amy leaned against her, small hands cupping her chin, and both elbows resting firmly on Amanda's right thigh. She looked down at the little girl, who had welcomed little Marc into her life and happily allowed him place as the center of attention. She loved him and never wanted to be away from him. Amanda placed her right arm around Amy, leaned over and kissed her cheek. The child snuggled closer and sighed in contentment.

"Lady, will I have a baby when I grow up?"

Amanda wasn't certain that she could answer that correctly. She went with her instincts. "When you get married, you and your husband will decide about your family. You will be a wonderful mother." Amy giggled and reached out to touch Marc on his tiny hand. Amanda encouraged her to touch him, but to do so gently.

"I take good care of Peter," she said of her little stuffed rabbit, "just like you take care of me and Marc." She thought for a minute. "And Daddy, too. Daddy takes care of all of us, doesn't he, Lady?"

Amanda hugged her. "Yes he does, darling. Daddy is a wonderful man, and that makes you a lucky little girl." She hadn't really stretched the truth, she told herself. After all, he wasn't the one spending the money; that wasn't in their contract. But he was there for them, a strength that they needed.

Thinking himself unseen, Marcus stood in the doorway leaning against the doorjamb watching a scene that warmed and fascinated him. It was also a sight that shook him to his very core. The tranquility. The love flowing among them. Here was indisputable evidence that his first marriage had been a sham. They hadn't been a family. Just three individuals needing much more than they received. Amy and Amanda loved each other without reservation just as he had known they would. How was he going to take Amy away without breaking her heart? And did he even want to?

He had wondered why Amy wasn't jealous of Marc, and now he realized that Marc hadn't taken Amy's place in Amanda's life.

He was merely an addition, another joy to her, and Amy understood it. He watched his namesake pulling on his wife's nipple and felt a pang of envy before turning quickly away to avoid discovery. What had he done to himself? He could barely look at Amanda without wanting her, a craving that was rapidly exceeding want and becoming need. A genuine marriage was out of the question, and he knew that she wanted no less. He didn't consider marriage a logical arrangement. You gave another individual control over your emotional well-being and exposed yourself to whatever treachery and deceit she cared to lay on you. And then you paid for it with your sweat and blood. With heartache and despair. He didn't want any part of it. He raced down the stairs on his way to no place, trying to escape what his heart needed and his body demanded.

Amanda saw him there, but pretended that she didn't. She knew that he often stealthily watched her nurse Marc. And she knew, too, that her husband avoided her son. Maybe he didn't want to become attached to the baby. She tried not to think of it, but she did, and it hurt.

The days grew cooler, and most of the trees were bare. It would soon be Thanksgiving Day, Amanda remembered, and this year, she would be a part of a family. Amy barreled noisily down the stairs and ran into the kitchen. Neither Marcus nor Amanda cared how much noise she made running in the house; the sound of Amy running was music to both of them. She found her place at the breakfast table and asked her father, "Daddy, why does the man sit in the garden? Is he a nice man, Daddy?"

Marcus glanced at Amy and asked her indulgently, "What man, sweetheart?" Amy's imagination was boundless, he thought, with some pride.

"The man that's in the garden. He's there a lot. I see him out of my window." Decidedly alert now and tense, Marcus got up as casually as he could and walked out on the back porch. A man sat on the stone bench beneath the trellis, casually, as though he belonged there. Amanda stilled his hand as he reached for the knob of the screen door.

"Are you sure it's safe to go out there?" Marcus was already moving away from her. "But he might be armed, Marcus. Please be careful."

He nodded. "Not to worry. He may be armed but, with that potbelly, he's out of shape. I'm not." He walked rapidly toward the rear of the garden, sizing the man up as he approached him.

"Did you lose something here, buddy?" he asked, his aggressive stance belying the innocuous words. "Who are you and what do you want?"

The man raised his hand to deflect the sunlight from his face. "Don't get antsy, mister. I'm not hurting anybody. Just doing my job."

Marcus observed the man through narrowed eyes. "And what, precisely, is your job?"

The man sighed deeply, rising slowly as he did so. "I'm a private investigator for K. T. Trayhill Construction. I'm no threat, Mr. Hickson."

Marcus bristled. "Well, well. Your company nearly killed my daughter. Take a hike. This is private property. If I find you here again upsetting my family, I'll be less reasonable, believe me." It pleased Marcus to know that the company was desperate for information that would exonerate it. Well, it didn't have a case. Watching the man walk off, he thought, *Just another brother trying to make it,* and breathed deeply of the fresh morning air. He looked around at the nearly bare trees on either side of them and facing the house, comparing what he saw with the same midsummer scene, and wondered if Amanda realized how susceptible to prowlers she had been. Perhaps he gave her something, after all. He could protect her.

* * *

The Saturday morning before Thanksgiving, on Marcus' birthday, Amanda and Ellen took the children into town to buy gifts for him. Bouncing along on her first shopping expedition, Amy treated it as a grand adventure. Both women were overjoyed when she finally chose a red collared T-shirt for her daddy. It was Amy's day. At Caution's Coffee Bean, where they went for hamburgers and soda, the owners treated her to a wide sampling of ice cream flavors and gave her some lemon lollipops.

"This kid attracts people like a magnet," Ellen whispered to Amanda, as they watched Amy get the attention of practically every person in the restaurant within minutes of their arrival. When she saw that a man at a nearby table was watching her, Amy waved at him and said, "Hi." And when they were leaving, she walked over and told him goodbye. Amanda thought he looked familiar, though she couldn't recall where she might have seen him.

Sam was sweeping the street nearby when they stepped outside the café, and Amanda introduced Ellen and the children to him.

Amy looked up at the weather-beaten old man. "Are you tired?"

His smile made his old eyes twinkle. "I guess I am, but not from work. Just mostly from age." Amy giggled exuberantly and handed him one of her lollipops. "I'll see you next time Lady brings me," she told him, as they left. Amanda thought she saw pure joy shining in his old eyes.

Marc slept in his bassinet, and Amanda sat with Amy in the child's room where they wrapped Marcus' birthday gifts. One tag read, *Happy birthday, Daddy. Love, Amy.* A second tag read *For Marcus. Happy Birthday. Amanda.* And there she sat, chewing the pencil as she struggled with the tag for Marc's gift. No matter what she put on it, there would be questions. If she put the word *daddy* on it, Marcus might ask why she'd done it. If she didn't, how would she explain it to Amy? She didn't even know what Marcus had told Amy about the baby, and she hadn't told the child anything. She wrapped the box in iridescent green paper with gold ribbon and took the coward's way out. She'd tell him who it was from when she handed it to him. She put on a yellow silk caftan and started down the stairs with Amy. To her horror, the door opened at exactly the same time as she realized Marcus might guess what she'd planned when he saw she'd dressed Amy to match—in a yellow dress with a big yellow bow in her hair. And it was too late to change it, for the two brothers walked into the foyer.

Marcus looked up, saw them standing there and was about to ask her the meaning of it when Amy, racing down the stairs, reached him with outstretched arms.

"Daddy! Daddy! Happy Birthday, Daddy! Marc and me went shopping with Lady for your presents. I got you—"

Luke cut her off. "Honey, you don't tell him what the gift is. He finds out when he opens the box."

"Oh! Hi, Uncle Luke."

Marcus held Amy close in his arms, but his eyes were on Amanda. Had she declared war? She was so feminine and lovely in that flowing thing with her curly hair cascading down to her waist. And the lavender scent that she always wore teased him mercilessly. He wanted to be alone with her. He wanted... Marcus reined in his thoughts and his awakening libido as Amanda reached him at the bottom of the stairs. She kissed him fleetingly on the lips, surprising and startling him, and wished him happy birthday before turning quickly to greet Luke. Marc suddenly gave a loud greeting of his own, and he watched his wife turn to retrace her steps.

Luke stopped her. "Let me see if I can get him quiet. It's time he got used to me." Amanda let him pass but followed and watched from afar as he changed the baby's diaper and lulled him back to sleep.

Luke paused in front of her. "What's the matter, Amanda? Doesn't Marcus help you with Marc?" She shook her head slowly. "He hasn't touched him since he handed him to me right after he was born."

Luke frowned. "You wouldn't joke about a thing like this."
Amanda wished that she was joking.

She shook her head. "He watches me nursing when he thinks
I don't see him and calls me when Marc cries. He'll even warm
his water bottle, but he won't lift him or play with him. I think
he's afraid of getting too close."

"Yeah. Well, don't let it get you down. He'll come around."
Amanda wasn't that optimistic. She knew that Marcus was determined to end their relationship at the end of their contract; he
was taking great care not to become involved with her child.

"Daddy, you can put me down, now." Marcus had hardly
realized that he was holding Amy. He was still gazing up the
stairs where Amanda had disappeared behind Luke. When he
saw Amanda and Amy coming down the stairs in their yellow
dresses, holding hands and smiling, he'd been speechless, his
senses numbed and the blood roaring in his head. His heartbeat
had accelerated at a frightening pace, and an undefinable gut-
searing sensation had winded him more than if he had jogged
five miles.

"Wait here, baby." He started slowly up the stairs feeling as
if his feet had turned to lead. He had to find a way out of his
dilemma. Nearly five more months of it. Five more months of
despair at work and torture at home. He was married. He wasn't.
She was his. She wasn't. Worst of all, she had become Amy's
mother, and he couldn't deny it. He refused even to think about
the obvious solution. At the top of the stairs, he called to Amanda
and Luke who stood talking, "I need ten or fifteen minutes to
shower and change. Get yourself a beer or something, Luke."

After his shower, Marcus walked into the dining room and
stopped abruptly. Yellow flowers, lighted yellow candles, fine
porcelain, silver and linen adorned the table, and the members of
his family stood at their chairs waiting for him. "Wow," he
muttered to himself, "she's really clobbering me." But he wouldn't
let her knock him down twice in one hour. He took his seat at the

head of the table, gave her a deliberately intoxicating grin and quipped, "My two women are incomparable. Eat your heart out, Mr. President." The telltale glitter of Amanda's eyes and her sudden inability to look at him gave her away. *At least I'm not dangling here all by myself,* he thought smugly. *I get to her just like she gets to me.*

With the lights lowered, Amy strutted, beaming, into the dining room carrying Marcus' favorite chocolate cake adorned with thirty-six lighted candles. She stepped very carefully, and everyone present knew that her tuneless rendition of "Happy birthday, Daddy" would not be duplicated soon. Momentarily speechless with astonishment and delight, Marcus reached for the cake and placed it on the table for her.

"Make a wish and blow the candles out, Daddy," Amy commanded. He took a deep breath and felt it leave him unaided, when his eyes caught Amanda's gaze. No one had to tell him what she wanted him to wish for. It might well have been a neon sign blazing across her face. She wanted him to wish for her, to wish that she was his. He parted his lips to speak, but he saw her hand go involuntarily to her heart, knew what she felt and couldn't utter a word. He didn't deny that the heat sizzling between them, burning from their locked gazes was enough to make any adult onlooker squirm. Luke squirmed.

"What did you wish for, Daddy?"

The blood rushed to his face, sending his adrenaline into overdrive. Marcus reached over and lightly pulled a lock of Amy's hair, but his eyes were on his wife. "It's a secret, but I'll let you know if it comes true."

She giggled and licked her ice cream. "Do you think I'm pretty, Daddy?"

Marcus grinned. She was like every female other than Amanda and his mother that he'd ever known: crazy for compliments and never satisfied. "Of course I do, baby."

Smiling happily, she told him, "Lady thinks I'm pretty, too. And she always says I look just like my handsome daddy. She said—" But Marcus didn't have a chance to enjoy Amanda's embarrassment, because she called a halt to it.

"Finish your dinner, Amy. We have to give Daddy his presents."

Marcus hooted. "Yes. But we'll finish this conversation later. I want to know what you've been telling my daughter about me."

"She said—"

"Amy, *eat!*" The desperation in Amanda's voice made his blood rush. What could she have told his little girl about him? He joined Luke in the laughter, but he felt as if his soul had leaped out to her.

He looked into her eyes, and her energy seemed to wind around him, to sear him with the intensity of a lover's hot caress. As though shocked at what she saw in him, Amanda rubbed her sides with trembling palms, made an excuse and left the room. If he needed proof of his willpower, he had it, because he managed not to follow her.

Marcus pondered her behavior as she hurried out of sight, admitting to himself that he would have gone after her if he'd thought he'd be able to discipline his libido. He said the hell with common sense and got up just as Marc reminded them of his presence in the house. The infant's wail cooled his passion at once.

"I'll get him," Luke called out to Amanda. He changed the baby and brought him downstairs. Then, with what Marcus recognized as feigned innocence, Luke handed the boy to him. His heart thumped wildly, for he had once more to cross a threshold over which no return would be possible. With studied airiness, Luke explained that he was going to the kitchen to warm a bottle of water. Caught, Marcus had no basis for protest and held the baby awkwardly until he began to whimper.

"Put your hand under his head, Daddy. That's what Lady does." Amy leaned over and kissed Marc's cheek, and the baby smiled. Marcus regarded the children intently, realizing that a bond had developed between them. He looked around but saw no place to put the child, relaxed and let reason triumph over stubbornness. Amanda and Amy had tried hard to make his day special, and he wouldn't disappoint them. Clumsily, he shifted the baby closer to his chest and forced himself to look down at him, really look. The child chose that moment to yawn and smile. "I won't be captivated. I won't," he said fiercely, staring down at Marc Stuart Hickson. But the baby smiled and cooed, blissfully denting the tough man's armor.

Stunned, Amanda viewed the unfamiliar scene from the doorway. *Don't comment,* she warned herself as she set the tray on the coffee table. Luke tested the water on the back of his hand.

"Where did you learn so much about babies?" Marcus asked him.

"You know Alex, my brother-in-law, has a slew of kids. I used to baby-sit when he and Eunice couldn't afford a sitter. I got to be good at it, and I love kids." He relieved Marcus of his unwanted burden.

Marcus thanked Amy for his red T-shirt, smiling down at her when she stood beside him, her hands locked behind her.

"Open Lady's present, Daddy." She handed him the brown box with iridescent brown ribbon. "Lady says that the paper matches your eyes."

Enjoying Amanda's discomfort, he prodded, "What else does Lady say about me?" Amy ran over to investigate the handsome leatherbound business calendar and leaned against her father.

"She said she doesn't love Uncle Luke more than you." Marcus pursed his lips to hide a smile and put an arm around his daughter.

"I'm rather glad to hear it."

"She said she doesn't love anybody more—"

Luke cut in. "Amy, you must learn to keep a secret." He looked at his brother. "And Marcus, you're asking for more than you're giving. I'd have thought that it would be more fun to get such information firsthand."

Marcus shrugged nonchalantly. "'A wise man will *make* more opportunities than he *finds*.'"

* * *

Amanda had been sitting quietly sipping coffee. She hadn't drunk any while pregnant and was especially enjoying it now. She didn't mind Amy's chatter, because it wouldn't hurt Marcus to know that human beings didn't divine the course of history. God and Nature did that, and they didn't give a hoot what kind of contracts women and men made. He ought not to be surprised to learn that she loved him deeply, though he should already have known it; he wasn't exactly immune to *her*. She reflected on his quote and grinned at him. "I'll bet Sir Francis Bacon would have reprimanded you for taking advantage of a child's innocent trust."

Luke observed their easy bantering, his eyes dancing with merriment. She was his brother's match, all right. Marcus was an avid reader and so, apparently, was she. And this was a game that Marcus loved. Having this common interest enabled them to duel at will with their sexual attraction safely in drydock. He leaned back, enjoying himself.

Amanda decided to let Marcus have the last word and save him the trouble of fighting for it. "*Tsk. Tsk.* Low blows are unworthy of you," he told her. "'No one rises to low expectations.'" Amanda knitted her brows. She wasn't easily stumped.

"Give up?" he asked her. She guessed wrong.

"No way," he stated, triumphantly. "It's from Les Brown, the man who lectures on better living. I heard him say it with these ears." He pointed to them.

"Let some air out of your balloon and open the rest of your presents," she advised with a smirk.

"Who's this from?" Without looking, she knew what he held.

"It's Marc's present for you, Daddy. Lady and me found it in a anti store."

"Lady and I. And you mean antique store, darling," Amanda corrected her.

Marcus had the sensation of hot skin crawling on the back of his neck, irritating his nerves. He knew why she hadn't written anything on it. Unable to write what she wanted, she hadn't written anything. He looked at her, questions darting from his eyes, but Amanda made her face unreadable. He had rejected her child. Was he going to accept his gift? He could hurt and humiliate her with his next move, or he could make her heart sing. He unwrapped the box slowly, as though postponing the inevitable. He looked at the centuries-old, gold-plated tuning fork, his square jaw working as he checked his suddenly treacherous emotions. In his prosperous days, he had collected tuning forks from all over Europe, and there were dozens in his collection. But none such as this.

"Did Luke tell you that I collect these?"

Her surprise and pleasure were evident. "You collect them? I had no idea. I hope you like it. I mean, Marc hopes you like it." It was "showtime," and Marcus knew it. He didn't want to love the baby only to have another empty hole in himself on April twelfth. He got up slowly and kissed the infant who rested so happily on Luke's knee and got a smile and a waving first for his effort. Luke's expression clearly said, "That wasn't so difficult, was it?" Shaken by the child's easy acceptance of him, he turned toward Amanda. The unshed tears sparkling in her eyes affected him deeply and, with parted lips, he bent to her mouth, oblivious to both onlookers. She trembled at his touch, surprising him. And arousing him. Marcus raised his head and looked at her, at the bloom on her face and the stars in her eyes. Still clutching the tuning fork, he headed without a word for the back porch and the cold air that would dampen his arousal and put everything else back into perspective.

Chapter 10

She hadn't missed school, Amanda realized after nearly three months of maternity leave; having a family was both time-consuming and stimulating. Without her new family, she wouldn't have known how to fill the time. But she loved teaching and her new responsibilities as principal, and she planned to hold the principal's traditional Christmas party for the Caution Point Junior High School staff, even though she wouldn't return to school until after the first of the year. She hated leaving Marc at home with Ellen while she shopped for the party and for their own Christmas, but the crowds of shoppers made maneuvering Marc's stroller through the stores too cumbersome. She wanted their Christmas holidays to be perfect. Warm and loving. Binding. An experience that Marcus would never forget. And she readily admitted to herself that it might be the only truly happy Christmas she would ever know. Oh, happiness was a relative thing, she realized, and for her, it was simply being with Marcus. She didn't let herself imagine how happy she would be if he acknowledged that he loved her and consummated their marriage. He did love her. She just knew it.

She sat on an upholstered bench in her bedroom, pulled on a pair of thick socks and was about to go to the closet for her boots when Amy handed them to her. Surprised, Amanda pulled the little girl into her arms and hugged her longingly. If only…but she wouldn't permit herself to finish the thought. Amy wrapped her arms around Amanda's neck and whispered, "Do you want me to go with you and help you, Lady?"

Amanda couldn't help being amused. Laughing, she kissed Amy on each cheek and studied the look of longing on her little face. They hadn't spent much time alone together since Marc's birth. Time devoted especially to Amy.

"All right, love."

Amy chatted nonstop during the drive into the town's central shopping area. And it was revealing chatter. "Lady, why doesn't Daddy like to hold Marc? He just likes to stand and look at him in his little basket."

Shocked at Amy's astuteness, Amanda searched for the right response. She hadn't known that Marcus paid any attention to Marc and wondered why he carefully hid from her his interest in her son. She looked down at the child who awaited her response.

"It's been a long time since you were a baby, and he just has to get used to him." At least he'd gotten around to *looking* at Marc.

"Uncle Luke doesn't have any children, and he plays with Marc all the time." Now, what was the answer to that? She ought to leave it for Marcus to deal with Amy, she thought, resentfully. Before she could answer, Amy let fly a tornado.

"Maybe daddies aren't like uncles."

Horrified, Amanda glanced down at Amy, who didn't appear to be the least perturbed. After all, no child could ask more of a father than Marcus gave to his daughter. But she knew that she and Marcus had a problem that they hadn't foreseen: Amy was clearly under the impression that Marcus was Marc's father. What explanation had Marcus given her? Probably none. "I will let Mr. Hickson deal with that," she muttered to herself and changed the subject.

They shopped for Christmas tree decorations, presents and clothing for Marc and Amy, who accepted it as natural that Amanda would buy things for her and give her money to buy

Christmas gifts. All morning, the child clung to her in a way that
deeply affected Amanda. She showed none of her usual independence and assertiveness, reaching for and holding Amanda's
hand, leaning against her and trying to help her with packages.
At one point, she corrected an inattentive salesman.

"Lady told you she didn't want a blue sweater for Marc. She
wants any color but blue and pink."

The salesman smiled indulgently at Amy and commented as
one would to any proud mother, "You've got a smart little girl
here." Amanda was about to correct him when a glance at Amy
caused her to pause. The child was giving the man one of her
happy, charismatic Hickson smiles, clearly delighted that he
thought she was Amanda's own child. When Amanda didn't correct the man, Amy leaned possessively against her and wrapped
an arm around her thigh. She had intended that the two of them
would have lunch in a nice restaurant, but her emotions, her conscience and her intelligence were waging a three-way war inside
of her, and she only wanted to get home as quickly as possible.
She and Marcus needed to talk, and one of them had to talk to Amy.

Face reddened by the fierce cold, Marcus turned up the collar
of his green-and-brown mackinaw and tightened his grip on the
nine-foot spruce that was to be their Christmas tree. He regarded
it with fierce pride, a beautiful tree—the first he'd bought. Helena
had preferred white, artificial trees with silver bells and, for
himself and Amy alone, he'd bought only one tree, a very small
one that she could help decorate. Last Christmas, there had been
no tree, because Amy had been too sick to appreciate one. Before
he could ring the bell, the door sprang open, and an exuberant
Amy greeted him with Amanda right behind her. He tried to
control the racing of his heart and the sudden joy that suffused
him like heat. He fought accepting what his heart proclaimed—
that this part of his world had righted itself. But their welcoming smiles were intoxicating, and he wanted to believe, needed
to believe. He leaned the tree against the outer wall of the house

and opened his arms, feeling a constriction in his chest as Amanda went into one arm and Amy into the other.

Marcus lifted his daughter with one arm and hugged her, not realizing that he had tightened his hold on Amanda until it almost pained her. But she didn't seem to mind; instead, she appeared to revel in it. He looked down at her and gasped at the glistening warmth radiating from her eyes. Her tenderness and unselfish, unstinting sweetness was his, and he needed it as much as he needed the air that he breathed. How had he been so lucky? His defenses crumbled when she reached up and pulled his head down until she could find his mouth with her parted lips. When her tongue teased his bottom lip, he groaned and opened up to her, kissing her with all the hunger and need he'd stored up in the weeks since Thanksgiving when he had last tasted her sweetness.

"Can she breathe while you're kissing her like that, Daddy?" Marcus laughed. He didn't find it amusing and he didn't feel like laughing. It was a nervous reaction. He took a deep breath, looked at Amy and was about to reply. What he'd say, he didn't know, but he made it a point always to try and answer her questions. But Amy didn't always need answers.

"Lady, do you like it when my daddy kisses you like that? Do you, Lady?" Amanda had promised herself that she would fight for Marcus at every opportunity, and she didn't waste that one.

"I love it." She looked the disconcerted man in the eye and told him, "I love it when you kiss me, and I want it when you don't."

Releasing them both gently, he treated it lightly. "What's a man to do when one female brings out a hammer and the other one declares war?"

"I don't have a hammer, Daddy," Amy informed him.

"Well, at least you know who declared war," he murmured under his breath. Amanda appeared unconcerned, as one who'd made her point. He liked kissing her. He liked it a lot.

Marcus and Amanda worked together to prepare a simple dinner of spaghetti, meat sauce and salad. Apple turnovers and creamy vanilla ice cream completed the meal. As soon as she had gotten the kitchen in order and Marc asleep, Amanda joined Marcus and Amy in trimming the big spruce. Marcus tried to treat it as if it were an ordinary occasion, but couldn't. Amy's unrestrained childish glee and the quiet but joyous peace that radiated about Amanda and seemed to permeate the house were consistent reminders that something very special was happening in his life. Suddenly flustered and finally glimpsing the truth—that his happiness was once more out of his hands—he sat back on his heels and exploded without warning.

"This is a business arrangement. It's not supposed to get into my gut like this!" He didn't believe that his words left Amanda unperturbed, that she wasn't astonished, that by some miracle, she understood what had caused his outburst. He had a sense of frustration when she continued tying a gold winged bird on the tree, refusing to look at him, pretending she hadn't heard him. He knew he was being unreasonable, but he was beyond caring.

"You heard me," he said softly, gently gripping her shoulders. She looked pointedly toward Amy, warning him. Chastened, he gave her a gentle shake.

There he goes again, mixing up his signals, she thought crossly. "The dead probably heard you, too," she replied, caustically, wanting him to know that she resented the outburst. "A little consistency on your part might cure what ails you. I know it would work miracles for what's bothering me."

She watched his shoulders slump for a second before he corrected his posture. "That's right, don't give in to it. Don't ever give in to your emotions, and especially not where I'm concerned." She stood, turned and walked up the stairs. His gaze followed her until she was out of sight.

"Are you mad at Lady, Daddy?" Amy missed nothing, and he'd do well to remember that.

"No, Amy. I'm not angry with Amanda."

"Yes, you are." Marcus declined to respond. He looked down

at his daughter and wondered how she always sensed the mood of his relationship with Amanda. Right now, she wasn't pleased with him. She was *his* child, but she was identifying with Amanda. Sighing, he got up and started up the stairs to straighten things out between them. It didn't escape him that Amy, who always wanted to be on the same floor if not in the same room with them, remained where she was, pensive and withdrawn. That was out of character for her, and he found it disturbing.

"May I come in?" He had stood there for a minute or two observing the tenderness, the sweetness with which she mothered Marc. Amy had been deprived of that special bonding between mother and infant, and he never tired of seeing Amanda bestow such loving care upon her son. When she nodded, he walked into the room, thinking that Amanda made up for much of what Amy had missed in a mother's care.

"You wanted to speak to me?"

He wasn't accustomed to chilliness in Amanda, but she was cool toward him now, and he deserved it. "Yeah, if you don't mind." The forefinger and thumb of his left hand pressed into his square chin. "I was out of line back there, and I spoke aloud without meaning to. I hope you won't hold it against me, because I never intended to make you uncomfortable or to destroy such a pleasant atmosphere. Amanda, things are getting away from me. Here. At work. Even Amy is mad with me, because she doesn't like the way I spoke. Look. I want us to have a good Christmas. Please don't let what I said spoil it."

What Amanda knew about the male psyche, she had learned living with Marcus. And with this particular male, you stood up for your rights, because he practically demanded it. She pasted what she hoped was a cool smile on her face and told him, "As apologies go, that one was pretty lame."

He knew that what she said was true. Besides, he hadn't much felt like apologizing, but had done it for the sake of harmony. He felt as a pacifist might feel defending his home against intruders. He didn't want her to get inside of him, but if he didn't fight he was lost. Even as he thought it, he knew he wasn't being completely honest with himself. She was already lodged in his heart, precious to him, as much a part of him as the skin on his arms and the nails at the tips of his fingers.

"Amanda." It was a plea for understanding, but she remained unyielding. And when he started toward her, she held up a hand to stop him.

"Don't, Marcus. I want us to have a happy Christmas together, and I understood why you spoke as you did. But you can't kiss me as if I'm precious to you and behave a half hour later as if I'm a nuisance that you can't wait to be rid of. We're separating on April eleventh. If you dig a hole for yourself, all four of us will have to climb out of it. I've scrambled up enough times in my life."

"I don't want you to hate me, Amanda. And if I get us into a hole," he growled, "I'll get us out of it." He could see that she hurt, and he wanted to reach out to her, to protect her, even from him. "If there is an excuse for me," he told her, "it's that I never anticipated what living with you would be like." *How could I know that you would teach me what the relationship between a man and a woman is supposed to be?* He stepped closer, but she moved backward, and he struggled with the feeling of strangulation that stole over him as he tried to come to terms with his need for her.

"Let me hold you, Amanda. Just…just let me hold you for a minute."

It was the closest he had come to telling her what she longed to hear. She took in his agonized expression, the pain that clouded his beautiful eyes, and she thought of the Christmases to come, of the holidays that she would not spend with him. She visualized family occasions when they wouldn't be a family, wouldn't be together and felt her heart spin.

He opened his arms to her, and she walked into them feeling warm and contented while they held each other. Silently drawing love and strength. Pushing back time. Denying their day of reckoning.

"You're not mad at Lady anymore, Daddy?" How long had she been standing there, and what had she heard?

"I told you I wasn't angry with her, Amy. Now, will you please go downstairs or in your room while we talk?" But instead, she ran to him and raised her arms for a kiss. He obliged her, and she ran off, her demeanor that of one whose little world was now resting on its proper end.

Seeing his puzzlement at Amy's behavior, Amanda told him as gently as she could, "Any coolness between us threatens her sense of security. All of us will pay a price when you and I separate."

"I know," he said, taking her hand and walking toward the stairs. "Don't I know!"

She had planned to ask Marcus to speak to Amy about the relationships between the three of them and Marc. But he was nearly bent out of shape as it was, and she couldn't risk it. She disliked having to postpone anything so important, but she didn't want to push Marcus further away from her. It would have to wait.

The day of the school party finally arrived. Marcus lit the fire in the living room fireplace and took a deep breath. It was as though he was reliving his childhood, experiencing again the fairy-tale Christmases that his parents provided for Luke and him. The scent of pine and bayberry, the lights twinkling on the huge spruce with its myriad colorful decorations gave an aura of magic to the house. Amanda and Amy had hung elves, fairies, munchkins, angels and cherubs on the tree along with the bells, and he had added the colorful lights. Green garlands and huge red poinsettias nestled strategically about the house. Not since he was a small boy had he anticipated Christmas with such impatience. At last, his child would know what a family's Christmas should be. He suddenly wished they weren't having guests, that he, Amanda and the children would have it all to themselves. The caterer set a huge bowl of mulled wine on the coffee table, and one of his aides followed wheeling a multitiered table

laden with nuts and hors d'oeuvres. For one minute, Marcus
tried to stifle his feeling of well-being. And then he gave in to it
and went to find Amanda.

The doorbell rang, and Amanda started for the door. Marcus
restrained her with a gentle hand on her arm. "We do this
together, Amanda. I know this is the school party, but they are
our guests." She hoped that her smile communicated to him her
gratitude. He was always there for her when she needed him, but
was he doing this because he felt that their contract demanded
it, or was it because…?

"Sometimes I wonder what I would do without you." It came
out naturally, but the implications of her remark struck them
both. He tipped her chin up with his index finger.

"We aren't going to let anything prevent us from enjoying this
season. Do you understand?" She nodded, forcing a smile. Hand
in hand they greeted their first guests—the athletic coach, his
wife and five-year-old son. Amy immediately shepherded the boy
upstairs to play. Much later, Luke came prepared to stay until
after Christmas, and the minute he walked in the door, Iris Elms
went for him, having had no success with Marcus. Amanda had
refused to respond to Iris' challenge and relished the heady
feeling she'd enjoyed when Marcus ignored the woman.

Sixty-three people were soon milling through the living, dining
and breakfast rooms, and a few had wandered out on the enclosed
porch. Marcus turned sharply to find Amy tugging at his leg.

"Daddy! Daddy! Something's wrong with Marc, and I can't
find Lady." He took the stairs three at a time, still holding his
glass of wine. He found the child with a bad case of hiccups and,
without hesitating, lifted him and held him upside down for a
second. Remembering his experiences with Amy when she was
an infant, he laid the baby across his lap and patted him gently
on the back, noticing his soiled diaper as he did so. Then, as if
he did it every day, he placed him on Amanda's bed, removed
the diaper and went to find a washcloth and basin. When he

returned, he saw Iris Elms standing by the bed staring down at the infant with a smirk on her face.

"Don't tell me you've got a raspberry on your behind, too," she told Marcus, gloating. "I never would have guessed that they were so common."

"What are you talking about?" He went about freshening up the baby and was trying to ignore her, when he saw the birthmark on the child's little bottom.

"If you don't know, I wouldn't be so bold as to tell you. Ask your wife." She sauntered out triumphantly, passing Luke, who had witnessed the exchange from the doorway. She gave Luke a frank, wordless invitation before telling him, "Your brother got screwed real good."

Luke must have noticed the perspiration beading on his brother's face, for he walked over to him, glanced down at little Marc and saw the birthmark. "I'll do it," he told Marcus, referring to the diaper.

Marcus shook his head. "No. I will. I don't mind it. It's just that I can't stand that woman. I would have thought you'd have cooled her off by now."

Luke nodded. "Yeah. Well, just give me another five minutes." He loped down the stairs, found Iris Elms and ushered her to the front door. "I see you're just leaving. I'll get your coat." Taken aback, she stammered her objection, but Luke's steely hazel eyes commanded compliance.

"This is a Christmas party, and it's a time and place for goodwill, not for spewing venom. And if you think you've caused a problem between my brother and his wife, let me tell you that you haven't."

"Just who do you think you are?" she asked.

"I'm Lieutenant Detective Luke Stuart Hickson, and I don't care *who* you are. Just leave." Luke stood at the door watching her walk toward her car, wondering what she knew and why she knew it. He made a mental note to remind Marcus that he should alert Amanda to beware of Iris Elms. He didn't know whether Amanda knew the origin of that birthmark, but he suspected that Iris Elms had seen it on Pearce Lamont, Jr., and he didn't care much for the implication. He also suspected from the look of hatred on her face that he hadn't heard the last of her.

Christmas Eve was like nothing Amanda had previously experienced. Though her parents had cared for her, they had never taken the time to show her the pleasures and mysteries, the enchantment of Christmas. She felt as if she could fly; maybe it wouldn't last beyond Christmas, but she sensed a change in Marcus. A stranger would have thought them a happy family of four. At breakfast, Marcus had announced that they should all wrap their presents and place them under the tree.

"We're going out," he told them, "and I don't know for how long." This brought a quizzical expression from Luke, and Amanda realized that he, too, had noticed a difference in Marcus, who was behaving as if he was head of the house.

"Mind cuing me in on our itinerary?" Luke asked him.

"I've no idea. We're going to enjoy Christmas. Marc and Amy have to see Santa Claus, and Amanda wants to see the decorations downtown. Beyond that, it's anyone's guess. Get a move on, everybody."

Amanda could hardly contain her happiness, and she couldn't help smiling at Luke's knowing look and approving nod. Questions milled around in her head, but she didn't need the answers; the important thing was Marcus' acceptance of them as a family with himself as its principal decision maker. She rushed upstairs to begin wrapping her packages, and Luke caught her on the steps.

"You may be the smartest woman I've ever known. You don't question the change in him; you merely welcome it. Let me tell you that it's real. One of your teachers—a short, dark woman with dyed red hair and whose name I forget—issued you a challenge at the Christmas party that brought a few things home to him, and what you saw back there a minute ago is part of it. Just be yourself; you're halfway there."

Amanda controlled her tremulous smile for fear that tears would flow.

"Oh, Luke. If I could have had a brother, I'd have wanted him to be just like you." She thought she'd embarrassed him.

"What do you mean, 'could have had'? I *am* that brother, and I will be no matter what. Hurry, now." She watched him for a second as he bounded up the steps. How had she been so fortunate as to find a husband such as Marcus and a brother-in-law who championed her cause? Luke paused at the top of the stairs, and she realized that he was waiting for her.

"Amanda, is that birthmark on Marc's bottom one of your family's traits?" She shook her head.

"Not that I know of. Why?" He took his time answering, as though deciding how much or what to tell her.

"It seemed to mean something to that teacher. Did she know Pearce Lamont, Jr.?" He must have noticed her embarrassment, because he patted her shoulder in a consoling gesture.

"I don't know where Marc got that, Luke, and I didn't know any of Pearce's friends. He was very popular with women, but if she knew him, I wasn't aware of it."

"Amanda, I don't want to upset you, especially not this morning, but I want you to tell me this: did Pearce have that mark?"

She fought to stave off the memories that his question triggered. "I don't know. I didn't see that much of him."

"All right, sis. Just be careful of her." Amanda nodded. She had already decided to maintain a safe distance between herself and Iris Elms.

Marcus made Robert's house their first stop, so that Amy could give the boy his present. "I'll be over tomorrow with yours," he told her. Then they paid a visit to the Christmas tree in the town square and to Santa Claus and his reindeer, joined the carolers in the mall, watched the skaters and ate roasted chestnuts. Along with dozens of other revelers, they followed street musicians and sang carols in their wake. It amazed Amanda that she could have known of these Caution Point traditions most of her life without ever having participated in them, and she knew she would never forget that day with Luke, Marcus and their children.

In mid-afternoon, Amanda asked Amy whether she was tired.

"No, Lady, but maybe Marc is." Amanda had been wondering how it happened that Marcus contentedly pushed Marc's stroller wherever they went, that he had held the baby while they were in the department store and that he'd given him the bottle when they stopped at Caution's Coffee Bean for lunch. She had been bottle-feeding Marc for the past two weeks in preparation for her return to school. As far as she knew, this day was only the second time he'd touched the child since just after his birth. She was too happy to question it.

"Daddy will know whether Marc is tired," she told Amy.

Hours later, they ate a simple supper at home and sat around the lighted tree near the roaring fire to exchange gifts. Marcus disappeared and returned with Marc. "Everybody's supposed to be in on this," he explained. He didn't give the child to Amanda, but kept him, a move that wasn't lost on anyone present, including Amy. Amanda accepted Luke's present, a framed photograph of five-year-old Marcus wearing a baseball cap turned backward and pulling at the pants that he seemed to be losing, and knew that the expression on her face as she looked at it was all the thanks he needed. Her gaze fell on Marcus, and she thought he nearly lost composure when, forgetful of her onlookers, she clutched the picture to her breast. What had brought on the change in him?

Christmas morning came, and Amanda felt that she couldn't bear any more happiness. She would always remember how that Christmas began. Luke cooked breakfast while she and Marcus tidied the house, and Amy helped by keeping Marc company. They found him cooing happily while the little girl told him the story of Daddy Goose, and her heart soared when Marcus brought her baby down to the breakfast table.

"This is time for togetherness," he told them again.

Maybe with this to think back on, I'll be able to endure whatever comes, Amanda thought, as the day wore on. Warm. Loving. Idyllic.

After the traditional Christmas dinner early that evening, Luke put the dishes in the dishwasher, turned it on and announced that he had a stop to make. He had observed the fire between Amanda and Marcus, and he was hoping that they'd finally do something about it.

"I've got a couple of calls to make," he explained.

"Anybody I know? Is it serious?" Marcus demanded, obviously in a carefree mood.

"No and no. I'm not making a move until I find a woman who's Amanda's equal." He kissed Amy goodbye and hugged Amanda.

"Thanks, sis. It was really great." Then he whispered, "If you don't get him tonight, you never will. Remember that your pride won't keep you warm, but *he will*." Barbara Whitfield had told her to "go for broke." She hoped she understood what that meant.

Her thoughts of what the night could bring, of Luke's words sent tremors through her. Excited and nervous, she walked around aimlessly until time to put the children to bed. Marcus sang a lullaby to Marc and read Amy the story of *Little Red Riding Hood.* Did he think she was pestering him? She couldn't keep her hands off her husband. Throughout the day, she'd touched him every time she was near him. A hand on his long back. A fingertip to his muscled arm. A tiny pinch on his brown cheek. A clutch for support when none was needed. She remembered how he had looked at her when she had playfully slapped his buttocks, and her imagination fueled desire in her.

Marcus sang to Marc until he slept, then leaned over and brushed the baby's cheek with his lips. *This child has a claim on me,* he told himself, *has had since before he was born.* He had known that if he let himself get close to the baby, pretty soon he wouldn't want to be away from him. He didn't regret it. Amanda had done everything possible to make their Christmas a memorable one. Her sweetness, the joy and wonder of it all shining in his daughter's eyes, and Marc's acceptance of him had given him welcome respite from his constant worries over his business. He knew that Iris Elms' certain vendetta against Amanda had made him anxious for his wife and increased his protectiveness toward her. But once he'd given in to his feelings, he'd been happier than he could remember being before.

He had made Amanda happy, too, and he was glad, but he had also gotten one more hook that he would probably carry forever. He raised his head and looked straight at her, directly into her love-filled, passion-drenched eyes. She had kept him dangling from a live wire all day without even being aware of it, and like nail to magnet, he marched straight to her feminine lure. They might have been bodies frozen in time, as they stood for what seemed like minutes mesmerized by each other, close enough to touch, but not touching. It was time, and they felt it to the depth of their starved souls.

"Amanda. *Amanda.*" He hardly recognized his voice. His emotions, all that he felt, the sweetness with which she had given of herself to him and Amy at Christmas and before were more than he could push aside. His feeling, his awesome, driving need for her bubbled up inside of him like molten lava. He reached for her.

"Amanda. Oh, sweetheart, what have you done to me?"

She went silently into his arms and lifted her lips for his kiss, knowing that nothing could have prepared her for the force of it. The hot, consuming passion with which he took her mouth sent shivers racing through her. Her knees buckled when she felt the power, the sudden strength of his arousal against her belly, and her own answering desire took complete possession of her. Excitement and anticipation of his loving battered his senses, and she spread her legs, unconsciously inviting invasion, undulated helplessly against him. She wondered if he heard the furious pounding of her heart when he parted her lips with his searching tongue and finally made love to her eager mouth. As though she'd been wound up like a mechanical toy, her arms wrapped around his neck, and she tried to climb up his body. He bent to lift her but, as he did so, Marc whimpered. The child went back to sleep, but Marcus stared down at the woman in his arms, suddenly distant as if she had dashed cold water over him. Shaking his head, trancelike, he turned and left without a word.

Devastated. How could he switch from hot to cold in seconds? *It wouldn't take much for me to hate him,* she told herself. She heard the front door close, and pretended that she didn't care where he went. But she did care. Where could he go in thirty-degree weather on Christmas night? The thought of another woman brought a searing pain to her chest. She had been so sure that he would finally give in to his need and take her. The way he'd looked at her, had moved to her, searing her with his hot gaze. And oh, how he had held and kissed her, as if he had wanted to eat her up. Yes, he had wanted her; his hot arousal pressing against her belly was proof of it.

Marcus had not misled her, she knew; he had made his position clear and maintained it throughout. He weakened sometimes, but she had lived with him long enough to know that he had iron control; his head ruled the rest of him.

She showered, went to check on Amy and then got ready for bed knowing that she wouldn't sleep. What a shattering end to what she had thought was the most wonderful Christmas of her life! Dispirited, she pulled on a red lace teddy—bright colors always made her feel better—and sat on the edge of the bed, reliving the wonder of the past two days. Marcus had been so caring and so attentive and, somehow, he had finally accepted her child. She mulled over what Luke told her and decided that a liaison with Pearce was the reason why Iris disliked her. She hadn't even known that Pearce was involved with Iris. A sigh escaped her as she saw trouble with the modern-dance teacher as inevitable. The woman couldn't have seen that birthmark unless Luke…could it have been Marcus changing that diaper? She saw it clearly then. Iris had taunted Marcus about the birthmark, and he had defended his wife. She didn't doubt that the incident had made him more protective of her and Marc. If so, perhaps she should be grateful to Iris. And to Marcus. He'd given her more than she had hoped for, but it wasn't enough.

"Why can't he love me just once? Is it too much to ask? I won't make demands on him. I just want to know what it's like all the way with him." She spoke aloud, her words ending on a sob.

Marcus grabbed his mackinaw and was out of the door before he got it on. A blast of cold air rocked him as he ran down the steps, onto the walk and into the slippery street. He welcomed the discomfort. It had been close, too close. He had almost sealed his fate and the course of the rest of his life. He wasn't fool enough to believe that once he knew her completely, once he sank into her sweet body, he would ever be able to leave her. He walked rapidly toward the Albemarle, punishing himself as he leaned into the biting wind. He hadn't spent such a joyous Christmas since he'd left his parents' home. She had enveloped them all—Luke, the children and himself—in love and warmth. Amy had finally known a child's magic Christmas. And Marc. It had taken little more than seconds for the baby to wrap himself around his heart. He hadn't wanted to love the boy, to become attached to him, just as he hadn't wanted Amy to get too close to Amanda. But he hadn't reckoned on the power of a child's faith and trust. Marc was as comfortable with him as with his mother. And he hadn't anticipated the strong bond that immediately formed between Amy and Marc.

Marcus wasn't confused; he knew what was happening to him. He was just looking at the pros and cons, he assured himself. The houses were becoming fewer and more widely separated but, through the windows of each one, he saw the evidence of families joined in the holiday spirit, of family love and a woman's special touch. In his mind's eye, he could see Amanda as she had been that Christmas day with Marc, with Amy, with Luke. And with him. And he could feel her hands, her fingers touching, caressing endlessly, each time she was near him. He had walked well over a mile, and the freezing weather hadn't blunted his desire for her. He hadn't ever wanted a woman as he wanted Amanda. Never. It was more than lust, and he knew it. Far more. With the wind howling around him, he stopped and looked out at the Sound. At the desolation, the churning winter. *Just like my life,* he thought, bitterly. And suddenly, like a homing pigeon, he spun around and followed his heart.

Marcus knew she heard his rap on her door, that if she didn't answer, it was because she was either angry, upset or both. He rapped again. Louder.

"Yes."

He hoped the tremor in her voice signified desire and not rage. "I want to come in, Amanda."

"Marcus, don't promise me what you're not going to give me. I hurt enough without the pain of having you walk away from me. I don't like it, and I'm starting not to like you. Just go away."

Marcus opened her door, walked in and locked it behind him. Then he went into Amy's room, assured himself that she was asleep and locked the door between her room and Amanda's. He turned around and looked at his wife, but she was concentrating on her feet, refusing to look at him. He threw off his coat, walked to her and braced himself down on his haunches.

"Look at me, Amanda." She raised tormented eyes to his, and he spoke in lowered, husky tones. "You didn't expect that it would come easy for us, did you?" When she looked perplexed, he explained.

"The day we met in Jacob's garden, you knew there was fire between us, because you felt it just as I did. You're like no one I've ever known, except possibly my mother. You're sweet, as she was. You make a home a place of peace and comfort, just as she did. You're inside of me, Amanda. Deep inside of me." He rested his hand on her bare thigh, and she jerked as if he had touched her with a hot iron poker. He quickly pressed his advantage, letting his hand roam upward toward the seat of her passion. It dawned on him then that she was nude except for that transparent slip of nothing that allowed him to see her nipples and the curls that covered her womanly folds. His arousal was swift and full.

Amanda raised her hand to push him away. He was getting next to her, but she wasn't going to let him have the advantage.

"Don't start what you can't finish."

She had almost said *won't* but, instead, had challenged him.

"What do you mean?" Amanda couldn't imagine that any woman had ever questioned his masculinity or that he would let one get away with it, and she felt better for having done it.

"I can finish anything that I start." He glared at her, clearly aware that she was baiting him.

The sparks that flew from his eyes only made her more reckless. "That's probably what Napoleon told his army of men as he led them to Waterloo, where they were later beaten by the Duke of Wellington."

He grabbed her shoulders, though his touch was gentle.

"If you want me, just say so, and I won't leave this room until tomorrow morning." The urgency of his tone and the tenderness in his voice sent tremors ricocheting through her.

"And just what will you be doing while you're in here?" She was beginning to feel the power of her advantage, and it only heightened her desire for him. His incredulous look told her that she had won. And when he pulled her to her feet and opened his mouth over hers, she was ready for him. It was all she wanted. *You're not getting away this time,* she vowed, silently. She pulled his tongue into her mouth and sucked it vigorously. When he groaned in passion, she put one hand in his hair and the other one on his hard arousal. She stroked him, and he cried out. But she refused to give quarter and began to push her advantage. He snatched her hand away and locked it behind her. Her belly tightened with desire and fire coursed through her when he lowered his head and fastened his lips on a fully erected aureole that winked at him through her lace teddy. Her knees buckled.

"Marcus. Marcus." She moaned his name as he suckled her. She wanted his mouth on her bare skin, not through that lace.

"What is it, love? Tell me." He lifted her until his arousal pressed the apex of her thighs. With his hands splayed across her bare bottom, he moved against her. "If you want me, let me know it. I can't walk away from you this time. I need you. Oh, Amanda! *I need you!*" She brought her knees up and wrapped her legs around him. Only his slacks separated them, and she began searching for his zipper. He stopped her, knowing that it would be over before he could properly attend to her needs. She looked at him, shaken and with a feeling of déjà vu.

Seeming to read her thoughts, he smiled, lifted her and lay her on the bed. With gentle care, he reached down, pulled the teddy over her head, threw it aside and stared down at her, entranced.

"Oh, sweetheart. You're so beautiful, so beautiful." She started to cover herself with her hands, but he wouldn't allow it.

"You were beautiful when you were swollen with Marc. Don't you know that you're even more beautiful now?"

She wanted to believe him, and she wanted to believe what she saw in his beautiful eyes. She looked up at him, her eyes revealing her vulnerability.

"I want to see you, too. I saw a lot of you that other time, and I hadn't known that the male body could be so…so enticing," she said, her tone shy. "But I missed something." He grinned, flinging off his clothes as fast as possible. Then he stood bare before her, proudly ready, proudly male. She held out her arms, welcoming him.

"Do you really think I'm that…that I can accommodate…?" She struggled with the thought, pointing to the obvious place.

His seductive laugh sent frissons of heat to the well that

housed her passion. "You'll fit me, sweetheart. Mother Nature was smart."

She frowned, and anxiety gripped him. "What is it, Amanda? We can't have any secrets here."

"I just…Marcus…I want you to go all the way. I want you inside of me this time," she blurted out.

"Don't worry, honey. It's what I want, too." He stretched out beside her and slowly, gently gathered her into his arms and held her. Amanda trembled, overcome with the sensation of his body naked against hers.

Fire roared through her, and she trembled helplessly, nearly bursting with passion as he feathered kisses over her face and worked his way down to her neck and throat, his lips barely grazing her flesh. How had she ever lived without his tantalizing kisses, the unearthly experience of his loving that irritated and splintered her nervous system?

"Kiss me," she begged him, but he was charting his own course, giving her everything that a woman needed, assuring her complete satisfaction. She thought she would die when he teased the pulse of her throat with his devilish tongue while his fingers barely skimmed up and down her arms.

"Marcus…please," she moaned. He bent to her breast, licking first one nipple and then the other one before drawing one deep into his greedy mouth and feasting voraciously. Sucked into a vortex of passion, she cried out from the pleasure of it, her fingers digging into his shoulders. When she began to undulate against him, he stilled her with his hand.

"Easy, sweetheart. Don't rush it. I want this to last, and I'm not made of wood." He rose above her, put an arm under her shoulder and kissed her. She parted her lips to his kiss and almost went mad, as his tongue claimed every crevice, every centimeter of her mouth while he fondled her breast. Remembering that she could make him want, too, she slipped her hand down, aiming for the most vulnerable part of him, but he was too quick for her.

Taking both of her hands and placing them over her head, he feasted on her body, before releasing them and seeking out the seat of her passion with his knowing, deft fingers. She gave herself up to the powerful sensations, crying aloud and writhing beneath him when he began to stroke her. Then she found the swollen length of him, parted her legs and attempted to pull him to her. He could wait no longer.

"Look at me, love. Open your eyes and look at me." He was poised above her, waiting.

Frustrated almost to the point of exploding, she asked him, "Are you waiting for an invitation?" He smiled and nodded.

"Yes. Oh, yes, Marcus. I've waited for you so long." Suddenly, he stilled, and she almost panicked.

"Has the doctor released you?"

"Yes. Yes," she told him impatiently.

"When?"

"Two weeks ago."

He sighed deeply with relief and joined them with one powerful stroke. She cried aloud. He was silent and still, struggling for control that he needed as never before. *Home!* He was home at last where he belonged. Slowly, he began to move. Amanda grasped his tight buttocks and hung on, meeting his every thrust. He tried not to hear her soft cries of pleasure, tried not to feel too keenly the hot, tight sheath that had begun to pulse around him threatening to push him over the edge. He had to make certain that she never wanted any man but him, and he needed his control. Her breathing accelerated and her movements quickened as the convulsive clenching and tightening began. She moaned beneath him, begging him for complete release, but he strung it out. Bringing her to the edge time and again until she finally went wild in ecstasy, wringing the essence of life from him. He shouted in a powerful release, collapsing upon her as it enthralled him.

* * *

Marcus attempted to move, but she restrained him with her arms and thighs.

"I'm too heavy for you." He raised his head from her shoulder and kissed her long and tenderly. Amanda squeezed him to her with every ounce of strength that she had. She knew that it might be her only chance to love him.

"No you aren't," she corrected him. "I love the feel of your weight on me." But he rolled to one side, taking her with him and holding her close.

"I love you so." She had shouted it in ecstasy. Had he heard her? She was afraid to guess his reaction. Nervously, Amanda turned on her side facing the man who was now her husband in truth as well as in law. Perhaps she was being foolish, but she had to know.

"Are you sorry, Marcus?" It was barely a whisper. He raised up on his left elbow and looked down at his wife.

"How could I be sorry? I feel like a whole man for the first time in my life." Amanda could hear her heart pounding. She dared not hope, but he was looking at her expectantly, openly defenceless, vincible to her for the first time and not trying to hide it. She couldn't think, so she just burrowed into him, trying to get as close to him as was humanly possible.

When she did find her voice and looked up at him, she surprised herself. He hadn't altered his gaze. "I don't want us to go back to the way we were, Marcus. I couldn't stand it. Not after now… I mean, after I know what it's like to be with you." He leaned closer, so close that his breath warmed her face. So close that he was almost a blur.

"What do you want? Tell me what you want." It was her chance, maybe her only one and she was going to take it. Honesty was the best policy, Aunt Meredith had always preached.

"I want you to move all of your personal things in here. I want to sleep with you every night and wake up with you every morning. I want to be your wife, Marcus." *There! She'd said it.*

Marcus sat up. He had hesitated only a second and she seemed terrified by it. He stroked her jaw in an effort to ease her anxiety, but the clouds began to gather in her eyes nevertheless. Gently, he kissed her.

"Don't cry, love. I think it's what I want, too, but there are rough roads ahead of us, rougher than you could imagine, and this may not be the time for firm commitments. I'm willing to try it, though." He paused. "What am I saying? *I want to try it!* But would you agree to our taking this as we go along? Don't be hurt by what I'm saying. I am not in the position to give you my word unequivocally, Amanda, and I won't, because I keep my word. There's no other woman, but there are problems. Do you understand?" She nodded.

"Where are you going to sleep?" she asked him, doggedly, satisfied now that she had a chance to win him. Marcus laughed a genuine belly laugh, and playfully slapped her bottom.

"You like the idea of sleeping with me, do you?" She nodded and watched his handsome face split into a satisfied male grin. Remembering Barbara Whitfield's advice, she refused to be ashamed of it; her only concern was in getting what she wanted. *Marcus!*

"Then this is where I'll sleep."

"You've smiled more in the past two days than in all the time I've known you. Why is that?" He shrugged it off. If that was true, he hadn't realized it.

"I guess things just started to sort themselves out," he hedged.

She sat up to look at him, and her gaze strayed to his broad chest and washboard firm belly. The black curls had teased her breast when he held her, and she had gloried in the feel. She lifted her hand to touch him and jerked it back, not certain that she was allowed such boldness. His eyes had been intent upon her face and her every move.

"Touch me, Amanda. I want you to touch me whenever and wherever you like. I want to know the feel of your hands on my body. Go on. Do it." His voice had grown hoarse and his breathing harsh. She buried her fingers in the hairs on his chest, accidentally caressing one of his pectorals. He flinched, and she would have withdrawn her hand, but he pressed it to him.

"That didn't hurt?" she asked him.

"No. No, baby, it felt good. Just like you feel when I touch you there." Slowly, she let her hand graze it gently, tantalizing him.

"Amanda, please, for God's sake." He increased the pressure, but she removed his hand and teased him with her tongue.

"Keep that up, and I'll have you on your back in seconds." That was music to her ears, and she tried to suckle him. When he bucked violently, she slid her hand down and cradled him. He pulled her into his arms and rolled over. This time he didn't linger over preliminaries, but ran his fingers gently over her feminine heat, found her moist and ready, slipped into her and swallowed her cry of joy into his open mouth.

Amanda struggled under the hairy weight that pinned her hip to the bed as she slowly journeyed from sleep to consciousness. Something also had a firm grasp of her breast. Momentarily alarmed, she looked down at the hair-streaked arm that held her close. *Marcus!* It came back to her then. Their night of love and loving. Of tenderness and the greatest joy she had ever known. Not even when she had held her son for the first time had she known the sheer bliss she had experienced with Marcus deep inside of her, holding her, loving her. And he had brought her to ecstasy time and again, all through the night. She should be tired. She should be sated. She was neither, and she tried to turn over and face him. Didn't she have the right to ask for what she wanted? He had many ways, she'd learned, of asking her. She twisted around to find him awake, watching her and looked for signs of resentment. Wariness. Regret. She found none of those. He smiled warmly and her heart began to race.

"Good morning, sleepyhead." He turned her gently in his arms and pulled her to him, and she buried her face in his shoulder and mumbled, "Hi."

He pulled back in order to look at her. "What's this?"

"I don't know anything about morning-after etiquette."

Marcus laughed. "Well, baby, you sure had night-before etiquette down to a fine art."

"You did, too." She kissed his neck, but he appeared not to respond.

"Take what you want, sweetheart. I'm here for you."

Encouraged, she dipped her tongue to the pulse at the base of his neck. He hardly breathed. Frustrated and feeling a little peevish, she ran a hand over his nipple, circling it until he began to shift his body. Encouraged, she bent to the other one and teased it with her tongue. His breathing accelerated, and his fingers pressed into her shoulder and thigh. To make him her own was her only thought as she held him to her, caressing, kissing and stroking him, loving him wantonly and telling him in breathless whispers that he was all any woman could ever want.

"You sure you want what you're asking for?" he ground out, hoarsely. If she didn't, he was in trouble.

For an answer, she threw one leg across his hip, grazing his arousal. He flipped her onto her back and leaned over her.

"Do you want me? Do you?" He said it as softly as he could. As gently as possible. But his blood rushed to his head, and his breathing faltered. To have this proof that she wanted him because he'd given her ecstatic pleasure before was almost more than he could bear. In almost five years of marriage, Helena had never made a single overture to him that suggested she wanted to make love. Had never shown pleasure in his body. Never tried to seduce him. Amanda reached up to him in an unmistakable invitation, and he fell, trembling, into her arms.

Shattered by her selfless loving, he tried to contain his galloping passion. He needed for her to know that she was more to him than the solution to his financial woes and surcease from the raging desire she'd stirred up in him from the moment he'd met her. Unable to find words adequate to express his feelings, he gathered her to him and, poised above her parted thighs, lowered his lips to hers and kissed her with more tenderness than he'd ever felt for any human being. It was light, without pressure, but he sensed that it shook her from the top of her head to the soles of her feet. Gazing into her wide, passion-glazed eyes, he made them one. *One!* Would he regret it? He pushed the thought out of his mind and sank into her warm loving body.

Chapter 11

Marcus scrambled eggs while Amanda poured the milk, almost overflowing Amy's glass. She couldn't concentrate. She couldn't help glancing furtively at him, wanting to touch him, unable to get her mind off what had been happening between them less than an hour earlier. Amy chattered away about Christmas and how she wished it came every day, and Amanda was grateful for it. She didn't understand Marcus' silence; maybe he had second thoughts. They sat down to eat, but Marcus immediately got up, pinching Amanda's nose as he passed her. Reassuring her.

"I'm going to get Marc. I know he's not hungry, but he should be with us." He bounded up the stairs, whistling as he went. Amanda breathed easier. That didn't sound like a man having regrets about the night before. He brought the baby down and held him while he tried to eat his breakfast.

"Daddy, how come you were in Lady's bed?" The two adults stared at her, speechless. Amanda wondered how she'd known, since both doors had been locked. "Were you feeling bad, Lady? Daddy used to put me in his bed when I was feeling bad."

Marcus shook his head as if to clear it of foreign matter, and looked at his daughter.

"How do you know that I slept in her bed?" The only way to deal with Amy was straight.

"'Cause you weren't in your bed, and it was all made up when I went in there. I heard you and Lady talking, and I saw you come out of Lady's room wearing a towel like you do when you just had a shower." Marcus didn't try to contain a smug laugh. His five-year-old kid was already into deductive reasoning. But he could see that Amanda was horrified, primed to lecture him that he had confused the child.

"Amy, sweetheart, Amanda is my wife. We are married. That means we can sleep in the bed together whenever we want to. It's one of the nice things about being married."

"Oh!" She pursed her lips and frowned, as she regarded him intently. They waited for her next question, but the problem was apparently too much for her and she finally smiled at Amanda. "I'm glad you didn't feel bad, Lady." He hadn't gone far enough, he realized.

"We've decided to share a room, Amy. Now, when Uncle Luke spends the night he won't have to sleep on the sofa." The child looked puzzled. Then she beamed.

"You mean like Tommy and Rachel Culpepper's mom and daddy?"

Relieved, Marcus nodded. "Right."

Amy seemed satisfied. But only for a moment. "Rachel said Tommy is her little brother. Is Marc my little brother, Daddy?" Marcus nearly choked on his coffee. He dealt with all kinds of people in the course of his work and socially, as well. Governors, orchestra conductors, opera divas, all kinds of musicians, deans of the country's finest schools of music. And not one of them had ever been able to stump him the way Amy could. Dumbfounded, he looked to Amanda for help.

She had seen it coming, and she was glad that they could deal with it together. "Marc is your stepbrother, darling. That's a little different from regular brother, though."

Amy smiled happily. "Am I gonna have a regular brother?"

Before either of them could answer, she said, "It's okay. We can let Marc be my regular brother." Amanda didn't look at Marcus. She couldn't. Yet, she sensed his withdrawal, his darkening mood.

Marcus was clearly nonplussed. She knew he suspected it wasn't her first acquaintance with that topic, and he seemed put out because she hadn't mentioned Amy's questions about Marc. She had learned the advantage of letting him act first, so she said nothing. He put Marc in his stroller.

"Look. I...I'm going for a walk." They heard the front door close, and Amy got up, walked around to Amanda and leaned against her. Amanda had learned that, when things weren't to Marcus' liking, he was liable to take a walk. He would discuss the problem later, after he'd cleared his head and made up his mind on his own terms.

"Did I do wrong, Lady?"

Amanda looked down at the worried, upturned face. "No, darling, Daddy just has a lot on his mind."

"But..."

"It's all right. Really. Keep Marc company while I straighten things up." But his behavior worried her. She knew that Marcus had not completely come to terms with the idea of their having a bona fide marriage. He hadn't wanted to remarry, and he could easily feel as if he'd been trapped. Maybe he had been. She'd lived with him for eight months, but she sometimes felt as though she hardly knew him. She couldn't go back. She couldn't live in the house with him and not share his bed, his body, his life. She loved him with every atom of her being, and he knew it. Amanda looked down as Amy wrapped her little arms around Amanda's thighs.

"Are you going to cry, Lady?"

She knelt and gathered the precious child to her. "No, sweetheart. There's no reason. I'm fine." But Amy held her tighter, wordlessly saying that she didn't believe her. Marcus found them that way.

He had walked to the end of the block without even donning his coat. But he knew he had probably upset Amanda, so he had turned back and slowly retraced his steps. He hadn't thought about the relationship between Marc and Amy. He was her stepbrother, but his birth certificate said he was her half-brother, her blood kin. He had a legally contracted marriage of convenience with Amanda with a stipulation that, if either of them wished, it could be dissolved by annulment on April the eleventh. But he had consummated the marriage, and it could only be terminated by divorce. A divorce that he knew Amanda did not want and that he wasn't sure he wanted. He also wasn't sure that he *didn't* want it. How had events closed in on him so suddenly? He had nothing to offer Amanda and, in another three weeks, he probably wouldn't even be able to support his child. Yet, he couldn't deny that they had become a family. And he didn't want to deny it. He walked into the house and found his wife and his daughter wrapped in each other's arms, giving and receiving support. He gathered them both to him and, with unspoken tenderness, quieted their fears. But he knew he was looking into a stark future.

Amanda busied herself first with the children's recreation and then with lesson plans for the coming semester. She tried without success to shake the feeling that Marcus was deeply concerned about something. His periodic lapses into silence told her that something was wrong. Fearing that he really did regret the change in their relationship, she put out a feeler.

"Had you planned to go to the factory today?"

"No. I always let my employees have the day after Christmas as a holiday. This year, we'll be closed for the weekend, as well. As soon as I move my things into our room—" she noticed the emphasis upon *our* "—I have to get down to work on my accounts." She nodded, but his deep sigh did not escape her. Something weighed heavily on him, and he wasn't sharing it.

By eleven o'clock, riddled with anxiety, she decided she had to do something. Taking coffee and a hot apple turnover, she went up to Marcus' old room where he sat working on his accounts. As she reached the door, he propped both elbows on the desk and dropped his head into his hands before releasing a deep groan. She stood there stunned as she watched him shrug first one shoulder and then the other in frustration. Amanda knocked then, because she didn't want to embarrass him, and walked in with the morning treat. He took the coffee, seemingly grateful, and gave her a weak smile.

She stepped behind him and began to massage his neck and shoulders, silently telling him that she was there for him. He didn't speak, but she knew that he was enjoying that bit of attention. As she worked out the tenseness of his muscles, she recalled that, on Christmas Eve, he'd said in a fit of pique that things were getting away from him at home and at work. She faced the glaring truth then that he did not intend to confide in her.

"Marcus, what is it? I know that you're terribly worried about something. Is there anything that I can do?" She felt him tense.

"Thanks. But I don't think so. I have to get through this myself." She pushed back the offense that she felt. Now was not the time to be self-centered, she thought, as she sat down on the floor beside his chair and laid her head against his knee. Amanda searched for the words that would make him realize that they were a couple, a team, that they were closer than they had been only one day earlier. She had to make him see that her problems were also his, and that his problems were hers.

"Maybe I can't help, Marcus, but maybe I can. Don't you know that whatever hurts you hurts me? Can't you at least tell me what it is that's hurting us both? I've lived here all of my life, and I know a lot of people. Can't we work through whatever it is together?" She felt the tightening of his muscles beneath her hand and sensed his withdrawal from her.

"I told you I'll deal with it," he insisted. "You don't have to solve every one of my problems, Amanda. A man's entitled to his own soul, even if it's damaged." She gasped at the bitterness of his tone, but she wasn't about to cower; there was too much at stake, and she didn't bend easily. Amanda knew she had always possessed innate strength, but Marcus had enhanced her self-assurance and had made her even stronger with his tender loving.

Standing, she placed a hand lightly on his shoulder and told him, "You're my husband, Marcus, and I love you. It saddens me that you can't share your troubles with me, but I'm here for you, no matter what. And I always will be." She patted him lightly and left the room. She'd have loved to box his ears but, as Aunt Meredith used to say, more flies were caught with honey than with vinegar. Amanda paused at the top of the stairs. She had just told Marcus Hickson that she loved him, and he hadn't uttered a word nor moved a muscle.

On Monday, January the second, Amanda was back at school, Ellen had gone to the University of California, Amy was spending her first day in kindergarten, the Hicksons had a full-time house-keeper and Marcus was at the factory, pacing the floor. In the ten weeks since the water-main break had caused flooding in the factory, they had managed to overhaul and refinish only three concert grands and six small-string instruments. The damage had been more severe than either Marcus or any of his crew had en-visaged. Work had been slow and tedious. It had been necessary to order parts, some from as far away as Germany. And all of the income had gone toward salaries and the restoration and upkeep of the factory. Not one penny for the mortgage and nothing for Marcus. He would begin to see some profit only after complet-ing work on the rare, antique harpsichord, for which he was awaiting parts from Germany. Jerzy Heiner, his specialist in small-string instruments, walked over to where Marcus leaned against a water-mottled doorjamb, contemplating his options.

"Would you look at this one, Marcus?" He held a priceless Stradivarius. "It's the same with every piece that was in that room. These pegs seem to be rusty, and the scroll won't move." Marcus examined the prized violin.

"Doesn't look too good, but you can fix it. It's just going to take longer and cost more to straighten this mess out than I'd figured."

"What about the insurance company?"

Marcus shrugged. "I didn't have a separate clause covering water damage, but there is a provision for coverage, though I'll get less than if I'd had a water-damage clause." Jerzy tilted his head and looked inquiringly at his boss. Marcus glanced at Jerzy. He knew he was behaving as if this was happening to someone else, but that was the only way he could deal with it.

His mood of detachment had taken him mentally out of his surroundings, and the sound of the front door buzzer almost startled him.

"You've been misinformed, buddy, this place is not for sale," Jerzy told the visitor. Marcus ignored the mumbling voices, preferring not to hear the exchange but, with his inner vision, he could see the vultures circling ever lower over his business.

He went into his office, found the mortgage and read the fine print. It contained nothing that gave the bank the right to pawn off his mortgage without his agreement or to initiate a sale of his property prior to foreclosure. He knew he could seek an injunction to stop the harassment of the brokers who behaved as if they had the right to snoop around his factory, but he didn't want to add to the staggering amount that he already owed his lawyer. Besides, in three weeks, one of them might own it. He wiped the sweat from his forehead and leaned back in the executive chair that he'd bought and enjoyed in more prosperous times. He needed his life's work, the factory he'd worked so hard and so long to build, his reputation and the sense of well-being to which he'd become accustomed. But he realized that he needed it more for Amanda than for himself. He wanted her to be proud of him, but who had ever admired a fallen angel, a crumbling statue or a failed man? He wanted to give her the world, but pretty soon, he wouldn't own an inch of it and he'd have nothing to offer.

While Marcus, miles away, staggered beneath the burden of their future, Amanda walked briskly down the hall to her office, greeting teachers and students as she went. She found a bouquet of miniature yellow carnations on her desk with a note from her assistant principal welcoming her back to school. She had called a staff meeting for three-thirty that afternoon, and she knew that some people would be disgruntled, but she didn't intend to call meetings during school hours when students would be unattended. For once, everybody assembled promptly. They seated themselves freely and, to Amanda's amazement, Iris Elms placed herself directly in front of Amanda, close enough to reach out and touch her. Amanda noted Iris' air of mockery and her arrogant smirk and recognized it as an attempt to intimidate. She dismissed it as pettiness until she noticed that Iris' six followers and fellow troublemakers had taken seats just behind her. Amanda moved to the side of the room and stood while she talked, satisfied that she had thwarted the woman's attempt at nastiness.

During dinner, she was tempted to tell Marcus about it, but decided it was unwise to burden him with a problem that he couldn't help her solve. Iris had become a problem, and she planned to initiate her transfer away from Caution Point Junior High as soon as she could locate a suitable replacement. She wouldn't tolerate subversion of her program. It occurred to her that Iris wouldn't be so brazenly antagonistic if she didn't have strong, influential support. She'd worry about that when she had to.

Amy bubbled with stories about her afternoon with Beanie Miller, the new housekeeper and, though Marcus entered freely into the spirit of her chatter, Amanda was very much aware that he was worried. After they got the children to bed, she showered, pulled on her burnt orange caftan, let her hair down and wondered how to approach him. Humming off-key, she walked barefoot to the kitchen, got two long-stem glasses of cold sherry and carried them into the living room where Marcus sat viewing a blank television screen. He hadn't touched her nor shown her any affection since the morning when she'd awakened in his arms. He had rejected her offer of help, ignored her confession of love for him and withdrawn from her. But he had continued to show tenderness and love to Amy and Marc. The little boy wiggled and gurgled with glee each time he saw the man whom he would call father.

He looked up at her when she touched his shoulder lightly, and a careful smile moved over his worried face. She handed him the drink and sat down on the sofa beside him, waiting to see if he would share the moment with her. Marcus grimaced slightly as he raised the glass briefly before taking a sip.

"Would you rather have had something stronger?" she queried.

He threw his head back for a second, then leaned forward and gave her a level look.

"Don't be nice, Amanda. I don't deserve it, and you know it."

"I won't deny that living with you this past week has been difficult," she told him, "but this isn't about what you do or don't deserve."

"Exactly what is it about, Amanda?"

She had the advantage, but she didn't want it. Marcus fought hardest when he was down. Trembling with the false nerve that she was about to exhibit, she whispered, "It's about I want my husband back. *I need my husband, Marcus!*"

He looked at her. "What are you saying?"

He placed his glass on the table, untouched but for one sip. "I said, what are you telling me, Amanda?"

She stuck her chin out and waded in. "I'm telling you that I need you. I'm through lying in that bed beside you while you pretend I'm not there. I need my husband, damn you!"

Marcus faced her. "I thought that after what passed between us that morning, after what I said, you'd never want me to touch you again."

"Are your feelings so fragile that they won't withstand a little breeze?" she needled. "What will happen when we get a real storm?" She stood up, scared to death, but hiding it, and held out her hand to him. "'Love is not love which alters when it alteration finds.'"

She caught her breath as Marcus burst into the first real smile she'd seen on his face in a week. "Ah, the Bard would be proud of you. As for me," he added with his own homage to Shakespeare, "'I may command where I adore.' Come with me." He picked her up and carried her effortlessly up the stairs and to their bed.

Marcus looked down at the woman sleeping in his arms. When she had come to him, the essence of femininity with her thick, curly hair falling across her full breasts and her lovely wide black eyes sparkling against that orange thing she wore, he had needed her so badly that he had felt frozen inside. And he had hardly believed his ears, had expected anything but that she still wanted him. It had even occurred to him that she might ask him to leave. She had needed him, all right; she hadn't overstated that one bit. Never had a woman responded to him as she did. She had gone wild beneath him. And still, she had remembered his needs and preferences. He'd been hungry for her, more starved for her sweetness, her soothing love than he had ever been for any woman. But she hadn't questioned nor withdrawn from his awesome demands; she had gloried in satisfying him. He had never known a woman to give so selflessly, so completely, to open herself so unabashedly to the fulfillment of his needs. He had been unconsciously holding her closer, and she sighed as she burrowed into him, clutching at his heart. Luke's words came back to him: *"You will never forget her."* Knowledge of it brought pain, and it brought a stealthy peace. No, he wouldn't forget Amanda. Not ever. He stared into the darkened ceiling, suddenly feeling as though he'd been sucked into a whirlwind. *Oh, my God! What have I done? I love her! I love her and I have nothing, absolutely nothing to give her.* He held her closer as he faced reality. He would give his life for her, if need be. He stifled a groan that sprang from deep inside him. She needed nothing *from* him. *Only himself!*

"Hello. Dr. Hickson speaking." She swiveled around in her desk chair to get a better view of the playground.

"Hi, sweetheart." He had nothing to tell her, and she knew it, but for weeks he'd been calling her at school just to "touch base," as he phrased it. There was something different about Marcus, but Amanda wasn't sure what it was. He was still worried about the business, she guessed, but there was something else; he seemed to be courting her. She laughed. That was a silly notion. After all, they were married, and he didn't have to court her. But he awakened her each morning with loving—almost as if he couldn't get enough of her—called her at work though he had nothing special to say and, when he arrived home, he kissed her as if he hadn't seen her in years. She felt that his feelings for her had deepened, but he had never confirmed it, never said the words. Never told her that he loved her. But she knew that Marcus wasn't afraid of love, even though he might think so, because he told Amy regularly that he loved her. She had more than she'd ever dreamed of, she reminded herself. She was happy. Or she would be if he would let her into his life. If he would share his concerns with her. Perhaps it was too much to ask—to be his friend as well as his wife.

Amanda opened the door to Marcus and to the warm, early March breeze that heralded the coming spring and soon thereafter, April eleventh. He was home earlier than usual and, as she searched his tired face, she knew she was looking at a beaten man. He didn't reach for her as had become his habit, so she opened her arms, and he went into them. But only after a moment's hesitation, she noticed.

"What is it, Marcus? Darling, what is it?" she persisted, when he remained mute. Marcus drew away and regarded her with almost lifeless eyes, and yet he seemed to be trying to see into her soul.

"Marcus?"

He shook his head slowly in dreamlike denial. "I'm going to lose it. Lose everything. I've put my blood into it, and my crew has sacrificed so much, but it's all hopeless. Hopeless from the start. Ten days from now that mortgage is due, and that's the end of it."

Though horrified, she contained it. She knew better than to offer help; he didn't want any more of her help, and he had let her know it.

"What will you do?" She felt like a fool asking such a question, for she was certain that Marcus had explored every conceivable option before telling her.

"I don't know. Right now, I have no contingency plans; I'll figure it out when the time comes. My last chance was to get the work on that antique harpsichord completed. I stood to make a bundle on that, but the parts that I ordered from Germany aren't available and won't be until a master craftsman makes them, and he makes them by hand. It will take weeks, maybe months, if he's very busy." He released a long breath. "I didn't count on that flooding. The insurance company has to investigate and won't get around to that until the first of April. I don't know why they're taking so long; the flooding is a matter of record."

Amanda took Marcus' hand and walked them up the stairs to their room. She had never loved him so much as now, and her heart was breaking for him. Marc cooed happily in his crib, and she watched in awe as Marcus dropped her hand and knelt down to tease and play with the happy little boy. Marc's waving fist and bubbling smiles richly rewarded him.

"This kid makes me feel like a giant, like I'm one hell of a man," he told Amanda, as he rose to his full six-feet, three-inch height. "Where is Amy?" Her constant patter kept the house so alive that her absence could never go unnoticed for long.

"Amy is over at Myrna and Jack's house." He sat on the bed, and she walked over and began to knead his shoulders. He looked up at her with eyes that didn't shine.

"I'm not out, Amanda; just down right now," he offered defensively.

She continued to minister to him. "I know, love. I know."

Marcus yanked off his tie and shirt, kicked off his shoes and lay across the bed, drained. She didn't want Amy to see him that way, so she phoned Myrna and asked if Amy could spend the night, saying that she would explain later. Then she sent the housekeeper home, put on her burnt orange caftan, let her hair down and crawled onto the bed. Marcus glanced up at her, raising an eyebrow in question as she pulled his head onto her lap. Gently, she brushed his forehead with her lips and then began to stroke his cheeks and his hair, whispering to him that it would be all right and that she was with him no matter what. That he wasn't alone.

Marcus welcomed the peace that stole over him and the easing away of his burden as she continued to stroke him, to whisper encouragement and to console him. Slowly, he opened his eyes and pierced her with the intensity of what he was feeling. Feeling for her. Then he turned and pressed his face into her belly, wrapped his arms around her and held her. After a moment, he lay on his back, his head still resting in her lap and looked up at her with eyes that were no longer vacant, no longer sad, but luminous.

"I love you, Amanda. I love you so." She gasped aloud, unshed tears misting her eyes, and stammered something incoherent. He placed a finger on her lips. "Shhh, darling. Don't you know that you are my life? Ah, Amanda, sweetheart, I do love you so."

I'm not fooling myself, she thought. For a man of Marcus' pride and abilities, losing all that he had worked for and then having to hire himself out to another man would be a crushing, devastating blow. She hurt for him and watched him for any sign that he might have found a way to save his life's work. His desperate lovemaking night after night gave her a sense of foreboding and a feeling that he saw himself hanging from a precipice.

She managed to get Iris Elms transferred and, after staring out of her office window for more than an hour, unable to work more, she called in her assistant principal and told him that she would be away for the remainder of the day. Worry accomplished nothing; Marcus needed concrete help. She walked out into the March mist to the principal's parking place and got into her car.

"I'm probably going to regret this," she told herself, "but I can't let him go down." She pulled into the Culpeppers' driveway, got out and walked around the back where she found Myrna in the garden setting out lettuce plants. The other woman looked up in surprise. Seeing Amanda's distress, she pulled off her gardening gloves and went to meet her.

"Girl, aren't you supposed to be at school?" Myrna looked more closely. "Amanda, what is it?" They walked into the kitchen, but Amanda still hadn't managed to speak. Myrna put on a pot of coffee, pulled out a chair and took Amanda's hand.

"What can I do to help?"

"I'm going to do something that Marcus will hate, and he'll leave me," Amanda blurted out. "I love him, Myrna, but I have to do this, and I know he will never forgive me."

Myrna's face mirrored surprise. "I thought you and Marcus agreed in advance to separate at the end of a year if the marriage hadn't blossomed into a relationship you both wanted. Jack and I think you're good for Marcus, and we've been hoping that the two of you would make a go of it. Actually, we had begun to think you would." Amanda shook her head.

"He's going to leave me, Myrna."

"Honey, Marcus loves you, too. I'm sure of it. What is so bad that it can't be resolved if two people truly love each other?" She got up and poured them each a mug of coffee. "Cream and sugar?" Amanda declined both.

"I know he loves me now. But Marcus is proud, and he has to eat his pride every day when he walks into my door, because he's not head of his house. He's not footing the bills."

"But wasn't that your contractual agreement?"

"Sure. But Marcus has taken one hard knock after another, starting with Helena's antics, and our contract is the blow that could beat him to the ground." She asked for the other woman's confidence and proceeded to tell her as much as she could of

Marcus' financial situation without exposing him unduly. Then she told her what she planned to do. Myrna sat there, pensive, sipping her cool coffee.

"We knew Marcus was in difficulty, but we hadn't guessed it was so bad. You want my opinion; here it is. If it were Jack, I would do exactly what you intend to do and take my chances. A man's pride is wrapped up in his woman, his work and his kids. He can handle disappointments with his children—though that will hurt him—but his work is *what* he is and his woman is *who* he is. If he can't support himself and his family, he'll leave you. He won't let you take care of him. Then he'll have nothing. If you do what you're planning, at least he'll have his work. Child, I'd run under my man, even if somebody was holding a gun to my back."

Amanda leaned back in the chair, closed her eyes and let her troubled mind do its damage. She couldn't hurt worse nor be more afraid if a priest were walking her to her execution. She sighed heavily. That was it exactly: she *was* going to her execution. Determined not to let it beat her down, she gave Myrna a thumbs-up sign and smiled.

"Love doesn't conquer all, and I can only die once, so I'm going to do what I know is right. When he leaves me, I'll just have to accept it. Thanks for being my friend. Nothing that you could have said would have caused me to change my mind, but it helps to know you would have done the same." She glanced at her watch. "I've got to hurry." Myrna stood and clasped Amanda in a warm embrace.

"If you need to cry, honey, I'll be here. I want us to be friends, no matter what happens." Touched and deeply grateful, the words hung in Amanda's throat, so she merely nodded. Ever since her friend Julie had married and moved to Scotland, Amanda had wanted and needed a close woman friend; maybe she had finally gotten lucky.

She went home and searched the desk until she found what she wanted. It was exactly noon, and she had plenty of time in which to drive to Portsmouth and back before Marcus got home at six-thirty. She paused only briefly, then prayed that she wouldn't see him there.

Days had passed, and Amanda was beside herself. She had procrastinated about telling Marcus what she had done, postponing the time when she would have to take her medicine. She couldn't forget his reaction to her having visited Amy without his knowledge. And she was certain that, this time, he might terminate their relationship. He had told her explicitly that he didn't want her help with the mortgage, and this was the second time she had knowingly gone against his wishes. But most important of all, he had opened his heart to her, told her that he loved her and taken her for his wife. He would see her action as the height of deceit, and she knew that, in a few more days she would have to pay the piper. She wasn't lily-livered, she told herself, she just wasn't rushing the moment when her husband would walk out of her door for the last time.

Her lovemaking had become frantic. Desperate. Driven by her fear that each time would be the last. That night, when they finally came down from the pinnacle to which her wild passion had hurtled them, Marcus gathered her to him and questioned her.

"Honey, what's the matter? You've been a nervous wreck for days, now. Even Amy has asked me if you're all right."

Now was the time to tell him, but she couldn't bring herself to spoil what they'd just experienced. So she lied a little.

"The closer we get to April eleventh, the more anxious I get."

That apparently didn't make sense to him, and he told her so. "I thought that was behind us. Stop worrying over nothing." He pulled her spoon fashion to him, with her bottom nestled against his groin and his left hand beneath her breast and went to sleep. Amanda lay awake most of the night.

Chapter 12

Marcus walked into Hickson's String Instrument Restoration and looked around to where Jerzy Heiner sat on a concert grand with his long legs dangling before him, waiting for his boss's signal to begin work. He swore. All the years of hard work down the drain. He couldn't even declare bankruptcy and salvage his expensive tools, because the bank had title to everything there but the instruments awaiting repair. He squared his shoulders back and walked over to Jerzy.

"I'm going to have to close down, friend. I couldn't make last month's mortgage installment and another one is due today. I've done everything that I can, but this is beyond me. You've stuck with me, and I appreciate it. Lock the door. I don't want any of those vultures in here. Let's start the inventory." He whirled around resolutely, went into his office and closed the door. The bank wouldn't open for another twenty minutes. He thought of calling Luke and decided there was time enough for that. Luke was already worried for him. The telephone rang. He relaxed when it proved to be a wrong number. He looked at his expensive Rolex, a remnant of better times, and saw that only three minutes had passed. It was almost like phoning the grim reaper for a date and then waiting for him to come and get you.

After what seemed like hours, he was able to contact the bank and ask for his loan officer. "Good morning, Allen. This is Marcus. I'm not going to be able to meet the mortgage, and I'd like to know what your foreclosure procedures are."

The man took care of the niceties, Marcus noted, offering his regrets before getting down to business. "I'll have to check the records, Marcus. The computer is down just now, but I should be able to call you back in about an hour." Marcus swore to himself, anxious to get it over with. He paced the floor for a few minutes, and then got in Luke's car and drove down to Hampton Roads, the roadstead waterway leading to the Chesapeake Bay. It was very narrow at that point, separating Portsmouth and Norfolk. He watched as the sun, shrouded by the morning fog that hovered over the roadstead, peeked through the low-lying clouds. He was seeking a moment of peace, but the scene depressed him more, and he went back to the factory.

Jerzy jumped down from his perch on the piano when Marcus walked into the door.

"Allen Baldridge wants you to call him at the bank. His number's on your desk."

"Thanks." He went into the office, closed the door and dialed.

"Marcus Hickson." He listened, disbelieving, to the voice on the other end. "*What? What did you say?*"

"I said you must be mistaken, Marcus. These loans have been paid in full. You don't owe the bank one cent. In fact, we'll be glad to extend you any reasonable amount of credit you want."

Marcus got his breath back and spoke in an abnormally controlled voice. "You're sure of this, now? When was it paid?"

"A week ago," the man replied, apparently confused.

Marcus thanked him and hung up. Then he called his brother. "Detective Hickson speaking."

"Did you pay off my bank loan?" Even before he'd dialed Luke's number, Marcus had a premonition that he would be asking the wrong person. He was praying that his hunch was wrong.

"Good morning, Marcus." Luke didn't pull punches. "You

know me, and you know very well that I wouldn't do such a thing without discussing it with you first."

"I just wanted to be certain before…"

Luke interrupted him sharply. "What the devil are you so put out about? You know it must have been Amanda who paid that bill, and you're just getting all fired up to raise hell with her. If I'd had that much readily available cash, I wouldn't have let you make that loan in the first place. Calm down, Marcus. Why don't…" Marcus was sure that the dial tone had stunned his brother, and he regretted it, but he didn't need the additional indignity of a lecture.

Marcus walked out his office and over to where Jerzy was still perched on the grand. "We're not closing, but you can take the inventory. And you can call the crew and tell them to report to work tomorrow morning."

"Yes sir!" A delighted Jerzy grinned at him.

Marcus scowled. "I'll be gone for the rest of the day." He had trusted her, told her his goals and his dreams and shared his problems. And he had told her specifically that he didn't want her help with his financial situation. She had offered, and he had bluntly refused. In a moment of despondency and uncertainty he had confided in her, but he hadn't wanted her to start waving her magic bankbook around. And what had she done? She had a compulsion about fixing things. Pushing Luke's car well above the speed limit, Marcus fueled his frustration. He'd been stupid to fall for her, but he'd get over her, he assured himself.

He parked in front of the house, went directly to Amy's room and began packing her things. He didn't want to take anything that Amanda had given her, but he couldn't make his child suffer just because he'd been a fool. He packed the rabbit, knowing that it would always be a constant reminder of Amanda not only for Amy, but for him. Then he packed his own belongings, put everything in the trunk of the car, and pondered his next move. He didn't want Amy to hear what he had to say to Amanda. When he discovered that Myrna wasn't at home, he phoned Robert's mother and got permission to leave Amy with her for a while.

The telephone rang, but he ignored it; he had no desire to hear any of Luke's wise counsel, he told himself. A look at his watch confirmed that Amanda would be leaving school in an hour or so, and it was time to pick up Amy from kindergarten. He got Amy, left her at Robert's house and went home to wait for his wife. *Not for long she is,* he thought, though momentarily saddened when he realized that Marc was out somewhere with the housekeeper and he wouldn't see him again. He dismissed it. "The hell with it," he muttered to himself, "I'm out of here, anyway."

Her stomach churned, and her heartbeat accelerated when she saw the big car parked in front of the house at three-thirty in the afternoon. Marcus usually got home after six, and he always parked in the garage. She drove into the garage and sat there trying to summon enough courage to face him. Why hadn't she told him? It would have changed nothing, she told herself. She'd taken a calculated risk…but maybe, just maybe.

When she entered the foyer, she could see his reflection in the hall mirror, sitting on the sofa with his long legs stretched out in front of him and both arms languishing on the back of the sofa. His appearance was casual, relaxed, but she knew that was for her benefit; inside, he was like a coiled snake, ready and anxious to strike. And strike he did.

"Here's your key. You may want to give it to the next hard-luck guy you pick up." He felt a twinge of guilt at having said it, but he was hurting. He shook it off.

"Such meanness doesn't become you, Marcus. I knew I was risking a lot, but I risked it anyway rather than see you lose what you've struggled so hard to build. I did it knowing that you would probably never forgive me for it, and I'm not sorry. I'd do it all over again." She didn't reach for the key, but walked to a table near the window and placed her briefcase there. She turned and faced him, composed and proud.

"What are your plans?"

He had to admire her coolness, because he doubted, indeed, he would have sworn that she didn't feel cool and wasn't nearly as composed as she looked.

"I'm leaving right now and taking Amy with me. You couldn't leave me with my pride, could you? Did it occur to you that it is I and not my wife who is responsible for any predicament I get into? I don't lean on women, honey. You set yourself up to take care of me and my child, and then you decided to be my fairy godmother and wipe out my debts." She winced, and he knew that the pain and anger he felt were mirrored in his eyes.

"Well, I don't consider myself out of debt, Amanda. As soon as I can, maybe early next week, I'll work out some conditions for repayment and send them for your approval. Then you or your attorney can sign it."

She stared at him, appalled, both at the strength of his anger and at the venomous words with which he chose to express it. Unable to resist getting some of her own, she shot out, "Are you asking me to believe that a contract actually means anything to you? How amusing! You're breaking the contract that we have, and I'm not going to waste time entering into another one with you." She hurt, and she wanted him to leave if he was going. She didn't want him to see her fall apart.

"I release you from that contract. Before you took me to bed, I would have held you to it, but I'm damned if I'll beg a man to share my bed. I only ask you not to drive a wedge between Amy and me. That you let me see her sometime. That's all I ask."

"You're asking a lot, baby." He sneered.

"I never ask for more than I give," she threw at him over her shoulder, as she mounted the stairs. *Let him think about that one!* "Goodbye, Marcus."

He sat there for one moment, his heart breaking, cursing himself for loving her and fighting to control his urge to go after her, to hold her one last time. He jerked himself up, stuffed his hands in his pants' pockets and looked out of the living room window at the bleak afternoon. He told himself the world wasn't coming to an end, walked out and closed the door softly behind him.

She didn't feel bitterness, only hurt. She'd acted out of love for him, but he didn't understand that or seem to care. She'd battered his male ego, singed his pride, and he wouldn't forgive her. Would he rather have lost everything than have her save it for him? Her anguish escalated into a stabbing pain. And as if he had timed it perfectly, the flood of tears and the racking sobs came as she heard the door close. She wouldn't have been able to hold back for another second. She had known he would be angry, but she hadn't imagined that he would be cruel because she had averted what would surely have been personal and financial disaster for him. She lay across her bed for what seemed like hours. *He was gone!* He'd left her. Amanda got up and went to the bathroom where she washed her face with cold water. Then she got out of her school clothes and into jeans and a sweat shirt and smiled at what she had done. Marcus had bought her her first pair of jeans. Aunt Meredith had thought them disreputable.

Mrs. Miller, the housekeeper, arrived with Marc, put the groceries away and left. Amanda cradled her baby. "It's just us from now on, love. You and me." She had wanted a child to love and who would love her, but she knew that no one and nothing could replace Marcus or banish the emptiness that he had left inside of her.

"Where are we going, Daddy?" *Here it comes,* Marcus thought, as he moved into the interstate.

"We're going to Uncle Luke's home."

"Is Lady coming, too?"

He took a deep breath. "No, baby, she isn't coming." He tuned the radio to classical music. Amy liked music, but he didn't believe for a moment that music or anything else would divert her from the route her mind was on right then.

"Why?"

"Because she isn't. That's why. Amy, I'm tired and I would appreciate it if you would stop asking me so many questions." He knew he might as well be speaking to the clouds.

"When are we going back home, Daddy?" He heard fear in her voice this time, but he couldn't help it.

"We are going to be living with Uncle Luke for a while, Amy."

"And then are we going back home to live with Lady? Are we, Daddy? Huh?" Marcus swore under his breath. Might as well tell her.

"We're not going to be living with Amanda anymore, Amy."

She was quiet. Too quiet. Marcus looked over just as the child began trying to unbuckle her seat belt. He glanced over his shoulder, quickly shifted lanes, and pulled into the next rest stop.

"What are you doing, Amy?" He looked down at an infuriated replica of himself. She didn't answer, but continued trying to release the strap. *Thank God it's too much for her to manipulate,* he thought. "I said, what are you doing?"

She poked out her bottom lip and faced him defiantly. "I'm going home to Lady and Marc."

He understood her pain, because his own sprang from the same source. Marcus looked down at his daughter, at the tears that flowed and that she refused to wipe. "I'm sorry, baby, but I'm going to be living with Uncle Luke, and your place is with me. With your father."

She began to sob then. "I don't want to leave Lady and Marc, Daddy. I don't. I don't."

He put an arm around her. "I know, Amy. Believe me. I know."

Luke stared at his brother. "You mean you've left her? For good? I don't believe you."

"Yeah. That's exactly what I said." He ran his left hand ruthlessly across his chin. "I was a fool. And I swore I'd never, *never...*" He was searching for words, when his unforgiving daughter walked into the living room and informed him that she was hungry.

"We'll send out for a pizza in a minute. What do you want on it?"

She cocked her head, just as he frequently did, and looked at him. "Daddy, I don't want a pizza. I want stuff like we always have at home." Marcus regarded her almost with amusement. So she was determined to be difficult, was she?

"Amy, we do not live with Amanda anymore. It's pizza tonight or nothing." Without another word, she turned and went back into the twin-bedded room she was sharing with her father and closed the door.

"She's not going to let you off easily, Marcus. She loves Amanda, and she loves Marc, and you've just dynamited her sense of security," Luke told him, pushing his beer aside.

"It can't be helped. I told Amanda clearly that I did not want her to interfere in my financial affairs, and she decided she knew better than I did what was best for me. That's just what Helena did."

"Oh, save it, man. If you even consider comparing those two women, it's because you're having difficulty justifying what you've done. And what about your contract with Amanda? It's still valid."

"We had a fight about her paying off the mortgage, and she volunteered to release me from the contract."

"Are you getting an annulment?"

Marcus groaned and dropped his head into his hands.

"What's the matter? Don't you want one?"

Marcus shrugged his shoulders. "I can't. It has to be a divorce."

Luke gaped. "What are you talking about? The contract calls for an annulment, if things don't work out. Isn't that right?"

"Yeah. It does. But I consummated the marriage."

"You what? When?"

He would have enjoyed punching Luke right then. He didn't need the man's mocking, satisfied grin. Luke's face was all innocence. "Well, I'd have thought less of you if you *hadn't* taken Amanda to bed. Any red-blooded man in your place would eventually have done the same."

Marcus walked over to the bar and got a cube of ice to put in his beer. He hated warm beer. "When? Christmas night and many times thereafter." Disgusted, he went into the kitchen and threw the beer into the sink, his taste for it and anything else gone. The thought of lovemaking with Amanda had him perspiring profusely. "My God. I'm in trouble."

"You're damned right, you are." Marcus didn't realize that he had spoken aloud or that Luke had followed him. "You married her, and you made her your wife. You can't walk out just because of a misunderstanding."

"Don't sound so righteous, Luke. This didn't happen to you. If it had, you'd still be in an unappeasable rage. I've taken and taken from Amanda, and I have nothing to give her. She knew that bothered me, but what does she do? She takes out her almighty checkbook and, with the lick of her gold-plated pen, she throws two hundred and forty-five thousand dollars at me, even though she knows I don't want it. Back off, Luke. It's bad enough without your disapproval."

"Marcus, I just don't want to see you make the worst mistake of your life, because of pride. Would you rather have seen the fruits of twelve years of labor, your life's work, down the river? Would you? There's no woman worth knowing who wouldn't have bailed the man she loved out of a situation like yours, if she could have. And Amanda loves you. She loves you, Marcus; don't bother to deny it. I watched the two of you together Christmas Eve and Christmas Day. That woman looked at you as if she thought the sun rose just to shine on you. Don't make any final moves until you're sure. She cares deeply for you, Marcus."

"I know she loves me; she has for months. But love doesn't justify deception, and it doesn't make deceit palatable." He put a hand on each knee and raised himself up gradually. "Where's Amy? She's awfully quiet." He walked to their room and opened the door.

"Right now, Robert. And tell her I'm going to call her soon as I can. I love you, Robert, 'cause you're my friend." He wondered at the long pause.

"Me, too. Right now, Robert. Bye." She hung up and remained

sitting on the side of the bed. Marcus walked in and sat beside her. She looked at him, but this child who had seemed to wear a permanent smile for the past eight or nine months, showed him a solemn face.

"What is Robert doing for you?" He had guessed, but he wanted her to tell him.

"He's getting Lady's phone number for me, and he's calling her and telling her where I am."

"Why didn't you call her?"

"'Cause I don't know her number, but Robert can get it from his mother, and I know Robert's number."

"I see. Why didn't you ask me?"

"'Cause you're mad at her. I know you are, Daddy." He watched her bottom lip go out in defiance. "Could you give me a pencil and some paper, Daddy?" He got it for her and remained there, knowing he had lost some points with his precious daughter. Amy answered the phone when it rang and copied down the number.

"Thanks, Robert. What did she say?" Marcus wondered at the long silence. "Oh, good. Thanks, Robert. Bye."

Marcus read the correct area code and phone number over Amy's shoulder. For a five-year-old, she was certainly resourceful. And it was just one more thing for which he had to thank Amanda. Only five hours since he'd left her, and he felt as if his world had been shattered. As if he'd lost his right hand. Losing that factory wouldn't have hurt nearly as bad. He loved the factory, but Amanda had become his life.

Amanda walked into the kitchen carrying Marc, who laughed and bubbled. The happy child didn't cry unless he was hungry or uncomfortable. She hugged him, inhaling his sweet baby scent, before putting him in his stroller. In a few days, he would be five months old. His hair was losing its brownish cast, and he had begun to look more like her. Thank God, she murmured, grateful not to be reminded constantly of Pearce Lamont. At the thought, she recalled the anonymous note she'd received at school the day before. It had a Portsmouth postmark and had stated that she wasn't as clever as she thought. She'd come home planning to discuss it with Marcus, but their conversation had been of a different sort, and he'd left her. The last time she'd received a letter with that postmark had been two days before she'd conceived Marc. Pearce, Jr., had written to say that he'd be in town that weekend. She shook off a premonition and got busy preparing French toast for herself and oatmeal for Marc. When she placed the baby in her lap, he tried to sing, clapping his little hands as he did so. "I hope you'll be able to sing," she told him, "because I can't. I don't even try." Then the spoon slipped from her fingers and her appetite went with it: Marcus had sung to Marc at breakfast while he held and fed him. Could Marc be missing Marcus? She looked down and saw her tears spattering her baby's cheek.

Amanda didn't want to be alone, and she didn't want Beanie Miller's company. She liked her housekeeper well enough, but the woman's attitude of endless suffering would have worn upon a saint. She dressed herself and Marc, strapped him into his car seat and drove downtown. It seemed to her as if half of Caution Point had ventured out that Saturday morning, the first day of spring, and she had never before realized how much people tended to move around in pairs or as families. She didn't remember ever having felt so lonely. She turned into State Street, deciding to have coffee and a doughnut at Caution's Coffee Bean, but as soon as she sat down, she knew she'd made a mistake. Her last visit there had been with Marcus, their children and Luke on Christmas Eve. So she finished it quickly and wheeled the baby outside just as Sam, the ragman, crossed the street. He greeted her warmly.

"I ain't see'd you much recently, Miss Amanda. Where's your little girl? She's a cute thing, that one." Though it cheered her to see her friend, she didn't want to explain about Amy and Marcus. She told him simply that Amy was with her father. When the old man bent down to look at Marc, Amanda took the baby out of the stroller and held him so that Sam could get a better look. They chatted for a while, and she waved him goodbye. It was one time that he gave her as much solace as she gave him.

I'm not going to start feeling sorry for myself, she swore, driving into her garage. *I knew what I was doing, and I knew the consequences. Oh, Lord. I hope he's all right,* she thought. Then she laughed. Had she been mothering him, for heaven's sake? He had taken care of himself before he met her, and he was probably good at it. She answered the phone.

"Hello." Her voice seemed odd, almost an echo.

"Lady. It's me, Lady."

Amanda sat on the edge of her bed, too weak to stand. "Amy, darling. Oh, I'm so happy to hear from you. How are you, darling?" She had expected to hear Amy's happy giggle, but she heard sobs instead.

"Amy, what's the matter?" Amanda tried to control her anxiety. She didn't want to upset the child.

"I want to come and see you and Marc. Daddy says we don't live with you anymore. Are you mad at my daddy, Lady?" She wouldn't expose Marcus, but she wouldn't lie, either.

"Amy, I am not angry with your father. I love your father, and I love you. If your father can't bring you to see us, ask him if we can visit you. Where is he? I'll ask him"

She heard the sniffles. "He's at the supermarket, Lady, but Uncle Luke is here. We can ask him." Amanda heard Amy yell for her uncle and knew that the child had called her without her father's knowledge or permission, had waited until Marcus was out of the apartment before making the call.

"Hello, Amanda. How are you?" She hadn't realized how much alike their voices were, and hearing Luke gave her a shock that she could have done without.

"I'm not going to lie and say I'm fine, Luke. I'm not. I'm devastated, but I will survive it. And I'm not going to say I've experienced worse, because I haven't. But I took a carefully considered risk. I don't think I lost, but I had to give up two people that I love, that are so much a part of me. And it hurts. How are you?"

"I'm sorry about this, Amanda. I wasn't surprised at what you did nor at Marcus' reaction. You're a loving, giving woman, and my brother is proud and stubborn."

"You don't think I acted improperly?" She held her breath, realizing what Luke's approval meant to her.

"What else could you do? You're human, and you love him. No, you didn't act improperly."

"But I knew he wouldn't like it, Luke."

"Don't be too hard on yourself. If he's so mad about it, why doesn't he close down? It isn't over. I have never known him to be as happy as he was those six weeks when the two of you were man and wife."

Her voice trembled and nearly broke, but she controlled it. "How is he, Luke? Is he all right?" She heard Luke clear his throat.

"For Pete's sake, Amanda. Marcus is just as miserable as you are."

"Uncle Luke, ask her to come. Ask her, Uncle Luke," she heard Amy say in a determined voice.

"Amanda, I didn't hear my phone ring. Did Amy call you? Really? When did she learn to dial?"

"Yes, she called. I taught her to dial several numbers, including yours, before Marc was born. She wants me to bring Marc to visit her."

"Any time you want to come, you're welcome."

"But what about Marcus? He may not like it." She didn't want to go against her husband's wishes again.

"That will be too bad. Any loving, caring mother has the right to see her child."

"But I'm…" She stopped, as she pushed back the tears.

"Not even Marcus would disagree with that." Luke seemed impatient even with the idea. But he wasn't Marcus, and Marcus was the man whose approval she wanted.

"What is it that I wouldn't disagree with, Luke?"

"It's really for you." Marcus ignored the challenge in his brother's unreadable face, nodding his thanks as he took the phone.

"Hello." He heard the catch in Amanda's breath. Could it be…?

"Hello," he repeated impatiently, as he realized who was on the other end. *Say something! For heaven's sake, say something to me. Anything!*

"Hello, Marcus. Amy wants me to bring Marc to see her, and I'd like to, if she can't come here."

"I'll bring her next Saturday." He heard his deeper, softer tone, that betrayed his feelings. "How are you, Amanda? And how is Marc?"

What did he expect her to say? She wasn't going to tell him what his leaving had done to her, so she raised her voice a pitch higher and informed him, "We're making it, Marcus. The only problem is that Marc has to sing to himself now, because I can't carry a tune. How are you?"

"Fine," he snapped, and she knew she'd disappointed him when she downplayed her feelings for him. *Well,* she thought, *I'm through wearing my heart on my sleeve.* Behind him, she heard Amy's shout of glee and smiled at the thought of seeing the child. Luke had said that Amy was her daughter. How she wished it were true!

Amanda turned her car into Myrna's driveway, braked and got out. The day had turned chilly as the March wind whipped a cool breeze in from the Atlantic. She tried to put a spring into her steps, but she couldn't fool herself into believing that she wasn't miserable. She was. And she was lonely. Hearing Amy's and Marcus' voices had done that to her. Marcus' coolness had hurt, even though she had invited it with her flippancy. She hadn't bothered to call Myrna, but had given in to a sudden over-powering need for the warmth of another person, someone who would put an arm around her. Myrna had said that she was there for her, Amanda kept reminding herself. *Well,* she thought, if Myrna was sincere, *I'll soon know it.*

Myrna must have sensed Amanda's distress as she opened the

door, for she didn't have to be told of it nor of its source. Wordlessly, she enfolded Amanda in her arms and rocked her gently.

"He left you." It wasn't a question. Amanda nodded without raising her head. "Where are they?" was Myrna's next query.

"They're with Luke. I knew that their leaving would be difficult for me, but I never dreamed that I could suffer like this. Knowing that I was pregnant and unmarried was far easier." She tried to smile. "I shouldn't dump on you like this, but Myrna, *I hurt!*"

"Of course you do. You love your husband and you love Amy. Come on in, and let's get a glass of wine or something. Where's Marc?"

"I left him with Beanie Miller." Amanda never thought of the woman by her given or surname, but by both.

Myrna laughed. "She is an imposing figure, isn't she? She used to keep Rachel for me when I was working, and I always felt as if my mother was looking over my shoulder, cataloging every wrong move I made." Myrna had deftly switched the conversation to a safe topic, as though she knew that if they talked about Marcus, Amanda would make her visit a short one. Amanda followed Myrna into the living room, where her hostess had spread several travel brochures over the coffee table. Myrna brought some chilled white wine, raised her glass to Amanda and sipped it.

"Jack and I are taking the children to Europe this spring. We're going to the Low Countries and Germany, and it'll be wonderful to visit Brugge in Belgium, where we got engaged."

Amanda leaned forward, no longer listless. "Marcus ordered something important from Germany. If he had been able to get it soon enough, the mortgage crisis would have been averted, and we'd probably still be together. When will you be in Germany?" Myrna told her they would be in Germany mid-April and would be back home the first of May.

"Unless it weighs a ton, we'll be glad to bring back whatever it is," she added. "Just find out what it is and where we can collect it."

"Me? I think Marcus has had all the help from me that he wants."

Myrna's indulgent smile was such as she might bestow on one of her children. "Learn something about men, Amanda. Marcus will be flattered that you think of him. And by now, he isn't angry with you. He's probably wondering why he was in such a hurry to cut off his nose just because he had a cold. You said he loves you."

"Yes. He loves me."

"That's what Jack and I think. Follow your instincts. Since he's your husband, behave like it. All the time. Act like you're his wife, and that will frustrate him plenty." Amanda laughed a solid good laugh for the first time in two weeks.

"Oh, Myrna, I'm so glad I came here today. Thank you." Amanda stood, and Myrna walked her to the door.

"Remember that old adage," Myrna advised. "All's fair in love and war. Just keep it honest." Amanda got into her car, feeling hopeful for the first time since she and Marcus had separated. Marcus loved her, and she was entitled to do everything possible to get him back. And she would. To begin with, an annulment was illegal, and he wasn't getting a divorce because she hadn't given him a reason. Helping your husband out of a financial bind did not constitute grounds for divorce. "What on earth got into me?" she asked herself. "I was always a fighter. Why have I suddenly decided to sit down and let life get a stranglehold on me? I'll show Mr. Hickson one or two things." She walked into her house a changed, resolute woman.

Amanda left her office the following Monday afternoon in a cool, misty rain, walked to her parked car and looked down at its left front tire. Flat. She threw her briefcase and handbag into the car and went back to her office to call Bond's Garage for service, but didn't get a response. She tried Bond again and learned from his answering machine that he was busy for the rest of the day. She got her things, called a taxi and went home. Beanie Miller met her at the door with a frown of disapproval for having had to work fifteen minutes overtime and left. Hardly a word was exchanged between them.

"I'd love to drop a wet frog down her oversized bosom," Amanda said aloud. "It would serve her right. I'll bet that would make her talk."

She checked on Marc, who was still asleep, changed into a bright green caftan, let her hair down and started down the stairs. She answered the telephone on its second ring.

"Hi, Lady. It's me, Amy. Am I s'posed to be getting therapy? Daddy thinks I finished."

"Hello, Amy, darling. I'm not sure, but I'll ask the therapist tomorrow and let you know." *Just talking with this child by phone gives me so much joy,* she thought. "How is your father?"

"Daddy's working. I'll tell him you want to talk with him."

Amanda gulped. She hadn't said that. "I didn't say I wanted to talk with him, Amy."

"You do, Lady. You have to tell him about the therapy. I'll see you and Marc Saturday when Daddy brings me. I love you, Lady. Bye." She didn't wait for a response, but hung up. Amanda stood holding the phone. That child seemed to have her own agenda.

Amanda was sitting up in the bed she had shared with Marcus, trying to read, when the phone rang. She looked at her bedside clock. Nine-thirty.

"Hello." She knew her voice sounded hoarse and panicky.

"You wanted to speak with me?" He didn't sound unfriendly; just not friendly.

She sighed. Still fuming, was he? "Amy said you wanted to know whether she was supposed to be getting therapy."

"She said what?" He sounded as if the very notion was preposterous.

"Didn't you?"

"Amanda, Amy's next appointment is with the doctor, not the therapist. What is she up to?" Amanda grinned. Surely he could see that the child was trying to bring them together. Matchmaking. And only five years old.

"I have no idea. Tell me how you are." She was surprised when her voice took on a low seductive quality.

After hesitating, he told her, "Like you said, I'm making it. How about you?" She remembered her promise to herself just in time to swallow a dull, meaningless response.

"Oh, Marcus. Beanie Miller is such a sourpuss that I hate for Marc to spend so much time with her, but she's very good to him, so I tolerate her. And I have a flat tire and had to leave the car at school. So—"

He interrupted. "Didn't you call Ken Bond?"

"I did, but I only got his answering service." She heard him swear and could imagine what his left hand was doing to his hair.

"If you're not sleepy, wait up and I'll call you back in half an hour." He hung up.

"Hello." This time, her voice was filled with anticipation, and she didn't try to hide it. Didn't want to hide it.

"Marcus here." As if she wouldn't know his voice among thousands. "Gage Motors in Edenton will take care of it. Your car will be parked in front of your house when you're ready to leave tomorrow morning." She thanked him, spun an idea around in her mind and decided to take a chance.

"Marcus, I'm not trying to take over, but I thought you might like to know that the Culpeppers are returning from a vacation in Germany the first of May. They might be able to do business for you there." He was silent so long that she feared his rejection.

"When did you learn this?" His voice gave away nothing of what he was thinking or feeling.

"Saturday afternoon. I had a glass of wine with Myrna over at her house. If you're interested, you could give them a call." A long pause.

"Thanks. I will. I'll call Jack tomorrow morning. It just might expedite things. Thanks a lot, Amanda." Another pause. "Look, we…we'll be in touch."

"Good night, Marcus." It was all that she could manage. He hadn't rejected her help, and he'd managed to get a garage service miles away in Edenton to look after her car. How were they going to open the car and drive it to her house? she wondered. Then she remembered that Marcus had a key. She wasn't going to question him about it, but she stored the precious knowledge that he'd looked after her problem. He had acted like a husband. Maybe Myrna was right. Amanda turned out the light and slipped into a sound, blissful sleep.

Marcus was less fortunate. Hearing her soft, sweet voice. Talking with her. He knew that if he hadn't called and that, with taxicabs at a premium there in the mornings, she might have had to trudge to work in the rain. It occurred to him, too, that she could have other serious problems that he wasn't there to handle for her, and he became depressed in spite of himself. She had sounded so wistful. He couldn't stop thinking about how vulnerable she was there alone with Marc. And when she'd told him about the Culpeppers' plans, she had acted as if he might blow up at her. Why should she be afraid of him?

He turned over for the nth time, wishing he could sleep and that the top of his cotton-knit pajamas wouldn't twist around his waist. He hated pajamas but he couldn't sleep in the room with his daughter without them. The lease on his house would expire in another three weeks, and he'd be able to move back into his own home. His own house. How were he and Amy going to find each other in that huge cavernous place with the cold, inhospitable chrome and glass that Helena had imposed on him? He hated it, but just when he'd decided to make the place into a warm, livable home, Amy's doctor bills had soaked him financially. He had a mind to sell it. Amanda's house had been warm and inviting, a place where a man could feel at home. He'd known happiness there, he reflected. It could have been wonderful if he had been in a different position. But a man couldn't take from a woman, no matter what the circumstances were, and have his self-respect. If only he had met her at another time, before he'd learned what being emotionally at a woman's mercy could cost a man. His conscience pricked him. Amanda didn't have the willowy figure of a model, so he wouldn't even have seen her. He turned over on his stomach and groaned in self-disgust.

Four hours later, Marcus awakened moaning Amanda's name, his body on fire. Dawn had just begun to filter through the darkness, but he got up, knowing it was useless to try and sleep. He walked down the hallway toward the kitchen intending to make coffee and stopped, feeling nothing short of evil.

"I ought to call her right now," he muttered in frustration. "Why should she sleep?" *I'd do it,* he assured himself, *if I wasn't sure I'd wake up Marc.* But Marcus knew that he would never do that or anything else that would bring Amanda discomfort. *Marc!* He missed that child more than he would ever admit to anybody, and he hated to see how the separation had hurt Amy. She longed for Amanda and Marc most at dinner and bedtime, when she would either refuse to eat, sulk or go to sleep in tears, depending on her mood. He hoped that time would make it easier for her.

Why hadn't Amanda stayed out of it? He could have survived losing the factory, he assured himself, but being without her was killing him. "What the hell!" he muttered. If he were honest, he would admit that losing the shop, after everything else he'd had to endure, would have devastated him. And she knew it, his treacherous heart told him. He had finished his third cup of coffee and was rinsing the mug in the sink when a glance at the wall clock told him that it was five-fifteen. Making a sudden decision, he dressed quickly, put Amanda's car keys in his pocket and started toward the door.

He tripped over Amy's prized book, *Winnie the Pooh,* and remembered to leave a note for Amy's kindergarten teacher telling her that Luke's brother-in-law would get Amy from school when he picked up his own child. He had arranged for her to stay with Alex and Eunice until he went for her, a solution that he welcomed in the hope that being with the couple's children would take Amy's mind off of her preoccupation with "going home" to Marc and Amanda. He got in Luke's car and headed for Edenton where he intended to be certain that Gus delivered Amanda's car to her door on time.

* * *

When you faced a day of reckoning, time seemed to fly, but when you were looking forward to something pleasant, it moved at a snail's pace. Marcus would know a good quote to support that bit of truth, Amanda mused. The weekend seemed to have been months coming, the longest four days in her memory. She arranged the flowers on the breakfast room table for the fourth time. In less than two hours she would see them. She was frying a batch of apple turnovers when she remembered one of her aunt Meredith's iron-clad rules: "If you want success, you must never leave a stone unturned." She lowered the flame, went to the hall phone and punched Luke's number.

"Detective Hickson speaking."

"Luke, this is Amanda. I'm glad it was you who answered. Why don't you come along with Marcus and Amy today?"

"Sure thing. I almost called to invite myself, but I didn't want to interfere with your plans. Marcus is out, but I don't think he'll mind."

"Luke, I'm fixing lunch. Please don't let Marcus stop at a fast-food place on the way here. I want us all to have lunch together."

Luke laughed aloud. "I like what I'm hearing, and I'm with you all the way, sis. Pull out every one of the stops, and let it all hang out; he can be had, believe me. We'll be there around twelve-thirty."

The heat of her embarrassment settled in her face, and she was grateful that he couldn't see her. "Thanks. I guess Amy is with Marcus."

"Yeah. She gave him a hard time at breakfast. Demanded pancakes when she knows that Marcus doesn't know how to make them. He took her with him to appease her. She's doing her part, and if you do yours, this thing ought to work itself out pretty soon." She heard the amusement in his voice and knew that she had in Luke a more than willing ally.

Amanda opened the front door as the car came to a halt, and Amy scrambled out and ran squealing up the walk. She bent with her arms outstretched, and the child raced into them, almost knocking her down.

"Why are you crying, Lady? We're here." Amanda wiped her face, smearing makeup as she did. She hadn't realized how lonely she'd been for Amy. And she chided herself for having applied eyeshadow when she knew that Marcus knew she never wore it.

"I'm just so happy to see you, darling. I missed you." She glanced at the mascara on her fingers and grimaced.

Amy giggled, happily. "I missed you, too, Lady. Where's Marc?" Without waiting for an answer, she went looking for him.

Amanda forced herself to look up then and found Marcus' unsheltered gaze devouring her. She gasped aloud, slowly straightening, and opened her mouth to greet him. But no sound came. His effort to speak was as futile as hers. Luke broke the silence.

"Hi, sis." He knew that it needled Marcus to hear him call Amanda *sister.* "I never realized a woman could look so good with mascara smeared across her nose." He bent and kissed her on the cheek. Then he turned to Marcus. "Eat your heart out, brother."

Amanda grinned, but it was clear that the joke, if it was one, escaped Marcus altogether. He moved up, stopped in front of her and stood there without speaking. Amanda looked into his shuttered gaze, wondering where the look that she'd seen moments earlier had gone. Finally, she could stand his silence no longer.

"Sometimes when I'm not looking at you, I almost forget how big you are." She wished immediately that she had let him speak first when she realized that his sense of humor had taken a walk. He singed her with a mocking smirk.

"I don't forget anything about *you.* Nothing. Not ever."

Amanda had resolved that they would have a pleasant afternoon, and that she would ignore his barbs and behave civilly and sweetly no matter how much Marcus challenged her to do otherwise. Responding to impulse, she reached up and pinched his cheek. "Stop scowling and smile," she admonished him. His startled expression amused her; the Amanda he knew would stand her ground, but she was hardly aggressive.

At his inquiring look, she went on, "It's cloudy. We need some sunshine around here, and your breath-robbing smile usually does the trick." Marcus' blush fueled her daring. She stepped a little closer and patted him on the buttocks before quickly turning around and walking toward the kitchen.

"Come on in," she threw over her shoulder.

Luke laughed aloud at Marcus' stunned reaction.

"What's so amusing?" Marcus wanted to know.

"You are," was Luke's smug reply. "If my woman had paid me a compliment like that one, I'd have half of her clothes off her by now."

"Yeah. I'll bet. Right here in the foyer in front of all of us." Marcus observed, dryly.

Luke turned on the charm, grinning broadly. "I see you were thinking about it," he ventured. But he walked quickly past his brother and followed Amanda toward the kitchen. As a child, he'd learned not to push Marcus too far.

Marcus sped up the stairs, taking two steps at a time, as he acknowledged his longing to see Marc. He found Amy enjoying the baby, who cooed, laughed and slapped his hands. He stood for a moment, looking down at them, his heart pounding away in his chest. In three weeks, the boy seemed to have almost doubled in size, and his face had gained maturity. Marcus balanced himself on his haunches and got Marc's attention. The boy looked at him for a moment and then raised his arms toward Marcus as he bounced and grinned.

He reached for the child and pulled him into his strong arms, hugging and kissing him. "You missed me, didn't you, fella?" The baby bounced and bubbled and seemed to be trying to hum a tune. Marcus picked him up, took Amy by the hand and went downstairs. He wasn't behaving the way he'd told himself he would—cool and aloof. Amanda had demolished his intentions with that one wispy brush of his face, and then she had declared war on him with that slap and slight squeeze of his backside, gestures that she well knew would heat him up. He shook his head as if to affirm his immunity to her. But she had his number. She knew how he loved to have her hands on him, how he responded to her soft touches. And she had to remember how aroused he became when she teased him. He came back to the present. Marc was trying to get a grip on his nose, and Amy was demanding an answer to a question that he hadn't heard.

"Can't we, Daddy? Can't we?" Get a hold of yourself, man, he silently ordered.

"Can't we what?"

"Spend the night. I want to spend the night. Lady won't mind. Then I can have pancakes for breakfast."

"No, Amy. We are not spending the night. You asked if we could visit, and that is all we're doing. Visiting." The little fox. He looked down, knowing he'd see her bottom lip pushing out, but she surprised him.

Her smile couldn't have been broader. "Okay, Daddy. Then we can come back next Saturday. Okay?" Manipulator was what she was. She knew him too well.

"We'll see," he said lamely. They reached the kitchen as Luke finished filling the water glasses.

Marc responded brightly to Luke's greeting, but when Luke tried to take the boy from Marcus, he whimpered and refused to go. Assured that he was remaining with Marcus, he fell back into his smiling, playful mood. Marcus glanced at Amanda, who had observed it all with a look of wonder. Their eyes clung. No, she thought. It isn't over. It just can't be.

Amanda had prepared the kind of meal that her family had always loved and, when she served the apple turnovers, gleeful shouts of pleasure from Amy and Marcus were her cherished rewards. Marc clapped his hands and made humming noises, so Marcus sang to him while the child chirped and bubbled with glee.

Feeling as though she couldn't stand any more, Amanda went

out on the porch while she calmed herself. Marc had really missed Marcus, and she hadn't thought it possible. After a moment, she straightened her back and returned to the others.

"Marcus, I hope you've got your tools in that car," she said, brightly, hiding her emotional turmoil. "The knob on the screen door back there is loose."

"Okay. I'll fix it. Anything else you need done?" He didn't look at her, and she couldn't determine whether he was pleased or displeased.

"Well, if you don't mind. One of the balcony windows in Amy's room has been rattling when the wind is strong, and it's kind of hard to sleep. But I could get a handyman to do that."

"I'll take care of it," he growled.

Marcus finished his third apple turnover. "If you've got any more of these, how about a doggie bag? Otherwise, I may make myself sick right here." She assured him that she'd prepared adequate takeout. He patted his pockets, then asked Luke for the car keys.

"I'm going to the hardware store to get something for that window. Be back shortly."

"Daddy," Amy called after him. "Can I go, too?" She shrugged it off when he refused and turned to Marc.

"Daddy is a bad boy, Marc. Say *Daddy*. Say *Dad-dy*."

Amanda gasped when the child repeated it after Amy. And to her horror, Luke hooted with glee. "It's time somebody taught him," he told her in a mildly accusatory tone.

Darkness had descended by the time Marcus completed the repairs and prepared to leave. "It's been nice, Amanda." Suddenly ashamed, he gave her a quick peck on the cheek and, without looking at her, beckoned for Amy. His uncooperative daughter insisted that she wanted to tell Marc a story and sing him to sleep. Frustrated, Marcus told her that they could do it next time.

She jumped up, squealed and told Amanda, "We can spend the night next Saturday when we come."

Marcus glared at her. "You little demon, let's go." He lifted Marc to kiss him goodbye, and the boy clapped his little hands together, smiled and said, "Da da." Marcus almost dropped him. He looked at Amanda, but his proud daughter forestalled any accusation that he might have made, silently or verbally.

"I taught him, Daddy. I taught him today. Say *Daddy,* Marc. *Dad-dy.*"

The happy baby smiled and proclaimed, "Da da." Luke compounded his brother's frustration by taking the child from him and telling him, "Now tell your uncle Luke goodbye." Marc looked at him briefly and then reached for Marcus. Luke must have decided not to pour oil on the fire when he picked Amy up and started out.

Amanda took the baby. "I'm so glad you came today. I missed you. And I missed Amy, too. See you next week."

Marcus wanted to sock somebody, and he wanted to hold Amanda and kiss her. But all he did was shove his fists in his pockets, nod to her affirmatively and leave. She yelled after him.

"You forgot this." He retraced his steps and walked back into the foyer where she stood holding a large bag.

"What's all this?"

"It's supper and turnovers for the three of you." He took the bag and stood looking down at her. Then he dropped it on the floor.

"Oh, hell, Amanda." His arms went around both of them, and his kiss on her upturned, hungry lips wasn't brief. He loved her mouth as if he'd been starved for it, but when he felt desire grip him, he eased away.

"I didn't mean to do that." He picked up the bag.

"I know. And don't worry. I know it didn't mean anything." He scowled, wanting to shake her.

"See you." He walked fast.

Chapter 13

Amanda heard nothing from Marcus until the following Friday morning. She knew he was probably angry with himself for kissing her, and that he was capable of eliminating any chance that it would occur again. He telephoned just as she walked into her office. She had let the phone ring, thinking that Patsy, her secretary, would answer it. Finally, she picked it up.

"Hello." The response both surprised and pleased her.

"Dr. Hickson, please. This is Marcus Hickson, her husband." She felt the impact of his charisma through the telephone wire. Thick and winsome.

"I'd like to bring Amy over this afternoon around five, if I may. I'll pick her up Sunday about the same time."

"Hello, Marcus," she reprimanded. "I'll be happy to have Amy for the weekend. Are you making a trip somewhere?" A wife would ask that question, she told herself. Evidently, he didn't agree.

"Amy wants to spend the weekend with you and Marc. We'll see you around five. Goodbye." She couldn't believe he'd hung up, and it depressed her. But only momentarily. *He's scared,* she thought, triumphantly. *He doesn't want to be alone with me and doesn't even trust himself to have a personal conversation with me. Francis Bacon wrote that knowledge is power,* she recalled. "Well, I know he wants me, and I know he's fighting it. But if he thinks he'll get any help from me, he's shopping with bogus checks," she told herself happily. The world had suddenly become a brighter, more hospitable place.

She had just finished bathing and dressing Marc and was walking down the stairs with him in her arms when the doorbell rang. A happy, enthusiastic Amy greeted her excitedly, but Marcus, appearing indifferent, shoved Amy's little case into the foyer, said "hi" and turned to leave. "Won't you stay for a cup of coffee?" Amanda asked him, more to aggravate him than to gain his company.

Marcus pushed his jacket back and hooked his thumbs into his belt. He didn't look at his wife; just being near her was temptation. And he was not going to give in.

"Thanks, but I've got to get going."

"Can I have a kiss, Daddy?" He reached down to accommodate his daughter, but straightened up as if he'd touched a live wire when, with arms outstretched, Marc greeted him with a clearly pronounced "Da da." The baby attempted to hum and tried to lean toward him, shattering Marcus' resistance. He took the child who clapped his little hands together gleefully while Marcus sang a few bars.

He had to get out of there, he told himself. He wasn't going to let circumstances direct his life. Then Marc patted his cheek, and the big man succumbed and hugged and kissed the baby. He quickly thrust the child back into his mother's arms, said a hurried goodbye and left. But after one lonely hour, he faced the truth: the three people that he had left in the house on Ocean Avenue meant everything to him; they were his reason for living. All three of them. And what could he do for them? Nothing.

The next day, Monday, Amanda sat in the doctor's waiting room holding a six-month-old magazine upside down, her bravado slowly petering out. Marcus had been even more distant when he'd returned for Amy than when he'd brought her. And that morning, when she had come to herself, Beanie Miller was pouring cold water on her face. The woman had arrived for work to find Marc crying uncontrollably and Amanda out in a dead faint. Since she had never fainted before, Amanda thought it best to see a doctor immediately. She had left the baby with the housekeeper and taken the morning off from school. She could still envision Beanie Miller hovering over her, frightened. "Miss Amanda!" she had screamed. "Lord, child, what's going on here?"

"The doctor will see you now, Mrs. Hickson." Being addressed as Mrs. Hickson always gave Amanda a feeling of immense pride. Most people either called her Dr. Hickson or Miss Amanda. She thought her husband an exceptional person, honorable, strong, yet tender, and she was proud to be his wife and to carry his name.

Amanda had known the doctor all of her life, but they had never been friends. Neither had any of the other women she'd played with as a child, she realized. Dr. Lillian McCullen was Judge McCullen's niece, and seeing her reminded Amanda that the judge had promised to expedite Marcus' case. After thoroughly examining Amanda, she told her to dress and wait in her office.

"I want you to take these vitamins as directed. You probably remember the regimen I want you to follow, but in case you've forgotten, please read this pamphlet. You're not to ingest any nonprescription medicine, alcohol or caffeine, but eat plenty of fruits, vegetables and drink four glasses of skimmed milk daily. I'd also like you to gain a little weight. You're much too thin. As your doctor, I have to ask whether you're under stress of any kind." Amanda assured her that she wasn't, though it was barely the truth.

The doctor beamed. "Good. Your baby should be born about September the twenty-third. Come in Friday for an amniocentesis. Did you have one with your previous pregnancy?" Dumbfounded, Amanda answered the questions, made an appointment for the test and trudged out to her car. Pregnant. She was pregnant with Marcus Hickson's baby.

* * *

Outside, she looked around her as if the world were new. It wouldn't do for the principal of Caution Point Junior High to dance wantonly in public, but she had the urge to do exactly that. She hadn't thought that she might get pregnant, because her period had never returned, and she'd considered it normal. She hadn't taken into account that she had stopped nursing Marc after one month. Suddenly fear curled inside of her. She sat in her car, too upset to start it. In exactly eleven days, she was supposed to meet Marcus at their attorney's office and dissolve their marriage. He had been frigid toward her the last two times she'd seen him, and he was sure to think she'd tricked him. Well, she reasoned, he didn't have to know anytime soon. He could find out the way everybody else did. She was married, and if she'd gotten pregnant, it was her business. This time, she didn't have to find a husband. God forbid! If she put another man's name on the birth certificate of Marcus Hickson's child, the result when he found out would be national news. The thought cheered her so much that she laughed aloud.

Friday, shortly before noon, Amanda received the results of the amniocentesis, she was carrying Marcus' son. It threw her into a quandary, because she had named her firstborn son for Marcus. Well, she would find a way. When she reached home, she discovered two letters addressed to him. One was from his attorney and the other one was from the clerk of the county court. She decided against driving to Portsmouth to deliver them, in view of her recent fainting spell, and called Braden's delivery service from Edenton. She placed them in a larger envelope and enclosed a note.

Dearest Marcus,
I hope these bring a change of fortune for you, and that you will soon have good news. Marc and I love you and miss you. Your wife, A.

She had hesitated to say that she and Marc loved him. But what the heck, she reasoned, love begets love. Hadn't she read that somewhere?

Saturday morning, she called Luke, knowing that Marcus would be at the factory. "Did Braden deliver an envelope for Marcus?" she asked Luke after greeting him.

"Yes, right after supper. Didn't he call you? Well, I guess he didn't. What's going on with the two of you?"

"He's backing away."

"Is that why he's been up most of the night for the past ten days? Last night, even Amy asked him to go to bed and please stay there." He chuckled. "Amy usually stays with Alex and Eunice while Marcus is working and she's not in school, but she went to work with him this morning, claiming he needed 'pretection' in case he went to sleep at the factory."

On impulse, she asked him her husband's middle name.

"Marcus is his middle name. His first name is Todd, but he wanted to be called Marcus. You know that our dad's name was Marc, don't you?" They spoke for a while, and she hung up without giving him a message for her husband.

Marcus could hardly believe that his long ordeal might be nearing an end. The case would be heard Monday in Caution Point. The company had offered to settle out of court, but his lawyer had advised against it and he agreed. Pictures of the accident, of the dilapidated machinery that the company had used at that building site, and the police report of the crane operator's insobriety at the time gave him a strong case. He also had affidavits from a dozen doctors and three physical therapists, as well as a briefcase filled with medical bills as proof of the damage. He ought to call Amanda and tell her, and he ought to thank her for getting the letters to him. If she had forwarded them by mail, they would have arrived too late.

He should call her. But if he heard her voice... He knew she was nothing like his former wife. Amanda was—hell, she was wonderful. But could he count on her being like that for the rest of their lives? Would she change if he agreed to make them a permanent family? He couldn't risk it. But he wasn't sure that he could walk away from her, either. He needed her. He burned for her.

He locked his office, literally pulled Amy away from a piano and closed the factory. As they stepped out on the street, the little girl reached for his hand.

"Daddy, let's go home and see Lady and Marc."

He bent and picked her up so that she could see his serious eyes. At least he hoped they looked serious. They hadn't lived with Amanda for going on two months, and she still considered the place home. "Amy, honey, I have told you that we do not live with Amanda and Marc anymore."

She stared right back at him. "I know you said it. But I want Lady to be my mother, and I want to be with my little brother."

Stunned, Marcus walked around to the car, still carrying her, strapped her in and got behind the wheel. He spoke softly. "Amy, Marc is not…" The words got stuck in his throat. He thought for a moment. "I know what's best for us, Amy. You will have to trust me." She was silent. Then he learned that a five-year-old was capable of shedding silent, cascading tears without moving a facial muscle. He turned the car toward route seventeen and Caution Point. Maybe she had more sense than he did. The explanation he gave Amanda for their impromptu visit was that Amy wanted to see her and Marc and that he needed to get information from the hospital. He also used the opportunity to thank her. He wasn't being a coward, he reasoned, just careful.

Marcus endured two hours of misery knowing that he could be with Amanda, with his family instead of staring into space while he pretended to sip cold coffee. Disgusted with himself, he took a brisk walk around the mall trying to consume the energy that had been building inside of him since the last time he had sunk himself into her sweet, wild body. Wondering how much more he could take, he shook his head as if to erase those memories. Amanda wasn't responsible for his predicament, and she didn't deserve the kind of treatment he'd been giving her recently. He got back to the car, noticed that he'd parked in front of a florist, walked in and bought a dozen long-stemmed red roses. Then he went to get Amy. Amanda looked up at him, wide-eyed, when he handed her the box.

She watched them as they walked toward the car and until they sped from her sight. "Why do you continue to give me mixed signals?" she whispered. "Don't you know how cruel it is to be pushed and pulled like a yo-yo and spun like a top?" She went inside and opened the box.

The card read, "Whatever you can lose, reckon of no account. If it is of true value, you will have it for a lifetime. Always, Marcus." What did he mean?

Several days later, Marcus walked into Luke's apartment and picked up his mail. One letter was a copy of the court settlement of his suit against the building company. He let out a deep sigh of relief. At last, it was final and in writing. He was his own man again. He opened the other letter and read:

"A foolish consistency is the hobgoblin of little minds…" (Emerson). Therefore, I excuse you. "If now isn't a good time to tell the truth, I don't see when we'll get to it." (Nikki Giovanni). Your loving wife, A.

Marcus frowned and tucked the letter into his shirt pocket. A few minutes later, he took it out and read it again. Was she accusing him of being inconsistent in his behavior toward her? Yeah.

Amanda tucked Marc into his car seat and stored his stroller in the trunk. She breathed deeply of the balmy April morning, the light breeze that brought a mixture of fresh ocean air and the pungent perfume of hyacinth to her welcoming nostrils. She loved the spring. It was a time when she felt free, confident, full of hope. And what a difference a year could make! She parked on State Street in front of Caution's Coffee Bean, settled Marc in his stroller and went in. But she no longer enjoyed going there and left quickly.

She greeted Sam, the ragman, as she left the café and lifted Marc from his stroller so that Sam could see how he had grown. They talked for a while, before she bade him goodbye, put the baby in his car seat and went around to the back of the car to store the stroller. The trunk lid was up when she heard Sam yell.

"Stop! Stop!"

She bumped her head on the trunk top in her hurry to see what was the matter and only recovered in time to see a gray, stretch limousine pull away, while Sam stood there shouting and waving his arms.

"He got the baby," Sam screamed. "He took little Marc. Miss Amanda, he took the baby." Amanda looked at the backseat of her car, saw that it was empty and passed out.

A strange woman fanned her, and another held a glass of water for her to drink. Then she remembered why she was sitting on the curb against her parked car. When she saw a policeman, she got up, walked slowly into the café and tried but failed to reach Marcus either at work or at Luke's apartment. Then she called Luke at his office.

"I'll get there as fast as I can drive," he told her. "Go home and leave it to me. I'll find him." Ninety minutes later, when Luke ushered Amanda into the police station and identified himself, she knew from the officers' attitudes that her brother-in-law commanded reverence. An officer took them to a room where another patronizing policeman questioned Sam.

"I know what I see'd, and I remember the license number. I'm old, but I ain't stupid," Sam told the officer.

Amanda took the old man's arm. "Sam, this is Lieutenant Detective Hickson, my brother-in-law. Tell him what you know."

Luke shook hands with Sam. The old man's back straightened, and his head went up proudly.

"Well, sir, there was that long gray Lincoln that parked itself right in front of Miss Amanda's car as soon as she and the baby went in the café. And when she come out and was putting the stroller back in the trunk, the chauffeur of that Lincoln jumped out, opened her car door and snatched the baby. I see'd it with my own two eyes. The number on the Lincoln was Virginia, PRL 100, and the dealer what sold the Lincoln is in Portsmouth."

The examining officer scoffed. "You're telling us that a man your age can see that well and has a perfect memory."

Sam wiped his wrinkled lips, cocked his head and looked at the man. "I was standing right at the Lincoln. And I got picture memory. I always had it. I remember what I see, and I ain't never wore glasses. That officer that come in here. That woman. She got brown hair, blue eyes and part of her tooth is broken off." He thought for a minute. "Yes, sir, and she's missing a button up here." He pointed to his pocket and sat back as if in triumph. "And the tag on her said S. Morrell."

The officer stared at Sam. Then he called Sally Morrell and told her with a grin, "I never knew that part of your front tooth was broken off. And I see you've lost one of your buttons."

Luke thanked Sam before telling the sergeant, "The perpetrator is in my area of jurisdiction. I'll keep you posted." He drove a dispirited Amanda home and tried to console her.

"Stay here, in case I need you. I'm fairly certain who the culprit is and I'm positive that Marc is unharmed. But I have to hurry, in case they attempt to hide him somewhere. Call Marcus." He checked with his precinct and drove off.

What kind of man would take a baby from its mother? Amanda wondered. Would he hurt her child? She sat at her kitchen table trying to remain calm, while Beanie Miller paced the floor, wringing her hands and crying hysterically. The woman was so distressed that Amanda decided she might like her after all. She pulled herself up and went to the phone to let Marcus know what had happened. She had tried twice, but failed to reach him. Marcus exploded with a string of expletives, before telling her that he would see her as soon as possible.

"No, Marcus. Stay there. You may be able to help, and Luke may need you."

"Amanda, Luke has the whole Portsmouth police force to help him."

"I know that, dear, but Marc doesn't know them. He knows you, and you know him. I'll be all right."

"Maybe you're right. My God, Amanda! If anybody lays a hand on my kid, I'll kill him. I'll call Myrna and ask her to stay with you until I get there." At any other time, his reference to Marc as his child would have made her day, but she merely stored it in her heart and mind for future reference.

Luke stood beside his desk. "I feel as if my hands have been tied. I hadn't counted on my best sources being unavailable because today is Saturday."

Marcus paced the floor. "Luke, we both know who did this, and we've known all along that it might happen. Besides, it doesn't take a genius to figure out that, here in Portsmouth, PRL stands for Pearce R. Lamont."

"I know that. I checked that out before you got here. But the witness did not see Lamont take Marc; he saw the chauffeur take him and, with those tinted windows, he couldn't say whether anyone was inside the car. And as an officer of the law, I have to have a reason for arresting Lamont. I don't even have what I need to get a search warrant. How the—"

"Right! How did he know about Marc? The only person outside of this family, the Culpeppers and Doc Graham who had an inkling that I am not Marc's biological father is that woman who tried to get next to you at Amanda's Christmas party. And the reason I suspect her is because of her reaction to the birthmark on Marc's hip. Amanda doesn't have it, so I presume his father had it. And she wouldn't know that unless she'd seen him naked. If she had an affair with him, that might explain her animosity to Amanda." He thought for a moment. "Oh, yes. She and Pearce must have been intimate, and she knew he had a liaison with Amanda, though I suspect that Amanda didn't know he was also having an affair with the Elms woman. I remember her telling me that she and the Lamonts were close friends, but I could see that she wasn't in their class. She must be Joe Elms' sister. If the two of them are blackmailing Lamont, that would account for her conviction that she could be insubordinate to Amanda with impunity, because she can count on Lamont to get her out of any mess she gets herself into."

Luke frowned. "And I remember the eerie feeling I got from one of her remarks. She was jealous of Amanda, and she was a troublemaker. And don't be so smug. She only tried me after she got nowhere with you. I think she wanted something to flaunt over Amanda. She must have told Pearce, Sr., about Marc."

"I'm with you there. I'll get her full name and phone number from Amanda," Marcus said as he reached for the telephone. Amanda answered on the first ring. He consoled her as best he could and got the information he sought. Then he called Iris Elms.

"Miss Elms, this is Marcus Hickson." He interrupted her display of pleasure at his call. "My son was kidnapped today by Pearce Lamont's chauffeur in the presence of witnesses. Tell me why you informed Lamont about my son, or I'll have you indicted as an accessory to a kidnapping." Luke quickly pressed the recording button.

She sputtered. "I…I didn't…"

"Don't bother to lie, Miss Elms. I can prove that you did, and I want to know why you did it. Why you told Pearce Lamont that my child is his grandson."

The woman seemed suddenly nervous and frightened. "How was I supposed to know he'd want the kid? I didn't think he'd do anything like that." Agitated and scared. Right where he wanted her. He let her talk. "Well, don't blame me. Pearce, Jr., was my man until he started tailing after Amanda Ross. He just did it on a bet, and she actually believed he preferred her to every other woman in the world. If you can't see, that's your problem."

"How much did Lamont pay you?"

"Not half what it was worth to…" She realized that she'd been tricked. "Nothing. Nothing. I've got to go."

Luke picked up the extension. "Miss Elms, this is Lieutenant Hickson. I think I should warn you that you've just made a very damaging confession." His feral grin as he heard the dial tone would have unsettled her, had she seen it.

Marcus leaned over Luke's desk. "What now?"

"I'm taking this tape to Judge Long, my uncle-in-law, and I'll get a search warrant. All I needed was a scrap of evidence. Any scrap. Henry will give me the order."

"Pearce Lamont, Sr., is used to throwing his weight around," Marcus fumed. "The guy owns two newspapers, an FM radio station and several motels, and his contributions to political parties, local politicians and the policeman's benevolent fund makes him untouchable. I hear he likes to boast that he has the clout to have his security system wired to the police station."

"Yeah, and you wouldn't believe how much I'm going to enjoy getting a piece of him," Luke said as he deactivated the system with a flick of his finger. Luke took an unmarked squad car so as not to alert Lamont's guards. On the way to Lamont's estate, Marcus remained quiet. Somber. Berating himself with the notion that their problem wouldn't exist if he had been with Amanda and Marc.

"I wonder why a man of Lamont's prominence and prestige would risk a kidnapping charge," Luke said, breaking the pall-like silence.

Marcus shrugged. "He's getting his due, believe me. Think of the women—must have been three or four of them—who brought paternity charges against Pearce, Jr., and the old man used his power and money to defame each one of them. And of course, they got nothing but heartache for daring to take on the

Lamont machine. Now, he's lost his son, doesn't have an heir, and he's resorted to kidnapping in order to get one." Marcus expelled a deep breath. "I bleed for him."

Luke grinned. "Yeah. Me, too. I'm also going to throw him in the slammer.

"You can't come with me, Marcus," Luke told him, when they reached the Lamont estate. He should have guessed Marcus' reaction: his brother looked at him as if he'd just said the sky had fallen.

"Not a snowball's chance in hell, brother. It's my kid we're after, so move over."

Luke glanced at him. It was a heavy price to pay, he thought, but maybe it was worth it if it made Marcus realize what the boy meant to him. Made him see and feel that Marc was his son. It was more than worth it.

"All right, but stay behind me. Well behind me." He signaled to his backup that he was going in. They got through the gate with ease, walked up to the massive, ornately carved front door and rang the bell. A maid opened the door without asking the caller's identity. Luke grinned. Just as he'd thought; it was considered safe when there was no sound of the gate's alarm. The minute the maid saw them, she attempted to close the door, but Luke and Marcus were faster and smarter, and when the door closed, they were both inside.

Luke produced the search warrant and identified himself. "Any lack of cooperation on your part will be considered obstruction of justice, which is punishable by law. I want to see every person in this house under age two. And if you refuse to assist me, I'll search every room, cranny and nook in this house, if it takes all year." He pulled out his phone and punched in some numbers alerting the officers posted at the gates and doors. "Detective Hickson speaking. No one leaves this property as long as I'm in this house. Got it?" The maid raised a hand in compliance and stepped back to allow them access.

They were halfway up the stairs to the second floor, when an infant's wail pierced the silence. They took the steps two at a time. It wasn't difficult to find him.

"What do you mean barging in here like this? Who are you?" Louella Lamont asked them haughtily. Marcus thought: What a tiger! They identified themselves and Luke produced the search warrant.

"I'm looking for my son, Marc Hickson," Marcus growled, "and—"

"There's no such person here," she told them, attempting to block their entry into the elaborately decorated nursery. Marcus brushed past her as the baby continued its screams. He picked the child up, and immediately the crying ceased.

Marc looked at the man who held him and slapped his hands together. "Da da, Da da." It was music to Marcus' ears. "Da da, Da da," the child continued, happily.

The woman cringed as Luke censored her with his eyes. "If there's no such person here, why is this child addressing this man as Daddy? And why did he stop crying the minute he recognized his father?"

Marcus reached for the white, bambi-like telephone and dialed his wife. "I've got him, sweetheart. He's right here in my arms. I'll be there as soon as I can. Tell Myrna she can go home to Jack."

Marcus replaced the receiver just as Pearce Lamont, Sr., walked to the door. "What is the meaning of this? Who are you?"

"I'm Lieutenant Detective Hickson and you're under arrest for kidnapping. Your chauffeur will be arrested as an accomplice along with Iris Elms. What made you think you could get away with this? You're a powerful man, Lamont, but not as powerful as you suppose."

"Who let you in here?"

"One of your trusted staff," was the cryptic reply. "Shall I use handcuffs, or are you coming without them? What shall it be?"

The man looked at Marcus, attempting to take his measure, and hesitated, as if sensing that he might regret his next move. "I'm a responsible citizen, and it won't do our people in this city a bit of good to see me jailed like a common criminal. I didn't think it was a good idea, but my wife insisted that the baby belongs with us." He glanced at Marcus.

"I could make it worth your while. You don't stand to gain anything from all this." Eyeing Marcus cautiously, he reached for his checkbook.

Luke quickly stepped in front of Lamont. "He's my prisoner, and I'm responsible for his safety," Luke informed Marcus, who was placing the baby on the bed, preparing to retaliate with his fists. "I will not permit you to beat his brains out no matter how much I'd like to see you do it."

He closed the space between himself and Lamont. "Hands in front of you. Attempted bribery is also against the law." Pearce Lamont, Sr., walked out of his elaborate estate in handcuffs.

Amanda waited by her living-room window, the outdoor floodlights ablaze. It was nearly midnight when she saw Luke's car ease to the curb in front of her house. She was out of the door and down the walk before Marcus could get out of the car. Her tears flowed when, for a second time, Marcus, having delivered her son, handed him to her.

Gradually, she focused on her husband, who stood beside her. "I'm so happy. I can never thank you enough. Oh, Marcus, I have never been so afraid in my life. Thank—"

"Don't thank me, Amanda. I had just as much at stake here as you did. I've only hurt like that once before in my life, and that was when the ambulance was taking Amy to the hospital after that terrible accident."

When he handed Marc to her, he'd had a powerful sensation in his chest, as if his heart swelled. Ecstatic with a joy that threatened to overwhelm him, he had to dig deep inside himself to force the composure he needed. At last, he had been able to give her something. Something of lasting value. Something that she would remember forever. He stood quietly while she hugged and kissed the baby, tears streaming down her cheeks.

She couldn't help hearing what he'd said, but he knew she'd gotten so used to thinking that Marc was no one's concern but her own that the meaning of his words failed to penetrate.

"But I can never ever thank you enough for finding him and for being there for me when I needed you most."

"Luke is the one who masterminded this, not me."

"We did it together." Luke was loping down the stairs. "Without your help, Marcus, I might still be looking for him," Luke said quickly. Some day he'd tell Amanda how the kidnapping had affected Marcus and how he'd behaved in that crisis. But Amanda hugged Luke and tried to express her thanks nonetheless.

"I put Amy to bed, and she didn't even wake up," Luke told them. "I've got to drive back to Portsmouth tonight, but I need some coffee and a sandwich or something. Marcus, do you realize that we never got lunch or dinner?"

"I forgot about food. I'll get something together, Amanda. Or would you rather fix it, and I'll get Marc settled?"

Luke gazed in awe at Marcus' face, as his brother looked down at Amanda with an expression of knowing intimacy, and glanced away in embarrassment. The older man walked toward the kitchen, wondering if his brother hadn't just committed himself. He hoped so. How he hoped so!

Marcus made a pot of coffee, fried bacon, scrambled eggs and warmed the biscuits he found in the refrigerator. He didn't want to leave Amanda, but he didn't want to sleep in that guest room ever again. He knew she would let him share her bed, but he also knew there remained between them too many unresolved issues, too much needing to be said for them to reach the level of intimacy for which he yearned. Soul as well as mind and body. The three of them ate what he had prepared. Marcus looked at Amanda as she sipped something made of one of Aunt Meredith's herbal recipes and realized that she wouldn't understand why he was leaving. Well, he'd give it a shot.

"I have some things to do in Portsmouth tomorrow, things I should have done today. So I'm going back with Luke. If it's all right with you, Amy can stay here and miss school for a few days. Keep you company. She'd like that. She's already told me that she wants to be with her little brother."

Flabbergasted by that last revelation and by the fact that Marcus had let himself say the words, Amanda nearly missed an equally important fact: Marcus had voluntarily given her a reason for not spending the night with her. And he was a man who only explained his behavior grudgingly, if at all.

She walked to the door with them. She should have been happy, exuberant, because her son was safe in this own bed, unharmed. Instead, a feeling of dejection, of melancholia settled over her. She needed Marcus, wanted him with her.

Luke hugged her goodbye and walked out, giving them privacy. But Marcus just stood looking down at her, wanting to take her in his arms and erase the fragility, the defenselessness mirrored in her eyes. He knew they needed to lose themselves in each other, to wipe out all memory of what they had just been through. They needed to make love. He fought the temptation to step over the gulf that separated them, take her in his arms and carry her up to that bed. But he kept his counsel and merely dusted her cheek with the back of his hand.

"I'll be back in a few days. Then we'll talk."

Chapter 14

Amanda looked up at him, wanting in every chamber of her soul to feel his arms around her. But she wouldn't beg. She had asked him to marry her, but she wouldn't ask him to love her and she wouldn't beg him to stay with her. She had offered him her love, and he had walked away from it. She merely nodded in response.

She knew that Marcus sensed her subtle withdrawal, though he appeared to ignore it, and her heart thundered in her chest when he brushed her lips with his. Was it a promise, or would she be Amanda Ross again on April the twelfth? He teased her mouth gently, and she knew he was using every bit of control that he could muster.

Monday, April the ninth, two days later, and just two days from D-Day, Amanda arrived home from school, her nerves worn ragged from an eight-hour struggle to concentrate on her job, keep her mind off Marcus and tears off her face. For once, Beanie Miller wasn't waiting to rush out of the door, but sat on the back porch entertaining the children. The ordeal over Marc's kidnapping had changed the woman drastically. Amanda picked up the mail that lay on a table in the foyer and noticed Marcus' handwriting. She shivered with fear. It was the first letter that Marcus had ever written to her, and it had been delivered by mes-

senger. She went into the living room, sat down, took a deep
breath and opened it with trembling fingers. She read through
tear-blurred eyes.

> Dear Amanda,
> Thank you for giving my child her health and a mother's
> love, for giving me what I had never known and preserv-
> ing for me what I almost lost. I hope you won't mind if I
> invite myself to dinner at your place tomorrow evening,
> April tenth.
> Marcus.

Amanda cast her eyes toward the sky. Was this a civilized kiss-
off? A gentlemanly letdown after allowing her to believe that
there might possibly be something more for them? Feeling as
miserable as was humanly possible, she placed the note on the
coffee table, and a check dropped on the floor. It was for the sum
specified in their contract plus the amount she had given the
bank in full payment of his loans. She knew he had received a
very large settlement and remembered that he had sworn to repay
her. She didn't want the money she'd paid him under their
contract, but he was a proud man, and she knew he would insist
upon it. The note was neither warm nor cool, merely polite and
thoughtful.

"And cryptic," she said aloud as she walked toward the back
of the house to greet the children and send the housekeeper
home. The note told her nothing of his intentions or his feelings.
She didn't know whether he was coming to ask for a divorce or…
She couldn't make herself envisage the alternative.

Amanda slipped into the Chinese silk, brick-red caftan and
zipped it up, admiring the gold sunburst on the left shoulder. Then
she unplaited her hair and brushed it out to its full length, applied
a pale lipstick and made a face at herself in the mirror. She had
considered buying a hot number for Marcus' visit and thought

better of it, reasoning that she would never be a siren. She'd bought the caftan and a matching one for Amy during her lunch hour. Her designs might be obvious, but she didn't care; if Marcus walked away from her, he wouldn't do it with ease, because she intended to use every bit of the ammunition she had. Not quite all, a niggling voice reminded her. She remembered Barbara Whitfield's gift of Saint Laurent perfume and applied it in various places, including her navel and, to Amy's delight, sprayed a mild lilac scent in the child's hair. She reach for her gold ballet slippers, then brushed them aside. Marcus knew she didn't wear shoes in the house. The doorbell rang, shattering the silence and her nerves. Trembling and holding Amy's hand tightly, she opened the door.

Marcus stood there, jolted, neither moving nor speaking. Her feminine sweetness was a powerful elixir winding itself around his heart. And his child, healthy and beautiful, stood beside her trying to be just like her. Amanda was a wonderful role model for his daughter—soft, feminine and sweet, but strong, intelligent and decorous. She'd dressed them alike, he noted, and his daughter's pride in it was obvious.

"There aren't two lovelier females in the world," he told them in a husky voice. He fought his desire to take Amanda in his arms right then and was relieved when Amy raised her arms for a hug, temporarily cooling him down. Marcus handed Amanda a florist's box, picked up his daughter and kissed her, but he had eyes only for his wife. He set Amy down and gave her a slim box, silently thanking Providence that he'd thought of it. If Amanda was teaching her how to be feminine, he could do no less than show her what to expect of a man.

"Open it."

She couldn't stop looking at him. She had never seen him like this. She had always thought him handsome, but dressed as he was, in a hand-tailored suit and shirt and with a demeanor that matched his elegant attire, he bewitched her. She saw a subtly different Marcus. His strength and competence were not new to her, but this man projected power, authority and self-reliance. Had his eyes always sparkled with such impudence? She rubbed her arms, self-consciously reacting to the naked look in his eyes; the look of a man who liked what he saw and wanted it.

"You look…you're Saville Row personified," she whispered in reference to the British-like perfection of his attire. "So elegant. We're honored, aren't we, Amy?" The little girl smiled shyly and nodded.

"You're looking at the fruits of more prosperous days. I haven't been much in the mood to dress up in the last couple of years," he replied offhandedly. Then he grinned as if to banish any threatening cloud.

"Go on. Open them," he told Amanda and Amy, who looked at her stepmother with an expression that seemed to say, *what do I do now?* "Is Marc asleep?" he asked them before lightly pinching Amanda's nose and sprinting up the stairs.

Amanda opened the box of twelve red roses and read his note. "'Of all sad words of tongue or pen, the saddest are these: it might have been.'" She stared at Whittier's words, not knowing whether to laugh or cry, to hope or accept defeat. Amy pulled on her arm.

"Lady, my daddy gave me a yellow rose." Amanda looked down at her proud little face, enveloped in smiles. "Lady, ask Daddy if me and him can live here with you and Marc. Please, Lady?"

Amanda gave the only answer that she could. "He and I. We'll see, darling." She walked slowly upstairs with the roses to place them on the table beside the bed and found Marcus standing at Marc's crib holding the baby in his arms and talking to him.

"It's time you learned to say something other than Da da." He shifted the child's weight and grimaced. "You're wet again. Hickson men do not wet their pants, young man. Here, let Daddy change you." He placed the gurgling, bouncing baby in the crib, as the child happily repeated "Da da," as Marcus turned to go for a diaper. He turned right into Amanda, almost knocking her down.

"Where do you keep those things?" he asked, as if referring to himself as Marc's daddy was nothing out of the ordinary. She pointed, unable to speak. She was afraid to hope, afraid to believe what she had heard. It didn't really mean anything, she told herself; there were lots of absentee fathers. She rushed down to get the dinner on the table and to compose herself. She had to find a way to make him see that they belonged together, and she was not going to use the child she carried as bait.

Amanda had prepared Marcus' favorite meal, and he didn't have to be told that the dessert would be apple pie. She poured a glass of wine for him but none for herself.

"Aren't you having any?" he asked. "A meal like this deserves a good wine, and this one is excellent."

"Thanks, but I think I'll pass."

He regarded her intently. "Are you all right?"

Before she could answer, Amy informed him, "Miss Beanie says that Lady is sick every morning. She was sick this morning." She turned to Amanda. "Weren't you, Lady?"

Marcus stared at his wife, but her gaze didn't waver from her plate. *Well, well,* he thought, *just what is going on here?* He remembered that she had refused coffee and drunk some kind of herbal tea the night they rescued Marc. He smiled deceptively, luring her into an unwarranted ease.

"I guess that means you're not going to drink the champagne I brought. Well, it will keep. Luke loves champagne." He looked directly at her when he said it. Reading her. She almost panicked at the implication that he was going back to Luke's place, and he figured she deserved to do just that.

He had read Amy to sleep, and they still sat on the edge of her bed. He got up, offered Amanda his hand, and she placed trembling fingers in his palm and allowed him to lead her into her bedroom. He closed the door, locked it and turned to her.

"Thank you for a lovely evening, Amanda." He watched as anxiety mirrored itself in her face. He wanted to pour some sense into her, but that wasn't all he wanted. He could be patient when it suited him, and right then, it served his purpose. He waited.

Amanda wasn't sure of her next move. *If he leaves me tonight,* she acknowledged silently, *it's over between us.*

"Are you leaving?" That cracked whisper did not sound like her voice. She tried again. "Th-thank you for the beautiful roses. Won't you stay for a while?" What had happened to her aplomb, her ability to think even when she was nervous? She looked up at him, almost frantic with fear that he was planning to leave her and go back to Portsmouth. She knew that her emotions—the fear, the desperation and the need—simmered in her gaze.

He swore. She always got to him when she looked helpless. "You owe me an explanation, Amanda." He sounded harsher than he had intended, but he hurt. He had gone there intending to put his cards on the table, tell her what she meant to him and start on a new life with her and their children. But she hadn't been straight with him, and he wanted to know why.

"When were you going to tell me that you're carrying my child?"

She gasped, her face suddenly ashen. He walked toward her and stopped. When Amanda was in a corner, she came out fighting and her anger was obvious.

"I was not going to let you think I tricked you into staying married to me. So I was either going to tell you after our divorce was final or after you decided that we would stay married. It depended on you, Marcus. I knew it wouldn't be easy, but I prepared myself to go through it alone. I thought you cared for me, but you walked out of here and took Amy with you when I'd only done what any other woman would do if she loved her husband. But you would rather have lost your business than let me help you. Oh, I was going to tell you sooner or later."

* * *

He watched in amazement, as her anger disappeared like a puff of smoke in a gale force wind. "I'm not certain that I would react that way now." He paused. "No, I don't think I would. But my pride had taken such a shellacking in the previous eighteen months, and that was just another instance of your giving me something invaluable, when I had nothing whatever to give you." He ran the fingers of his left hand over his well-groomed hair, ruining the effect.

Uneasiness churned in her when his eyes suddenly mirrored a fierce agitation, an emotion as turbulent as the Albemarle in the clutches of a storm. He seemed reluctant to form the words.

"Do you want my child, Amanda?" His voice had become tinged with anxiety.

"Oh, yes," she whispered, unconsciously advancing toward him. "Oh, Marcus, I've wanted so badly to share this with you. I couldn't tell anyone, not even Myrna, because I was supposed to tell you first. I've even chosen a name." She stopped, alarmed at his silence. Did he want her out of his life?

"So…are you glad or sorry? I mean, do *you* want it?" She held her breath.

The words had barely passed her lips when he picked her up and swung her around. Then he set her on her feet and looked down at her with luminous eyes. Eyes that she prayed were windows of his heart.

"Did you think I could stay away from you forever? I've been almost useless since I left here. I love you, Amanda. I never stopped loving you, but I had nothing to offer you. Tell me you still love me in spite of what I've put you through these past months."

She rose on tiptoe, trying to reach his mouth, and he bent to her. A burning excitement coursed through her when he paused, his lips so close, but not touching. Then she trembled, and he crushed her to him, opened his mouth above hers and demanded entrance for his foraging tongue. Tendrils of pleasure racked her nervous system as his dancing tongue mated with hers, and her sensitive breast beaded, welcoming the caress of his big hand. Flames roared through her, and when she trembled, he lifted her, spread his hand across her round bottom and let her feel his hard passion pressing into the cradle of her femininity. Starved for him, she moved impatiently against him, signaling her spiraling heat.

Marcus flipped down the back zipper of her red caftan and watched it pool around her bare feet. She tried to unbutton his shirt, but he stepped back to gaze at the treasure before him, seeing beyond the scraps of red lace that hid nothing.

"I love to look at your body," he rasped. "You are so beautiful. These weeks and months when I could see you only in my imagination, in my dreams, I remembered every pore." He lifted her and fastened his hungry mouth to one nipple, making her cry out from the pleasure that he gave her. Wanting more, with trembling fingers, she opened the front hook of her bra and let her breasts spring free. Darts of fire singed every nerve of her body when he pulled her deeply into his mouth.

"Marcus, please. I…please." He let his hand wander until it cupped her intimately, and she buckled from the hot sparks that kindled her passion.

"What do you want, honey? Tell me. I need to hear it. Tell me."

Beyond false pride, she answered in a clear voice. "I want you. I need to feel you inside of me, Marcus." She poked him roughly in the chest. "And you know it. The first time you brought Amy to see me, you kissed me almost…almost vindictively when you were leaving, and you had to know that you left me bothered. I've been aching for you every minute since."

He picked her up, lay her on the bed and slowly peeled away her bikini panties, kissing every inch of her as he did so. She raised open arms to him, and he was out of his clothes in seconds and into her welcoming arms, breathless with anticipation, knowing the bounty that awaited him.

He begged her to slow down, but she was beyond any semblance of self-control, and he was catapulted almost to the brink by the force of her wild passion. As she gazed into his fevered eyes, he slowly found his home within her.

"Marcus. Oh, Marcus, I love you. I love you."

Shaken by the enormity of her release, he struggled to control his own rush to completion, to prolong their pleasure. But when she cried out in abandon, he gave up his essence in a vortex of ecstasy.

"My love, my wife, my life."

Slowly they climbed down to reality, and he rolled onto his back and tucked her to his side. He had to clear up a few things, and he wanted to do it before he went to sleep.

"We have to talk, Amanda. I want to tear up that contract, and I want you to accept the check I sent you. It's important to me. I won't put a price on the year I've spent with you. I also want to sell my house in Portsmouth, because I've never been happy there."

In a voice that suggested outward calm, she asked him, "Were you happy here?"

He pulled her closer. "This house is a home. And I found here with you what I had never had and hadn't known existed. Yes, I've been happy here, and I'd like us to live here, but I want to add three rooms and baths on the lawn side of the house. We'll be a large family."

"What about the factory?" Surely he wasn't planning to commute daily.

"I'll commute three times a week and you can still keep your job. That is, if you want to." He felt her snuggle up to him, rolled her on to her back and leaned over her.

"You didn't tell me how far along you are."

"Our child was conceived on Christmas night, Marcus, so I'm a little over three months." Marcus grinned, remembering that night as the one on which he'd learned what a woman could be to a man. He looked down at her belly.

"You're sure? You look flat to me."

She placed his hand on the little mound. "I'm sure. Todd Marcus Hickson, Jr., will be born September twenty-third."

Marcus shook his head as if to clear it. "We're having a son? My God! And you asked Luke my full name. Does he know?"

"I didn't tell him why I asked. Oh, Marcus. I didn't know I could be so happy."

"Nor did I. I feel like waking Amy up. She's been torment-ing me, telling me that she wants you to be her mother."

"I have felt almost from the beginning that I am her mother."

"And in my heart and mind, I am Marc's father. I love him, Amanda."

"I know, darling. I know." She yawned happily, threw an arm across his chest and went to sleep.

The second title in a passionate new miniseries...

THE BRADDOCKS

SECRET SON

Power, passion and politics
are all in the family.

Sex and the Single Braddock

ROBYN AMOS

Determined to uncover the mystery of her powerful father's
death, Shondra Braddock goes to work for Stewart Industries
CEO Connor Stewart. But her undercover mission soon
gets sidetracked when their sizzling attraction explodes
into a secret, jet-setting affair!

Available the first week of September wherever books are sold.

KIMANI™
ROMANCE

All work and no play…

SUITE
Temptation

Acclaimed Author
ANITA
BUNKLEY

When Riana Cole kissed Andre Preaux goodbye to conquer
the San Antonio business world, Andre had given up without
a fight. Now, years later, they are reunited, and memories
of delicious passion come flooding back. Andre is
determined to get her back, but this time he's negotiating
for one thing only—her heart.

"Anita Bunkley's descriptive winter scenery, likable,
well-written characters and engaging story make
Suite Embrace very entertaining."
—*Romantic Times BOOKreviews*

Available the first week of September wherever books are sold.

KIMANI™
ROMANCE

www.kimanipress.com

KPAB0800908

She was on a rescue mission;
he was bent on seduction!

SECRET AGENT
SEDUCTION

TOP SECRET
ROMANCE ON THE RUN

Favorite Author

Maureen Smith

Secret Service agent Lia Charles needs all her
professional objectivity to rescue charismatic
revolutionary Armand Magliore, because extracting him
from the treacherous jungle is the easy part—guarding
her heart against the irresistible rebel is the *real* challenge.

Available the first week of September wherever books are sold.

KIMANI™
ROMANCE

Where there's smoke, there's fire!

MAKE IT HOT

Gwyneth Bolton

Brooding injured firefighter Joel Hightower's only hope
to save his career is sassy physical therapist Samantha
Dash. But as the sizzling attraction between them
intensifies, Samantha must decide whether a future with
surly Joel is worth the threat to her career.

The Hightowers
Four brothers on a mission
to protect, serve and love.

Available the first week of September wherever books are sold.

KIMANI
ROMANCE ™

www.kimanipress.com   KPGB0830908

NATIONAL BESTSELLING AUTHOR

ROCHELLE ALERS

invites you to meet the Whitfields of New York....

Tessa, Faith and Simone Whitfield know all about coordinating
other people's weddings, and not so much about arranging
their own love lives. But in the space of one unforgettable year,
all three will meet intriguing men who just might bring them their
very own happily ever after....

Long Time Coming
June 2008

The Sweetest Temptation
July 2008

Taken by Storm
August 2008

ARABESQUE®

www.kimanipress.com

KPALERSTRIL08